Aristophanes: An Introduction

ARISTOPHANES

An Introduction

James Robson

B L O O M S B U R Y
LONDON • NEW DELHI • NEW YORK • SYDNEY

Bloomsbury Academic
An imprint of Bloomsbury Publishing Plc

50 Bedford Square	1385 Broadway
London	New York
WC1B 3DP	NY 10018
UK	USA

www.bloomsbury.com

First published in 2009 by Bristol Classical Press
an imprint of Gerald Duckworth & Co. Ltd.
Reprinted by Bristol Classical Press 2012
Reprinted by Bloomsbury Academic 2013

British Library Cataloguing-in-Publication Data
A catalogue record for this book is available from the British Library.

ISBN: PB: 978-0-7156-3452-3
E-pub: 978-1-4725-1962-7
E-pdf: 978-1-4725-1961-0

Library of Congress Cataloging-in-Publication Data
A catalog record for this book is available from the Library of Congress.

Contents

To Owain,
my *cariad* and *ffrind mawr*

Acknowledgements

Writing a book involves imposing on all manner of people. I am particularly grateful to Dr Amanda Wrigley of the Archive of Performances of Greek and Roman Drama in Oxford who kindly took time out to show me the archive and help me source images. I would like to note my appreciation to Siobhan Desouza and Simon Andrews, too, for letting me see a performance script of the wonderful Kaloi k'Agathoi *Clouds* (and for providing me with an image of the poster to boot). My colleagues at the Open University also deserve thanks: I feel very fortunate to work in a department – and indeed a faculty – staffed by such warm and engaging people. To single out three friends and academics who have generously given of their time, I would like to note my gratitude to Dr Felix Budelmann, whose brains I often picked in the early stages of writing and who commented on a number of chapters for me; Dr Anne Alwis, who provided helpful feedback on various chapters while in draft form; and Dr Thomas Jenkins, whose extensive knowledge of American slang terms for sexual acts and organs proved so valuable to me when writing Chapter 7.

My friends and family have supplied support and encouragement in bucket loads, especially my husband, Owain Thomas, and my father, Charles Robson, both of whom have patiently read through the whole manuscript and offered no end of useful comments. Much of this book was written at my parents' house in Lot-et-Garonne where not only they, but also their friends Bob and Sheila Parsons and Ted and Janet Vandyke, made me extremely welcome: my warm thanks to them, too. I should like to take the opportunity here to express my gratitude to Dr Judith Owen for undertaking the indexing of this book with such aplomb. Lastly, special thanks are also due to Deborah Blake and the team at Duckworth for the warm and efficient support I have received during the writing and publication of this book.

Preface

Aristophanes is one of the smartest, wittiest and most nuanced authors I
have ever read – a feat all the more impressive for the fact that he is also
a master of earthy humour, insults, slapstick and obscenity. On one level
his plays are extraordinarily accessible – so accessible that a modern
production can not only make audiences laugh heartily but also lead them
to see startling parallels between today's world and that of Athens 2,500
years ago. On another level, however, his plays can be somewhat difficult
to understand: the conventions of his theatre; his allusions to unfamiliar
people, places and objects – indeed, his whole conception of playwriting –
make for comedies that can seem as complex and intangible as the rich
culture they grew out of. Certainly for me it was not love at first sight.
When I first read Aristophanes as an undergraduate, I warmed to some
parts of his plays but not others, which I will freely admit to finding
baffling. But as I gradually developed a way of understanding his work,
my appreciation deepened until eventually I was hooked.

This, then, is the book that I wish I had read when I first encountered
Aristophanes. Its purpose is to bring his plays to life by casting light on
some of the more challenging aspects of his work, such as his literary
allusions, his songs and his politics (to give but three examples). This is
not to say that this book provides a set of clear cut 'answers' to the
problems that Aristophanes presents us with, however. Rather, it aims to
take readers to a point where they can study the plays intelligently for
themselves and make their own minds up about the scholarly debates and
controversies that still rage about Aristophanic comedy. To this end, I aim
not just to furnish readers with my own insights on the plays but also to
introduce them to some of the more influential and helpful approaches
taken by other Aristophanic scholars over the years. Nor do I shy away
from introducing readers to the occasional technical term or Greek word
when it aids understanding and helps to inform debate. The result, I hope,
is a book which communicates the power, richness and sheer vitality of
Aristophanes' work and which also provides readers with the wherewithal
and confidence to explore his plays in a dynamic way, to ask and answer
their own questions and, above all, to enjoy the plays for the wonderful
poetry and drama that they are.

This book is organized in a thematic way, with each chapter covering a
separate topic. Rather than trying to draw examples from every play in
each chapter, my practice (where possible) has been to hang the discussion

of a topic around a small number of plays: the plays concentrated on in a given chapter are listed in its introduction. This has inevitably led to some plays gaining more attention than others and my bias has generally been towards those works of Aristophanes that are most commonly read, studied and staged in the English-speaking world and/or which chime with the topics I have chosen to cover. The main casualty here, I fear, has been *Wealth*, which receives precious little attention. For this – and for any misunderstandings and misrepresentations of his plays I may have propagated – I sincerely hope that Aristophanes will forgive me.

Note on Greek Names and Words

The perennial problem for anyone writing on Greek civilization is how to deal with proper names. The general practice in this book has been to give the version of the name most familiar to English readers. Usually this has meant using the traditional Latinized versions of names: thus Cleon rather than Kleon or Kleôn. Where I have judged the Hellenized version of a name to be in relatively common usage (or, on occasion, where the Latinized version of a name simply looked too weird) I have altered my practice: thus Thorikos (rather than Thoricus), and so on. When key Greek terms have entered the English language, my practice has been to italicize the transliterated word (e.g. *orchêstra*) but not its English equivalent (orchestra).

Aristophanes and Old Comedy

Introduction

Who was Aristophanes? In one respect, of course, this is an easy question
to answer: he is classical Athens' most celebrated comic playwright – a
status to which he has been able to lay claim from ancient times and which
helps account for the fact that he is the only poet of the genre known as
Old Comedy to have his plays survive in anything other than fragmentary
form. On another level, however, answering this question causes us all
manner of difficulties. If we are keen to find out basic facts about the man
– what he felt about his own plays; what his political leanings were; where
he stood on the key debates of his day – then the information we possess
is often difficult to interpret. The aim of this book is to provide ways of
understanding, appreciating and enjoying the plays of this truly inspir-
ing and original playwright – in short, to offer an insight into the man
and his work. In this opening chapter, for example, we shall consider
what is known about Aristophanes' life and how he presents himself in
his plays as well as looking at the basic characteristics of the comic
tradition in which he was writing. Whilst Aristophanes' output will be
considered as a whole, the focus in this chapter will be on his early
career and, in particular, key passages from *Acharnians*, *Knights*,
Clouds and *Wasps*.

Aristophanes' life and times

As with most ancient authors, the information we possess about the life of
Aristophanes is very patchy. He was born some time between 460 and 450
BC and was a member of the deme of Cydathenaeum, a district in the heart
of ancient Athens.[1] We also know the name of his father – Philippus – and
the names of three of his sons, Philippus, Ararus and Nicostratus, all of
whom became comic playwrights in their own right.[2] He died either in or
just after 386 BC.

As for his work, we know the titles of forty-four plays written by
Aristophanes, eleven of which survive in full.[3] The shortest of these
extant plays is *Assemblywomen* comprising 1183 lines of Greek verse,
while the longest is *Birds* at 1765 lines (and it is the line numbers of the
Greek text which are used to refer to passages in the plays). In addition
we possess around 1000 fragments, ranging from single words ('mack-

erel','sailoress': frs 189 and 858) to ninety-plus lines of Greek (frs 590 and 591: both from tattered papyri). The Hellenistic *hypotheses* (introductions) to his works help us to establish the production dates of many of Aristophanes' plays and often provide details as to what prize they received in the dramatic contest and which of Athens' dramatic festivals they were staged at (either the Lenaea or the Great Dionysia: see Chapter 2). Combined with valuable information provided by scholia (notes made by ancient commentators on manuscripts of the plays) and internal references in the plays themselves, a rough chronology of Aristophanes' life and career can be sketched out. The following is a list of key dates:

460-450 BC	Aristophanes born
431	Peloponnesian War breaks out between Athens and Sparta
427	*Banqueters** (produced by Callistratus or Philonides)
426	*Babylonians** (Great Dionysia; produced by Callistratus)
425	**Acharnians** (Lenaea; produced by Callistratus: first prize)
424	**Knights** (Lenaea; produced by Aristophanes: first prize)
423	*Clouds** (Great Dionysia: third place)
422	**Wasps** (Lenaea; produced by Philonides? or Aristophanes: second place)
	Death of Cleon
421	Peace of Nicias: suspension of hostilities between Athens and Sparta
	Peace (Great Dionysia: second place)
418-416	**Clouds** (revision of 423 BC play: not performed)
415-413	Sicilian Expedition (Athens' military campaign in Sicily)
414	*Amphiarus** (Lenaea; produced by Philonides)
	Birds (Great Dionysia: second place; produced by Callistratus)
413	Sicilian disaster; resumption of fighting between Athens and Sparta
411	**Lysistrata** (Lenaea?; produced by Callistratus)
	Women at the Thesmophoria (Great Dionysia?)
	Oligarchic coup in Athens (Rule of the Four Hundred; Rule of the 5,000)
410	Democracy restored in Athens
408	The first *Wealth**
406	Athenian victory in the naval battle of Arginusae
405	**Frogs** (Lenaea: first prize)
404	Peloponnesian War ends with the defeat of Athens
	Rule of the Thirty Tyrants
403	Democracy restored in Athens
399	Trial and Execution of Socrates
392 or 391?	**Assemblywomen**

2

1. Aristophanes and Old Comedy

388	The second **Wealth** (produced by Aristophanes)
387?	*Cocalus** (Great Dionysia; produced by Ararus)
386?	*Aeolosicon** (produced by Ararus)
386?	Aristophanes dies

[* denotes a lost play; **bold type** denotes a surviving play]

Of course, a list of dates does not tell us much in itself, but when we are dealing with an author whose work is as topical as Aristophanes' a historical perspective is particularly important, since the plays are so intimately bound up with what was happening outside the theatre. This chronology will therefore serve as an important reference point throughout this book.

Useful as this chronology is, however, part of what makes Aristophanes such a fascinating figure is that we do not have to rely simply on bare scraps of biographical information to build up a picture of the man. Not only do we have Plato's lively pen portrait of Aristophanes in the *Symposium* (which may or may not have much basis in reality) but, in addition, Aristophanes' personality seems to shine through in the plays themselves. The details we glean from his comedies even extend to their author's physical appearance: at *Knights* 550, for example, the chorus informs us that Aristophanes has a 'gleaming forehead' – a reference to his baldness, which is echoed at *Clouds* 545 and *Peace* 771-4.[4] More revealing than this, however, are the numerous passages in Aristophanes' plays where what appear to be personal opinions of the poet are communicated to the audience. Characters in Aristophanes' dramas – and more often still the chorus – claim to speak on their author's behalf, delivering comments about politicians, poets and other real-life personalities as well as matters of personal interest and public policy.

One real-life figure who features heavily in Aristophanes' plays is Cleon, an outspoken politician and fellow demesman of Aristophanes'. The exact details are unclear, but following the production of *Babylonians* in 426 BC – in which he had evidently been made an object of ridicule – Cleon apparently (i) publicly criticized the play for ridiculing Athens' citizens in front of foreigners; and (ii) initiated some form of legal proceedings against Aristophanes (although whether the legal proceedings concerned the play or not, we cannot be sure).[5] Mention is made of these events the following year in *Acharnians* (377-82, 502-6, 628ff.), staged in 425 BC, but Aristophanes' most vicious counter-attack comes a year later in *Knights* (424 BC), where one of the play's central characters, Paphlagon, is a thinly disguised and grotesque caricature of Cleon. A series of insults are made, and the chorus (which claims to hate the same men as the poet: 510) even fantasizes about Cleon's destruction and the benefits it would bring to Athens:

Most pleasant will be the light of day
For those who dwell here
And those who come here
Should Cleon be destroyed.

Knights 973-6

Cleon continues to be attacked in later plays right up to his death in 421 BC. In *Wasps*, for example (422 BC), he appears in yet another guise: a litigious dog (*kyôn* in Greek, cf. *Kleôn*) of the deme of Cydathenaeum accusing another dog of theft.[6]

Perhaps more intriguing are moments in Aristophanes' plays when the chorus or a character speaks as if they were the poet. Before his pro-Spartan speech to the hostile chorus of *Acharnians*, for example, Dicaeopolis ruminates on the nature of public discourse in Athens, bringing into question the ability of certain groups of citizens to make sound judgements. As elsewhere in the play, during Dicaeopolis' meditations, the first person singular comes to refer not (just) to Dicaeopolis, but also to Aristophanes himself:[7]

> I've got a lot to be afraid of. I know the ways of country folk – they're very pleased if a glib man praises them and the city, whether the praise is merited or not. That's how they get bought and sold without even realizing. And likewise I know what's in the hearts of old men, that all they care about is causing a sting with their voting pebbles [i.e. when they serve on juries in the law courts]. And I know what *I* suffered *myself* at Cleon's hands because of last year's comedy [i.e. *Babylonians*]. ...
>
> *Acharnians* 370-8

How are we to judge these personal comments? This is a highly controversial point amongst scholars of Aristophanes and a huge variety of positions have been taken. On the one hand, it is tempting to take them as straightforward opinion pieces offered up by the poet to his audience. If these passages do not reflect Aristophanes' personal views then why are they in the plays? On the other hand, however, it is worth bearing in mind that these comments hardly comprise a spontaneous outpouring on Aristophanes' part, but rather a set of artfully crafted lines delivered by the chorus and characters of a comic drama. We would not normally expect every line uttered by every character in a play to reflect the author's personal opinions, so why should these comments be judged any differently? There are no easy answers here and these questions, in different forms, recur again and again when we read Aristophanes' plays and try to get to grips with his work.

Aristophanes on his own plays

One topic about which Aristophanes' choruses make a series of particularly muscular claims – once more, seemingly speaking on behalf of the poet – is the quality of Aristophanes' plays themselves. An especially rich set of comments emerge following the poor showing of *Clouds* in the dramatic competition of 423 BC. The defeat of this play appears to have been a particular source of annoyance to Aristophanes and elicits the following rebuke to the audience from the chorus of *Wasps* (produced in 422 BC):

> Last year you betrayed him beyond measure when he sowed some brand new (*kainotatos*) ideas which failed to take root because you didn't understand them properly – although he swears by Dionysus over countless libations that no one has ever heard comic poetry better than that. ...
> But in the future, my good people,
> Cherish and nurture more
> Those poets who seek
> To say something new (*kainos*).
> Keep hold of their ideas
> And keep them in your clothes-boxes
> With the citrons.
> And if you do this, after a year
> Your cloaks
> Will smell of cleverness (*dexiotês*).
>
> *Wasps* 1044-7; 1051-9

Aristophanes revised *Clouds* some time between 418 and 416 BC – and it is this later, unperformed play that has come down to us. In this reworked version, the disappointment of the play's defeat is once again writ large and, as in *Wasps*, the chorus makes some strong assertions about the originality and cleverness of the first *Clouds* when they address the audience in the section of the play known as the *parabasis* (on which see below). They speak in the first person singular, evoking Dionysus, patron deity of drama, as their witness and impugn Aristophanes' rival playwrights as 'vulgar men':

> Spectators, I shall speak frankly and tell you the truth, I swear by Dionysus who reared me. So I might be victorious and be thought intelligent (*sophos*), I took you to be smart (*dexios*) spectators and saw fit to let you have the first taste of this, the cleverest (*sophôtatos*) of my comedies – a play into which I had put a great deal of effort. Then I withdrew, defeated quite undeservedly by vulgar men. It's the clever ones (*sophoi*) among you that I blame for this – the ones for whose sake I put in all that hard work. But even so, I shall never willingly abandon the smart ones (*dexioi*) among you.
>
> *Clouds* 518-27

It is not only *Clouds* that the chorus claims is 'new' (*kainos*) and 'intelligent' (*dexios, sophos*) either. They go on to claim novelty and ingeniousness as characteristic of Aristophanes' work in general:

> I don't try to deceive you by bringing the same things on two and three times; rather I always skilfully contrive to introduce new (*kainos*) styles of comedy, all ingenious (*dexios*) and completely different from one another.
>
> *Clouds* 546-8

5

Similar claims are still being made in Aristophanes' plays in 405 BC, when the chorus of *Frogs* assures Aeschylus and Euripides during their battle of words that the audience 'understands clever things' (*ta dexia*: 1114). And this ability of the spectators to comprehend subtleties is not simply due to their natural intelligence, but is also a product of the fact that they have been taught to think (1116) – presumably by Aristophanes' plays themselves!

In this same *parabasis* of *Clouds*, Aristophanes also has the chorus outline the ways in which his play is more sophisticated than those of his rivals. The lines are revealing as they give us an insight into some of the less refined techniques used by comic writers to raise laughs, such as the use of leather phalluses with red ends (i.e. made to look like circumcised or erect penises), outrageous comic dances and pseudo-violent slapstick (the topic of humour is explored more fully in Chapter 4). The chorus personifies the play as a young girl, saying:

> Look at how modest her nature is. For a start, she has not come with a bit of stitched, dangling leather, red at the end and thick so as to give the boys a laugh. Nor has she made fun of bald men, nor danced a cordax. Nor is there an old man (one with a speaking part) hitting whoever's around with a stick in an attempt to disguise bad jokes. Nor does she [i.e. this comedy] rush on with torches, nor shout 'help, help!' Rather, she has come trusting in herself and her script.

> *Clouds* 537-44

What makes this passage particularly interesting, however, is that the claims made are largely refuted in the course of the play. At *Clouds* 1298, for instance, Strepsiades – an old man and the play's main character – pokes one of his creditors with a goad (i.e. an object similar to a stick); at 1321 he yells 'help, help!'; at 1490 he asks for someone to bring him a torch; and at 1493 another character rushes on crying 'help, help!' – this time one of Socrates' students. What is more, a few years later Aristophanes puts erect leather phalluses to devastating use in his staging of the consequences of the sex strike in *Lysistrata* (411 BC) and at the end of *Wasps* (422 BC) we find a comic dance-off between Philocleon and the sons of the tragic poet Carcinus (whom Aristophanes dresses as crabs, inspired by the fact that their father's name means 'crab' in Greek: 1485ff.). In fact, the only technique listed here which the bald Aristophanes does not employ in some form or other in his plays is making fun of bald men!

So what are we to make of Aristophanes' claims to cleverness and originality? Such assertions are made consistently throughout his work and certainly it seems counter-intuitive on reading Aristophanes' plays to deny that they are clever and original. It should be added, however, that the numerous fragments we possess of other comic playwrights of the era suggest that 'cleverness' and 'originality' were not in short supply (whatever Aristophanes' criticisms of his rival poets might imply to the

6

contrary). What is more, the fact that no complete play by any other comic playwright of the classical era survives makes a rounded assessment of Aristophanes' originality and cleverness difficult, if not impossible (especially in terms of, say, plot development and characterization, where a whole play would be necessary to make a useful comparison with Aristophanes' work).[8]

The question still remains as to how we are to understand this passage from *Clouds* (537-44).[9] That is to say: what are we to make of the fact that Aristophanes has the chorus make a series of specific claims about how his comedy is superior to his rivals' only to have most of them undermined as the play progresses? Surely Aristophanes cannot be unaware of the content of his own play, so is this a case of the playwright being playful? And if *these* comments are playful, where does this leave us in respect of Aristophanes' broader claims to originality and cleverness or, indeed, any other claims he makes? In short, are such claims playful, heartfelt – or something else?

An important factor to take into consideration at this point is that it seems to have been conventional for Old Comic poets to criticize their rivals. Aristophanes himself is a victim of snipes in the fragments of other comic playwrights: he is accused of plagiarism by Eupolis, for example (frs 60 and 89), and is often ridiculed for not producing his plays himself (Ameipsias fr. 27; Aristonymus fr. 3; Plato comicus fr. 107 and Sannyrion fr. 5: see also Chapter 2). So, one way of understanding *Clouds* 537-44 is as a conventional piece of rhetoric: a dig by Aristophanes at his rivals of a kind that his audience would readily recognize and enjoy – without necessarily subjecting the claims to close scrutiny. A fruitful point of comparison here is a passage from *Knights* (424 BC) where, unusually, we find a piece of sustained *praise* of comic dramatists. At *Knights* 518-40, the chorus sympathetically cites a series of poets – Magnes, Cratinus and Crates – who, it claims, were heartlessly tossed aside by the Athenians once past their prime. It is instructive to note that, unlike the comic poets criticized and ridiculed in Aristophanes' plays, the pitiable Magnes and Crates both belong to a former generation and are therefore not current rivals of his. Cratinus, however, was not only a contemporary of Aristophanes' but was even up against him in the comic competition that very year – but the insinuation is, of course, that Cratinus, too, is a has-been! Here, then, we have a set of seemingly heartfelt sentiments interlaced with a barbed jibe at a rival, with pathos and bathos, fact and fiction combined – and there is only a certain extent to which these elements can be unpicked. Significantly, though, the audience is given little if any time to focus on the truthfulness of what is said: rather, an idea is put out there, a conventional point is made (namely that Aristophanes' rival playwrights are inferior to him) and the play moves on.

Once more, then, we are faced with a range of intriguing problems when we try to get to grips with passages containing 'personal' sentiments. And one factor that is clearly relevant is the role of convention. The very fact that the expression of personal opinions was a normal and expected part of Old Comedy should perhaps make us wary of taking all of Aristophanes' claims at face value – especially when it is conventional for poets to express certain views, such as the superiority of their own work to that of their rivals; and especially, as we have seen, when the claims made by Aristophanes in this regard do not always stand up to scrutiny. But being wary about 'personal' statements and being sensitive to context and convention are not the same as seeing all such comments as mere posturing or playfulness on Aristophanes' part. The problem of how we interpret 'personal' comments remains a live issue for as long as we read Aristophanes' plays and, indeed, will crop up regularly in later chapters of this book.[10]

The conventions of Old Comedy

Piecing together the characteristics of the comic dramatic tradition that Aristophanes inherited is no easy task. Aristotle talks briefly about comedy's origins in the *Poetics*, but admits that the early stages in the development of comedy were not recorded 'because it was not taken seriously' (1449a38-b1). As with other drama, comedy certainly originated in Dionysiac ritual, but Aristotle specifically talks of comedy emerging from 'Phallic Songs' (*ta phallika: Poetics* 1449a11-12) – songs which perhaps resembled the exuberant song to Phales (the personified god of the Hard-On) found at *Acharnians* 263-79 – and adds that it was only in the generation prior to Aristophanes that Crates became the first Athenian playwright to abandon comic lampoons in favour of more fully worked out plots (*Poetics* 1449b7-9). Aristotle is also responsible for the division of ancient Greek comedy into three phases: Old, Middle and New. Modern scholars usually use the term Old Comedy to refer to the period from 486 BC (when comedy was first officially produced in Athens) until roughly 400 BC; Middle Comedy for plays dating from 400 to 320s BC (and thus taking in Aristophanes' last two extant plays, *Assemblywomen* and *Wealth*); and New Comedy to describe comedy dating from the 320s onwards – and specifically the plays of the comic poet Menander.

The genre of Old Comedy as inherited by Aristophanes was, then, a product of both long traditions and recent innovations. At its heart lay what may seem like an anarchic mixture of humour, topical abuse, social commentary, obscenity, slapstick, song and dance; but, as is evident from close study of Aristophanes' work, his plays were also structured (albeit loosely) according to a conventional pattern. Old Comedy made use of six building blocks in the construction of a play – prologue, *parodos*, *agôn*, *parabasis*, consequences of the *agôn* and *exodos* – giving Aristophanes' dramas a distinctive form. Each of these elements of his plays has its own norms and conventions.

1. Aristophanes and Old Comedy

Prologue

This is the opening scene of the play before the arrival of the chorus, usually beginning with a monologue (such as Dicaeopolis' soliloquy that opens *Acharnians*) or a two-handed dialogue (such as one between two slaves as in *Knights* or *Peace*). Comic prologues tend to be three or four times longer than those of tragedy, largely because they have a lot of work to do: in a comedy (unlike tragedies, which are generally based on well known myths) the play's premise, its main characters, and any other relevant details all have to be presented to the audience at the start of the play. A favourite Aristophanic technique is to keep the audience in the dark at first as to who the characters are and/or what exactly they are doing, while peppering the script with tantalizing clues to rouse the spectators' interest. *Peace*, for instance, opens with slaves frantically kneading dung cakes to feed a mysterious creature, while in *Lysistrata* the first character we meet is the play's comic heroine pacing up and down waiting to discuss a 'far from trivial matter' with her fellow women (*Lysistrata* 14), the nature of which – the proposed sex strike – is not revealed until line 124 of the play.

Parodos

The *parodos* is the entry of the chorus, whose lines are either sung or chanted (i.e. something approaching operatic 'recitative'). The identity of the chorus, who typically either supports or is hostile to the play's main character, is also established at this point. The entry of the chorus was capable of being a point of high drama: not only did it introduce a new phase of action in the play, but could also mark the point where the chorus' elaborate costumes were revealed (e.g. *Wasps* and *Birds*) or – in the case of a chorus hostile to the play's main character – the beginning of some vigorous stage action. In *Acharnians*, for example, the chorus rush into the acting space in violent pursuit of Dicaeopolis' messenger, Amphitheus, shouting:

> Everyone, this way! Follow him! Chase him! And ask every passer-by where he is. It'll serve the city well if we lay hold of this man.
>
> *Acharnians* 204-6

Agôn

The *agôn* is the 'contest' or 'dispute' that arises between two parties and which constitutes the central issue of the play. This can take different forms: a dispute between two characters (such as Aeschylus and Euripides in *Frogs* over who is the better poet); between the comic hero and the chorus (such as Dicaeopolis and the chorus of *Acharnians* over whether it

9

is justifiable to make peace with Sparta); or, unusually, between groups of characters and semi-choruses (such as in *Lysistrata*, where female and male characters and choruses are opposed). An *agôn* proper comprises a formal debate between the two parties with paired speeches (as in *Knights*, *Wasps* and *Frogs*), but the dispute is often formulated more loosely than this. In *Acharnians*, for example, Dicaeopolis simply delivers a speech to the chorus in defence of his private peace treaty (*Acharnians* 490-626), whereas in *Women at the Thesmophoria* the Inlaw does not so much mount a defence of Euripides – the women's sworn enemy – in reply to their various speeches, as expose the women's most shocking secrets (372-519: see p. 86)! In other plays, such as *Birds* and *Assemblywomen*, the *agôn* amounts to little more than an extended act of persuasion by the main character as to the benefits of his or her scheme.

Parabasis

The *parabasis* is the 'coming forward' of the chorus during which the actors are absent from the acting space, leaving the chorus to address the audience directly. In Aristophanes' early plays, the chorus routinely takes the opportunity to praise the poet and attack Cleon: the *parabasis* sections of *Knights*, *Wasps* and *Clouds*, for instance, are the source of many of the passages discussed earlier in this chapter. There are certain formal elements to the *parabasis*, such as a speech by the chorus leader directly addressing the audience (called 'the anapaests' at *Acharnians* 627, *Knights* 504, *Peace* 735 and *Birds* 684 after the poetic metre in which they are composed). Other elements include a breathless, tongue-twisting song known as a *pnigos* (from the Greek word 'to choke') and various strophic songs (i.e. songs with rhythmically corresponding verses, or *strophai*), generally delivered by the chorus in their character as clouds, knights, birds, etc. (the technical name for these is the 'epirrhematic syzygy'). In Aristophanes' earlier plays there is sometimes a short second *parabasis*, whereas in later plays the importance of the *parabasis* diminishes: in *Frogs*, for example, there is *only* a second *parabasis* and in *Lysistrata* (as well as the Middle Comedies *Assemblywomen* and *Wealth*) there is no *parabasis* at all.[11]

Consequences of the agôn

Following the resolution of the *agôn* (and sometimes before the *parabasis*) the audience is presented with the consequences of the main character's victory. This often comes in the form of a stream of individuals, such as those who come to see Peisthetaerus in *Birds* hoping to benefit from the establishment of Cloudcuckooland. Similarly in *Acharnians*, characters come to Dicaeopolis hoping to benefit from his private peace treaty with Sparta, some of whom are allowed to share in his prosperity (i.e. those who are not responsible for the war), others not (most notably the general, Lamachus). These consequences are not always positive for the main character: the episodes following the female seizure of power in *Assembly-women*, for example, arguably show Praxagora's new regime in a morally ambivalent light; likewise the outrageous behaviour of Philocleon in *Wasps* shows that his son, Bdelycleon, has ultimately failed to educate him in the ways of polite society.

Exodos

The ending of the play and 'exit' (*exodos*) of the chorus. This often involves food, wine, sex and celebration – but not without exceptions. *Women at the Thesmophoria*, for example, ends in a very low key fashion with little jubilation accompanying Euripides' rescue of his Inlaw, whereas the famously problematic ending of *Clouds* sees Strepsiades setting fire to Socrates' Thinkery (*phrontistêrion*).

Important as these six structural elements evidently were to the genre of comedy, it is interesting to observe the way in which Aristophanes uses them more or less flexibly in different plays according to his requirements as a dramatist. The tendency is for his earlier plays to be structured in a more uniform fashion than his later work, and during the late fifth century changes were evidently afoot (most notably the eventual abandonment of the *parabasis*). In his Middle Comedies a new configuration is discernible: although traces of the old structural elements survive, *Assemblywomen* and *Wealth* are essentially made up of a prologue and series of episodes punctuated by five choral odes (although the text of most of these songs no longer survives).

The emotional structure of Old Comedy

Just as important as these formal elements for understanding Old Comedy is the basic emotional structure of the plays. There is routinely a main character in the play, the so-called 'comic hero', who more often than not is an ageing or older man, a country dweller and – perhaps most crucially – exercises no power within the city. Dicaeopolis in *Acharnians* and Trygaeus in *Peace* fit this pattern well, for example; other central characters, perhaps most notably Lysistrata and Praxagora, less so (the presentation of women and old men is examined further in Chapter 5).

At the play's start, the comic hero(ine) invariably has cause for dissatisfaction and comes up with what William Arrowsmith has called the 'Great Idea'[12] – some fantastic solution to the problem, such as bringing about peace by means of a private treaty (*Acharnians*) or by flying to heaven on a giant dung beetle (*Peace*) or by persuading the women of Greece to hold a sex strike (*Lysistrata*). This scheme faces problems and/or

11

opposition but is ultimately successful – which is in turn a cause for celebration. This formula of dissatisfaction, 'Great Idea', opposition, solution and celebration has been stated in a number of ways by scholars: Kenneth McLeish, for instance, prefers to sum up Aristophanes' plots with the simple model 'problem stated – solution sought – rejoicing'.[13] Naturally, this schema works better for some plays than others (as we saw above, not all plays see the problems overcome or rejoicing, for example), but this serves once more to underline the fact that Aristophanes was the master, not slave, of his art: he made intelligent and flexible use of the structural elements he inherited, tailoring them to fit with each play he authored.

Conclusions

In this chapter we have begun to look at some of the key issues surrounding Aristophanic drama, most notably the problems associated with interpreting the 'personal' views expressed in the plays and the characteristics of the comic tradition inherited by Aristophanes. These plays are important documents for helping us to understand the nature and development of comedy in the late fifth and early fourth centuries BC during a period when comedy – deeply influenced as it was by its conventions and traditions – was nevertheless undergoing some substantial changes. The fact that we know the production dates of most of Aristophanes' plays allows us an insight into the ways in which Aristophanes developed and changed as a dramatist over the years and also helps us to engage with the numerous topical allusions and political jibes we find in his work – one of the most fascinating aspects of which is his relationship with Cleon, which is neatly played out for us in his first five extant plays, from *Acharnians* to *Peace* (this topic is explored again in Chapter 9). In the next chapter we shall go on to consider further aspects of Aristophanes' early career as a playwright and producer and take a broad look at how the plays were produced and performed in their original context: namely in the context of festivals which played a central role in the civic and religious life of Athens.

Putting on a Show

Introduction

Whilst much of the subject matter and many of the themes of Aristophanes' comedies arguably have a timeless quality, there is little escaping the fact that his plays are also products of a specific culture, written to be performed at a certain time and place. Among the more obvious ways in which the plays are intrinsically tied to their fifth-century Athenian context are the topical and political references they contain; the prejudices and tastes that the audience members are assumed to share; and the theatre space for which the plays were composed (all topics examined in future chapters). Perhaps more subtle – though no less important – is the way in which Aristophanic drama was influenced by the civic and religious context for which it was written, namely the two dramatic festivals, the Lenaea and Great Dionysia, that played such a large part in the life of all classical Athenian dramatists, comedians and tragedians alike. In this chapter, we shall examine not only these festivals but also the whole production process which preceded the staging of Aristophanes' plays, including how they were funded and the way in which the actors were chosen and the choruses trained. As we shall see, all these different elements had their own impact on how Aristophanes composed his plays which makes getting to grips with them an important part of understanding his work.

Reconstructing the nature of dramatic festivals and the processes by which Aristophanes got to put on his 'shows' is no easy task. Indeed, despite the best efforts of generations of classical scholars, there is still a surprising amount of uncertainty and debate surrounding various aspects of the theatrical production process in Athens and the organization of the dramatic festivals. One option for an author of a book such as this is to dodge these uncertainties and to provide a filtered, 'common sense' version of events without highlighting the points of debate. This is not the approach adopted here, however. Instead, in this chapter we will look at the ancient evidence from which our picture of the dramatic festivals is built up – including passages taken from a range of Aristophanes' plays themselves – and consider some of the different conclusions that scholars working with this evidence have reached. In this way, we will not only be able build up a broad picture of how plays were staged in ancient Athens, but also explore some of the challenges of using Aristophanes as an historical source. An understanding of the civic, religious and cultural context of Aristophanes' plays will also form an important backdrop to topics discussed in later chapters, such as Aristophanes' portrayal of women (Chapter 4); his use of obscenity (Chapter 7) and above all Aristophanic politics (Chapter 9).

Dramatic festivals

All the plays we possess from the classical era were written for – and first produced at – one of two annual Athenian festivals: the Lenaea and the Great Dionysia. Both of these festivals were held in honour of Dionysus, a god linked primarily with wine, but who presided over other transformations besides drunkenness, such as madness, ecstasy, the mask – and dramatic imitation. The first recorded performances of tragedy in Athens are in 533 BC at the Great Dionysia, long before comedy gained official recognition; but this is not to say that comedy did not have a long tradition prior to the fifth century, merely, as we saw in Chapter 1, that in earlier times 'it was not taken seriously' (Aristotle, *Poetics* 1449a38-b1). In Aristophanes' day, comedy was performed alongside tragedy at both of these festivals and, at the Great Dionysia, alongside satyr plays, too (dramas featuring choruses of satyrs, the mischievous and lusty half-animal followers of Dionysus). Our sources are not as full as we might like them to be, but they nevertheless allow us to reconstruct the basic features of both the Lenaea and the Great Dionysia.

The Lenaea

The Lenaea was both the smaller of the two festivals and the one we know least about. It preceded the Great Dionysia by several weeks, beginning on the twelfth day of the Athenian month of Gamelion – at a time of year equivalent to late January in the modern calendar. The festival was spread over four days and, aside from drama, also seems to have involved a procession and various other religious rites. Comic plays began to be formally produced at the Lenaea in about 440 BC and tragic plays in 432 BC: probably five comedies were staged along with two sets of two tragedies.[1]

The official name of the festival was the 'Dionysia at the Lenaeon', the Lenaeon being the name of a sanctuary of Dionysus whose probable location was the Athenian market place (*agora*). We find references in Aristophanes and elsewhere to the plays being produced 'at the Lenaeon' (rather than 'at the *Lenaea*') which may well indicate that they were physically staged in or near the sanctuary, although it is often argued that this phrase is formulaic and that from 440 BC, if not before, productions would have taken place in the Theatre of Dionysus on the slopes of the Acropolis.[2]

2. Putting on a Show

Several of Aristophanes' plays were staged at the Lenaea, including *Acharnians, Knights, Wasps, Frogs* and *Lysistrata*, and for comic playwrights at least,[3] there was probably little or no difference in prestige between the two festivals (for tragedians, on the other hand, the Great Dionysia evidently had more standing than the Lenaea).[4] A much-quoted passage from *Acharnians*, however, does seem to imply a difference in the make-up of the Lenaea audience compared with that of the Great Dionysia. In an address to the play's spectators, the central character, Dicaeopolis, refers to the presence of citizens and resident immigrants (*metoikoi* or 'metics') in the audience, but says that foreigners – who apparently arrived in Athens *en masse* only in the better weather once the sailing season had begun – are absent.

> We are by ourselves: it's the contest at the Lenaeon and there are no foreigners here yet. Neither the *phoroi* ('tribute monies' or taxes) nor men themselves have arrived from the allied cities. No, we're all alone now, stripped of the husk. For I consider the metics (*metoikoi*) to be the citizen bran.
>
> *Acharnians* 504-7

An idea that has interested some scholars is whether the differences between the Lenaea and Great Dionysia – and especially the differences in the kinds of spectators that the festivals attracted – has left an impression on the plays themselves. Certainly it is in the early Lenaea plays – *Acharnians* (425 BC), *Knights* (424 BC) and *Wasps* (422 BC) – that Aristophanes' most vehement political and personal attacks appear, namely on his great adversary Cleon. What is more, it is in the later Lenaea plays, *Lysistrata* (411 BC) and *Frogs* (405 BC), that we find what appear to be some very specific pieces of political advice (discussed further in Chapter 9). Perhaps, then, some themes, sentiments and approaches did fit the mood of one festival more than the other and comparison of the Lenaea with the Great Dionysia therefore has the potential to be instructive.

The Great Dionysia

We possess far more information about the Great or City Dionysia, which was an altogether larger affair than the Lenaea. This festival was spread over five days, beginning in earnest on the tenth of Elaphebolion – late March in the modern calendar. The first event of the Great Dionysia's programme, however, happened two days *before* this date: this was the *proagôn*, or 'pre-contest', where poets appeared with their uncostumed actors to give the gathered onlookers a taste of what to expect from their plays (*Proagôn* is also the name of one of Aristophanes' lost plays). In Aristophanes' day, the *proagôn* took place in the Odeon, a building erected as part of the Periclean building programme in the 440s BC right next to the Theatre of Dionysus.

15

It is important to bear in mind that theatrical performances formed only one part of this religious festival – and, indeed, the next significant event of Great Dionysia had nothing to do with drama at all. This happened on the eve of the festival when a torchlight procession (the *eisagôgê*, or 'leading in') saw a sacred wooden statue of Dionysus taken from the god's sanctuary in Athens and escorted to a temple on the road to Eleutherae – the border town from where he was said first to have entered Attica. Here, in a ceremony probably dating back to around 530 BC, celebrants performed a sacrifice before bringing the image back to his sanctuary, just south of the Acropolis – and it is overlooking this ancient sanctuary, on the Acropolis' southern slopes, that the Theatre of Dionysus eventually took permanent form.

On the first day of the festival proper, Athens staged a huge procession (*pompê*) in which different sections of the city's population were demarcated: citizens bringing offerings such as sacrificial bulls and carrying wine were divided into their ten tribes (*phylai*), for example, and the resident immigrants (*metoikoi*) wore distinctive red robes and carried bowls for mixing the wine with water. Other groups, such as members of the city's executive council (the *boulê*) and its young men undergoing military training (*ephêboi*), were also distinguished. A characteristically Dionysiac touch to the procession came in the form of erect phalluses held aloft by participants.

This first day of the Great Dionysia was an occasion for dances, sacrifices, drinking – and also choral competitions. Each of the ten tribes was represented by one chorus of fifty men and another of fifty boys who sang and danced to Dionysiac songs called dithyrambs. The fact that 1,000 men and boys would have competed in these dithyrambic contests in any given year certainly has interesting implications for the way we think about the audience of the plays. Many of its members would be all too used to the cut and thrust of competitive performances both at the Great Dionysia and in other contexts and would thus have viewed the dramatic performances – especially the choral parts – with something of an expert eye. As befits a festival in honour of the god of wine, following the dithyrambic competition, the evening was given over to drunken revelry.

Once the rowdy celebrations of the first day were over, theatrical performances took place over the remaining four days of the festival – and it was probably at the Great Dionysia that the original version of *Clouds* (423 BC), *Peace* (421 BC), *Birds* (414 BC) and *Women at the Thesmophoria* (411 BC) were all performed. However, it was not only plays that the audience got to see, since – in the late fifth century at least – other pieces of civic business were enacted before the dramatic performances began:[5] the ten annually elected generals (each representing one of Athens' ten tribes) poured a ceremonial libation; the names of citizens who had benefited the city were read out along with details of the public honours they had received, and there was also a public display of the *phoros* ('tribute money' or tax) paid to Athens by its subject city-states.[6] In addition, there was a parade of war orphans who had reached manhood – these young men, whose fathers had died in battle and who had been raised at the state's expense, were honoured by being given armour and had the privilege of occupying special seats during the performances.[7]

In and of themselves, these pieces of civic business enacted before the dramatic performances may seem of only marginal interest, but their linking together by Simon Goldhill in his 1990 article 'The Great Dionysia and Civic Ideology' casts them in an interesting light.[8] Taken as a whole, these ceremonies can be said to raise interesting questions in the minds of spectators about key civic issues: not only what it is to be an Athenian citizen (through the honouring of the city's benefactors and the coming of age of the war orphans) but also questions concerning Athens' relationship to other city-states (through the display of tribute money and presence of foreign ambassadors). The role played by the ten tribal generals also recalls the tribal divisions so prevalent in the festival's organization (the separation of citizens into their different tribes in the procession and the choral competitions, for example). What is more, the fact that the resident immigrants (*metoikoi*) are *not* represented by any general (they had no voting rights and therefore elected no representative) highlights once more the way in which they are at once included in this festival yet at the same time marginalized: resident immigrants wore distinctive dress in the procession, as we saw earlier, and they were also excluded from direct participation as singers or actors in the dithyrambic and dramatic competitions.[9] In short, the Great Dionysia can justly be described as an occasion when Athens, its civic organization and its international standing are on display both to itself and to the world at large. And all this must surely have interesting implications for the way in which we read and understand the plays that were performed at this festival – especially the social and political commentary that they contain. (In Chapter 5 we will see how Aristophanes often has marginal figures like old men and women offer a critique of contemporary society and in Chapter 9 we will look at the nature of the 'advice' and political stances that occur with such regularity in Aristophanes' comedies.)

The festival programme

Comedies only began to be performed at the City Dionysia in 486 BC, taking their place alongside tragedies and satyr plays which had been staged at the festival for at least two generations by this time. One piece of information that we do not possess, however, is the order in which the different types of plays were put on. It is possible that the comedies were performed on day two of the festival and tragedies on the following three days. This is the order of events argued for by Douglas MacDowell, for instance, on the basis of a law quoted by the fourth-century orator Demosthenes:[10]

... when the procession takes place for Dionysus in Piraeus with the comedies and tragedies, and the procession at the Lenaeon with the tragedies and the comedies, and the procession at the City Dionysia as well as the boys, the revel, the comedies and the tragedies, and on the occasion of the procession and the contest of the Thargelia ...

Law of Euergus, quoted at Demosthenes 21.10

MacDowell suggests that, since this law lists Athens' festivals in their chronological order, the order in which 'comedies and tragedies' are listed here is likely to reflect their appearance in the festivals, too: thus tragedies preceded comedies at the Lenaea, whereas comedies preceded tragedies at the City Dionysia.[11] Supporting evidence for such an arrangement is also found in victory lists – inscriptions dating largely from the 340s but which are evidently based on earlier records. These give details of the winning dithyrambic choruses (both men's and boys') and plays (comedies and tragedies), as in the following example, which records the victory of Aeschylus' *Oresteia* at the Great Dionysia of 458 BC. Note that in the Athenian calendar each year is named after a senior public official called the Archon (also known as the Archon Eponymous):

[In the archonship of Philo]cle[s]: the boys of the tribe Oineis with Demodocus as sponsor (*chorêgos*); the men of the tribe Hippothontis with Euctemon of Eleusis as sponsor (*chorêgos*). In the comedies: Eurycleides was sponsor (*chorêgos*), Euphronius producer (*didaskalos*). In the tragedies: Xenokles of Aphidna was sponsor (*chorêgos*), Aeschylus producer (*didaskalos*).

IG II² 2318

Once more, the order in which the victories are recorded may well reflect the traditional order of the performances: boys' dithyrambs, men's dithyrambs, comedies, tragedies – and certainly such an arrangement is understood by a number of scholars. This gives us the following programme for the festival.

Eve of Festival	torchlight procession (*eisagôgê*)
Day 1	procession, dithyrambic contests, sacrifices, revelry
Day 2	5 comedies
Day 3	3 tragedies + 1 satyr play
Day 4	3 tragedies + 1 satyr play
Day 5	3 tragedies + 1 satyr play

Not every scholar is convinced by this running order, however. Many prefer to work on the assumption that comic plays came at the end of the festival, providing light relief after three days of tragedies. Reversing the order of comedies and tragedies in this way gives the following running order.

Eve of Festival	torchlight procession (*eisagôgê*)
Day 1	procession, dithyrambic contests, sacrifices, revelry
Day 2	3 tragedies + 1 satyr play
Day 3	3 tragedies + 1 satyr play
Day 4	3 tragedies + 1 satyr play
Day 5	5 comedies

To complicate matters further, there is also a school of thought which maintains that, for both the Great Dionysia and Lenaea, the number of comedies was reduced to three for much of the Peloponnesian War (431-404 BC). This makes yet another configuration possible, namely that during this period the three comedies were performed, one at the end of each day, allowing the number of days of dramatic performances to be cut to three.

Eve of Festival	torchlight procession (*eisagôgê*)
Day 1	procession, dithyrambic contests, sacrifices, revelry
Day 2	3 tragedies + 1 satyr play + 1 comedy
Day 3	3 tragedies + 1 satyr play + 1 comedy
Day 4	3 tragedies + 1 satyr play + 1 comedy

This idea of a curtailed wartime festival has proved stubbornly popular, despite the fact that the evidence to support it is relatively slight.[12] And while there may be good reasons for finding this scenario unconvincing – not least because days two to four of the festival would have been hugely drawn out, and the festival's traditional pattern significantly disturbed – such an arrangement would at least make good sense of a passage from the *Birds*, where the chorus extols to the spectators the virtues of having wings:

> There is nothing better or more pleasant than growing wings. For instance, if one of you spectators had wings, and you'd been hungry and bored with the choruses of the tragedies, you could have flown off home, had some lunch, then flown back to us again once you were full up.
>
> *Birds* 785-9

The implications of this passage have been much discussed, since our concept of the order of events alters greatly depending on what we make of it. But here, as so often when we try to use Aristophanes as an historical source, we come up against a set of imponderable questions. Is the joke behind this passage that a winged spectator could skip the boring parts of a tragedy but return in time for a comedy (assuming that is what is implied by 'us' in line 789)? If so, does this joke only work if his comedy is being performed at the end of a day of tragedies, or is the truth being stretched for the purpose of the joke? And if the truth *is* being stretched, does the joke rely on the idea that comic performances generally follow tragic ones – thus adding weight to the view that comedies were performed on day five of the festival – or could it still work if this play were being performed on day two? There are no easy answers here. And yet given the number of allusions there are to tragedy in Aristophanes' plays (explored in Chapter 6), it would clearly be interesting to know whether the audience watched his comedies with that year's tragedies fresh in their minds, or whether they were watching on day two of the Great Dionysia – the day which David Wiles has dubbed 'a day of hangovers'.[13]

The production process

The process by which the plays came to be produced at the festivals sheds further light on Aristophanes' work. Once again, we are better informed about the Great Dionysia, though what little we know about the Lenaea would suggest that the production process was similar for both festivals.

Late in the summer preceding the Great Dionysia, prospective playwrights would formally 'ask for a chorus' by submitting outlines of their plays to a state official – the Archon (also known as the Archon Eponymous: see above) – whose job it was to decide which three tragedians and which five comic poets would get to stage their dramas. A different official, the Archon Basileus, performed this function for the Lenaea. Here it is worth bearing in mind that the main concern of both of these annually allotted posts would have been the overseeing of various aspects of Athens' religious life, with theatrical productions forming just one element of this. In other words, these officials were not chosen for their expertise in drama and on what basis they would have made their decisions about which plays to stage and which poets to turn down is not known. However, reputation probably counted for a good deal and it would no doubt have taken a brave Archon to turn down one of the city's favoured poets.[14]

It was at this juncture that a successful poet would have been assigned a *chorêgos*, a wealthy citizen who was leant on to provide the funds for the production.[15] The *chorêgia* was a form of 'liturgy' (*leitourgia*), a wealth tax levied on Athens' wealthiest families in order to meet certain public expenses, notably the training of dithyrambic choruses (such as those which took place at the Great Dionysia), theatrical productions and the

20

equipping of warships. In a speech by the orator Lysias, delivered in the late fifth century, a *chorêgos* is said to have spent a sum of 1,600 drachmas on a comic production – a drachma being the wage that a skilled labourer might expect for a day's work.[16] The reason why this was such an expensive business is that it involved paying for the maintenance of the chorus members (24 in number for comedies) and the provision of their masks and costumes, which were often highly elaborate: the outfitting of the choruses of *Frogs*, *Wasps* and *Birds*, for instance, can have been no cheap affair. What is more, the *chorêgos* was also responsible for providing a place for the chorus to practise; paying musicians to accompany the performance, and even for appointing and remunerating a choral trainer (*choro-didaskalos*) – though this was often the poet himself.

Chorêgoi whose choruses were successful in the Great Dionysia's dithyrambic competitions erected small monuments to their victories in the form of tripods – and celebratory inscriptions set up by *chorêgoi* who were victorious in the dramatic contests also suggest that these men regarded their play's success as something of a personal triumph (the recording of the names of the *chorêgoi* in the victory lists also suggests a strong identification of *chorêgos* with play and *vice versa*). Both the winning poet and the winning *chorêgos* originally received an ivy wreath as a prize (later a bull and a tripod were awarded respectively), and as a result of the victory the *chorêgos* was also responsible for a further expense: providing the play's cast and crew with a victory party (*epinikia*).

An interesting question to pose is what influence a *chorêgos* may have had – or tried to have – over the production in return for his investment. Complaints we hear about mean *chorêgoi* (e.g. *Acharnians* 1150-73; Eupolis fr. 329) coupled with boasts we hear from lavish *chorêgoi* (such as the 1,600 drachmas supposedly spent by the speaker of Lysias 21) suggest that the extent to which this figure was inclined to be generous with his money held great importance. And since the *chorêgos* was appointed while the play was probably still only in outline form, there must also have existed a temptation for him to influence the content of the play. Given the amount of personal invective that most of Aristophanes' plays contain (a topic explored more fully in Chapters 7 and 9), one wonders in particular whether a *chorêgos* would have sought to have any say over which individuals were (or were not) singled out for attack.

Actors

Along with a *chorêgos*, a poet whose play was chosen for production was most probably allotted, rather than chose, his principal actors. These were paid for from the public purse – presumably because the work they were undertaking formed part of a public, religious festival. Once more, we can only speculate as to how the end product may have been affected by this allotting of actors, which again occurred when the play was at an early stage of development. Presumably each actor had his own strengths, weaknesses and specialisms which both the playwright and actors would work to accommodate as the production developed. And it would no doubt be naive to suppose that the relationship between the state-appointed (and therefore presumably unsackable) actor and the playwright would always have been a smooth one! It should also be mentioned that there was an earlier tradition in tragedy of playwrights appearing in their own plays. There is no evidence that Aristophanes ever acted, but some scholars have nevertheless speculated that he may have appeared in *Acharnians* – a suggestion inspired by the fact that in the play Dicaeopolis often claims to speak on behalf of the playwright – as well as in other plays (e.g. as Xanthias in *Frogs*).

With the possible exception of the playwright, then, the actors were publicly appointed semi-professionals, in contrast with the chorus which was made up of talented amateurs assembled by the *chorêgos*. In common with the chorus, though, all actors were male with the consequence that all female roles in the plays – as well as the female choruses of *Lysistrata, Women at the Thesmophoria* and *Assemblywomen* – would have been played by men. The chorus would also have heavily outnumbered the speaking actors of which only three (sometimes four) were required for Aristophanes' plays – with the chorus leader or 'coryphaeus' also making occasional contributions to the dialogue. (The portrayal of women and the function of the chorus are discussed further in Chapter 5.)

The general practice of the Greek theatre was for the principal actor, the 'protagonist', to take the lead role in a play (e.g. Dicaeopolis, Lysistrata) and for the other parts in the play to be divided up between the second and third actors (the 'deuteragonist' and 'tritagonist'). This explains the occasional occurrence of unmotivated exits in the plays ahead of the entrance of a new character, since the practicalities of performance dictate that if there are already three speaking actors on stage one must leave and change his costume in order to reappear in a new guise. When Euripides and his Inlaw pay a visit to Agathon in *Women at the Thesmophoria*, for example, Agathon's servant opens the door, but disappears at line 70 never to be seen again, just ahead of Agathon's appearance at line 101. In a similar way, when Peisthetaerus and Euelpides pay a visit to the Hoopoe in *Birds*, his servant disappears at line 84 ahead of the Hoopoe's entrance at line 92.

Comedy occasionally requires a fourth speaking actor on stage (which is only very rarely the case in tragedy). Modern attempts to reconstruct the way in which the various parts in Aristophanes' plays may have been divided up reveal that this fourth actor would probably have had very few lines assigned to him, however. Perhaps the role of fourth actor served as something of an apprenticeship.[17] Non-speaking actors were also required. On the assumption that the fourth speaking actor was to be given as few lines as possible (which may or may not have been the case in reality), the division of parts in the *Birds*, for example, may have been as follows (the numbers in brackets are the line numbers for which the actors must be on stage):

Protagonist:	Peisthetaerus
Deuteragonist:	Euelpides (1-846); Priest (863-94), Oracle-Monger (959-90), Inspector (1021-31), First Messenger (1122-63), Iris (1202-59), Young Man (1337-71), Sycophant (1410-68), Poseidon (1565-1692)
Tritagonist:	Servant of Hoopoe/Tereus (60-84), Hoopoe/Tereus (92-675), Poet (904-53), Meton (992-1017), Decree-Seller (1035-51), Second Messenger (1170-85), First Herald (1271-1307), Cinesias (1372-1409), Heracles (1574-1692), Second Herald (1706-19)
Fourth Speaking Actor:	Triballian God (1565-1693)
Non-Speaking Actors:	Four Birds (267ff.), Two Servants (435), Two Slaves (656), Slave (850), Aulos-Player/Crow (859), Slave (1311)

What emerges from these part-divisions is the sheer versatility required of the second and third actors, given the range of parts they are required to perform. And if the allocations are at all correct we also gain an impression of the time available to the actors to change costume and prepare for their next part (sometimes as little as eight lines). Presumably, for different parts (e.g. women, old men, non-Greeks, etc.) an actor would appropriately modify not only his movements but also his voice which – given that the plays included both speech and song – and must have been a highly demanding task.[18]

The playwright and director

One role that has not been mentioned so far is that of the director. It is probable that this key role in the plays' production was usually undertaken by the playwright. However, in Aristophanes' case, it seems that this was not always so. In 424 BC – three years after Aristophanes' first play, *Banqueters* (427 BC), was performed in Athens – the chorus of *Knights* addresses the audience in the play's *parabasis* as follows:

> But the thing that he says that many of you approach him about and are amazed about and question him about – namely, why he didn't ask for his own chorus long ago – he has asked us to talk to you about this. For he says that it was not through stupidity that he put up with this situation for so long, but because he considered that being a comic director (*komoidodidaskalos*) was the most difficult task in the world.
>
> *Knights* 512-16

To take this statement at face value, *Knights* was the first play for which the young Aristophanes acted as his own *didaskalos* – a word probably best translated in a theatrical context as 'director', but which also carries the connotation of 'teacher'. The fact that Aristophanes did not direct his own plays is confirmed by the scholia and the writers of the Hellenistic *hypotheses* (introductions) to his plays, too. We are told that the lost *Babylonians* (426 BC), and the extant *Acharnians* (425 BC), *Birds* (414 BC) and *Lysistrata* were all presented 'through Callistratus' and that *Frogs* (405 BC) and the lost *Amphiarus* (414 BC) were presented 'through Philonides' (*Wasps*, staged in 422 BC, is also said to have been produced 'through Philonides', though the factual basis of this is disputed by some). Furthermore, Aristophanes' last two plays, the lost *Cocalus* and *Aeolosicon*, were said to have been presented 'through Ararus', that is to say Aristophanes' son, later a comic dramatist in his own right.

Quite what producing a play 'through' another man meant is not wholly clear, but it is probably a safe assumption that these men acted in the capacity of director (*didaskalos*) for plays which Aristophanes wrote. Taken together with evidence from victory lists – where along with the *chorêgos*, the name of the winning play's *didaskalos*, not poet, is cited – the *Knights* passage also raises interesting questions about what public recognition, if any, Aristophanes received for his writing prior to *Knights*. The following passage from the *parabasis* of *Wasps* has proven a particularly rich source of discussion in this regard. The chorus talks of Aristophanes as having helped other 'poets' in secret, before taking risks openly.

> And now, o ye people, pay attention, if you want to hear some straight talking. For our poet has a bone to pick with the spectators now. For he says that they have wronged him, without provocation, despite the enormous benefits he's conferred on them. At first he did this not openly, but secretly, by giving other poets (*poêtai*) assistance ... He got into other men's stomachs and poured forth comedy in abundance, but afterwards – and openly this time – he took his chances on his own account, controlling the reins and mouthpieces of his own (and not other men's) Muses.
>
> *Wasps* 1015-22

Most scholars interpret this passage as referring to the period when Aristophanes' plays were produced *through* others, the assumption being that the *poêtai*, 'makers'/'poets', referred to here are simply directors such as Callistratus. However, few facts about Aristophanes' life are wholly uncontroversial, and an alternative interpretation of these lines has been put forward, namely that Aristophanes served a form of 'apprenticeship'.[19] According to this theory, the reference in this passage is to a time before Aristophanes wrote comedies of his own when he helped other playwrights with their plays by providing them with material. Certainly there are problems with this theory. For instance, given that Aristophanes may only have been in his early twenties when his first full plays were produced, we would have to imagine him as serving this 'apprenticeship' when still extremely young. However, this interpretation does have its appeal, not least because it provides an explanation as to how Aristophanes was able to hone his talent at such a young age.

The dramatic contest

One unusual element of dramatic festivals to modern eyes has already been alluded to: that is, the fact that they were organized as a competition. Before the performances the judges were chosen by lot from amongst the citizen body. This was done by the presiding Archon who would draw a name from each of ten urns, one for every Attic tribe (*phylê*). It is not known whether there was any qualification for being a potential judge aside from being a tribe member and thus an Athenian citizen. Once chosen, however, the allotted judges came forward and swore an oath to vote for the best performance before taking their seats in a part of the theatre that was specially reserved for them (presumably near the acting space). Also chosen by lot was the order in which the plays were performed.

The voting procedures themselves are something of a mystery. It seems that after the performances the ten judges' votes were collected together and then drawn out at random in such a way as to determine a winner – with second and third (and during certain periods fourth and fifth) places awarded, too, as victory lists record. Tentative reconstructions of the way in which votes were counted when awarding the tragic prize may go some of the way to solving the puzzle. It has been suggested that, first, five randomly chosen votes were counted, then, if necessary, seven, nine, and eventually ten votes until a winner emerged – and the number crunching shows that such a system is highly effective for determining a rank order among the three tragic competitors.[20] However, an equivalent procedure for awarding the comic prize would be far less efficient: here the number crunching shows that if the same procedure were applied to comedy there would be a tie amongst two or more of the five competitors far too often for the system to be practical.

Whatever its exact nature, this complex voting mechanism has a number of interesting aspects. For example, the use of citizen men as judges and their selection from every tribe may be seen as underscoring the civic-orientated nature of the festival. What is more, the random way in which votes were counted and the use of lots to choose not just the judges but also the order in which the plays were performed could also be said to be democratic – since no one could influence the outcome – and at the same time to provide an opportunity for divine intervention.[21] Whatever its merits, however, what the system of selecting judges for the dramatic competitions certainly did *not* amount to is a rigorous means of ensuring that the poet who wrote the greatest work of art won. The citizens who judged the plays may have had any number of reasons for voting the way they did, and we should certainly resist the temptation of drawing conclusions about the relative merits of plays on the basis that some, such as *Acharnians, Knights* and *Frogs* won first prize, whilst others, such as *Wasps, Peace* and *Birds* did not.

Whatever peculiarities and weaknesses this voting system may have had, the question of winning first prize was evidently of great importance to the poets themselves. The chorus in *Assemblywomen*, for example, appeals directly to the judges not to overlook the play simply because it drew a disadvantageous position in the lot.

> I wish to make a small suggestion to the judges. To those who are clever: remember the clever bits and vote for me! To those who like a laugh: remember the funny bits and vote for me! So obviously I'm telling nearly all of you to vote for me! Don't let the fact that I drew the first position in the lottery count against me. No! You should remember all of this and, in accordance with the oath you swore, always judge the choruses fairly, and not behave like those miserable prostitutes (*hetairai*) who can only ever recall their last client!
>
> *Assemblywomen*, 1154-62

Here it is cleverness and laughter that are singled out as the elements of the play with the most potential appeal. As we saw in Chapter 1, Aristophanes' boasts tend to centre on the intelligence and originality of his plays (as well as his good advice), and so the claims made here come as little surprise. What is interesting to note, however, is that whereas the chorus of the *Assemblywomen* directs their comments to the judges in particular, elsewhere it is the audience at large who are held responsible for the fate of a play in the competition. In the revised version of *Clouds*, for example, it is the *audience*'s (and not the judges') failure to appreciate the intellectual qualities of Aristophanes' work that are blamed for the failure of the original version of the play (see Chapter 1, p. 5). Is the focus on the audience's reaction both here and elsewhere simply an indication that the judges were thought of as a microcosm of the audience? Or was it the case that the audience's reaction held great sway over the judges when they voted? If nothing else, the importance given here to the audience's verdict on a play would suggest that the spectators' and the judges' verdict varied less than one might have suspected.[22]

Audience

Who watched Aristophanes' plays? The audience must have consisted predominantly of citizen males, and presumably city-dwellers would have far outnumbered country-dwellers for the simple reason that urbanites would have had less far to travel and no accommodation to find in the city. During the early years of the Peloponnesian War, when many rural folk were herded into Athens to escape the Spartan raids on the Attic countryside, the make-up of the audience would no doubt have changed – and Dicaeopolis' longing in *Acharnians* to return to his village would consequently have struck a chord with many spectators (*Acharnians* 32-6: as we shall see in Chapter 5, the theme of the countryside features heavily in Aristophanes' plays from the 420s). Plutarch (who lived AD 46-120) tells us that Pericles (who died in 429 BC) established the so-called 'theoric fund' to allow poorer citizens to afford the entrance fee for the dramatic festivals (although many scholars date the introduction of this fund to the fourth century).[23] Since non-citizens did not benefit from this allowance, it is probably fair to assume that, after the fund's introduction, citizens were more likely to be able to afford the entry fee than non-citizens.[24] That said, references in the plays certainly imply that boys attended as well as resident immigrants (*metoikoi*), who are expressly mentioned in Dicaeopolis' speech to the chorus of *Acharnians* in a passage which also implies the presence of foreign visitors to Athens at the Great Dionysia (quoted at the beginning of this chapter).

Great controversy surrounds the question of whether or not women attended the plays: compelling arguments can be made either way and the evidence from Aristophanes' plays themselves is somewhat contradictory. In the continuation of a passage quoted earlier from *Birds*, for example, where the chorus outlines the advantages of having wings, it is assumed a woman will be at home and able to receive a lover during a theatre performance:

> If any of you happened to be having an affair with a married woman and you'd seen her husband sitting in the seats reserved for the council members, you could have taken wing, flown off from among your ranks, fucked her – and then flown back again!
>
> *Birds* 793-6

However, in *Lysistrata*, in an ode addressed to the audience, both women and men are exhorted to ask the chorus for loans:

> Let every man and woman make their demands ...!
>
> *Lysistrata* 1050

Whilst it would clearly be of great interest to know if there were female spectators (especially of plays like *Lysistrata* and *Assemblywomen*), we simply cannot be sure either way, since evidence from outside comedy is contradictory, too.[25] Regardless of its actual make-up, however, the audience is generally *conceived of* as all male when it is addressed: in the *parabasis* of *Women at the Thesmophoria* (e.g. 786-99, quoted in Chapter 5, p. 71), for example, the chorus' comments about the 'harsh things' said about the female sex are clearly aimed at men.

One interesting perspective on the audience is to consider their role in the creation of the dramatic moment: spectators are, in an important

27

sense, an essential part of any performance, both as witnesses to an ephemeral event and, especially in the case of Old Comedy, as active participants. On the one hand, the actors refer out to the comic audience in Aristophanes' plays: to the spectators as a whole; to various sections of the audience (e.g. to different ages and ranks at *Peace* 50-3 and specifically to the *boulê* at *Peace* 872); and to named individuals. On the other hand, the audience must also have communicated with the actors, inasmuch as each play would have been punctuated by the spectators' laughter, applause and heckling. Indeed, comments from the audience are even invited at *Wasps* 73-85 when they are asked to guess at the nature of Philocleon's disease.

Xanthias:	[Bdelycleon]'s shut his father up inside so that he can't get out. He's got an extraordinary disease, you see, the name of which no one will ever find out or hit upon unless we tell them. [*To the audience*] Go on, guess! ... [*Pretending to hear a suggestion*] Amynias here says he's addicted to playing dice.
Sosias:	He's not even close, by Zeus! He's just assuming that other people are suffering from the same malady as himself!
Xanthias:	But he's right that the old man's an *addict* of sorts ...

Wasps 70-7

Local festivals

The Lenaea and the Great Dionysia were the two major dramatic festivals in Athens and represent the two contexts in which all of Aristophanes' extant plays were first performed. However, they were certainly not the only occasions at which drama was staged in Attica. Any attempt to reconstruct the theatrical life of the city-state beyond these two festivals is hampered by a shortage of evidence, but such literary references and relevant archaeological evidence as we do possess suggest that there were dramatic performances at a number of so-called Rural Dionysia: festivals in honour of Dionysus celebrated in Attica's demes and villages (such as the Rural Dionysia we find Dicaeopolis celebrating at *Acharnians* 247-79, though to be sure no dramatic performances are mentioned there). One major local Dionysia took place in Piraeus, for example, as mentioned in the Law of Euergus quoted earlier, where we find a specific link between a local Dionysiac festival and the staging of drama:

When the procession takes place for Dionysus in Piraeus *along with the comedies and tragedies* ...

Law of Euergus, quoted at Demosthenes 21.10

A late anecdote from Aelian (second or third century AD) also implies that Socrates saw a new tragedy of Euripides' at Piraeus – and if it had competitors of this calibre, presumably the Dionysia at Piraeus was not without prestige.[26] From inscriptions we also know of numerous other Dionysia in Attica where comedy was performed in the classical era such as Thorikos, Aixone and Kollytos (and given that the latter was an urban Athenian deme there is good reason to suppose that its Dionysia made use of the Theatre of Dionysus). Were only new plays staged at these local Dionysia or were plays that had been successful at the Great Dionysia and Lenaea also restaged? This question is made all the more intriguing by an inscription dating from the last decade of the fifth century which informs us of a tragic victory by Sophocles and a comic victory by Aristophanes at the Dionysia at Eleusis (*IG* II² 3090).[27] Were the citizens of Eleusis lucky enough to witness world premieres of works by these literary giants at their local festival?

Conclusions

In this chapter we have looked at the basic characteristics of the festivals at which Aristophanes' plays were first performed and considered, too, some of the ways in which the logistics of 'putting on a show' in Classical Athens were a very different proposition from staging drama in the modern world. Inevitably these differences in the production process and staging have left their mark on the plays themselves, just as the religious and civic aspects of the dramatic festivals must surely have influenced not only how Aristophanes conceived of his plays but also how his audience understood them.

Aristophanes died some time in the 380s and during the fourth century the popularity of Athenian theatre grew hugely outside Attica, with drama becoming a major cultural export. Theatres sprang up across the Greek-speaking world – one benefit of which is that we are able to gain an impression of theatre design in the classical era and to gain insight into another important element we have to consider: the theatrical space for which Aristophanes composed his plays. The physical appearance of ancient Greek theatres and the way in which they would have been used form the subject of Chapter 3.

Setting the Scene: Theatre Space
and Costumes

Introduction

Understanding the physical shape, size and arrangement of the fifth-century theatre is a key part of getting to grips with Aristophanic comedy. The theatre space, just like the costuming and staging conventions of classical drama, has left a deep impression on the plays themselves – and all these elements are hugely important for us to study not least because they must have made for a very different experience from anything that most modern Western theatre audiences are used to.

Reconstructing the conventions and physical appearance of Aristophanes' theatre is not without its complications, however, as our sources – be they literary, archaeological or visual – are not always easy to interpret. Aristophanes' plays themselves provide a useful starting point since they often refer to the physical theatre itself (e.g. the entrances, seats), to the people occupying it (e.g. the actors and audience) and to costumes and stage machinery in a way that tragedies rarely do. What the plays do not contain, unfortunately, are stage directions (nearly all stage directions in modern versions of the plays are put there by translators) and so another problem that faces us is to reconstruct from the characters' speech how actors made use of the theatre space and interacted with one another and the audience.

The challenge in this chapter, then, will be to use the plays as sources to aid our understanding of how classical drama was staged, whilst also considering the ways in which Aristophanes exploits the theatrical resources available to him to write engaging drama. The passages considered (in conjunction with relevant archaeological, visual and other literary evidence) are taken from a variety of Aristophanes' plays, with special attention given to extracts from *Clouds*, *Birds*, *Women at the Thesmophoria* and *Assemblywomen*.

Theatre space

The ruins of the Theatre of Dionysus that lie on the southern slope of the Acropolis may be spectacular, but they can only help us to go part of the way to imagining the site with which Aristophanes was familiar in the late fifth and early fourth centuries. This is not just because the site was

allowed to fall into ruin: successive phases of reconstruction have also left their mark on the theatre we see today. Most significantly, the Theatre of Dionysus was rebuilt in stone and marble by Lycurgus in the late fourth century (around 330 BC) and further reconfigured in the Roman period. So while the ruins we see today *do* occupy roughly the same physical location as its fifth-century counterpart and give a useful impression of scale and layout, these remains are not necessarily indicative of the appearance and organization of the site in Aristophanes' day.

The plan of the Lycurgan theatre – built roughly 100 years after Aristophanes produced his first play – displays a number of key features of ancient theatres. The curved auditorium (*theatron*) with its raked seating is built on a natural incline – the southern slopes of the Acropolis – and would have accommodated a vast number of spectators: perhaps somewhere in the region of 15,000. The bulk of the performance space is given over to a circular *orchêstra* (dancing space) with a central altar (*thymelê*). A large, rectangular stage building, the *skênê*, stood facing the auditorium, to either side of which were the two long *eisodoi* (alternatively called *parodoi*) which provided access to the orchestra.[1] In the Theatre of Dionysus, the front row of seats, or *prohedria*, were reserved for privileged spectators such as important public officials and were distinguished from the other bench-like rows of seats by being carved in marble in the form of thrones, with a particularly elaborate central throne reserved for the

31

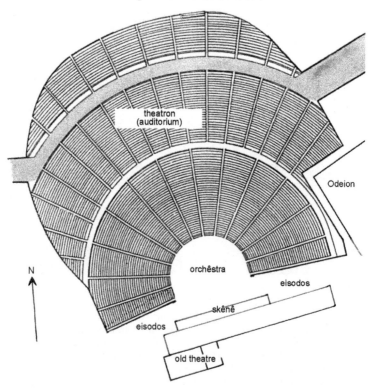

2. Plan of the 'Lycurgan Theatre': the Theatre of

Priest of Dionysus. Theatres of this era would also have boasted a raised stage accessed from the *skênê* by three doors and probably linked to the *orchêstra* by means of stairs.

How would the fifth-century theatre have differed? The seating would originally have been built out of wood rather than stone but since it has left no trace in the archaeological record, even its shape is uncertain. Theatres from this period excavated in other parts of Attica – namely at Thorikos and Trachones – suggest a more squashed shape for the auditorium and an orchestra which is more oblong than circular. At the very least, then, we should resist the temptation of assuming that the Theatre of Dionysus boasted a perfectly round orchestra and elegantly curved auditorium in Aristophanes' day. Recently, doubt has even been cast on the archaeological evidence that we thought we *could* date to the fifth-century: for example, the remains of a stone wall forming the base of the stage building is now thought by some to date from the mid-fourth rather than the late fifth century. The stage building itself – which would have housed stage properties (props), provided a place for actors to change, and whose roof was occasionally used as an acting space – would have been wooden in Aristophanes' day.[2] The number of doors the *skênê* possessed in the fifth century has proven a particular source of controversy amongst scholars: anywhere between one and three has been suggested, but all that is certain is that there would have been a sizeable set of inward-opening double doors in the centre of the *skênê*. Scenes in *Wasps* and *Assembly-women* also suggest the presence of windows in the *skênê* (a detail later attested in fourth-century theatrical vase paintings).[3]

The stage

The fiercest debates surrounding fifth-century theatre design concern the question of whether or not there was a raised stage in front of the *skênê*. The archaeological evidence from the Theatre of Dionysus is difficult to interpret, but a projection and holes in the middle of a late fifth-(but perhaps mid-fourth-)century wall (a wall which would have formed the base of the stage building) may suggest that it was designed to accommo-date a wooden stage. Perhaps more persuasive is the existence of a small number of vase paintings dating from the late fifth and early fourth centuries which clearly represent comic scenes and which depict a small wooden stage, perhaps a metre high, connected to the orchestra by a flight of wooden steps. Although these theatrical vases come mainly from South-ern Italy rather than Athens, the close links between the two dramatic traditions have been used to justify their application to Athenian theatre.

Most scholars are persuaded by the evidence of these vases that a stage was in use in Aristophanes' day, and data from the plays themselves can be used to back up this assumption. Perhaps the best example of an exchange that suggests the presence of a stage is to be found in *Wasps*. The ageing Philocleon has just left a drinking party where he has behaved riotously, taking away with him a young flute-girl, Dardanis. In the following passage, he appears to be guiding her up a flight of stairs: he offers her a 'rope' to steady herself – which in fact turns out to be the leather phallus that would have formed part of his costume (see below).

> Come up here, my golden little cockchafer: take hold of this rope with your hand. Here you go! Mind how you go as the rope's decayed. All the same, it doesn't mind being rubbed, though!
>
> *Wasps* 1341-4

The joke here appears to rely on there being some sort of a step or steps in the acting space – and so it seems a reasonable assumption that at this

33

3. Comic actors on a raised stage. Red-figure wine bowl (bell-crater)
attributed to the MacDaniel Painter, *c.* 380-70 BC.

point in the play Philocleon would have led Dardanis up from the orchestra
onto the stage *via* some stairs.[4]

So why doubt the presence of a stage? Not only has the interpretation
of textual and archaeological evidence been disputed but other compelling
points have also been made. David Wiles is a particularly persuasive
advocate of the stageless theatre, for example, and offers arguments based
on modern directors' experience of staging Greek drama, comparative
archaeological evidence and the practicalities of production.[5] He considers
the evidence of other theatres in use in the classical era – namely at
Thorikos in Attica and Megalopolis in the Peloponnese – whose design
would appear incompatible with the notion of a stage. He also makes the
further forceful point that in the theatre of Dionysus a north-facing stage
would be cast into shadow by the *skênê* to its rear on a sunny day – with
the result that actors on the stage would be difficult to see, especially in
contrast with the chorus in the well-lit *orchêstra*.[6] One might also wonder
what the advantage of a raised stage would be in a theatre where the
majority of the audience was looking down on the actors from raked
seating.

One way to accommodate many of the points made by Wiles whilst still

34

preserving the notion of a low stage is, of course, to imagine actors as moving more or less fluidly between the stage and *orchêstra* during the performance (and Wiles is surely right to stress the importance of the emotional and physical contact between actors and the chorus – especially in tragedy – which is lost if we imagine the chorus confined to the *orchêstra* and the actors to the stage). The fact that actors entered and exited not just through the doors in the *skênê* but also by the *eisodoi* – that is, by the preferred entry and exit route of the chorus – in itself suggests a certain mingling of the spaces occupied by the two.[7] When the large groups of women converge for their secret meetings at the beginning of the *Lysistrata* and *Assemblywomen*, for example, the majority evidently enter *via* the *eisodoi*. In the *Lysistrata*, these women are all played by actors who appear at a different time from the chorus; in *Assemblywomen*, however, the actors even enter at the same time as the chorus (27-42), and the line between non-speaking actors and chorus is deliberately blurred – no more so than when Praxagora and the Chorus Leader both begin to name individuals in the emerging throng:

> Praxagora: And now I can see Cleinarete – and here's Sostrate coming now – and Philaenete.
> Chorus Leader: Hurry up, won't you? Glyce swore on oath that the last of us to arrive would pay a fine of three offerings of wine and a measure of chickpeas.
>
> *Assemblywomen* 41-5

The merging of the identity of the actors and chorus helps to seal the impression of a huge group of women here – one sufficiently large to fulfil Praxagora's plan of flooding the assembly with her followers and forcing a vote to put women in charge of the city.

Many other entrances in comedy are also made through the *eisodoi*. At one point in *Birds*, for example, Peisthetaerus announces the arrival of a messenger, coming to report progress on the construction of the wall in the air that he is having built to separate gods from men:

> But now here's a guard running on, with a war-dance look, coming to tell to us what's happening there.
>
> *Birds* 1168-9

If we choose to believe that actors only ever delivered their lines on the stage, we should have to imagine characters such as this running on and then clambering up the steps before they spoke. It makes more sense, then, to imagine this messenger delivering his lines in the *orchêstra*.

A fluid use of the *orchêstra* by actors also helps counter objections that the stage may simply have been too small to stage some of comedy's larger scenes (such as the feasts and celebrations that end plays such as *Lysistrata* and *Peace*) since we can imagine the action as taking place in the *orchêstra*. All this said, the existence of a stage can neither be proven nor disproved. And as with so many other aspects of late fifth-century theatre, we can only weigh up the evidence and make informed guesses rather than definitive assertions about the theatrical conditions in which Aristophanes worked.[8]

Using the theatre space

The theatre space in which Aristophanes' plays were performed would have had a large impact on the way in which his plays were experienced by his audience: certainly attending an ancient dramatic performance would have been quite a different affair from watching a play in a modern, western theatre. Particularly interesting to contemplate is the audience dynamic. In the Theatre of Dionysus, perhaps 15,000 people sat in close proximity, watching the same set of events unfold – and since the productions took place in daylight in a semi-circular theatre, an audience member would inevitably see other spectators' reactions and have their own reactions observed. Comparisons have been made with large spectator events in the modern world, such as open air concerts and sports matches, and certainly it is instructive to consider the ways in which individuals react differently when they are part of a group from when they are alone (or at least isolated by the darkness of a modern theatre).

There are also practicalities to take into consideration with ancient open air theatre. An obvious point to make, for example, is that spectators and actors would have had to have taken the weather in their stride, be it heat, cold, wind or rain. The absence of stage lighting and a curtain would also have made for a different theatrical experience from the one that modern western theatre-goers are used to. There would have been no dimming of lights to mark the beginning of the performance, for instance, and no intervals or even pauses in the action made possible by a darkened stage: instead, such breaks in the action as do occur are by necessity accompanied by a choral ode or a distracting piece of stage business. Any props that the actors did not carry into or out of the acting space themselves (and comedy abounds in various pieces of paraphernalia) would presumably have been manoeuvred by slaves acting as stage hands.

Of course, the theatre space for which Aristophanes conceived and wrote his plays has also left its mark on the scripts themselves. For instance, when a new character enters the acting space, the audience is generally told who is arriving, a case in point being the arrival of the messenger in *Birds* considered above ('But now here's a guard running on ...'). Indeed, in the absence of theatre programmes such information was vital, especially in the context of comic drama, where (unlike the mythical figures of tragedy) the characters are generally unfamiliar to the audience. The numerous addresses and references to the audience also make better sense when we bear in mind that the spectators were fully visible both to the actors and each other. Towards the beginning of *Knights*, for instance, Demos' slaves, Nicias and Demosthenes, debate whether they should explain the plot of the play to the audience and even refer to the spectators' faces:

Demosthenes:	Do you want me to explain to the spectators what's going on?
Nicias:	Not a bad idea. But let's ask one thing of them: to make it abundantly clear by the expressions on their faces whether they're enjoying our words and actions.

Knights 36-9

When the characters in a play step outside the dramatic frame and refer to the theatre itself, the play's audience, or talk about themselves as actors in a play, scholars call this 'metatheatre' – and so the characters here, for example, can be described as making 'metatheatrical' comments.

Dramatic space

Old Comedy's use of the dramatic space is complex. On the one hand, Aristophanes sometimes uses techniques familiar to us from tragedy, most notably making the *skênê* door the dramatic focus of a play. Perhaps the best example of this is *Lysistrata*, where for much of the play the sealed doors of the stage building mark the physical division between the women who have seized the Acropolis and the men who are locked out. The impenetrability of the doors and the female control of the *skênê*'s inner reaches neatly complement the central theme of the play – the sex strike – where men are similarly shut out from interior female-controlled space. Other plays which exploit the ability of the door to form a barrier between private and public worlds include *Wasps*, where Philocleon is initially held captive inside the house and is thereby prevented from inflicting harm on the world at large. In *Peace*, on the other hand, the release of the goddess Peace from the *skênê* (envisaged in the play as a cave) marks the arrival of her blessings in the public domain, including an abundance of sex, food and wine.

Nick Lowe's illuminating study of 'Aristophanic Spacecraft' has done much to help us understand the way in which spatial identity is created and exploited in these plays.[9] He points out, for example, that at the beginning of Aristophanes' plays it is often the case that the audience is given no clear idea of where the action is unfolding. Rather, it is only during the prologue or with the arrival of the chorus in the play's *parodos* that the stage building is given any clear identity. In *Lysistrata*, for instance, it is not until the end of the prologue at lines 240-6 that it is hinted that the women are to be thought of as standing near the Acropolis, and plays such as *Birds* and *Wealth* both begin with characters wandering in anonymous locations. Indeed, as mentioned in Chapter 1, the prologues of these and other plays are carefully constructed by Aristophanes to tease his audience with clues as to who and where the characters are and what they are doing – only later is all made clear.[10] This is even true of plays like *Wasps*, *Knights* and *Assemblywomen* where the play's location (but not other such data) is revealed in the plays' openings lines.

Another feature of Aristophanes' plays with which Lowe has to grapple is the way in which spatial locations change throughout the course of the play. In tragedy, the action is generally confined to a single location (exceptionally two). In comedy, the action can leap around from place to place, with some of these locations being more strongly defined than others. In *Acharnians*, for instance, Dicaeopolis certainly visits the Pnyx in the heart of Athens, his own village and Euripides' house, but exactly where other parts of the play take place is not wholly clear – and it is only the most literal-minded spectator who would be tempted to ask just where Dicaeopolis makes his speech to the chorus, for example. Even in plays where the location *is* strongly defined, there are nevertheless lapses into spatial anonymity. In *Knights*, for instance, the *skênê* is generally to be identified as Demos' house, but after the *agôn* we find the Sausage-Seller and the Paphlagon both rushing inside to collect their oracles (line 972). As Lowe explains, there is no reason to suppose that the oracles have been previously stashed away inside Demos' house – rather it is simply the case that in comic fetching-and-carrying scenes such as this, Aristophanes often has 'the *skene* ... momentarily reverting to an anonymous prop-store "inside" '.[11]

In tragedy and later comedy, the *eisodoi* are often given distinct identities – most commonly the right (western) *eisodos* being the route into the city, the left (eastern) *eisodos* leading to the countryside. It is doubtful that the *eisodoi* were given such strong identities in Aristophanes' plays (though not impossible that in *Birds*, for example, the world of the gods and that of humans were approached *via* different *eisodoi*). What Aristophanes *does* often evoke, however, is a sense that off-stage is a different world from on-stage: thus in *Wasps*, for instance, the city lies off-stage, whereas Philocleon's domestic world is represented by the acting space and the *skênê*. Likewise in *Assemblywomen*, the utopia created by Praxagora lies off-stage, whereas problems in the establishment and workings of her new world order are played out in the acting space in front of the audience.

Stage machinery

Modern western dramatists and producers regularly employ special effects and technological devices to create sophisticated theatrical experiences for their audiences. The Greek theatre had few such resources at its disposal, but two pieces of theatrical equipment which Athenian audiences would regularly have seen pressed into service were the *mêchanê* and *ekkyklêma*.

The mêchanê

The *mêchanê* or crane was a device onto which actors were harnessed and brought into the acting space, suspended in mid-air. This is how Medea would have appeared at the end of Euripides' play as she rode off to Athens in her serpent-drawn chariot, for example, and how a number of gods would have appeared – especially in Euripides' plays – when they delivered the prologue or epilogue to the play. In the *Poetics*, Aristotle criticizes tragedians such as Euripides who use 'a god from the *mêchanê*' (*apo mêchanês theos*) to resolve a complex plot (1454b: a phrase better known in its Latin translation, *deus ex machina*).

The *mêchanê* was used at least three times in Aristophanes' extant plays – and not simply to parody its use in tragedy as is sometimes claimed.[12] In the *Birds*, for instance, the goddess Iris appears suspended by the *mêchanê* in a piece of staging that allows Aristophanes to reinforce the spatial relationships in the play: Cloudcuckooland is a skyborne city which lies between the gods and men and so it is only right that gods should appear from above. In *Clouds*, Socrates' otherwordliness is cleverly underscored by his entrance from above, also made possible by the *mêchanê*. In an unparalleled *coup de théâtre*, he appears suspended in a basket and when asked by Strepsiades what he is doing, Socrates demonstrates his head-in-the-clouds logic by replying:

> I could never have made correct discoveries about celestial phenomena without hanging up my mind and mixing the fine particles of my thought with the air which it so resembles. If I'd been on the ground and tried to observe the upper regions from below, I would never have made these findings. For it is beyond question the case that the earth draws the moisture of thought to itself. Just the same thing happens with cress.
>
> *Clouds* 227-34

Perhaps Aristophanes' most famous use of the *mêchanê* comes in *Peace* (82-179), however, when Trygaeus is enacting his 'Great Idea' to fly to heaven on the back of a dung beetle. This scene parodies a similar flight made in Euripides' lost play *Bellerophon* where the eponymous hero makes a comparable journey riding the winged horse Pegasus – the comic twist being that Trygaeus' chosen form of transport will not require the carrying of surplus supplies of food, as he can simply feed the beetle with his own excrement (137-9). Here Aristophanes draws attention to the play's theatricality (in a moment of 'metatheatre') to make fun of the *mêchanê* as a dramatic device. The actor playing Trygaeus addresses the crane operator not in character, but *in propria persona* as an actor in a play, seemingly agitated at the jerkiness of its movements:

Help! I'm frightened! I tell you, I'm not joking either! Crane Operator, pay attention, won't you? There's already some wind bubbling up around my navel, and if you're not careful, I'll end up giving the beetle a meal!

Peace 173-6

The ekkyklêma

The *ekkyklêma* poses somewhat more of a problem than the *mêchanê* – not least because it is not at all clear what form it took. The verb *ekkykleô* means 'to wheel out', and what this device probably comprised was a platform on wheels that was somehow manoeuvred through the central double doors of the *skênê*. The *ekkyklêma* evidently allowed the revelation of an interior scene – in Aeschylus' *Agamemnon*, for example, the dead bodies of Agamemnon and Cassandra (who are murdered in the palace) would have been displayed to the audience on the *ekkyklêma*.

As far as Aristophanes' plays are concerned, it is difficult to state with absolute certainty that the *ekkyklêma* was (or indeed was not) used in any given scene, but likely candidates for its use include the scenes when the playwrights Euripides and Agathon emerge from their houses in *Acharnians* and *Women at the Thesmophoria* respectively. The script certainly supports the idea that both of them were wheeled out on the *ekkyklêma*: Dicaeopolis tells Euripides, 'Get yourself wheeled out!' (*Acharnians* 408) and Agathon is initially described as 'the one being wheeled out' and at the end of the scene asks, 'Someone wheel me in as quickly as you can!' (*Women at the Thesmophoria* 96 and 265). If the device *was* used in these scenes then we also have here further instances of Aristophanes referring to the theatre's machinery in the course of the play.

Not all scholars believe the *ekkyklêma* was used in these scenes – and, indeed, we simply have no way of knowing just how extensively and in what circumstances the *ekkyklêma* was used in comedy. One thing does seem certain, however, namely that we should not expect it to be used in the same way as it was commonly used in tragedy (that is to show static, internal scenes). After all, as we saw above, Aristophanes was at liberty to include shifts in location in his plays and, importantly, to have internal scenes played out in front of the audience (in tragedy this is not true: in each play the acting space is generally conceived as a single location, always *external*). As we have seen, Aristophanes' plays do not always make it clear exactly where a given piece of action is taking place, but to be literal minded for a moment, in a play like *Clouds* there would appear to be at least two 'internal' locations: not only does Socrates' Thinkery seem to be indoors but one might also suppose that Strepsiades and Pheidippides are to be thought of as sleeping inside rather than outside in the play's prologue. Both these scenes, then, are very *un*tragic in that they contain action and dialogue which are taking place inside.

How does all this relate to the *ekkyklêma*? One role that this device seems to have played in comedy was to contribute to such internal scenes: that is, to help to bring the inside outside. Not perhaps in the prologues to the plays (where the precise location of the action is often only poorly defined), but in other scenes, such as the Agathon and Euripides episodes. In *Clouds*, then, when the Thinkery's students suddenly appear following Strepsiades' demands for the doors to be opened, it would make good sense if they entered the acting space – complete with all their paraphernalia – on the *ekkyklêma*:

> Hurry up, hurry up and open up the Thinkery and show me Socrates as quickly as you can: I'm simply dying to learn! Come on, open the door! [*Reacting to the appearance of the students*] O Heracles! Where *do* these creatures come from?
>
> *Clouds* 181-4

Again in *Peace*, the emergence from a cave of the statue of the goddess Peace along with her two attendants, Theoria and Opora, may have been staged using the *ekkyklêma* (*Peace* 508-19), and so on – scholars have also suggested a number of other occasions where the *ekkyklêma* may have been employed by Aristophanes, some more routine, some more intriguing than others.[13] Our lack of knowledge as to its workings, size and what weight it could bear also add to the difficulty in assessing its suitability to stage given scenes.[14] If, for example, the note on the single surviving manuscript of *Women at the Thesmophoria* is right (unlikely as it seems), that a temple (presumably the Thesmophorion) is 'pushed out' into the acting space at line 277,[15] then it would raise a whole raft of questions about what other objects might have emerged on the *ekkyklêma*, unsignalled in the script of the plays.

Costumes and masks

Vases from the classical era depicting theatrical performances provide important information about the costumes worn on the comic stage. Like their tragic counterparts, comic actors would have sported clothing which covered the whole of their bodies and a helmet-like mask covering the whole head, complete with hair. However, the difference between comic and tragic costumes and masks was stark, as can perhaps best be seen from the so-called 'Choregos Vase' (Fig. 4), painted around 350 BC (that is to say, around 30 years after Aristophanes' death, although the imagery is similar to that found on earlier vases, contemporary with Aristophanes' plays). The (unmasked) figure on the left wears the long, flowing robes of the tragic actor, whereas the three figures to the right sport typical comic attire: they wear padding on their bellies, rumps and even chests and beneath each actor's short cloak (*chitôn*) can be glimpsed the oversized, stitched leather phallus. The features on the masks are distorted and

41

4. Comic actors (two of whom are labelled *chorêgoi*) and a tragic actor
(labelled 'Aegisthus') on a raised stage. Apulian red-figure bell crater,

wrinkled – and also wrinkled is the 'skin' on the actors' arms and legs. In
short, these comic figures represent the antithesis of the classical Greek
physical ideal of the handsome, athletic (and small-penised) youth that we
find in so much art of the period.

Old and middle-aged men, like those depicted on the Choregos Vase,
account for only a limited number of Aristophanes' characters and there
will of course have been variations in costume and mask for other character-types. Obviously clothing and masks (which were made from linen,
cork or wood) have left no trace in the archaeological record, so any
reconstruction of theatrical costume must by necessity rely on pictorial
evidence – such as vases, terracotta figures and carved monuments such
as grave *stelai* (all mainly from the fourth century) – and later literary
evidence, in conjunction with data provided by the ancient plays themselves. From a study of such sources, it seems fair to suppose that even by
the late fifth century there already existed a number of standard masks
(e.g. young man, old man, poor man/slave, etc.) which gave clear indications about the social status of the character being portrayed (e.g. for a
male character, a beardless and/or pale mask suggests effeminacy). This

said, special costumes and masks were also made. On the one hand, the prominent public figures which appear in Aristophanes' plays may have been represented on stage by actors wearing portrait masks;[16] on the other, unusual or distinctive characters, such as the Persian official Pseudo-bartes in *Acharnians* or Dionysus in *Frogs*, would evidently have required special costumes. More spectacularly, though, the members of comic cho-ruses often required exotic garb: perhaps not in the case of the old men who form the chorus of *Acharnians* or the female chorus of *Women at the Thesmophoria*, but the necessarily lavish costuming of the choruses of *Wasps* and *Frogs* would have given an ideal opportunity for Aristophanes – and, moreover, a generous *chorêgos* – to introduce a show-stopping element of spectacle into a play. The chorus of the *Birds* even appears to have been equipped with individualized costumes, since Peisthetaerus and Euelpides identify each of the twenty-four strong chorus with a different bird as they enter: partridge, francolin, widgeon, halcyon, barbur, owl, jay, turtledove, lark, marsh-warbler, wheatear, pigeon, vulture, hawk, ring-dove, cuckoo, stockdove, firecrest, porphyrion, kestrel, dabchick, bunting, lammergeyer and woodpecker (*Birds* 297-304). Indeed, in *Birds* even the *aulos*-player seems to have been dressed elaborately – as we learn in a metatheatrical moment, when Peisthetaerus addresses him directly:

> Oi you, stop your blowing! By Heracles, what on earth's this? In the name of Zeus, I've seen a load of weird things in my time, but never a crow wearing a musician's mouthband!
>
> *Birds* 859-61

Merely providing the costumes for the chorus and cast for a play like *Birds* must have cost a substantial sum – an outlay all the more remarkable for the fact that each play was written for just a single performance in the dramatic festival.[17]

The implications for performance

The costuming conventions of Greek drama have important implications for the performance of the plays themselves. On a practical level, for instance, the fact that the actors' bodies are completely covered by their costumes and masks underpins the plays' capacity to be performed by just three or four speaking actors: that is to say, with the aid of a costume change it is relatively straightforward for an actor to go off-stage and later re-emerge as a new character. As Wiles notes, the restriction to three (occasionally four) speaking characters in a given scene must also have had its practical benefits: in a large theatre where the actors were masked, it would be all too easy for the audience to become confused about which character was talking if a larger number of speaking actors were used.[18] There must also be a relationship between the nature of actors' costumes and acting styles. For example, the difference between the long robes of tragedy and the short *chitôn* of comedy suggests a physicality to comic acting, for which we have ample evidence from the plays themselves. The comic costume's grotesqueness, with its open mouth, leather phallus, padded belly and buttocks also serves to underscore comedy's interest in bodily functions such as eating, sex and defecation.

It is all too easy to think of the ways in which masks *restrict* performance. To be sure, in an enormous open air theatre the clear delivery of lines – both spoken and sung – through the aperture of the mask must have required both significant natural ability and considerable training on the part of the actor. The playwright Sophocles is even supposed to have given up his acting career because of the weakness of his voice. In relatively intimate, modern theatre spaces, audiences are used to seeing the expressions on the actors' faces – indeed in a theatre tradition built on realist conventions and unused to masked performance, the ability of an actor to express emotion through the face is key to successful performance. But in the context of the Greek theatre, actors must have employed techniques which their modern Western counterparts experimenting with masked acting only learn through trial and error: how the use of 'dynamic poses' brings the character to life and how 'meaningful gestures of both head and body' can project emotion on the unmoving mask.[19] Padding, a larger-than-life mask and acting with the whole body would also have served to make the players more visible to an audience member who might have been sitting up to 100 metres away from the actors in the upper rows of the Theatre of Dionysus.

In the light of this discussion, it is interesting to note that there are perhaps more references to the facial expressions of characters than one might expect in a modern western drama: this is a technique used by Aristophanes to endow the actors' masks with expression and to convey the subtleties of these projected emotions to all members of the audience – even those sitting right at the back of the theatre. Earlier, we encountered the messenger in *Birds* running on with a 'war dance look', for example; and in a similar fashion, at the beginning of *Lysistrata*, Calonice conveys Lysistrata's mood and facial expression with the lines:

> What's disturbed you so terribly? Don't look cross, child. Knitted brows don't look good on you.
>
> *Lysistrata* 7-8

As well as characters' facial expressions, detail that might not be visible to all spectators is also conveyed to the audience verbally. For instance, Aristophanes often takes the opportunity to provide his audience with descriptions of how his characters are dressed – especially when the costumes are unusual and/or when the clothing worn is important to the plot. The *Assemblywomen*, for example – who, for the play's plot to work, will have to pass for men in the assembly – inform the audience about their shoes, body hair, suntans and men's clothing in a series of statements.[20]

> – I was just putting my shoes on when ...
> – Don't you see Smicython's wife, Melistiche, hurrying along in his shoes?
> – I've got armpits that are bushier than a shrubbery ... I oiled myself all over and stood in the sun all day to get a tan.
> – And have you got the beards ...?
> – ... you've got Laconian shoes, and walking sticks, and men's cloaks, just as we said.
>
> *Assemblywomen* 36, 46-7, 60-4, 69, 74-5

The scene in *Women at the Thesmophoria* in which the cross-dressing tragic poet Agathon lends clothing and other items to Euripides' ageing male Inlaw is a particularly rich source of references to clothes. When the Inlaw examines the objects that Agathon keeps in his house, for example – some of which the Inlaw will later employ himself when he dresses as a woman in order to infiltrate the all-female Thesmophoria festival – he comments on the way in which female clothing and a mirror lie alongside objects that belong to the male sphere, namely: musical instruments (such as the seven-stringed lyre, or *barbitos*), an athlete's oil flask and a weapon.

> What mix-up of life-styles is this? What does a *barbitos* have to say to a saffron gown? And what does a lyre have to say to a hairnet? Why an oil-flask *and* a breast-band? How incongruous! And what can a mirror and a sword possibly have in common?
>
> *Women at the Thesmophoria*, 137-40

Agathon's unusual physical appearance is also communicated to the audience. When Agathon enters the acting space as Euripides and the Inlaw look on, the latter likens him to Cyrene, a celebrated courtesan:

> Euripides: Be quiet!
> Inlaw: What's the matter?
> Euripides: Agathon's coming out.
> Inlaw: Eh? Where is he?
> Euripides: What do you mean 'where'? There – the one being wheeled out!
> Inlaw: What, am I blind or something? I don't see any man here at all – what I see is Cyrene.
>
> *Women at the Thesmophoria*, 95-8

Euripides also describes Agathon's appearance in great detail later in this scene when he explains how easy it would be for a man like Agathon to attend the Thesmophoria undetected:

... you're attractive, pale-skinned, clean-shaven, with a woman's voice, soft
skin – and you're easy on the eye.

Women at the Thesmophoria, 191-2

Presumably the actor playing Agathon would have worn a feminine-
looking mask as indicated in the script: pale and beardless.

In addition to the physical appearance of an unusually dressed character such as Agathon, intricate stage business is also described to the
audience. For example, when the Inlaw's cheeks are shaved while he is
being disguised as a woman, actions that might not be wholly visible to all
members of the audience are skilfully integrated into the accompanying
dialogue:

Euripides:	Agathon, *you* always carry a razor: could you lend us one?
Agathon:	Sure. It's there in the razor-holder: take it.
Euripides:	You're a gent. [*to the Inlaw*] Sit down. Puff out your right cheek.
Inlaw:	Owwwww!

Women at the Thesmophoria, 218-22

This tendency for intricate stage business to be related verbally has the
welcome benefit of allowing modern readers of the plays to reconstruct
much of the actors' physical actions and to make informed judgements
about what props were used (none of which information is given inde-
pendently in the scripts that have come down to us). Where we are less
well informed is about large-scale actions, timing and slapstick. The short
exchange above, for example, in which the Inlaw is shaved by Euripides,
offers huge scope for comic stage business in the hands of talented actors
– but how this scene was managed in the original performance is something at which we can only guess.

A final point worth making about masks and clothing is their potential for rapid scene setting. In contrast to unusual (and unusually
dressed) characters such as Agathon, when the majority of figures
entered the comic stage, the actor's mask-type and clothing would have
immediately communicated to the audience the kind of character being
represented (old woman, slave, young man, etc.). This is turn would
have evoked a conventional set of characteristics associated with each:
e.g. women are conventionally portrayed as alcohol- and sex-mad;
slaves as devious, and so on. In common with other Old Comic playwrights, Aristophanes makes extensive use of stock jokes connected
with established character-types. Clothing and masking conventions
thus provide a powerful tool for Aristophanes as a writer of humorous
drama (comedy's stock character-types will be looked at in more detail
in Chapters 4 and 5).

Conclusions

In this chapter we have seen how the physical size and shape of the theatre and the various theatrical resources available to Old Comic poets had a deep impact on how Aristophanes composed his plays. We have also seen how this impact is visible in the scripts of the plays that have come down to us and how certain questions are still a matter of fierce scholarly debate – not least the question as to whether or not there was a raised stage in Aristophanes' day. The visual and physical elements of Aristophanes' theatre continue to feature in the discussion in the following chapter, too, since masks, props and physical routines play an important role in the topic we turn to now – namely the devices that Aristophanes used in his plays to create his distinctive brand of humour.

4

Aristophanes the Humorist

Introduction

At the very beginning of *Frogs*, Xanthias, who is riding on a donkey and carrying a heavy bundle on a stick over his shoulder, turns to Dionysus and asks:

Xanthias: Shall I tell one of the usual jokes, Master: the ones that always get the audience laughing?

Frogs 1-2

What ensues is a fascinating exchange, where Dionysus and Xanthias talk not only as if they are master and slave, but also as characters in a comic play, recalling some of the standard quips that playwrights use to amuse their audiences:

Dionysus: Say whatever you like, by Zeus. Only not 'this weight is *crushing* me!' ...
Xanthias: Well then, can I tell the *really* funny one?
Dionysus: Yes, of course, be my guest. Only whatever you do, don't tell ...
Xanthias: Which one?
Dionysus: ... the one where you shift your stick from one shoulder to the other and say that you're busting for a crap. ...
Xanthias: Then what on earth was the point of me carrying this luggage?

Frogs 3; 6-9; 12

Of course, one of the clever aspects of these lines from Aristophanes' point of view is that he is able to entertain his audience with a series of well-worn and popular jokes while at the same time implying that he is above such cheap routines. Or in other words, he gets to have his cake and eat it, too. And so this passage serves as a useful starting point for anyone interested in Aristophanic humour since this exchange not only highlights the existence of certain stock jokes, characters and routines that Aristophanes could draw on (a hugely important element in his comedy, as we shall see), but also hints at another important fact: that some kinds of humour could be presented as inferior to, and less sophisticated than, others.

In this chapter, we shall examine the different techniques that Aristophanes uses to amuse his audience. In part, this will involve looking at some of the large building blocks that Aristophanes relies on to create humour: stock routines, stereotypical characters and comic ideas that can be drawn on throughout a whole play all fulfil important roles here. In addition to this, we shall look at some of the more specific joke-types that Aristophanes uses, such as what I shall call the 'unnecessary question', the 'stupid answer' and 'comic logic'. This survey of Aristophanic humour will bring us into contact with both the bawdy and the high brow; the verbal and the physical; the innovative and the clichéd; the genteel and the offensive. The central purpose throughout, however, will be to gain a flavour of Aristophanes' humour and to discover how we can characterize his instincts as a humorist: what comic techniques are favoured by Aristophanes, for example, and where does the balance lie between, say, sophisticated and non-sophisticated, original and non-original humour? The quips, jokes, puns, comic insults and humorous routines discussed in this chapter are taken from a broad selection of plays – and are no doubt none the funnier for being quoted out of context, analyzed and 'explained'. The bulk, however, come from four plays: *Acharnians, Clouds, Peace* and *Frogs*.

No discussion of Aristophanic humour is without its challenges. Working with the texts that we have, much of the visual and physical humour of the plays is difficult to reconstruct, and factors such as timing and the manner of delivery would also no doubt have played hugely important roles in making the original audience laugh. What is more, there are numerous comic allusions in the plays (to people, objects, works of literature, beliefs, and so on) that we do not fully comprehend. Given how much of the humour of the original performances we inevitably miss out on, though, what is perhaps extraordinary is the amount of humour that we *are* able to understand, appreciate and, indeed, find amusing ourselves 2,500 years later.

A further challenge comes in finding the vocabulary for discussing humour. What *is* humour, after all, and what are we to understand by words such as 'laughter', 'funny' and 'joke'? To address this last set of questions, let us begin by taking a brief detour into the world of Humour Theory in order to consider some of the terms, concepts and ideas that can help inform our understanding of this complex and intriguing phenomenon.

Laughter, jokes and 'serious' humour

One of the difficulties facing anyone wishing to discuss humour is the fact that terms such as 'humorous', 'funny' and 'joke' are used fairly loosely by speakers of English – and this includes many scholars who write about humour, too. In this section I shall aim to clarify the way in which a number of such key words will be used in this chapter so as to allow our discussion of Aristophanic humour to proceed on a more informed basis. The definitions which follow aim to provide some food for thought while at the same time reflecting fairly closely the way in which native speakers use the words in everyday speech.

Laughter

Laughter is a physiological phenomenon which can be caused by a number of factors. One stimulus for laughter is, of course, humour – and so we *may* laugh, for example, when we 'get' a particular joke (although other reactions are also possible: e.g. smiling, grimacing, or doing nothing – especially if we find the joke uninteresting or offensive, say). However, laughter is also caused by many other stimuli, such as relief, tickling, social awkwardness, intense joy, fear or even grief. It is important to bear in mind, then, that laughter is neither roused every time we 'get' a joke, nor is it provoked only by humour. Humour and laughter are certainly connected, but the relationship is not an uncomplicated one.

'Funny'

Essentially, most English speakers would describe a thing as 'funny' if (i) they viewed it as being humorous, and (ii) it caused them to laugh. Many individuals would no doubt also describe a text or event as 'funny' if they recognized its *potential* to cause them or even someone else to laugh.

'Humorous' and 'humour'

Compared to 'funny', the term 'humour' has the advantage of covering areas such as wit and satire that might not always be describable as 'funny' (i.e. causing laughter), but that are nonetheless recognizable as something other than sober discourse. On repeated telling, for example, a joke might cease to be 'funny' for a listener, but can still be described as 'humorous'. In other words, 'humour' is a relatively broad and objective category, whereas 'funny' is a narrower category and a matter of more subjective judgement. Humour appears in all sorts of guises: spontaneously in conversation; written or scripted in books, plays, films and on the radio; in non-verbal contexts, e.g. visual and even musical humour (e.g. a *scherzo* or a badly played piano). As we shall see in the following section, the precise definition of humour is still a subject of live debate and theorizing amongst scholars, but is generally understood to be a special type of incongruity. Whereas there were various Greek words which expressed the ideas of 'laughter' and 'funny', there was no word equivalent to the English 'humour'.

4. Aristophanes the Humorist

'Joke'

The word 'joke' can be used to indicate a variety of things in English. It is often used simply to indicate that something is humorous ('I was only joking', 'Was that meant to be a joke?'). However, 'joke' also has a semi-technical meaning; that is, a short, amusing text in the form of a story or puzzle, which a speaker might relate independent of context – sometimes scholars call these 'canned jokes' (we shall look at a number of such 'canned jokes' in the next section). In this chapter, the word 'joke' will be used in a broad sense (and not just to indicate 'canned jokes' which are, in any case, very rare in Aristophanes).

'Serious'

A further word that it is useful to define at this point is 'serious', since it is often used to indicate the opposite of humour ('Was that a joke or were you being serious?'). In his 2000 book, *Aristophanes and the Definition of Comedy*, Michael Silk suggests that discussions of Aristophanic comedy are all too often hampered by the fact that critics fail to appreciate that the word 'serious' has three distinct meanings in English: not only 'non-humorous' ('his face looked serious') but *also* 'honest' ('a serious proposal of marriage') and *also* 'substantial' ('a serious candidate').[1] As Silk points out, problems can arise when critics assume that because comedy is generally non-serious in *one* sense (i.e. humorous) it is also non-serious in *others* (i.e. *dis*honest and *in*substantial) – but this is clearly not always the case.[2] A racist or sexist joke, for example, may well convey the *honest* opinions of the person who tells it – and political humour and satire is, I would argue, perfectly capable of conveying *substantial* ideas (this topic is explored more fully in Chapter 9, which deals with the topic of Aristophanic politics). That said, one interesting aspect of humour is that a speaker can (whether with a clean conscience or not) deny the import of what he or she has joked about: 'It was just a joke – I didn't mean anything by it!' This slippery quality of humour makes it a convenient medium for broaching difficult, 'serious' topics as numerous modern sociological studies show: subjects like sex and death can be referred to in a jokey way and then, if the speaker is made to feel that their comments are inappropriate, he/she can claim that to have been 'only joking'.[3]

Humour theory: what is humour?

Theorists since Aristotle (and probably before that) have grappled with the thorny problem of humour. When it comes to answering the question 'what *is* humour?', the common response from scholars is that *incongruity* and *surprise* are key factors – but that these must be accompanied by a further element, i.e. what Aristotle calls 'painlessness' (*Poetics* 1449a): we rarely

51

find it amusing to be on the receiving end of a brutal physical or verbal assault, for example, however surprising it might be. Incongruity theories continue to dominate Humour Studies in the twenty-first century, with one particular theory of humour having achieved something of a leading position in the field: the General Theory of Verbal Humour (or GTVH) developed by the American scholars Salvatore Attardo and Victor Raskin.[4] At the core of Attardo's and Raskin's complex theory is what they call 'script opposition': put simply, their claim is that jokes typically contain two distinct ideas (or 'scripts') which are shown to be incongruous with one another (or 'opposed') at a key moment, namely the joke's punch-line.

There is a further key aspect of this modern theory – one which can be traced back to at least the eighteenth-century. In *The Critique of Judgement* (1790), the philosopher Immanuel Kant notes that 'the jest must contain something that is capable of deceiving for a moment' and certainly the element of deception is essential to how verbal jokes work.[5] 'Canned jokes', in particular, often operate on a 'garden path' principle, whereby the listener is initially led to understand a word, phrase or situation in one way, but later finds out that it must be understood in another way entirely. Take the following joke, for instance:

There are two fish in a tank. One says to the other, 'Where's the gun?'

Here, the word 'tank' will initially be understood by most listeners to mean a glass *fish* tank. It is only when we meet the word 'gun' that we are forced re-evaluate our initial assumption and understand the word 'tank' to mean something different altogether: namely, a *military vehicle*. Here, then, we find all the key elements of a joke: incongruity (i.e. the second meaning of 'tank' is at odds with the first), deception, surprise and painlessness (that is to say, the listener does not get hurt!).

To reiterate, when a joke is based around the different meanings of an ambiguous word, there is often one meaning of that word which is *initially* presented as the more obvious – but later in the joke, the listener is made aware of a *secondary* or alternative meaning. A further example of a joke that can be neatly analyzed in these terms is the following much-quoted witticism attributed to the comedian W.C. Fields (1880-1946), in which two meanings of the word 'club' are exploited:

Reporter: Do you believe in clubs for young people?
W.C. Fields: Only when kindness fails.

In a similar vein to the 'tank' joke, this quip relies on the fact that the word 'club' has more than one meaning (i.e. club[1] = 'society' or 'group'; club[2] = 'bludgeon' or 'cudgel'). Humour theorists call the ambiguous word or phrase around which a joke is built the 'connector': and so 'club' is the connector in this joke. To introduce another technical term, verbal jokes also characteristically contain what is known as a 'disjunctor', namely a phrase which forces the listener to re-evaluate his or her initial expectations about the meaning of the 'connector' (i.e. the ambiguous word or phrase). In this last joke the disjunctor is the phrase 'when kindness fails'. When the listener meets this phrase, he or she is both made aware of the potential ambiguity of the word 'club' and also reinterprets the sentence with reference to a secondary meaning of the word (i.e. 'club' as a 'bludgeon' or 'cudgel').

Often the connector and disjunctor are united, as in the following joke:

Have you heard about the new corduroy pillows?
They're making headlines.

Here the word 'headlines' is both the source of the ambiguity (headlines[1] = 'newspaper headlines'; headlines[2] = 'lines on the head') and is also the word in the text that forces the reader to look for an ambiguity in order to make sense of the joke.

Not all jokes are based on the double meaning of a word or phrase, however. Many are 'situational'; that is to say, based around a *situation* that can be understood in different ways. Take the following joke, for example:

A pair of suburban couples who had known each other for quite some time talked it over and decided to do a little conjugal swapping. The trade was made the following evening, and the newly arranged couples retired to their respective houses. After about an hour of bedroom bliss, one of the wives propped herself up on her elbow, looked at her new partner and said, 'Well, I wonder how the boys are getting along'.

Here, the punch line leads the listener to reassess his or her initial expectations – or in other words, 'Well, I wonder how the boys are getting along' acts as a 'disjunctor', leading the reader to re-evaluate the scenario as an instance of homosexual rather than heterosexual intercourse. Once more, then, the joke works on a 'garden path' principle with the reader's initial expectations frustrated. The important point about 'situational jokes' is that they contain no identifiable 'connector': the ambiguity is not inherent in a specific word or phrase, but rather in the *situation*.

Whereas modern humour theory is relatively good at accounting for the structure of 'canned jokes' like those quoted in this section, analysing the humour of Aristophanic comedy is not always so straightforward. Nevertheless, incongruity, verbal puns, frustrated expectation and careful phrasing all play important roles in the humour of his plays, as we shall see.

Humour, aggression and classical views of laughter

Incongruity theories are just one way in which scholars have sought to get to grips with humour. A further important group of theories are so-called 'social' theories, which focus on the role that humour can play in shaping interpersonal relationships.[6] Many social theories view humour as a substitute for aggression, the basic model being that one person derides another by making a joke at their expense and by encouraging others to laugh at their victim, too. Some social theories take a very different tack, however, and highlight the ability of humour to bind a group together. The suggestion here is that laughing at the same things can help individuals to identify with one another and therefore cohere as a unit (a process which can often involve there being an 'us' who are doing the laughing, in contrast to a 'them' who are being laughed at, making *in*clusive and *ex*clusive laughter two sides of the same coin).[7]

Social models of humour have interesting implications for the way in which we view Old Comedy. Arguably it is possible to see Aristophanes' audience as an 'us' who are bound together by their laughter, and the various individuals and groups attacked in the plays as a 'them' – figures of fun held up for mockery. But social theories can, perhaps, only take us so far and those scholars who seek to equate *all* humour with aggression are surely mistaken.[8] After all, whilst some jokes clearly *do* have 'butts', it is difficult to see who or what is the target in, say, the 'tank' joke or 'corduroy pillows' joke quoted above. And can we even claim that the 'partner swapping' joke is made *at the expense of* suburban couples who engage in casual sex or homosexuals? I would be tempted to say 'no', though maybe it depends on who tells the joke to whom and in what context. Perhaps it is safest to conclude that humour *can* be used aggressively (just as it *can*, on occasion, fulfil the role of binding together a group), but that this is not *always* the case. And so we find out once more that humour is slippery and difficult to pin down, its uses varied and complicated.

One reason to focus on social theories of humour is that Greeks of the classical era clearly saw laughter very much in these terms, recognizing its potential not only to bind a group together but also to do great harm. In his various studies of Greek attitudes towards laughter, Stephen Halliwell differentiates between what he calls 'playful' laughter and 'consequential' laughter and looks at the ways in which both of these were regarded.[9] As he stresses, 'consequential' laughter, was evidently a source of considerable concern to Greeks of the classical era who viewed it as harmful, derisive and highly shaming for its target: Euripides even has Medea cite her desire to avoid being laughed at by her enemies as one of her reasons for killing her children (*Medea* 1049-50). Consequential laughter is often represented in our sources as aggressive, violent and insulting: in a fourth-century legal speech by Demosthenes, for example, the fact that Ariston's enemies not only physically attacked him but are now prepared laugh at him in court is presented as the last straw (*Against Conon* 13 and 20). Conversely, the idea that laughter had the power to relax and unite people was also prevalent in the classical era: as Laurie O'Higgins shows in her study of female cults in ancient Greece, *Women and Humor in Classical Greece*, laughter played an important role in religious rituals in helping diverse groups of female initiates bond as a group.[10] As outlined above, the laughter roused by Aristophanes' comedies might usefully be seen as simultaneously fulfilling very different roles, then: while shared, 'playful' laughter may often have served to relax the audience and bring them closer together, targets of specific jokes may not always have enjoyed the 'consequential' laughter directed towards them.

From theory to practice: the building blocks of Aristophanes' humour

Having dealt with the important task of looking at humour in the abstract, we can now turn to the key question of this chapter and start to consider Aristophanic humour in closer detail. To this end, the rest of this chapter will chiefly be taken up with examining two overlapping phenomena. First, we shall look at the main building blocks that Aristophanes uses to create humour in his plays: devices like stock characters and routines and the use and abuse of real-life individuals that form the cornerstones of his plays' humour. Second, we shall consider specific joke-types and small-scale devices that Aristophanes uses: 'comic logic', puns and the like. This is not to say that there is any hard-and-fast dividing line between large-scale devices on the one hand and specific joke-types on the other (a stock character may make only a brief appearance in a play, for example, whereas one specific joke-type may form the basis of a long scene), but using these categories has the advantage of giving the discussion a clear structure. Towards the end of the chapter, we shall also consider ways in which Aristophanes' text can be 'playful' without necessarily being humorous and reflect on the larger question of how Aristophanes' instincts as a humorist might be characterized.

Use of stock characters

One of the most important resources that Aristophanes had at his disposal when creating humorous scenarios for his plays was the set of stock characters which existed in Old Comedy. We have already seen one example of a character-type in the introduction to this chapter, the clever slave, Xanthias in *Frogs*, who aids and abets and sometimes outsmarts his master (similar slaves are to be found in *Peace* and *Wealth*). Xanthias is perhaps the most mischievous slave we meet in Aristophanes – a fact that becomes more than apparent when we find him comparing notes with the Slave of Pluto as to how they both outmanoeuvre their masters:

Slave:	I feel like I'm in heaven, when I curse my master in secret.
Xanthias:	What about going outside and grumbling when your master's given you a bad flogging?
Slave:	Now that I *do* enjoy.
Xanthias:	And what about meddling in other people's affairs?
Slave:	Oh, there's nothing like it, by Zeus!
Xanthias:	Way to go, friend! And eavesdropping on your masters when they're being indiscreet?
Slave:	I'm absolutely mad about it!
Xanthias:	And then blabbing to everyone you meet in the street about what you've heard?
Slave:	What me? Why, when I do that I simply come in my pants!

Frogs 745-53

Other recurring character-types we find in the plays include grumpy old men, who are initially antagonistic to the central figure's 'Great Idea' (*Acharnians*, *Wasps* and *Lysistrata* all feature choruses of this kind, for example: see also Chapter 5) and the much-discussed *bômolochos* or 'buffoon', a figure who causes amusement by mocking and undermining other characters either throughout the whole play or in a given scene – often by means of direct address to the audience. Examples of such 'buffoon' figures include Dicaeopolis in the prologue of *Acharnians*; Calonice in *Lysistrata*; Dionysus in the *agôn* of *Frogs* and Blepsidemus in *Wealth*. As we can see in the following extract, for instance, the characters that Dicaeopolis mocks and undermines at the beginning of *Acharnians* include the Athenian ambassadors who, although they have apparently grown hugely rich during an enjoyable trip to Persia, nevertheless complain in the Athenian assembly about the privations they have suffered.

	[*The ambassadors arrive, richly attired.*]
Dicaeopolis:	Wowee! ... What a get up!
Ambassador:	You sent us the Great King on a salary of two drachmas a day in the archonship of Euthymenes. [i.e. eleven years previously!]
Dicaeopolis:	Alas for the drachmas!
Ambassador:	And so we wore ourselves out wandering through Caystrian plains in covered carriages, bedded down in soft sheets. It was hell!
Dicaeopolis:	Well I must have been in seventh heaven, then, bedded down in the rubbish next to the ramparts!

Acharnians 64-72

Perhaps the group from which Aristophanes makes the most comic capital is women, who are routinely portrayed as sex mad, deceitful and lovers of wine. The presentation of women in the plays is explored in Chapter 5.

4. Aristophanes the Humorist

One key question that the existence of stock characters raises is how they relate to the kind of 'incongruity' theories we looked at earlier which see surprise as so central to humour. After all, given that slaves, say, or female characters tend to give rise to a very similar set of jokes each time that they appear, one might be tempted to see their portrayal as anything *but* surprising. The answer here must be that there is something innately humorous about such characters being unable to diverge from their stereo-typical character traits and behaving in extreme ways. In the case of slaves and women in particular, much of the behaviour they exhibit in drama would, of course, have been totally unacceptable in real life – so here is a further incongruity, i.e. between the conduct expected from these kinds of characters *outside* the theatre and the way in which they are portrayed *inside* the theatre. So once more, we do find that a kind of frustrated expectation lies at the root of humour. What is also apparent from the extracts quoted in this section, however, is that exaggeration and distor-tion, too, play an important role in Aristophanic humour.

Original character types

Rather than always rely on stock character-types that are already known to the audience, Aristophanes often creates original character-types in the course of a play. For instance, young men are not presented as sex-mad throughout all Old Comedy, but are characterized as such in *Lysistrata*. Similarly, the old men in *Wasps* are characterized as obsessed with jury service. Once a character-trait of a certain group or individual has been established, Aristophanes is then free to exploit it in the rest of the play to comic effect. The desperation of the young men in *Lysistrata* when they are feeling the effects of the sex strike, for example, is the inspiration for a good deal of humour in the second half of the play – and in performance this would no doubt have made for some memorable scenes in which the male characters were vainly trying to hide their large erect phalluses. The script gives some strong hints as to the kind of comic stage action the audience would have witnessed: for example, when the Spartan ambassa-dors arrive towards the end of the play they are said to be wearing something like a 'pig-pen' around their thighs, and their Athenian counterparts are said to be bent over 'like wrestlers' (1073; 1083). Further comic capital is made from the fact that the sexual desires of both sets of ambassadors are so strong as to influence the way in which they carry out their official duties. The process of peace negotiations, which in real life would no doubt have been a formal and sober affair, is made into a highly comic scene, where the ambassadors eye up the young woman, Reconciliation, whose body becomes a map of Greece to be divided up. The *double entendres* flow thick and fast as the Spartans ask for the 'protuberance' at Pylos to be conceded to them (the reference is to Reconiliation's buttocks), whereas the Athenians in return ask for

57

'Hedgehogtown' (i.e. Echinus in Thessaly, 'hedgehog' also being a slang term for female genitalia) along with 'the Melian gulf behind it and the legs of Megara' (*Lysistrata* 1162-70).

A particularly good example of a character-type being created for a specific play is that of the students who inhabit Socrates' Thinkery (*phrontistêrion*) in *Clouds*. Since they spend so much time inside working on their various intellectual pursuits, they are said to be pale-skinned – an idea introduced right at the beginning of the play (they are described as the 'pallid' at *Clouds* 103). This characteristic is then used as the basis for numerous jokes as the action progresses. When Strepsiades first sees the students, for example, he is astonished at their appearance ('O Heracles, where *do* these creatures come from!' *Clouds* 184) and says that they resemble prisoners of war ('the men captured at Pylos' (186): a reference to the Spartan soldiers imprisoned in Athens between 425 and 421 BC). The joke is developed further: Strepsiades' student guide in the Thinkery displays concern for his fellow-students, ushering them inside the building and saying that 'they are not allowed to spend too much time outside in the air' (198-9), and later on Socrates' companion philosopher in the Thinkery, Charephon, is said to look 'half dead' (504). Presumably the students wore the kind of pale masks usually reserved for female characters making their pallor all the more obvious to the audience (and this would in turn have served to underline the supposed unmanliness of the students' lifestyle).

The idea that the students are too lost in thought to attend to their physical well-being and appearance is exploited for further, more elaborate jokes about them, too. At one point, for instance, Strepsiades leaps to the students' defence, comically putting their unpleasant habits down to 'thrift'. He says to his son:

> Don't badmouth men of intelligence and learning – men who, for reasons of thrift, have never cut their hair or anointed themselves, or even gone to a bathhouse to wash!
>
> *Clouds* 834-7

Quoted on the page, running jokes like these can often appear somewhat lame, but there is the potential in performance for them to be developed into a highly effective source of humour.

Original character-types are to be found in most (if not all) of Aristophanes' plays, not least because the central 'Great Idea' of the play usually provides plenty of scope for humorous creations – from the lawcourt-obsessed old men of *Wasps* and the sex-mad old hags of *Assemblywomen* to the various winners and losers in the new economic system that we find in *Wealth*. Unusual choruses, such as those found in *Birds* and *Frogs*, also allow Aristophanes to hatch original jokes and spawn new humour: such choruses provide an offbeat take on the world and audiences are often invited – particularly during the *parabasis* – to see the world through their eyes (more on this below).

Real-life individuals: abuse and caricature

One of the aspects of Old Comedy that attracted considerable attention in later ages was the extent to which it contained jokes made at the expense of real-life Athenians. The whole issue of personal invective will be explored more fully in Chapter 9, but for now it is worth spelling out some of the different ways in which various individuals are attacked in the plays. Some figures are the targets of repeated abuse from Aristophanes, most notably the politician Cleon, who is the subject of numerous vigorous attacks throughout the 420s. In the *parabasis* of *Peace*, for example, he is described as having:

> ... the voice of a torrent as it wreaks destruction, the stench of a seal, the unwashed balls of a Lamia, and the arse of a camel.
>
> *Peace* 757-8

Other figures also recur time and time again in Aristophanes' plays as the butt of jokes, politicians being the most common targets. The following joke from *Clouds*, for example, is made at the expense of Hyperbolus, who first came to prominence as a public figure towards the end of the 420s. At this point in the play, Socrates is in the midst of saying that Strepsiades' son, Pheidippides, will never make a good student of oratory when he suddenly recalls how one person who had no natural gifts for speaking whatsoever nevertheless managed to learn the necessary skills – by paying teachers of rhetoric huge sums of money.

> How is [Pheidippides] ever going to learn the art of acquittal, or the summons, or persuasion by obfuscation? ... And yet Hyperbolus learnt them – for a talent [i.e. 3,600 drachma].
>
> *Clouds* 874-6

The joke here is not just that Hyperbolus is ungifted and has used his wealth to buy influence – these lines also contain a jibe against Socrates himself, the implication being that he is prepared to teach anyone anything if the money is right.

Other real-life Athenians who come in for repeated abuse include the long-suffering Cleisthenes, mocked by Aristophanes over a twenty year period for his supposed effeminacy. When he appears as a character in *Women at the Thesmophoria*, for example, he rushes on and addresses the women as follows:

59

Aristophanes: An Introduction

My dear ladies, whose lifestyle I share: it must be obvious from my hairless cheeks that I'm a friend of yours. I'm just *mad* about femininity and have always acted as your ambassador ...

Women at the Thesmophoria 574-6

Cleisthenes was a socially (and perhaps politically) prominent figure and so in this respect a typical target for comic abuse. Precisely why he was singled out for attack as an effeminate is not known, but it was most likely for no more reason than the fact that he was unable to grow a beard. Whatever its origin, though, once Aristophanes had developed this comic caricature of Cleisthenes that was successful with his audiences, he used it again and again in plays stretching from *Acharnians* (425 BC) to *Frogs* (405 BC).

A figure with a similar history is Cleonymus, a political associate of Cleon, mocked numerous times for being a 'shield-thrower' – a serious charge indeed, since it implied cowardice and desertion (i.e. throwing away one's shield in battle). Whether Cleonymus did in fact throw his shield away in battle, or whether his supposed cowardice took some other form (such as the evasion of military service, perhaps) has been the subject of much debate. What we *can* be sure about is that, for whatever reason, Aristophanes found this joke about Cleonymus to be one that bore much repeating.[11]

Whilst some figures – most prominently politicians and poets – came in for persistent abuse, there are plenty more of Aristophanes' fellow-citizens at whom just one or two throwaway jokes are directed. Take the following extended sequence from *Clouds*, for instance, in which Aristophanes combines digs at some of his favourite targets (namely Cleonymus and Cleisthenes) with jibes at some less common figures: the poet Hieronymus (here named as the son of Xenophantus) and the politician (and supposed embezzler) Simon. This extract comes from the point in the play where Socrates is explaining to Strepsiades why the members of the cloud-chorus who have just appeared 'look just like mortal women' (*Clouds* 341):

Socrates:	Have you ever looked up and seen a cloud that looked like a centaur, or a leopard, or a wolf, or a bull?
Strepsiades:	Yes I have, by Zeus! What of it?
Socrates:	They can assume any shape they like. So, if they see some hairy, wild-looking guy – one of those shaggy fellows like the son of Xenophantus – they make fun of his passions by taking the form of centaurs.
Strepsiades:	So what do they do if they catch sight of an embezzler of public funds like Simon?
Socrates:	They immediately show him up for what he is by turning into wolves.
Strepsiades:	Right! So that's why, when they saw Cleonymus the shield-thrower yesterday and recognized what a great coward he is, they turned into deer.

4. Aristophanes the Humorist

Socrates: And now, because they have seen Cleisthenes – do you see?
Because of this they've turned into women!

Clouds 346-55

One of the interesting points about this passage is that Aristophanes tends to 'explain' the basis of the joke each time: that is to say, the audience is informed that Hieronymus is 'shaggy' (hence the Clouds turning into centaurs); that Simon is an 'embezzler' (hence wolves) and that Cleonymus is a 'shield-thrower' (hence deer). In short, for every character mentioned (with the exception of Cleisthenes), Aristophanes is careful to tell his audience the basis of each joke before he makes it.

Real-life figures also appear in Aristophanes' plays as characters. We have already seen how Socrates features as a character in *Clouds* and how Cleisthenes appears in *Women at the Thesmophoria*, for example, and other contemporaries of Aristophanes' that appear in his plays include Cleon (*Knights*), Euripides (*Acharnians* and *Frogs*) and Agathon (*Women at the Thesmophoria*), to name but three. Sometimes these figures seem to represent 'types' of individual: the way in which Socrates is represented in *Clouds*, for instance, suggests that Aristophanes was more concerned with creating a figure who embodies certain striking features of the new intellectual movements of the late fifth century rather than producing a portrait of Socrates *per se*. Similarly, we find figures like Lamachus in *Acharnians* who is the archetypical war-mongering general. Whether or not Lamachus took a pro-war stance in real life was probably of less importance to Aristophanes' decision to cast him in this role than the fact that his name suggests a fondness for fighting: since *machê* is Greek for 'battle', a general whose name included the element *mach-* must have seemed like too good an opportunity for a satirist to pass up.

When other real-life figures are represented in the plays there is always a strong element of caricature, with much of the humour relying on distortion and exaggeration as well as the wholesale invention of outlandish character-traits: this is the case with the blustering, ruthless Cleon of *Knights*, who appears in the guise of the slave Paphlagon, for example (see Chapter 9). It is also the case with tragic poets such as Agathon in *Women at the Thesmophoria*, who dresses as a woman to compose female parts for his plays, and Euripides and Aeschylus in *Frogs* whose poetry and dramatic technique are heavily satirized: indeed, the playful use and abuse of tragedy is also a rich source of humour in the plays, as we shall see in Chapter 6. What is more, Aristophanes uses other genres besides tragedy as a springboard for humour, too, especially dithyrambic poets and their poetry (e.g. *Peace* 828-31; *Clouds* 333-9; *Birds* 1372-1409) and oracles (most prominently at *Knights* 960-1099).

Stock routines

As well as stock characters, Aristophanes makes use of certain stock routines in his comedies to amuse his audience. A particular favourite, for instance, is the 'slave at the door' routine, where the main character of the play knocks on the door of a house and is answered by a slave who then engages the hero in a brief conversation. Typically the humour of these scenes stems from the fact that these slaves resemble the master we are about to meet in some key respect. The kind of complex reasoning and ingenious expression employed by Euripides' slave in *Acharnians*, for instance, gives a strong indication of the kind of a man that his owner will later turn out to be.

Dicaeopolis:	[*Knocking at the door of the stage building*] Slave! Slave!
Servant:	Who's there?
Dicaeoolis:	Is Euripides at home?
Servant:	He is at home and not at home, if you understand.
Dicaeopolis:	What do you mean 'at home and not at home'?
Servant:	Just what I say, old man. His mind is *not* at home since it is out collecting scraps of poetry; but he *is* at home himself ... composing a tragedy, with his feet up.
Dicaeopolis:	O thrice-blessed Euripides, to have a slave who gives such clever answers! Call him out now, please!
Servant:	Impossible!
Dicaeopolis:	But do it all the same!

Acharnians 395-402

In *Birds*, it is the physical appearance of Tereus' servant that is the source of the humour: rather than being human he is a bird, just as Tereus will prove to be. This slave, whose comically gaping beak elicits a stunned reaction from Peisthetaerus, comes as all the more of a surprise to the audience since he is the first bird-figure that we meet in the play.

Peisthetaerus:	Slave! Slave! ...
Slave:	Who's there! Who's this shouting for my master?
	[*The door opens and the slave emerges.*]
Peisthetaerus:	Apollo preserve us! What a gaping mouth this is!

Clouds 57; 60-1

Clouds provides us with a variation on the theme of the 'slave at the door' since, in this play, it is not a slave but a Student of Socrates' who greets Strepsiades at the entrance to the Thinkery. This Student introduces the new arrival to some of the unusual (and seemingly pointless) intellectual discoveries that Socrates has made there – and these would no doubt have been the source of much amusement to the original audience. For example, the Student relates the way in which Socrates has accounted for the humming sound that gnats make.

Student:	He said that the intestine of a gnat is narrow and that the air is forced through this slender tube right the way to the rump. Then, since it is a cavity lying adjacent to a narrow pipe, the arsehole resounds as a result of the force of the wind.
Strepsiades:	Ah, so the arsehole of gnats is a trumpet! O thrice blessed man! What amazing perspica*ssity*!

Clouds 160-6

A scene-type that is found in a number of plays is that of the main character warding off unwelcome visitors who come either to profit from, or spoil the success of, his/her 'Great Idea'. In *Peace*, for example, we find an arms-dealer and weapons-makers whose goods are mocked by Trygaeus and in *Birds* we find a whole series of individuals arriving at the newly founded city of Cloudcuckooland, only to be seen off by Peisthetareus: these include a priest, a poet, an oracle-monger, an inspector and a decree seller. A common figure of this type is the 'sycophant' or informer as found in *Acharnians*, *Birds* and *Wealth*: these were men who looked to bring legal suits against their fellow citizens purely for personal financial gain. The humour of these 'warding off' scenes might well be considered cruel by modern standards, since it routinely depends on the interfering figures being humiliated in some way, including being beaten or whipped.[12] Here is a typical example from *Clouds*, where Strespsiades drives an uppercrust creditor away with a goad.

Strepsiades:	Won't you chase yourself away from my house? [*He calls to his slave*] Someone bring me the goad!

[*A slave brings Strepsiades a goad, which he then wields in the Second Creditor's direction.*]
Second Creditor: Witness, please!
[*Strepsiades strikes him with the goad.*]

Strepsiades:	Giddy up! What are you waiting for? Aren't you going to trot off, you branded bronco?

Second Creditor: This is absolutely disgraceful behaviour!
[*Strepsiades strikes him again.*]

Strepsiades:	Get going, won't you? Or I'll prod you up your pampered, equestrian arse!

Clouds 1296-1300

Slapstick and physical humour

This last extract is just one of a number of passages from the plays that could be used to illustrate the importance to Aristophanes of slapstick and physical humour. Physical violence in particular is a standard feature of the plays and underpins, for instance, the episode in *Frogs* where both Dionysus and Xanthias (who has been imitating Dionysus) offer to be beaten. The idea behind this offer is to prove to Aeacus (one of the judges in Hades) which one of them is really the god, the point being that the 'real' Dionysus will not feel pain. As things turn out, however, both Xanthias *and* Dionysus cry out every time they are hit and come up with increasingly transparent excuses to explain their reaction. In the following extract, for example, it Xanthias' turn to be struck.

> [*Aeacus strikes Xanthias with a whip.*]
> Xanthias: Aaargh!
> Aeacus: What is it?
> Xanthias: [*Quickly thinking of an answer*] I ... see horsemen.
> Aeacus: OK. But why are you crying?
> Xanthias: Er ... I can smell onions!
> Aeacus: So you didn't feel the lash at all?
> Xanthias: No, no. It didn't bother me one bit.
>
> *Frogs* 653-5

All sorts of other physical humour exist in the plays, too, from the conflict between the male and female choruses in *Lysistrata* where the men are doused in water (381); to Philocleon's attempt to escape from his son's house through the chimney (*Wasps* 143-51) or strapped to the underside of a donkey (in imitation of Odysseus' escape from the Cyclops in Book 9 of the *Odyssey*: *Wasps* 177-202); to the elaborate routine in *Women at the Thesmophoria* where Euripides' Inlaw is shaved and dressed as a woman (212-65: see Chapter 3, p. 46). In this regard, we should not forget the important role that costume and clothing play in creating humour, too. There are other cross-dressing scenes in *Women at the Thesmophoria*, for example, involving Agathon and Cleisthenes; the dressing up of women as men in *Assemblywomen*; the attempt by Dionysus to disguise himself as Heracles in *Frogs*; the shabby costume of Tereus in *Birds* (whose beak 'looks funny' and whose feathers have fallen off: 93-106); and the outlandish attire evidently worn by the Persian Pseudartabas in *Acharnians* (the 'King's Eye', who enters at line 94).

One scene in *Assemblywomen* in which costume plays a key role is that featuring Blepyrus and his neighbour. Blepyrus is the first male character that we meet in the play when he emerges from his house in the clothing of his wife, Praxagora, who has gone off to the assembly dressed in her husband's cloak and shoes. Blepyrus emerges at line 311 wearing a saffron undergarment and a woman's Persian slippers and his ridiculous appearance is exacerbated by the fact that he is portrayed as desperate to defecate – and so this scene not only serves to highlight the role of clothing but also the importance of a common form of lowbrow humour found in the plays, namely the sexual and scatological (i.e. toilet) jokes that are found in such abundance in Aristophanes. In the following extract, a Neighbour, who has been talking to the squatting Blepyrus for quite some time, comments on the evident difficulty he seems to be in:

Neighbour:	It looks like you're shitting a cable there! Anyway, it's time for me to go to the assembly ...
Blepyrus:	Me, too – just as soon as I've finished my dump. But right now there's something like a wild pear locking everything inside. ... But what am I to do? It's not just that it's causing me pain *now*: where are my turds going to go in the future? For the moment this fellow from Pearsville, whoever he is, has got the door firmly bolted!

Assemblywomen 351-62

The humour generated by obscene, sexual and scatological references will be dealt with in greater depth in Chapter 7.

Specific joke types

So far we have been looking at some of the major building blocks that Aristophanes uses to create the humour in his comedies: above all stock characters, routines and situations around which the humour in a scene or a play can be built. From here on, the focus will be on shorter sequences: namely, the 'types' of joke that feature in the comedies. As stated above, there is no hard-and-fast line to be drawn between the larger scale comic techniques that we have been considering so far and the specific joke-types we shall be looking at now, since many joke-types can be expanded into long sequences, as we shall see. It should also be said that the following by no means represents an exhaustive list of joke-types, nor is it the only way in which Aristophanic jokes might be classified. Rather is intended as a cross-section of some of the more common devices that Aristophanes employs.

'Unnecessary' and 'stupid' questions and answers

One technique regularly used by Aristophanes is what I shall call the 'unnecessary' or 'stupid' question. These questions – the answers to which are either blindingly obvious or impossible to provide – are put by a character simply to act as a feed for a joke. A good example of a 'stupid question' comes in *Clouds*, when Socrates' Student first introduces the rustic Strepsiades to the various intellectual pursuits taking place inside the Thinkery. Strepsiades inquires as to what different groups of students are doing, such as 'those looking at the ground' who, we are told, 'are trying to discover what is under the earth' (188). Then, Strepsiades asks about the activities of a further group:

Strepsiades:	And what are these fellows doing – the ones stooping all the way over?
Student:	They are scrutinizing the nether darkness below Tartarus.

Clouds 191-2

At which point, Strepsiades poses his 'stupid question':

Strepsiades: Then why is their arse looking at the heavens?

Clouds 193

An honest 'answer' to this question might be to point out (as if it needed saying) that the students' arses are not *looking at* anything – how could they be? – and that it is a simple fact of nature that when people are bent over, their arses tend to point upwards. However, it is not an honest answer that we get – instead, it is a jokey one:

Student: It's learning astronomy all by itself.

Clouds 194

Here, then, the whole point of the 'stupid question' has been to provide a foil for a humorous response.

In addition to 'unnecessary' and 'stupid' questions, we also find the 'unnecessary' and 'stupid' answer. Take the following extract from *Peace*, for example, where Trygaeus' slave greets his master on his return from his recent trip to heaven. First, Trygaeus provides an unnecessary and perhaps sarcastic response to his slave's rhetorical question:

Slave: Master, are you really back?
Trygaeus: Well, so someone's told me!

Peace 824

Trygaeus then follows this up with a 'stupid' answer to the slave's next question:

Slave: What happened to you?
Trygaeus: I got sore legs from walking all that way!

Peace 825-6

This last answer puns on the fact that the Greek *tí d'epathes*, 'what happened to you?', can also be understood as 'what did you suffer?' (the Greek verb *paschô* having the double meaning of 'suffer' and 'experience'). These questions in fact form part of a longer sequence, where the Slave's questions provide a feed for a number of humorous replies from Trygaeus – or in other words, a whole series of unnecessary and stupid questions and answers, with Trygaeus acting as the comedian and the Slave playing the part of the 'straight man' or 'stooge' (*Peace* 824-41).[13]

Comic logic

A rather neat technique used by Aristophanes to create short humorous sequences is what I shall call 'comic logic'. This typically consists of a character coming up with a suggestion which, on the face of it, seems at best bizarre and at worst ridiculous and then offering up a seemingly

logical defence of it. A good example of this comes in *Peace*, when Trygaeus
explains to his daughter why he has chosen to make his journey to heaven
on a giant dung beetle rather than, say, on the winged horse, Pegasus. Part
of the humour here depends on the fact that the Greek word for beetle,
kantharos, was also the name not only of a kind of boat but also of the main
harbour in Athens' port, the Piraeus.

Daughter:	Should you not have harnessed the wings of Pegasus, so as to appear more like a tragic hero in the eyes of the gods?
Trygaeus:	But then, my dear, I should have needed double rations. This way I can feed the creature on whatever food I eat myself.
Daughter:	But what if it should fall into the watery depths of the ocean? How will this winged creature be able to glide to safety?
Trygaeus:	[*Showing her his phallus*] I shall use this rudder which I brought along specially. And my vessel [*indicating the beetle*] will be a beetle-boat made in Naxos.
Daughter:	But what harbour will receive you as you drift?
Trygaeus:	The Beetle Harbour in Piraeus, of course!

Peace 135-45

Note that this extract contains more than its fair share of 'unnecessary'
questions – as well as 'stupid' answers!

A further example of 'comic logic' comes from the prologue of *Assemblywomen*, where the women are rehearsing what they will later say in public
in the assembly. Praxagora gives one of her fellow women a garland –
which as well as traditionally being worn by those about to speak in the
assembly were also donned at Greek drinking parties. This is the cue for
Aristophanes to play on one of the stereotypical traits of women mentioned
above, namely their fondness for alcohol.

Praxagora:	Go on, speak!
Second Woman:	What? You mean speak before I've had a drink?
Praxagora:	'Drink' indeed!
Second Woman:	Well, my dear, why did you put this garland on me if I'm not getting a drink?

Assemblywomen 132-3

Aristophanes then has the woman follow the logic through and reason that
there *must* be alcohol present when the men meet at the assembly. To
argue her point, she draws on various pieces of 'evidence', such as the fact
that libations were customarily poured there and that Scythian archers
were also present at the assembly (these were Athens' nearest equivalent
to a police force):

Second Woman:	What then? Don't they drink at the assembly, too?
Praxagora:	Drink? Just listen to you!

Second Woman: Yes, by Artemis, they *do*! And unmixed wine at that! At any
rate the decrees they make seem mad enough to anyone in
their right mind: they *must* be the work of drunks! And, by
Zeus, they pour libations as well. In any case, why would
they make so many prayers, if there wasn't wine there?
And they rail at one another, too, just like drunks, and the
archers carry out anyone who's worse for wear.

Assemblywomen 135-43

One place in which a particular kind of 'comic logic' is commonly found
is in the *parabases* of plays which have non-human choruses where the
chorus presents the case for their superiority to mankind. The chorus of
Birds, for example, employs comic logic when they reason that many of the
audience would be happier living among birds than humans ('If any of you,
spectators, wishes to spend the rest of his days living pleasant life among
us birds, come to us! ...': *Birds* 753-68) and extol the advantages of being
able to fly ('There is nothing better or more pleasant than growing wings
...': *Birds* 785-800: see Chapter 2, p. 27). The benefits that humans would
enjoy if they were birds include the ability to fly away from the theatre
during a dramatic performance to have lunch; to crap; or to sleep with one
of the councillors' wives (787-96)! In a similar vein, the chorus of *Clouds*
provides 'evidence' of how they 'benefit the city more than any of the gods'
and reproach the spectators for failing to honour them appropriately with
sacrifices and libations (*Clouds* 575-94).

The old ones are the best? Repetition as humour

The repetition of jokey lines, phrases and ideas also plays an important
role in Aristophanic humour, as it does for many comic writers. Sometimes, for instance, a lengthy sequence can depend on a single repeated
idea, as is the case with the long passage in *Frogs* where Aeschylus
ridicules Euripides' poetry. At line 1200, Aeschylus says to Euripides, 'I
will destroy your prologues by means of an oil flask' and subsequently,
whenever Euripides begins to recite from the beginning of one of his plays,
Aeschylus demonstrates that the phrase 'lost his oil flask' can be used to
complete the sense of a line whilst also fitting the poetic metre in which
the Greek is written. When Euripides recites the beginning of his lost play
Phrixus, for example, the result is as follows.

Euripides: Cadmus, son of Agenor, once left
Sidon's city and –
Aeschylus: Lost his oil flask!

Frogs 1225-6

And when Euripides quotes the opening lines of *Iphigenia in Tauris*,
Aeschylus once more interjects in the same way:

68

4. Aristophanes the Humorist

Euripides:	Pelops, son of Tantlus, came to Pisa With swift horses and –
Aeschylus:	Lost his oil flask!

Frogs 1232-3

This same joke is made to fill nearly fifty lines, with the openings of no fewer than seven of Euripides' plays 'destroyed' in the same way, thus underlining the supposedly formulaic nature of Euripides' verse (*Frogs* 1200-47).

Repetition can also be used in more localized contexts. We have already seen an example of one common technique employed by Aristophanes, namely that of a speaker being mocked by having their words quoted back at them.

Second Woman:	What then? Don't they *drink* at the assembly, too?
Praxagora:	*Drink*? Just listen to you!

Assemblywomen 135-6

This 'mockery' regularly takes a more full-blooded form, as in the following example taken from the prologue of *Lysistrata*. When Lysistrata talks about the difficulties that the current military conflict is causing the women of Athens, her friend Myrrhine initially says that she will do anything to stop the war.

> Oh yes, I think I'd even cut myself in two, like a flounder [a type of flat fish], and donate half of my body to the cause!

Lysistrata 115-16

However, when she discovers that Lysistrata's plan is to stage a sex strike, she takes a very different view and refuses to take part, saying, 'Let the war carry on!' (*Lysistrata* 130). Lysistrata then turns Myrrhine's earlier words back on her with the following comic rebuke.

> You say that, do you, Miss Flounder? Just a moment ago you said that you'd happily cut yourself in half!

Lysistrata 131-2

A good director could no doubt make a good deal of comic capital out of the interplay between Lysistrata and Myrrhine in these lines.

Of course, repetition is also important to Aristophanic humour in quite a different way, namely the reuse of stock characters and stock routines discussed earlier. This reuse of comic ideas is sometimes apparent on the level of individual jokes, too, that are repeated in different plays (indeed, the existence of stock jokes that Aristophanes could draw on is made more than apparent in the opening sequence from *Frogs* quoted at the beginning of this chapter). What is more, there are even examples of jokes repeated in the *same* play, such as the pun on the name of the general Lamachus in

69

Acharnians. At lines 269-70 of the play, Dicaeopolis celebrates his freedom from 'toils and fusses (*machôn*) and Lamachuses (*Lamachôn*)' and these words are subsequently echoed by a messenger at line 1070, who enters declaring, 'o toils, fusses (*machôn*) and Lamachuses (*Lamachôn*)!': clearly this was a piece of word play that Aristophanes was proud of. Nor is Aristophanes averse to repeating a punch line. Towards the end of *Lysistrata*, for instance, we find four light-hearted choral odes all based around the same basic idea: 'if anyone in the audience needs a loan, just ask – but they won't get it!' (1043-57); 'if anyone would like a nice meal, just come round – but the door will be shut!' (1058-71), and so on (1189-1202; 1203-15: one of these odes is quoted in full in Chapter 8, p. 151). In short, for all Aristophanes' claims about the originality of his plays (e.g. *Clouds* 518-62; *Wasps* 1044-7 and 1051-59), he was evidently prepared to draw out humorous sequences with repeated jokes and to recycle comic material when it suited him.

Puns

Puns are a particularly common form of humour in Aristophanes' plays. Take the following extract from *Peace*, for example, where we find a pun on the word 'paean' (*paiôn* in Athenian Greek). A paean was a celebratory song in honour of Apollo, so called because it traditionally began with the formula 'hey, Paean' (*iê Paeon*), Paean being an epithet of Apollo. When Hermes begins to sing such a song in celebration of Peace's imminent return, Trygaeus brings him up short, the apparent 'reason' being that Paean sounds too similar to *paiein*, the Greek for 'to hit' or 'to strike' – a far from appropriate word in peacetime!

Hermes: May we all enjoy blessings! [*sings*] 'Hey, Paeon, hey!'
Trygaeus: None of this 'striking' (*paiein*), please: just say 'hey'!

Peace 453-4

We later find another similar pun when Trygaeus and his slave are trying to find a suitable way of marking the installation of the goddess Peace in Athens. Trygaeus suggests sacrificing an ox (*bous*) – an idea his slave rejects on the basis of the word's similarity to *boêthein*, 'to help' or 'come to assist', a verb which often used in a military context (e.g. sending troops to help relieve a siege).[14]

Trygaeus: What do you think we should use? A fatted ox (*bous*)?
Slave: An ox? No way! There's no need for any *ox*peditions (*boêthein*)!

Peace 925-6

It could be objected, of course, that neither of these last two examples are true puns, but rather 'near-puns': that is to say, *paiôn* and *paiein* are different words that just happen to sound alike, and this is even more true

70

of *bous* and *boêthein* which only have a passing similarity to one another. This fondness for near-puns is somewhat characteristic of Aristophanes' style, however, and proper names in particular form the basis of a good deal of near-puns in the plays. In *Knights*, for instance, where Cleon appears in the guise of *Paphlag*on (i.e. a slave from Paphlagonia), the chorus says that he *paphlazei*, 'boils' or 'splutters' (*Knights* 919) and, as we have seen, in *Acharnians* Dicaeopolis celebrates his freedom from 'toils and fusses (*machôn*) and Lamachuses (*Lamachôn*)' (*Acharnians* 269-70). Later in *Acharnians*, Dicaeopolis also talks of citizens drawing exorbitant salaries when they act as ambassadors on trips to 'Camarina, Gela and Catagela'. The first two are real cities in Sicily, but the last, Catagela, is a name Aristophanes has made up to sound similar to 'Gela': at its base is the Greek verb *katagelaô* meaning 'deride' or 'laugh at' and so translates as something like 'Mockington' or 'Scornsville' (and is therefore a particularly appropriate place for mocking, scornful ambassadors to be heading, of course). Needless to say, such puns do not always come across very effectively in translation.

Typically, puns and near-puns are used to add a short-lived splashes of humorous colour to the plays, but at times they can be used to underpin longer sequences. This is especially true in *Acharnians* where, for example, the ambiguity of the word *choiros* is exploited during a lengthy scene in which the Megarian seeks to sell his daughters to Dicaeopolis, claiming that they are piglets (a passage we will encounter again in Chapter 7). The joke underpinning the scene is that whilst *choiros* does mean 'pig' when it is a feminine noun (*hê choiros*), as a masculine noun (*ho choiros*) it is a slang term for female genitalia.

Dicaeopolis:	What *is* this exactly?
Megarian:	Why, it's a pig (*choiros*).
Dicaeopolis:	What *do* you mean? Where's she from?
Megarian:	Megara. Doesn't she look like a pig (*choiros*) to you?
Dicaeopolis:	Not really, no.
Megarian:	That's just awful: what scepticism! [*To the audience*] He says that she's not a pig (*choiros*)! [*To Dicaeopolis*] Well, if you like, I'll happily bet you some flavoured salt that *choiros* is what Greeks call *this*! [*indicating the girl's genitalia*]

Acharnians 767-73

This pun then gives way to a long series of *double entendres* where the dual meaning of *choiros* is fully exploited.

Dicaeopolis:	This 'pig' isn't fit for sacrifice.
Megarian:	Why not? Why d'you say it's not fit for sacrifice?
Dicaeopolis:	It doesn't have a tail.
Megarian:	Ah well, it's still young. [*Gesturing with his leather phallus as he speaks.*] But when it's grown up it'll have a big, thick, red one!

Acharnians 784-7

A further example of a pun forming the basis of a long sequence in the play is when Dicaeopolis holds a basket of coals hostage in order to force the aggressive chorus of *Acharnians* to listen to him. The chorus' deme of origin, Acharnae, was well-known for the charcoal it produced – a fact which helps to make sense of their claim that 'this basket is a fellow-demesman of mine' (333). But the 'reason' why they treat the coals as if they were alive is based on a pun, namely the similarity between the Greek words for 'charcoal', *anthrax*, and 'human being', *anthrôpos*. Or as Dicaeopolis puts it:

> Go on, pelt me if you want! But if you do, I'll slaughter this little one. And we'll find out soon enough which of you has any regard for charcoalkind (i.e. *anthrakôn*, 'charcoal'; cf. *anthrôpôn*, 'mankind').   *Acharnians* 331-2

Comic coinages and lists

In addition to puns there are other ways in which the verbal playfulness that pervades so much of Aristophanes' writing can spill over into full-blooded humour. One example of this is his coinages: that is to say, words that Aristophanes has 'invented'. While we might hesitate to call *all* of his coinages 'humorous' there are nevertheless many which seem specifically designed to amuse his audience. Obvious candidates include some of Aristophanes' longer compound-words, such as *spermagoraiolekitho-lachanopôlides* 'market-spawned-porridge-and-vegetable-sellers' and *skorodopandokeutriartopôlides*, 'garlic-primed-inn-keeping-bread-sellers' which appear at *Lysistrata* 457-8 and, of course, the word that occurs at the end of *Assemblywomen* which can lay claim to being the longest attested in any Greek text. The word –

lopadotemachoselachogaleo-
kranioleipsanodrimypotrimmato-
silphioparalomelitokatakechymeno-
kichlepikossyphophattoperistera-
lektryonoptenkephalliokinklope-
leiolagôiosiraiobaphêtraga-
lopterygôn

– which refers to what will soon be served up at a feast, is translated by Alan Sommerstein in his Aris & Phillips version of the play as:[15]

dishy-slicy-sharky-dogfishy-
heady-left-oversy-very-strong-saucy-
silphiumy-bit-salty-honey-poured-overy-
thrush-upon-blackbirdy-ringdovey-pigeony-
chickeny-roast-cooty-wagtaily-
rockdovey-haremeaty-boiled-winy-dippy-
deliciousy-wingedy thing.

Assemblywomen 1169-75

4. Aristophanes the Humorist

It is not just *lengthy* coinages that can usefully be categorized as humorous. In the following extract from *Knights*, Aristophanes makes humorous capital out of a new trend in the late fifth-century, evidently fashionable amongst the young, of coining new adjectives ending in -*ikos* (cf. English 'nau*tical*', 'philosoph*ical*', etc.). The passage (which contains no fewer than eight of these adjectives in five lines) begins with Demos' description of how certain youngsters in Athens go about praising a contemporary politician named Phaeax:

Demos: I'm talking about those youngsters in the perfume market who sit around, spewing out things like: 'Smart chap, that Phaeax ... he's persausative (*synertikos*), conclusative (*perantikos*), inventative (*gnômotypikos*), clear, arrestative (*kroustikos*) and wonderfully restrainative (*kataléptikos*) of those who are shoutative (*thorybêtikon*).'

Sausage-Seller: So I guess you are stick-up-the-fingerative (*katadaktylikos*) at the whole chatterative lot of them (*lalêtikon*)?

                                                   Knights 1375-81

Another playful device that Aristophanes often uses in his plays is the comic list. Lists appear throughout his work – sometimes short, sometimes long – with many of the more memorable lists conveying a real sense of life and energy. Take the following list from *Peace*, for example. Here, Trygaeus describes the scent of the goddess Peace in a list that – given that it is *smells* he is ostensibly describing – contains some very surprising items:

She smells of harvest, hospitality, the Dionysia, flutes (*auloi*), tragedies, songs by Sophocles, thrushes, scraps of Euripidean poetry ... ivy, wine-strainers, bleating lambs, the breasts of women as they run about the countryside, a tipsy slave-girl, an overturned wine-jar, and many other good things besides.

                                                   Peace 530-8

The imagery of this extract is extremely rich and suggestive with a whole range of sights, sounds, smells and allusions conjured up in a hugely evocative way. There are arguably humorous qualities apparent here, too – there is incongruity and surprise in abundance, after all – although perhaps not everyone would rush to call this passage 'humorous'. Exuberant and playful, yes – but not humorous in the way that the following list from *Knights* is. Here Demosthenes lists the powers that the Sausage Seller will enjoy in Athens once he has ousted Paphlagon (Cleon) and become first citizen.

Demosthenes: Look here. Do you see those rows of people? [*indicating the audience*]

Sausage Seller: [*surveying the crowds*] I do.

Demos: You will be the leader of them all – as well as of the people

> in the agora, the harbours and the Pnyx. You'll trample on
> the council; you'll trim back the generals; you'll tie people
> up; you'll keep watch over them; and in the Prytanaeum ...
> you'll suck cocks!
>
> *Knights* 163-67

Here, then, the humour comes in the form of a final surprise item – and so this passage can be said to be structured in a similar way to a 'canned joke', since these, too, characteristically contain a surprise in their punch line, as we saw at the beginning of this chapter.[16]

To summarize, Aristophanes *sometimes* uses coinages and lists to create humour, but not all coinages and lists can usefully be called 'humorous': instead, perhaps it is more fruitful to see devices like coinages and lists as part of a larger set of what scholars have called 'playful' or 'exuberant' features of Aristophanes' plays – features that are *sometimes* used to comic ends. Thus, for example, Aristophanes will often deal his audience small surprises by juxtaposing words or ideas that do not naturally belong together: at *Knights* 631, for instance, where the members of assembly are said to have 'frowned and looked *mustard*'; at *Peace* 637, where the goddess is said to have been 'thrust away with two-pronged *shouts*', and so on (in Chapter 6 we will see how Aristophanes mixes tragic and colloquial elements, too). Whilst examples like these demonstrate a lively, tongue-in-cheek use of language, none of them, I would suggest, is obviously 'humorous'. And so not only do Aristophanes' plays contain much that is humorous but, as the discussion in this section has shown, they also contain an undercurrent of 'playfulness' or 'exuberance', an irreverent and experimental attitude to language that endows his text with a genuine sense of vitality.

Conclusions

This brief look at Aristophanic humour, condensed and selective as it has been, can nevertheless allow us to draw some useful conclusions about the kind of comic techniques that Aristophanes favours and the kind of humorist he is. Perhaps one of the key findings is that, despite the fact that Aristophanes evidently prized originality and cleverness (as we saw in Chapter 1 and in the discussion that opened this chapter), much of his humour is based on stock characters, stock routines and other well-worn methods of joke-making. Indeed, he was not averse to recycling jokes, either. This is not to say that he was unoriginal, however: each play demanded fresh ideas, fresh jokes, and a new situation (a 'Great Idea') that the plot and humour could be hung around. Given the huge supply of ideas needed for each play, and the fact that Old Comedy was a genre that was based on an evolving set of traditions, perhaps it is even inevitable that a playwright (and especially one as productive as Aristophanes) would place the old alongside the new; would reuse as well as invent; and would serve up some old favourites along with some new comic dishes.

A further point to make about Aristophanes' humour is the extent to which it catered for the masses rather than just the intellectual élite. To be sure, there are many subtle puns, clever pieces of word play and satirical takes on contemporary (and sometimes non-contemporary) personalities, events and literature in his plays, but the recurring types of jokes generally fall into the category what we might call 'low-brow humour', understandable by all. Slapstick, obscenity, *double entendres* and personal abuse all play extremely important roles in the humorous make-up of his plays – and whilst Aristophanes may, at times, have been keen to play down the importance of, say, physical and sexual humour in his play, it is worth bearing in mind that there is nothing *un*inventive or *un*original about slapstick and/or sexual humour *per se*. Indeed, keeping the large audiences in the Theatre of Dionysus amused no doubt required a good deal of imagination on the part of Aristophanes as a playwright (and director) and considerable skill and judgement on the part of the actors who had to deliver the lines and perform the physical routines. It is worth remembering, too, that if a joke or routine went down badly with the audience, the absence of laughter in the theatre would have made its failure all the more apparent.

Another fact that has shone through in our discussion is the extent to which Aristophanes' humour can be cruel and offensive. Whilst sexual and scatological humour may have been found uncomfortable by some members of the audience (more on this in Chapter 7), the truly offensive material is arguably that directed at individuals. Many real-life individuals are mocked in the plays, with politicians and playwrights coming in for particular abuse. Some caricatures seem to be particularly unkind: perhaps the most obvious case is the portrayal of Socrates whose teaching and beliefs seem to be distorted almost out of all recognition, and a figure such as Cleisthenes, whose victimization may simply have stemmed from his inability to grow a beard, evidently had to suffer jokes being made about him in comedy for a period of at least twenty years. It seems highly unlikely that comic ridicule was always 'deserved', so to speak, and being on the receiving end of such public abuse cannot always have gone down well with the individuals concerned – and may well have spawned further jokes and comments outside the theatre, too. In this regard, one also wonders how some of the popular stereotypes we find in comedy affected the way in which groups like women and slaves were regarded by male citizens: we shall consider this question when we come to look at the comic portrayal of women in Chapter 5.

There are two last points to be made. First, it is important to highlight something that has not emerged in our discussion so far, which is that humour is scattered somewhat unevenly throughout Aristophanes' work. Some sections of the plays are simply more jokey than others and Aristophanes is capable of long sequences containing little or no humour. Put another way, just because Aristophanes was writing comedy we should not assume that his aim was always to amuse: his plays can be sober, weighty and 'playful', too (although discovering just when he is being, say, weighty rather than playful, or sober rather than humorous, is not always an easy task: more on this in Chapter 9).

Second, it is worth stressing once more just how key the quality of 'playfulness' is to Aristophanes' text: unpredictable words, ideas and juxtapositions are a constant presence in Aristophanes' work. In Chapter 5 we go on to consider unpredictability further when we come to look at the fascinating topic of how figures in Aristophanes' plays are characterized, since many of his characters regularly act in unpredictable ways and say unexpected things. We shall also look at the portrayal in Aristophanes' comedies of women, old men, and the chorus.

The People of Aristophanes

Introduction

The people of Aristophanes are a large and varied bunch. The sheer number of characters in the eleven surviving comedies is enormous: if non-speaking parts played by extras are included, the figures run into the hundreds. The speed at which characters enter and leave the acting space at certain points in the plays must have made for an exhilarating experience for the spectators of the plays – not to mention the actors, who in *Birds*, for example, had to portray twenty-one speaking parts between them. Arguably, the accumulation of people in the plays, just like the accumulation of props during certain scenes (and for that matter the accumulation of words in Aristophanic lists), was a particular characteristic of Old Comedy. As we saw in Chapter 4, amongst this dizzying array of personnel in Aristophanes' plays certain character-types emerge again and again, such as slaves, oracle mongers and tragic poets.

This chapter has three main objectives. The first involves making some important observations about the way in which the people of Aristophanes' plays are characterized (the concentration being on the discontinuity that characters display). The next task is to look at two Aristophanic character-types in particular detail, namely women and old men, from whose ranks the central figures of comedy are so often drawn. Lastly, we shall go on to look at a further set of figures that play a key role in the plays, namely the chorus, and consider their role and function in Aristophanic drama.

The discussion in this chapter will take in a large number of plays, with the sections on female characters covering all three 'women' plays and the sections on old men containing references to all five surviving plays from the 420s. However, the plays which feature most heavily are (in rough order of appearance) *Lysistrata*, *Women at the Thesmophoria*, *Acharnians*, *Wasps* and *Clouds*.

Discontinuity of characterization and 'recreativity'

In previous chapters we have seen several glimpses of how Aristophanes uses what we might call 'discontinuity' in his plays. We have observed that there are sudden switches in time and place in Aristophanic comedy, for example, and on a smaller scale, discontinuity also surfaces in the surprising combination of words in a single phrase (e.g. 'two-pronged *shouts*': *Peace* 637) and in the unexpected juxtaposition of items in various comic lists (e.g. '... crowns, anchovies, flute-girls, black eyes': *Acharnians* 551). This 'discontinuity' which is so prevalent in the plays does not only display itself in the form of disjointed plots, phrases and lists, however: it also seems to infect Aristophanes' characters, too. Or to put it another way, Aristophanic figures often say or do surprising things or act in a way in which real-life figures do not tend to act.

We have already seen some examples of the unrealistic behaviour that the people of Aristophanes display in our discussion of humour in Chapter 4. Characters ask stupid questions, for example (e.g. Strepsiades asking of the bent over inhabitants of the Thinkery 'why is their arse looking at the heavens?': *Clouds* 193); or give stupid answers (e.g. the Student's reply, 'It's learning astronomy all by itself': *Clouds* 194). There are also numerous comments made in the plays (often by 'buffoon' figures) which other characters simply ignore. Such is the case in the following passage taken from the beginning of the *Lysistrata*, for instance, where the play's heroine is interrupted while explaining why she looks so worried:

Lysistrata:	Calonice, my heart's burning and I'm deeply grieved by us women. Men think that we're so very wicked ...
Calonice:	And so we are, by Zeus!
Lysistrata:	... and yet although I've told the women to meet here to discuss a far from trivial matter, they stay asleep and don't turn up.

Lysistrata 9-15

In a real-life exchange, we should either expect Calonice not to make such a crass comment or for Lysistrata to question Calonice as to her precise meaning. But in the context of Aristophanic drama, different rules apply: Calonice's comment is simply ignored and the dialogue moves on.

In his discussion of the phenomenon of 'Discontinuity of Characterization' in *Aristophanic Comedy*, Kenneth Dover cites another way in which characters act in unrealistic ways, namely when they undermine their own statements.[1] While asking a favour of the Prytanis in *Women at the Thesmophoria*, for example, Euripides' Inlaw makes a highly unflattering allegation against the very man whose help he is seeking:

Inlaw:	O Prytanis, by your right hand – which you're accustomed to holding out cupped when anyone offers you money – grant me a small favour, doomed as I am to die.
Prytanis:	What favour would you like me to grant?

Women at the Thesmophoria 936-8

Note once more that the Inlaw's comment is ignored. In a similar vein, too,

78

no-one asks Calonice what she means when she pledges her support to Lysistrata in the following way:

| Lysistrata: | Would you be willing to help me put an end to the war if I come up with a plan? |
| Calonice: | Yes, I would, by the two goddesses! I'd even pawn my dress – and drink down the proceeds in a single day. |

Lysistrata 112-14

Here the (comprehensible) offer to help Lysistrata's cause by raising funds is undermined by a cheap joke (one that relies for its effectiveness of women's supposed love of alcohol). However, Calonice's comment neither raises a laugh nor any eyebrows amongst the various women that Lysistrata has assembled, who simply continue their conversation. There seems little point in asking what it is about the personalities of the Inlaw or Calonice that makes them say what they do nor in wondering why those around them fail to react differently to their remarks: in each of the passages quoted so far, any realism is simply sacrificed by Aristophanes for the sake of a joke.

So far all the examples of discontinuity of characterization we have seen are connected with humour, but there are plenty of points in the plays where non-realistic behaviour serves no overtly comic purpose. There is, for example, the tendency of certain characters to use elevated words or allude to concepts with which we would not normally expect a real-life figure of their social class or education to be familiar. This phenomenon – which Gregory Dobrov calls 'ventriloquism' – can be seen in the language of characters such as Dicaeopolis and Trygaeus, both of whom litter their speech with quotations from tragedy at key points in their respective plays.[2] In *Acharnians*, Dicaeopolis quotes and adapts lines from Euripides' lost play *Telephus*, for example, whereas Trygaeus in *Peace* cites a number of lines and phrases from the lost *Bellerophon* (also by Euripides). Once again, to ask why these characters act in this way is to miss the point – characters simply can and do say things that in real-life, or in a more true-to-life play, would at the very least merit an explanation. But in Aristophanic drama, no such explanation is asked for or given: rather, inconsistency and unpredictability are simply part of the fabric of the play.

Perhaps the most influential account of characterization in Aristophanes is that of Michael Silk who has suggested that unrealistic behaviour should not simply be regarded as something that figures in Aristophanes exhibit *occasionally*, but that it is a *fundamental* part of the way they are characterized.[3] In *Aristophanes and the Definition of Comedy* he coins the word 'recreativity' as an umbrella term to describe the discontinuous way in which so many of the people of Aristophanes behave – and this would include the examples we have been looking at so far. To understand what Silk means by this term, it is important to consider how 'recreativity' differs from the 'realist' way in which the vast majority of figures in Western literature are portrayed. He describes 'realist' characters as follows:[4]

> The people presented [in most Western literature] have what we may see as a constant relationship with 'reality' – with the world outside as we perceive it or might be presumed to perceive it ... They impinge as sentient beings, each with a tendency to be (in Aristotle's language) 'appropriate', 'lifelike' and 'consistent' ... .

Silk concedes that 'some Aristophanic characters ... lend themselves better than others to realist interpretation' (Lysistrata and Strepsiades have fairly consistent 'personalities', for example, as do the characters of the fourth-century plays, *Assemblywomen* and *Wealth*). However, he argues that Aristophanic figures do not in general belong to this 'realist' tradition; indeed, he suggests that they 'are not strictly containable within any realistic understanding of human character at all.'[5]

The passage that Silk uses to introduce the concept of 'recreativity' is taken from *Women at the Thesmophoria* where the Inlaw suddenly volunteers to attend the all-female festival of the Thesmophoria on Euripides' behalf. Euripides has just failed to convince the cross-dressing tragic poet Agathon to take up this challenge – hardly surprising since the mission requires a man to go there disguised as a woman with the object of intervening in the debate due to take place as to whether Euripides should be killed. But what are we to make of the Inlaw's offer? As Silk points out, at the beginning of the play Euripides has shown himself to be an intellectual heavyweight, whereas his Inlaw has proven himself to be something of a buffoon figure, often slow on the uptake and frequently tactless. And so it might come as a surprise that the apparently clever Euripides accepts his Inlaw's offer quite so readily.

Inlaw:	Euripides, my dear, dear kinsman: don't abandon your cause!
Euripides:	So what am I to do, then?
Inlaw:	Tell him [i.e. Agathon] to go to hell! And take me and do whatever you want with me.
Euripides:	OK, then. Since you're offering yourself to me ... take off that cloak!

Women at the Thesmophoria 209-14

Perhaps more of a surprise still is just how good a job the Inlaw makes of impersonating a woman. Whilst his male persona does occasionally poke through his disguise (just as his leather phallus pokes through his female clothing) he is at times startlingly convincing in his new role as a female festival-goer. As soon as he is dressed in women's clothes and the signal goes up for the start of the Thesmophoria he delivers the following speech, for example, in which he displays an amazing knowledge of festival customs:

> [*Calling to an imaginary slave-girl*] Come on, Thratta: follow me! Look, Thratta, the lamps are burning. And what a crowd of worshippers there is coming this way, all shrouded in the smoke of incense! O most beauteous Thesmophoroi, receive me here at your shrine in all prosperity and deliver me thus back home. [*Addressing the imaginary slave-girl once more*] Take down the basket and bring out the flat cakes, so I can make my offering to the two goddesses. ...
>
> *Women at the Thesmophoria* 279-85

The point to be made here is not just that these events are not very true to life, but that (i) the Inlaw undergoes an *instant* transformation: we do not see him practising or learning to act like a woman, rather he just switches into a new mode; and (ii) as with other examples of discontinuity we have seen, this transformation is not commented on as being surprising or unexpected by any other character. In other words, the Inlaw is 're-created' and the discontinuity in his characterization is to all intents and purposes just part of the plot: an unremarkable event that is simply woven into the sequential (but not always logically *con*sequential) storyline of the play. Nor is the case of the Inlaw unique: other characters go through major recreative transformations, too, from the rejuvenation of Demos at the end of *Knights* to the ever-shifting Dicaeopolis in *Acharnians* who takes on numerous guises as the play progresses – from audience member to participant in Athens' assembly to speaking as if he is the poet himself. To make the connection with the various examples we have seen in this section, other types of discontinuous behaviour are, for Silk, simply smaller scale versions of these transformations – and thus the kind of 'inappropriate' asides and unrealistic reactions we have observed elsewhere in relation to other characters (such as Calonice) are also 'recreative' moments in miniature. 'Recreativity', then, is a characteristic that most of the people of Aristophanes display to some extent: as Silk puts it, they are *'inconsistently* inconsistent' and liable to undergo changes – be they large or small – that are unannounced, unpredictable and even unmotivated.[6]

The consequences of 'recreativity'

Not only is the idea of discontinuous, 'recreative' characters interesting in itself, but it also has important consequences for the way we think and write about the people of Aristophanes. In particular, ascribing thoughts or motivations to his characters becomes something generally best avoided. After all, the behaviour of characters such as Calonice in *Lysistrata* or Euripides' Inlaw in *Women at the Thesmophoria* simply does not resemble the way in which 'real' human beings behave: that is to say, 'real' people do not tend to make cutting jibes that undermine requests they are making or undergo radical shifts in their personality and speech. And so when talking about the people of Aristophanes, we should generally resist the temptation of trying to 'explain' why a character is acting in a certain way or make claims about what is going through a character's mind at a particular moment. The characters themselves have not made a conscious decision to act in a particular way nor, arguably, are they portrayed as 'capable' (in any meaningful sense) of making any decisions at all: rather it is their creator, Aristophanes, who has decided to have them act in a certain way or make a given statement ('And so we are by Zeus!'; 'Tell him to go to hell! And take me and do whatever you want with me'). The safest policy when discussing such characters, then, is not to say that 'the Inlaw decides to do X' or 'Calonice thinks Y', but rather to say that 'Aristophanes presents the Inlaw as deciding to do X' or 'Calonice is presented as thinking Y': a long-winded formula, maybe, but one which reflects more accurately the way in which most (if not quite all) of the people of Aristophanes are portrayed.[7]

One last point to consider is the consequences of the presence of recreative characters in a play for the realization of humour.[8] These are, in fact, far reaching. After all, in a comedy populated by realistic (i.e. 'realist') characters, we may legitimately expect a proportion of the humour to stem from the way in which these figures are characterized and their subsequent interaction and individual responses to the situations which they confront. In a 'recreative' genre such as Old Comedy, however, where only some of the figures we meet have consistent 'characters', humour relying on subtle characterization can hardly be expected. That is certainly not to say that an author working in a recreative genre will be at a loss when it comes to finding ways to make his audience laugh – Aristophanes' plays are, after all, rich testimony to how humorous a non-realist play can be. However, what we only rarely find in Aristophanes is subtle humour which relies on an individual character's 'personality'; and what we find more often (as we saw in Chapter 4) is humour based on caricatures of real-life figures and, in particular, character-*types* – such as women and old men. And it is to these two character-types that we now turn.

Female characters in Old Comedy

Old Comedy is a particularly important source for the study of women in antiquity. In a culture whose literature, laws, art and public monuments were almost exclusively produced by men, there are all too few glimpses to be gained of the everyday lives of women in classical Athens and their perspective on the world. Not that Old Comic plays are themselves unproblematic as historical sources: these were also written by men, for an exclusively or mainly male audience, and all the words spoken by female characters in the plays would, of course, have been delivered by male actors, too. What we find in Aristophanes' plays, then, are not snapshots of women's lives, but something more complex – and, perhaps, all the more fascinating as a result. The picture of women that we find in Aristophanes takes as its starting point plausible details of the lives of 'real' women but blends these with comic fantasy, humour and invention in such a way as to entertain his male audience and to serve the poet's artistic ends. Studying the female characters in Aristophanic comedy is not only important for building up a picture of women's lives, then, but also for revealing male attitudes towards women. What is more, observing how this image of women is built up in the plays is also highly revealing of Aristophanes' techniques as a playwright and humorist, as we shall see.

From what we can piece together from the fragments of other comic poets, female characters were a relatively new phenomenon in Old Comedy when Aristophanes was beginning his career as dramatist in the early 420s.[9] Certainly women do not feature very heavily in his earlier plays and such women as we do find tend to fall into one of three categories. First there are goddesses, such as Iris, or the semi-divine Basileia (Sovereignty) whom Peisthetaerus marries in *Birds*. Second, there are sexual playthings, such as the dancing girls with whom Dicaeopolis frolics towards the end of *Acharnians*. And third there are women who are both, that is to say, goddesses-cum-whores: the semi-divine Theoria in *Peace* (who, Trygaeus' slave says, 'we used to bang on our way to Brauron after a few drinks', *Peace* 873-4) falls into this category. The wives and mothers of citizen men are hardly in evidence at all and on the rare occasions that they do appear, we do not hear them speak: neither the wife of Dicaeopolis (who appears during the Dionysiac celebration at *Acharnians* 241-79) nor the newlywed brideswoman (a kind of matron of honour) who whispers in Dicaeopolis' ear at line 1058 of the same play deliver any lines, for instance. Indeed, the only non-divine female characters to deliver lines in the surviving plays up to and including *Birds* (414 BC) are either youngsters, foreigners or both. Examples include the daughters of the Megarian trader in *Acharnians* (who are dressed up as pigs), the bread-selling Myrtia in *Wasps* (who, since she gives the names of her parents at line 1397, is presumably to be considered unmarried and therefore probably still young) and Trygaeus' daughter in *Peace*. These are all minor parts.

All this stands in marked contrast to the two plays that Aristophanes produced in 411 BC, *Lysistrata* and *Women at the Thesmophoria*, both of which contain a whole host of female characters – a feature they also share with the later *Assemblywomen* (produced around 391 BC).[10] Whilst it may be interesting to speculate as to what inspired Aristophanes to write plays centring on women when he did (in particular, why 411 saw such a sudden flurry of comic women) we are destined never to reach any firm conclusions here.[11] A more fruitful line of enquiry, though, is to look at how female characters in general, and citizen wives in particular, are portrayed in these three 'women' plays. The following three sections will be dedicated to this topic: first, to looking at the comic stereotypes associated with citizen wives; second, at the way in which Aristophanes exploits the contrast between female domestic life and the male public sphere in his plays; and third the way in which Aristophanes' plays might provide an insight into the grievances that Athenian wives voiced in real life.

Drunken, lying tarts: the citizen wives of Aristophanes

Aristophanes has great fun in his plays at the expense of citizen wives, the typical comic stereotype being that they are lovers of wine, sex-mad and deceitful.[12] This far from flattering image of women has predictably drawn a good deal of attention from feminist critics who, quite rightly, see it as part of a broader set of derogatory attitudes held about women in classical Greece. What makes these particular stereotypes so interesting, however, is the fact that they are plausibly connected with a particular set of male anxieties: that is, men's fears about their wives' sexual behaviour.

Classical Athens was a society where the production of legitimate offspring was of utmost importance since it was integral to the continuation of a man's household (*oikos*). Adultery therefore had the potential to threaten the very fabric of the home since – if it went undetected – it might entail another man's child being born into the husband's household. The fact that adultery could be severely punished (even by death) is testimony to the seriousness with which it was taken – and, indeed, the relatively high degree of segregation between the sexes and the seclusion of many women (especially in upper class households) was also presumably born of a desire to keep inappropriate contact between men and women to a minimum. In real life, then, the stereotypical behaviour exhibited by younger married women in comedy would be a cause for the utmost concern: indeed, drunkenness might lead to a loss of inhibitions; a high sex drive might lead to adultery; and a wife's deceit might mean that her husband would never know that a child resulting from the affair was not his own. But in Aristophanic comedy, these 'serious' concerns become topics of humour – and inventive and exuberant humour at that. Let us now look at these stereotypical character traits in closer detail and see how they are exploited to comic effect in Aristophanic comedies.

Female drunkenness is a motif we find in all three 'women' plays. A passage that illustrates well its exploitation for humorous purposes comes in *Women at the Thesmophoria*, when Euripides' Inlaw is eventually suspected of being a male imposter at this all-female festival. When he is questioned about the secret religious rituals which took place the previous year he 'guesses' correctly that these all revolved around alcohol:

Critylla:	Tell me, what was the first of the sacred objects revealed to us?
Inlaw:	Let me think. Err. What was it now? [*suddenly inspired*] Oh! We drank.

84

Critylla: And then after that: what was the second thing?
Inlaw: We drank some toasts.
Critylla: Someone must have told you!
                                                          Women at the Thesmophoria 628-32

Similarly in *Lysistrata* when the women are making their promise to abstain from sex, they appear to be far more interested in the cup and wine jar over which they are swearing (in place of a more customary animal sacrifice) than the oath itself:

Lysistrata: Someone bring out a cup and wine jar from inside.
               [*A female slave arrives with a large cup and jar and the women crowd round.*]
Myrrhine: Wow! My dear ladies, what an impressive piece of pottery!
Calonice: [*Handling the cup*] Yes, just picking this up is enough to
               bring a smile to your face!
Lysistrata: Put that down! ... [*Praying*] O Lady Persuasion and Cup of
               Friendship, please receive this sacrifice and smile upon us
               women. [*She pours wine into the cup. The other women
               watch intently.*]
Calonice: That 'blood's a lovely colour and sure does spurt out well.
Lampito: [*Hastily agreeing*] Yes, by Castor, and how sweet it smells,
               too.
Myrrhine: [*Jostling the others out of the way*] Me first! Let *me* be the
               first to swear, ladies!
                                                          Lysistrata 199-207

The comic notion that women are unable to control their sexual urges also gives rise to a whole host of risqué jokes in the plays. A typical example comes in *Assemblywomen*, where Praxagora plans to fill Athens' assembly with her female friends disguised as men – the idea being that they will then vote for the running of the city to be handed over to its women. As they rehearse, however, one woman voices a concern as to how the plan might backfire when the motion comes to the vote:

How are we going to remember to raise our arms, when we're so used to
raising our legs?
                                                          Assemblywomen 263-5

Risqué humour at women's expense is especially common in *Lysistrata*, where the sex strike is the source of all manner of jokes throughout the play, not least because the women must struggle against their 'natural' urge to have sex. The women that Lysistrata has collected together at the beginning of the play are initially highly resistant to the idea of sexual abstinence, for example:

Calonice: I won't do it! Let the war carry on instead!
Myrrhine: Nor me, by Zeus! Let the war carry on! ...
Calonice: Anything, *anything* else! If I had to, I'd even walk through

85

fire – rather that than give up cock! There's just *nothing* else like it, Lysistrata dear.

Lysistrata 129-30; 133-5

Later in the play, we meet a whole set of feeble excuses as the women try to sneak away from the Acropolis where they are holed up – with the sexual motives behind their desire to escape all too apparent. Take the following example:

First Woman: I want to go home. I've got some Milesian fleeces at home and the moths are simply making mincemeat of them.
Lysistrata: Moths you say? And you'll come back, will you?
First Woman: Oh yes, I'll come back straightaway. Just as soon as I've … spread them on the bed, that is.
Lysistrata: You're not *spreading* anything: you're going nowhere!

Lysistrata 728-33

A particularly rich comic passage which relies for its humour on the various stereotypes associated with the female sex comes in *Women at the Thesmophoria*. Before his identity as a man is discovered, Euripides' Inlaw makes a long speech in which he lists all kinds of wicked deeds supposedly perpetrated by women – once more playing on their comic reputation of being sex-mad and deceitful. During the speech (which he delivers while still disguised as a woman), he says:

To start with, I myself (not to mention anyone else) have all kinds of wicked things on my conscience. But the wickedest was when I was a bride of three days and my husband was asleep next to me. Well, I had this friend who had taken my virginity when I was just seven years old. He was desperate for a bit of what I had to offer and came scratching at the door … and I went downstairs secretly … poured water over the door hinge and went out to meet my lover. And so next thing you know I was bent over next to the altar of Apollo, clinging to the laurel bush and getting a good old seeing to!

Women at the Thesmophoria 476-82; 487-9

We have already talked about the 'serious' male anxieties that may underpin these various comic stereotypes – and the same may be true for other motifs in the plays, too. The idea of women seizing the reins of power, for example – which is central to the plots of both *Lysistrata* and *Assemblywomen* – is not only a *comic* fantasy: similar story patterns are also found in Greek myth and legend (e.g. the myth of the Lemnian Women, where all but one man on the island of Lemnos is killed). Perhaps it is not too far-fetched to claim (as some scholars have) that such plot-structures reveal further male anxieties about women, their powers and their potential to get the better of men. What is more, it is also interesting to speculate on the extent to which Old Comedy, through a roundabout route, served to reinforce certain cultural attitudes, such as the idea that women were sly, potentially dangerous and should ideally be segregated from men, restricted in their movement and closely watched. In other words, it is a real possibility that the jokes made about women in Aristophanes' comedies played a role in shaping both men's views and, as a consequence, women's lives outside the theatre.

Housewives hit the town: private women in public spaces

One of the character-traits of citizen wives that Aristophanes foregrounds in his portrayal of women is their expertise in domestic activities. For many Athenian wives, life in the home would have involved a whole range of activities, including performing various chores (such as wool-working, weaving and preparing food); taking a role in managing the household's finances; overseeing certain religious activities (women played a key role in death cult, for instance), and so on. When women appear in the public sphere in Aristophanes' plays, they are often portrayed as bringing these indoor activities outdoors. Sometimes this is done in a literal way in order to raise a laugh: for example, one of Praxagora's followers in *Assemblywomen* brings her wool basket along with her so that she can do some carding while the assembly is filling up (lines 86-92), supposedly unaware that this would give the game away that she was a woman. On other occasions, though, female activities are neatly integrated into the action, plot and imagery of the play – sometimes with striking results, such as the emergence of a highly original 'domestic' perspective on the problems of the city at large, as we shall see.

Lysistrata is a play that exhibits the imaginative blending of the domestic and public particularly well. The scene setting begins in the prologue, where various Athenian women outline the difficulties they have in leaving the house undetected by their husbands, underlining the fact that they are essentially housewives (we find a very similar scene at the beginning of *Assemblywomen*). Establishing this 'housewifeyness' at the beginning of the play is important thematically, since there are numerous examples of concepts taken from the female, domestic sphere and brought to bear on the broader world of the *polis* (city-state). These include Lysistrata's suggestion that women's expertise in the management of household finances can be successfully applied to the city as a whole (493-5) and the women's dressing up of the Magistrate (*Proboulos*) as a corpse (reflecting women's extensive role in burial: 599-613). The most striking instance, though, is surely Lysistrata's solution to the city's problems, which she presents in terms of a metaphor of wool-working (567-86: discussed more fully in Chapter 9). When asked by the Magistrate how she will unravel the large confusion that currently exists in international affairs, she outlines how women intend to resolve it.

> It's just like when we've got a skein of wool that's all tangled. We take it like this, carefully drawing it apart with spindles, first this way, then that. And this is just how we will disentangle this war, too, if you'll let us: we'll sort it out by sending embassies first this way, then that.
>
> *Lysistrata* 568-70

As her speech continues, she goes on to talk about washing, beating, carding and weaving the wool, with each of these steps made analogous to an action that the city should take in order to solve its problems. The result of these actions, in the words of Lysistrata's metaphor, is that the women will be able to 'weave a nice warm cloak for the people to wear' (line 586).

It is also worth taking a closer look at the character of Lysistrata herself, since she is carefully characterized as different from the other Athenian wives. In contrast to them, nothing she says indicates any weakness for sex, alcohol, or indeed, any hint of frivolity at all. She also gains status in the play by being cast as something of a priestess figure. There are various indications of this: her first lines in the play, for example, contain allusions to religious festivals ('If someone had invited the women to a Bacchic revel … they'd all be here by now', 1-4) and we have already seen the way she presides over the 'sacrifice' of the jar of wine (p. 85). Perhaps most significant, however, is the fact that one of the most important priestesses in Athens at the time the play was produced (the priestess of Athena Polias – 'Athena protectress of the city' – whose precinct lay on the Acropolis) was called Lysimache, 'Dissolver of Battles', whereas Lysistrata's name translates as 'Dissolver of Armies'. Characterizing Lysistrata in this way has two advantages for Aristophanes. First, he at once endows Lysistrata with the kind of authority a female would need to organize other women and to command the respect of men, making her leadership appear all the more natural. Second, it allows him subtly to evoke the one occasion on which women could collect together outside their homes without men being present, namely a religious festival (such as we find in *Women at the Thesmophoria*) – so the female gathering at the beginning of the play seems less forced than it might otherwise.

As in all the 'women' plays, Aristophanes treads an interesting line in his creation of female figures in *Lysistrata*, blending true-to-life detail of women's everyday lives (e.g. weaving, managing the household budgets) with popular comic stereotypes (e.g. drunkenness and a constant desire for sex) and a far-fetched plot (women seizing the Acropolis and staging a panhellenic sex strike). And this interweaving of the realistic, fanciful and the absurd is, to a large extent, a characteristic of the play as a whole. After all, one vital point to bear in mind is that the premise underpinning the plot of the *Lysistrata* is essentially fantastic. A scenario in which women gather together in secret, where they plot and fight against men and take charge of the city's affairs (albeit temporarily) was unthinkable in the real world of fifth-century Athens. Aristophanes is constantly playing with the

88

topsy-turvy idea of women in power to great effect and much of the appeal of the wool-working metaphor, as we have seen, comes from the way in which he takes this domestic image from the woman's realm and cleverly applies it to the male, public domain. In so doing, Aristophanes almost makes the concept of female rule seem logical, whereas to his audience the idea of women running the city would have been quite ridiculous: a concept suited to myth or even barbarian societies (such as the man-killing Amazons we find in Herodotus 4.110-17), but not to real life in a Greek *polis*.

This blending of fact and fantasy is apparent in the other 'women' plays, too. The plot of *Assemblywomen*, for example – where women also gain power in the city and impose a communist regime – is equally fantastic. But the concept of female rule is also made to seem logical in its own way with Praxagora arguing that, as the upholders of tradition, women are to be trusted with the city far more than men. Once more it is an analogy from the domestic sphere she initially uses to establish her case, claiming that women:

> ...... maintain, one and all, their ancient tradition of dyeing wool in hot water, and you won't see them experimenting with anything different.
>
> *Assemblywomen* 215-18

In typical Aristophanic style, however, this ostensibly serious claim to be the upholders of worthy traditions is then undermined by a series of further examples of 'traditions' which range from the inconsequential to the obscene. Praxagora says of her fellow women:

> They roast corn sitting down, just like in the old days. They carry things on their heads, just like in the old days. They celebrate the Thesmophoria, just like in the old days. They bake flat-cakes, just like in the old days. They annoy their husbands, just like in the old days. They keep lovers in the house, just like in the old days. They buy extra food for themselves, just like in the old days. They like their wine undiluted, just like in the old days. They enjoy getting fucked, just like in the old days. And so, gentlemen, let's hand over the city to them ...
>
> *Assemblywomen* 221-9

Praxagora delivers these last lines in the context of a mock-assembly where the women are practising what they will say in the real assembly. This idea of a female assembly is also used in *Women at the Thesmpohoria*: when the women meet together we find that the Thesmophoria is run along parallel lines to the real-life (and all male) Athenian assembly held on the Pnyx in the centre of Athens (where the Thesmophoria festival was also held). Evidently the idea of women fulfilling male roles by delivering speeches in public and going through the same ceremonies and procedures as their husbands and fathers was one that particularly appealed to Aristophanes – and presumably greatly amused his audience, too. It is important for us to bear in mind just how extraordinary and ridiculous the idea of women acting like politicians (or dressing like men, as Praxagora and her followers do in *Assemblywomen*) would no doubt have been to the original audience – however unexceptional it might seem to us now.

Hearing women's voices? Aristophanes on female grievances

As we have seen, citizen wives in Old Comedy are subject to a number of negative stereotypes and a fair amount of mockery, but that is not to say that their portrayal by Aristophanes completely lacks sympathy. Not only are figures such as Lysistrata and Praxagora likeable and impressive in themselves, but the ideals that they espouse also have much to commend them: as we have seen, women are often characterized as the upholders of tradition (generally a positive virtue in Aristophanes' plays) and in *Lysistrata* it is the women's actions that lead to the peace and panhellenic unity we find at the end of the play (also presented in a positive light).

Aristophanes also allows his female characters to voice a large number of complaints about their plight as women.[13] Some of these may be low level grumbles, but others seem to be weighty in the extreme – none more so, perhaps, than when Lysistrata reminds the Magistrate about the effects that war has on women. She speaks of women's powerlessness (they must tolerate the political decisions made by men and have no means of intervening: 507-28); the fact that their sons die in battle (588-9), and that wives must sleep alone while their husbands are on campaign (591-2). More poignantly still, she reminds him of the fate that women must suffer if they remain unmarried.

Lysistrata:	I am deeply distressed about the unmarried girls growing old in their chambers.
Magistrate:	What? Don't men grow old, too?
Lysistrata:	Really, By Zeus! You're not comparing like with like. A man comes home and even if he's grey-haired he can find a young girl to marry soon enough. But for a woman time is fleeting, and if she doesn't seize the short chance she's got, no one wants to marry her and she's forced to sit there, hoping against hope.

Lysistrata 594-97

Another apparently weighty passage comes in the *parabasis* of *Women at the Thesmophoria*, where the chorus reprimands the male audience for the way that men speak about women and treat them. They allude in particular to the seclusion in which many women were kept, arguing that it is inconsistent for men to keep such a jealous guard on their womenfolk while at the same time characterizing females as something evil:

Everyone says many bad things about the female sex, claiming that we are an utter curse on mankind and that all manner of evils originate with us: disputes, quarrels, civil strife, sorrow, war. Come on now, if we're really a curse, why do you marry us? If we're really a curse, why do you forbid us from leaving the house and from being caught so much as peeping outside. And why do you take such efforts to keep a close guard on this 'curse'? If the little lady does go off somewhere and you find that she's not at home, you have an absolute fit, whereas you really ought to be pouring libations and paying thanks if you find that your 'curse' has disappeared and is nowhere to be found at home. And if we're having a nice time round a friend's house and get tired and fall asleep, then all of you go round the couches looking for the 'curse'. And if we peep out of a window, you all seek to get a look at the 'curse'. And if she's embarrassed and retreats, then everyone is all the more keen to get a glimpse of the curse when she peeps out again.

Women at the Thesmophoria 786-99

Speeches like this provide a unique insight into women's lives in classical Athens, especially when read alongside other passages from Aristophanes which contain so much important detail as to the daily activities of women (from cooking to carding) and such vital information about their interaction with men (from the excuses that a wife could make in order to justify leaving the house alone to the fact that young women are only marriageable for a short time). This rich detail certainly implies that Aristophanes was far from ignorant of how women lived their lives and the presence of a number of thought-provoking passages delivered by women in his plays, such as those quoted in this section, also suggests that he had given some serious thought to women's perspectives on the world. Taken as a whole, then, his plays provide a rich mine of information about the female condition in classical Athens – a fascinating mixture of men's prejudices and fears about women; women's views about the way they are treated, and the day-to-day routine of women's lives. The challenge, as ever, with Aristophanes is to read his work in a nuanced way so as to unpick comic exaggeration and fantasy from the underlying reality which informs the plots, jokes and speeches we find in the plays.

Old men in Aristophanes

If the two plays of 411 BC, *Lysistrata* and *Women at the Thesmophoria*, are dominated by women, the character-type that dominates Aristophanes' five surviving plays from the 420s is the old man. The comic heroes of *Acharnians* and *Peace*, Dicaeopolis and Trygaeus respectively, are both ageing rustics who struggle to achieve their own versions of peace; Strepsiades in *Clouds* and Philocleon in *Wasps* are both old men involved in intergenerational conflicts with their sons; and Demos in *Knights* (an allegory of the People, or democratic body of Athens) is also characterized as elderly ('a bad-tempered old man who's a touch deaf': *Knights* 42-3). Nor is it just among the plays' central characters that we find old men: the

91

choruses of *Acharnians* and *Wasps* are also ageing male citizens. In the followings sections we shall look at the way in which old men are portrayed by Aristophanes and consider some of the thematic and dramatic reasons why he may have chosen to feature them so heavily in these early plays.

Choruses of old men: *Acharnians* and *Wasps*

To begin this brief investigation, let us first turn to the characterization of the choruses of *Acharnians* and *Wasps*. In a number of ways, both the charcoal-burning chorus of *Acharnians* and the wasp-like chorus of jurors in *Wasps* display characteristics that are typical of many old men in Aristophanes, namely a bullish spirit and deep-seated discontentment with certain aspects of the modern world.[14] What we also find at key points in these plays is that Aristophanes chooses to emphasize one particular aspect of the choruses' old age, namely their diminishing physical powers. Indeed, their relative vulnerability *now*, contrasted with their reminiscences of their *past* involvement in the military glories of the Persian Wars, lends a real sense of pathos to their portrayal.[15] The following song taken from the *parabasis* of *Wasps* displays well this mixture of bullishness, discontentment and pathos: here the chorus laments not only its own fading physical abilities but also the lack of manliness displayed by modern youth.

> O how valiant we once were in choruses
> And valiant, too, in battle
> And when it came to this and this alone [*indicating their phalluses*] what
> valiant men we showed ourselves to be as well!
> But that was in the past ... in the past.
> Now it is gone and on our heads blooms this hair
> That is whiter than a swan.
> Yet even from these remnants we must
> Find some youthful strength.
> For I think that my
> Old age is still superior
> To the ringlets, fashions
> And buggery of the young.
>
> > *Wasps* 1060-70

The complaints that the old make against the young men of Athens in this song have something of a familiar ring about them even today: hairstyles and manners are not what they used to be and today's youth are far less hardy than their fathers and grandfathers were. But the complaints go deeper than that. One particular way in which the old are said to be maltreated (in *Acharnians* and *Wasps* in particular) is in the law courts where, in contrast to the practices of yesteryear, young men are now accustomed to prosecute the elderly for financial gain. In the play's *parabasis*, for example, the chorus of *Acharnians* grumbles that they are not

92

afforded the respect in their old age that they deserve – especially given the military contribution they once made to the city:

> We ancient old men have a complaint to make against the city. You do not care for us in our old age in a way befitting of the naval battles we fought: in fact, you treat us badly. You thrown elderly men into lawsuits and allow them to be humiliated by young whippersnapper speakers ...
>
> *Acharnians* 676-80

In *Wasps*, the fault-finding takes on a broader dimension still. Here, the chorus complains not just about malicious prosecution but also that the money coming into the city in the form of tribute from the various states in Athens' Empire (an Empire that the older generation was instrumental in establishing) is being siphoned off by young politicians. The mixture of spirited disgruntlement with the modern world, reminiscences of past military glories, and regret at the physical decline that the old suffer is perhaps nowhere better exemplified than in the following ode from the *parabasis* of *Wasps*:

> I was truly formidable (*deinos*) *then* – oh yes, I would have put fear into anyone
> And I trounced our enemies [i.e. the Persians]
> When I sailed over there in our triremes.
> For *then* we gave no thought to
> Whether we could make a good speech or
> Prosecute someone maliciously (*sykophantein*);
> We only cared about who was the best
> Oarsman. And it is because of this that
> We captured so many cities from the Persians.
> And we're the chief reason that
> The tribute (*phoros*) is brought here –
> For the young men to steal.
>
> *Wasps* 1091-1101

An interesting difference between the two choruses we have been looking at is that the old men of *Wasps* become increasingly invigorated throughout their play, whereas the chorus of *Acharnians*, once subdued by Dicaeopolis (with whom they are at odds during the early part of the play), becomes more passive. In this regard, it is also worth pointing out another important detail to emerge from this passage (as well as other points in the plays): namely that the association of old men with the military victories enjoyed by Athens during the Persian Wars marks them out as men of *action*, whereas the young men of the present tend to be characterized as men of *words*. In one sense, then, this makes the old men's grumbles all the more poignant: not only do the young have physical strength on their side, but their superior way with words means that they are bound to prevail over the old in the law courts – as well as in the

93

political arena where the chorus alleges that the young also benefit financially. And here we have identified an important way in which Aristophanes uses old men in his comedies: he portrays them as deserving yet vulnerable citizens who, because of the actions of certain young men in the assembly and law courts – men who are more powerful than them both physically and in terms of the influence they wield – fail to benefit appropriately from the city's prosperity.[16]

It is not just in *Acharnians* and *Wasps* that the presentation of the old as the undeserving victims of democratic institutions such as the law courts and assembly is a key theme. Indeed, these are just two examples of plays in which Aristophanes chooses to turn the audience's attention to sections of society for whom the political, social and economic situation in Athens was far from ideal: the same could also be said about women's plays like *Lysistrata*, for example, where wives are portrayed as suffering because of their husbands' decision to make war. But a further important motif in the plays is that socially marginal figures like women and old men often turn the tables on those in power: comic heroes like Dicaeopolis in *Acharnians* and Trygaeus in *Peace* (in addition to Lysistrata and Praxagora in their respective plays) are characterized as bold enough to take the system on – and canny enough to steer their plans to fruition. Let us look at some of these old, male heroes now.

Individual old men: the countryside, peace and rejuvenation

No two old men in Aristophanes are quite alike. Just as the choruses of *Acharnians* and *Wasps* have both their similarities and their differences, the old men who feature as central figures in the plays also tend to share certain character-traits, but are ultimately portrayed in their own distinct ways. Certainly the qualities that we have seen associated with ageing choruses – such as pathos, physical decline and a tendency for nostalgia – are regularly in evidence in other old men. However, these traits are probably best seen as a part of a broader set of characteristics associated with the old which Aristophanes either uses (or chooses *not* to use) when creating characters – depending, that is, on his overall dramatic vision for the play in which they appear.

One difference between the members of choruses in *Acharnians* and *Wasps* and most of the other old men we encounter is certainly worth highlighting: namely, their relationship with Athens' military victories of yesteryear. With the exception of Demos in *Knights*, none of the main characters in the plays is said to have fought in the Persian Wars. Indeed, the nostalgia shown by Dicaeopolis, Trygaeus – and, in the following extract, by Strepsiades at the beginning of *Clouds* – is not connected with the triumphs of *war* at all, but rather with the *peace*fulness of the countryside. Reminiscing about the life he led before marrying a rich city girl, Strepsiades says:

5. The People of Aristophanes

> I had a rustic life, as sweet as sweet can be, nice and mouldy and unswept, where I could stretch out as I pleased; a life full of honey bees and sheep and olive cake. Then I married the niece of Megacles ... I a rustic, she a city-girl.
>
> *Clouds* 43-7

For Dicaeopolis at the beginning of *Acharnians*, thoughts of rustic peace are particularly prominent. We find him waiting for the assembly to start:

> ... gazing at the countryside, loving peace, hating the town and yearning for my village (deme).
>
> *Acharnians* 32-3

This association with the countryside is a surprisingly persistent motif where the old individual characters in these early plays are concerned: even Demos, whose connections are very much urban (he is said to come from the Pnyx, i.e. the site in the heart of Athens where the assembly was held), is said to be 'rustic as far as his temper is concerned' (*Knights* 41). Certainly where an older man is not specifically linked with the workings of the democracy – either to the assembly (like Demos) or the law courts (like Philocleon) – then the place that he remembers with fondness is routinely a rural location.

Another concept that links most of the old men in these early comedies is the uplifiting rejuvenation they experience at the end of the play (Strepsiades in *Clouds*, whose 'Great Idea' is unusual in that it ultimately fails, is a notable exception here). These 'rejuvenations' take different forms but generally involve a reinvigoration of the character's physical, and especially sexual, energy. One particularly common scenario is for the central character to be found frolicking with sexually available young women towards the end of the play: Dicaeopolis enters with two dancing girls (line 1198); Philocleon with a flute-girl (1326) (although for Trygaeus in *Peace* it is the prospect of marriage to – as well as sex with – the semi-divine Theoria (Harvest) that makes him seem like 'an old man who has become young again' (*Peace* 860-1)). In the case of Demos this rejuvenation takes on a whole new dimension: relying on a pun based on the similarity between the Greek words *dêmos* ('people') and *dêmós* ('fat'), he is boiled down and reformed, re-emerging – in a truly 'recreative' moment – in youthful guise at line 1331 of the play.

The appeal of the old

So, why are so many of the central figures in Aristophanes' early plays old men? Part of the answer must lie in the traditions of Old Comedy and expectations of his audience, but in one sense this just puts the question back one: why are old men so suited to Old Comedy in the first place?

Much of their appeal for comic poets must surely stem from that fact, as we observed earlier, that the old can be portrayed as downtrodden

95

outsiders who play a marginal role in society. Old men (like women) have a struggle on their hands if they are to achieve the objective of, say, establishing peace (like Dicaeopolis and Trygaeus) – and a difficult fight resulting in a hard-won victory (i.e. the realization of the comic hero(ine)'s 'Great Idea') lies at the very heart of Old Comic drama. In other words, since he is naturally an underdog, an old hero is well suited to the narrative structure of Old Comic plays. Conversely, young citizen men do not make good heroes – indeed, this is a section of society whose fate in the plays is routinely to be humiliated or frustrated in their ambitions (a rare exception here is the chorus of *Knights* who, tellingly, allies itself with the Marathon generation rather than modern politicians).

There are other ways in which the old make appealing characters. The pathos that can surround the old, for example, can easily be used to garner the audience's sympathy and this can play an important role in shaping the audience's reaction to characters. Not all old men are equally appealing (the chorus of *Acharnians*, in particular, is initially highly aggressive, for example, and Demos, Philocleon and Strepsiades all have their rough edges) but when Aristophanes shows us glimpses of the vulnerability that old age can bring (e.g. when the members of the *Wasps* chorus move slowly, taking care not to trip over a stone in case they hurt themselves, *Wasps* 246-7; or when Strepsiades fears that he will not be able to learn anything because he is 'old, forgetful and slow', *Clouds* 129), most audience members would no doubt be inclined to feel compassion for their plight. There is also obvious comic potential in the struggles we see between the younger and older generations in *Wasps* and *Clouds*, where changes in social values and education take centre stage (this theme was also explored in Aristophanes' lost play *Banqueters*, produced in 427 BC, where a father had one of his two sons educated along traditional lines and the other according to modern principles). The rapid changes in Athens' social and intellectual climate was evidently a hot topic in the 420s and so for Aristophanes dramatizing conflicts between the old and the young was no doubt a way of tapping into strong undercurrents of feeling in the city and, presumably, of spawning further debate outside the theatre.

An added appeal for a poet looking for characters through whom he can critique society – and unflattering comments on the workings of the democracy are another central feature of Aristophanic comedy – is that old men can convincingly be portrayed as displaying a mature understanding of society and as being deeply affected by social trends and public policy. Crucially, too, as vulnerable members of that society, the outcome of public policy *matters* for old men – just as it does for women. In short, marginal figures like old men and citizen women make a convenient 'us' to struggle against the 'them' of the ruling classes and so once more we see how well the old fit the narrative structure of comedy. (The nature of the social criticism we find in the plays, especially the extent to which it was either heartfelt on Aristophanes' part or simply a conventional element of his comedy, is considered more fully in Chapter 9.) In Aristophanes' hands, then, old men become extremely resonant figures, capable of simultaneously fulfilling a variety of roles and functions to suit the dramatic needs of his plays and the themes that he wishes to explore.

The role and characterization of the chorus

For modern readers of ancient plays the presence of a chorus can prove somewhat problematic. In classical Athens, a chorus was evidently an expected and essential part of drama – something taken for granted to such an extent that in his *Poetics*, where Aristotle discusses so many aspects of classical theatre, he barely mentions the chorus at all. For those used to modern western theatre, however, the collective voice that the chorus provides is a challenging concept. What is more, where there *are* parallels in modern culture – such as the choruses of operas and musicals – it is not always immediately clear how these might aid our understanding of ancient practices. At first glance, the large gypsy chorus of an opera like *Il Trovatore*, for example, or the pitiable chorus of the musical *Les Miserables* seem to be very different animals (sometimes quite literally) from the choruses of plays such as *Acharnians*, *Birds* or *Frogs*. But this said, the comparison is not without value: the song, dance and spectacle that both ancient and modern choruses provide are no doubt key elements of the theatrical productions of which they form a part (Aristophanes' songs are examined further in Chapter 8).

But the role of the chorus in ancient drama is more complex than it is in opera and modern musical theatre – as scholars of the Greek theatre are all too aware. Interestingly, though, whilst those who work on Greek tragedy have long grappled with questions about what the chorus' function might be, Aristophanic scholars have, in general, paid the comic chorus far less attention. Given that scholarly concentration in this field has been on tragedy, it will prove instructive to consider briefly the approaches that have been taken to the tragic chorus. A number of theorists have sought to come up with a single unifying theory to 'explain' the function of the tragic chorus (e.g. Schlegel's concept of the chorus as an 'ideal spectator', famously rejected by Nietzsche),[17] but what discussion has tended to show is that the tragic chorus is simply not reducible to a single formula. Importantly, the role of the chorus often varies not just from tragedy to tragedy, but also from moment to moment in a play. Sometimes the chorus can be characterized as onlookers external to the action; sometimes as a group that is deeply affected by the outcome of events; sometimes they are partisan, sometimes not. What is more, the statements they make can range from the bland to the insightful and can also vary in tone from the ordinary to the elevated – indeed, in tragedy as in comedy, choral songs can be poetic and high-flown in the extreme (see Chapter 8).

Of course, in tragedy – which is essentially what Silk would call 'realist' in the way its figures are drawn – the presence of a group of characters that can shift their perspective on the events of the play and whose observations can switch from banal to penetrating is striking. But for Aristophanic scholars this is not so much the case. After all, the quality that choruses often exhibit is one that many characters in Old Comedy exhibit, too: namely, 'recreativity'. In other words, the shifts that choruses can make linguistically (e.g. from coarse and colloquial language to elevated poetry) or tonally (e.g. from weighty to light or from pathos to bathos) or even in terms of their identity (e.g. from amphibians to initiates to in *Frogs*) are not so dissimilar to changes that other Aristophanic characters undergo. The multiple and composite personalities that its choruses display are all part of Old Comedy's rich tapestry.

There are certainly similarities between tragic and comic choruses, but it ought to be stressed there are important differences, too. For example, the identity of the comic chorus is less restricted than that of tragedy: not only were there choruses of men and women in comedy (as in tragedy), but also animals and even places, such as in Eupolis' lost *Cities*, where presumably the various members of the chorus (like those of Aristophanes' *Birds*) each had an individual identity. The fact that the comic chorus had twenty-four members (as opposed to tragedy's twelve or fifteen) also meant that it could be split into two substantial halves, either permanently, as in *Lysistrata* (between old men and old women), or temporarily, as in *Acharnians* (half of whom briefly dispute with the rest about the rights and wrongs of Dicaeopolis' private peace: e.g. lines 557-71). Comic choruses also tend to be more partisan and combative than their tragic counterparts. Indeed, the comic chorus regularly plays a role in the central dispute (*agôn*) of the play, either aligning themselves with the hero (e.g. *Knights* and *Peace*); or against him (e.g. *Acharnians* and *Wasps*, where the choruses are eventually won round); or both (e.g. *Lysistrata* where the chorus is split; or *Clouds* where the chorus appears to be on Strepsiades' side in the early part of the play but later claims to be punishing his impiety).

At this juncture it is worth remarking on how choruses are typically characterized in the plays. The first point to make is that, in general terms, the chorus' identity is very strongly defined in the first half of the play. Or in other words, the clouds 'cloudiness' (and, for that matter, the knights' 'knightiness' and the wasps 'waspiness') is particularly prominent before the *parabasis*. In *Birds*, for instance, the individual identity of each member of the avian chorus is noted by Peisthetaerus and Euelpides as they file into the acting space:

Peisthetaerus:	This one here's a partridge.
Euelpides:	And that one there's a francolin, by Zeus.
Peisthetaerus:	And that one's a widgeon ...

Birds 297-8

5. The People of Aristophanes

Similarly in *Clouds*, the 'cloudiness' of the chorus is brought to the fore right from the moment that they first sing. Here are the chorus' first words, taken from the beginning the play's *parodos* (which, unusually in this play, is sung offstage):[18]

> Everlasting Clouds,
> Making visible our shining dewy form,
> Let us rise from deep-booming father Ocean
> And head for the tree-capped peaks
> Of lofty mountains ...
>
> > *Clouds* 275-80

This strong emphasis on the chorus' 'cloudiness' is not equally strong throughout the whole play, however. During the *parabasis* their identity could be said to fragment, since (in *Clouds* and other plays) this is part of the play where the chorus regularly displays multiple identities (most often providing critiques of contemporary people, practices and policies from a number of different angles). In *Clouds*, for instance, the chorus members briefly take on the role of mouthpiece of the poet, talking to the audience as if they were Aristophanes himself:

> When Cleon was all powerful, I hit him in the stomach; but I didn't have the audacity to trample on him again when he was down.
>
> > *Clouds* 549-50

Later in the *parabasis*, however, the chorus goes back to speaking in their own character, i.e. as clouds – such as here, where they rebuke the audience for not paying them their due respect:

> Of all the gods we benefit the city the most, and yet, despite the fact that we watch over you, we are the only divinities for whom you neither make sacrifices nor pour libations. For whenever you launch some pointless military expedition, we either thunder or rain. ...
>
> > *Clouds* 577-80

But there are more identities still that the chorus can assume. Later in *Clouds*, for instance, in the play's second *parabasis*, they even mix two identities, talking of themselves not just as clouds but also as members of a comic chorus in the theatre:

> We wish to tell the judges how they will benefit – if they pay us, the chorus, our dues, that is. First of all, when the right time comes to plough your fallow fields, we'll make sure to rain on you first, and everyone else later. ...
>
> > *Clouds* 1115-18

The general rule, then, is this: after the *parabasis*, the chorus' identity is less well defined and less relevant to the action of the play than it was before. That is to say, towards the end of Aristophanes' plays, the broad tendency is for the role that the chorus plays in the action to be less dependent on their identity as clouds, etc., and for their words and songs to be more generic in kind. Even the chorus of *Clouds*, whose identity as avenging spirits set on punishing Strepsiades remains important right up to the end play, often simply fulfils the role of commenting on the action in the latter half of the play. When Better and Worse Argument are about to begin their respective speeches, for instance, the chorus sings:

> These two, who trust
> In their super-dexterous
> Arguments and thoughts and
> Their phrase-coining pursuits,
> Will now show which of them
> Is the better speaker.
> For now the game is on
> And for my friends there begins
> A no-holds-barred battle for wisdom.

Clouds 949-57

In some plays, like *Acharnians*, the loss of identity undergone by the chorus is more marked still: once they are won over to the idea of peace, the fierce charcoal-burning old men of Acharnae are essentially transformed into blandly defined supporters of Dicaeopolis' schemes. But there are exceptions to the rule: in *Birds*, for example, while the chorus does display multiple personalities during the *parabasis*, their 'birdiness' becomes an important characteristic once more in the second half of the play.

Generalizations about the chorus can only take us so far, however, and the way in which the chorus is characterized and manipulated by Aristophanes changes greatly from play to play. Take *Lysistrata* as a case in point, where the chorus is managed in a far from typical way. In this play, Aristophanes is careful to ensure that the two half-choruses maintain a strong identity as old men and women throughout the vast majority of the play and not just at the beginning (and since there is no *parabasis* in *Lysistrata*, there is also no fragmentation of the chorus into the various identities that we noted earlier). The two choruses of *Lysistrata* are also made to play key roles both thematically and dramatically. Aristophanes shows the two choruses in dispute, thus mirroring the central conflict (*agón*) taking place between the young men and women (Alan Sommerstein neatly describes the choruses of this play as providing 'a counterpoint to the main melody of the action').[19] More crucially still, their behaviour is made to prefigure that of the younger characters. The *parodos*, for example, is the first glimpse we get of men and women in direct conflict (254-386), and towards the end of the play it is the choruses who are the first to reconcile their differences (1014-42).

Interestingly, these old choruses in *Lysistrata* are characterized quite

100

distinctly from the younger characters in the play. Arguably, both the old men and the women are more physically combative than their younger counterparts and (in a manner typical of old choruses, as we have seen) both are prone to reflect on past glories. Both groups claim to have served the city well in their various ways: the old men (somewhat predictably) as fighters at battles such as Marathon (285), the old women as active participants in the city's religious institutions and festivals (638-47). The two groups could, then, be said to have crucial qualities in common – first, an instinct to fight, and second, a common history and purpose – which makes their reconciliation all the more credible. In short, the portrayal of the two choruses in *Lysistrata* is nuanced in the extreme, and Aristophanes was evidently expert at adapting and moulding the chorus(es) to suit his artistic ends in any given play. While it is important to be aware of the general tendencies that comic choruses exhibit, then, the chorus of each play ultimately needs to be understood on its own terms.

It should be made clear at this stage that many of the comments in this section are relevant only to Aristophanes' fifth-century plays. By the early fourth century, the subtle changes that we can already see taking place in the late fifth century had brought comedy to the point where the chorus played a very different role in the plays.[20] Both *Assemblywomen* (produced around 392/1 BC) and *Wealth* (388 BC) are structured in a different way from the earlier plays, in that they comprise a prologue and five episodes separated by a total of five choral odes. More significantly still, these choral odes are for the most part lost and are simply marked by the word *chorou*, 'of the chorus', in our manuscripts. The fact that these songs are not preserved suggests that the chorus' role was largely conceived of as singing lyrical interludes – and certainly the choruses of these two plays (whose characters, we note, are far more 'realist' than their fifth-century counterparts) play only a small part in the action. The shift from Old to Middle Comedy had evidently begun in earnest, with the changes that were underway destined to result in a very different kind of comedy indeed: the New Comedy of the late fourth century as written by Menander.

Conclusions

In this chapter we have made some important steps towards understanding better the nature of the characters that populate Aristophanes' plays. The notion of 'recreativity' in particular has wide-reaching consequences for the way in which we think about and discuss figures in Old Comedy. What is more, observing how Aristophanes makes use of various character-types like women and old men in different comedies, and examining how he tailors his protagonists and choruses to suit the thematic and dramatic needs of the play in which they appear, provides a fascinating insight into the way in which he creates his comedies. In discussing the portrayal of women and old men, too, this chapter begins to raise some important questions about how we might use Aristophanes' plays as an historical source to comprehend better the place of these social groups in classical Athenian society – questions with which scholars continue to grapple. Crucially, too, the discussion has also raised the issue of where Aristophanes' personal sympathies lay in regard not only to these two groups but political and social issues in general – a topic that will be explored more fully in Chapter 9.

A further area of discussion that this chapter has opened up concerns the role and function of the chorus in Old Comedy. The nature of the songs that they (and other characters) sing will be explored further in Chapter 8. For now, though, we turn our attention to a different topic entirely: namely, Aristophanes' relationship with tragedy.

6

Tragic Fragments

Introduction

Tragedy evidently held a special fascination for Aristophanes. Whilst the poets of Old Comedy had a history of engaging with various forms of literature – *including* tragedy – no other comic playwright seems to have shared Aristophanes' peculiar *preoccupation* with the tragic genre. Aristophanes' older rival Cratinus, for example, wrote a play about poetry (*Archilochoi*) and another about comedy itself (*Wine Flask*) but, as far we know, none that focused on tragedy. In contrast, tragedy frequently took centre stage not just in Aristophanes' surviving work but in many of his lost plays, too.[1]

In this chapter, we shall look at a number of ways in which tragedy's influence is felt in Aristophanes' comedies: from small elements, such as individual words and phrases, to larger structural elements, most notably parodies of whole scenes from Euripides' tragedies and even the appearance of tragic poets such as Aeschylus, Agathon and Euripides as characters in Aristophanic drama. The focus will be on those plays which borrow from tragedy most heavily: namely *Acharnians* (which makes extensive use of Euripides' lost *Telephus* and features Euripides as a character); *Peace* (which borrows elements from Euripides' lost *Bellerophon*); *Women at the Thesmophoria* (which can boast both Euripides and Agathon as characters and reworks scenes from no fewer than four Euripidean dramas), and *Frogs*, where we find the famous contest between Aeschylus and Euripides as to who is the greater tragic poet. One question that will continue to surface throughout the discussion is why Aristophanes chooses to use and abuse tragedy in the way he does in his plays.

The chapter is structured as follows. We shall first look at some of the ways in which tragedy surfaces in the plays – such as in borrowings, adaptations and tragic-style lines – and briefly consider Aristophanes' relationship with Euripides. After this, however, the chapter will be given over to looking in detail at some examples of comedy's interaction with tragedy – and to considering three terms that are key to an informed discussion of the subject at hand: 'paratragedy', 'parody' and 'pastiche'.

Aristophanes and tragedy

Aristophanes' interest in tragedy is plain to see throughout his fifth-century plays. One prominent way in which tragedy features in his work is in the form of quotations, such as when Aristophanes borrows phrases word for word from tragedy (e.g. 'Persuasion has no temple other than speech': Euripides, *Antigone* fr. 170 = *Frogs* 1391). At other times, however, Aristophanes' 'tragic' lines are adaptations of tragic originals. When Dicaeopolis makes his pro-Spartan speech to the chorus of *Acharnians*, for instance, dressed as he is in the '*rag*ments of Telephus' (*Acharnians* 432) that he has borrowed from the poet Euripides, he begins:

> Do not begrudge the fact, o gentlemen of the audience, that I, although a beggar, mean to speak to the Athenians about their city ... .
>
> Acharnians 497-9

Famously, this is an adaptation of two lines from Euripides' *Telephus*, a play in which the eponymous hero made a similarly important speech to a hostile audience:[2]

> Do not begrudge the fact, o gentlemen lords of the Greeks, that I, although a beggar, dare to speak to my betters.
>
> Euripides, Telephus fr. 703 Nauck

Alongside these borrowings and adaptations we also find numerous examples of tragic-sounding lines and phrases that are original to Aristophanes. These appear throughout the plays, but a particularly rich vein of 'tragic' lines comes in the Euripides scene in *Acharnians* (during which the rags of Telephus are borrowed). Here, to great comic effect, Aristophanes characterizes the tragedian as employing high-flown phrases in his everyday speech: Euripides uses well-worn tragic words like 'ill-fated' and 'wretch', for example, as well as tragic-sounding coinages like the 'ragment' (*rhakôma*) we have already met (*Acharnians* 419, 454 and 432). After a series of annoying questions from Dicaeopolis, Euripides also communicates his frustrations in full-blown tragic style:

> Know thou art bothersome and depart from my house!
>
> Acharnians 456

This scene from *Acharnians* is just one example of a passage where Aristophanes makes use of tragic-sounding words and composes tragic-style lines. In this chapter we will meet other forms of tragic-style composition, too – in particular choral odes, some of which mock, others of which mimic those found in tragedy.

Evident even from this brief discussion is that Aristophanes is not interested in all tragic playwrights equally; rather, he has one particular obsession, a tragic poet whose work crops up in his plays with alarming regularity: Euripides. Euripides' plays, Euripidean quotations and even Euripides himself make regular appearances in Aristophanes' work. Nor did this fixation go unnoticed by Aristophanes' rivals; in a fragment of the comic playwright Cratinus we find a neat coinage that seems to sum up so much: the compound-verb 'to euripidaristophanize' (*euripidaristophanizein*: fr. 342 KA). This word has elicited a variety of comments from scholars who have wrestled with the question: what exactly does it imply about Aristophanes' relationship with Euripides' work? But one thing seems certain: Aristophanes' interest in Euripides was sufficiently marked that for his rival poets it had become food for satire.

Paratragedy, parody and pastiche

In the course of this brief overview we have already identified some of the major ways in which tragedy makes its presence felt in Aristophanes' plays: quotations, adaptations, tragic-style lines – even the appearance of tragedians as characters in the plays. The challenge now, however, is to put these into some kind of framework and to find terms which are useful for discussing the effects that Aristophanes achieves by engaging with tragedy.

Previous scholarly discussions have sometimes served to cloud rather than make more straightforward the analysis of Aristophanes' use of tragic material. In particular, the word 'parody' – which is potentially a highly valuable term – is often overused, its meaning stretched to such an extent that it ceases to have any clear significance (unhelpfully, it is regularly used to describe passages which are clearly not 'parodic' in any conventional sense of the word). However, I propose that 'parody' – along with 'paratragedy' and 'pastiche' – can, when clearly defined, be extremely useful words. The aim of the following sections, then, will be to clarify the way in which these terms will be used in this book and to look at different examples of words and passages that can usefully be thought of as belonging to these three categories.

Paratragedy

For anyone interested in discussing Aristophanes' relationship with tragedy, perhaps the most helpful word to be acquainted with is 'paratragedy' (a particularly useful discussion of which appears in Michael Silk's 1993 article 'Aristophanic Paratragedy'). The reason why this word is so valuable is that it can act as an umbrella-term to describe *any* way in which tragedy is evoked in comedy and it therefore allows us to collect together and discuss under one heading a whole range of phenomena. Thus every time we find a word, a quotation, a character or a plot line that has been taken from the world of tragedy and transplanted into Aristophanic comedy (or indeed into any other context) we can label this 'paratragedy'. And every tragic allusion that we find in Aristophanes is therefore 'paratragic', including all the examples we have considered so far – and this is true no matter what form the allusion takes. No matter, for instance, whether a tragic-sounding phrase is a direct quotation, an adapted quotation or an

Aristophanic invention: all are examples of 'paratragedy'. As we shall see, parody of tragedy and tragic pastiche are simply specific kinds of para-tragedy.

Paratragedy may, on the one hand, pervade a play (such as the repeated evocation of Euripides' *Telephus* in *Acharnians*), or part of a play (such as the paratragic use of the four Euripidean plays, one after the other, in the second half of *Women at the Thesmophoria*), or a choral lyric (such as *Birds* 209-22: discussed below as an example of 'pastiche'). On the other hand, though, paratragedy may appear in miniature. Silk cites the example of *Knights* 1195, where the high-flown, tragic-sounding *o thyme* ('o my soul') is introduced unsignalled into an otherwise unelevated passage. The word appears in the following extract, where Paphlagon and the Sausage-Seller are competing for Demos' affections by offering him various edible treats:

> Paphlagon: Go on: take this nice plump slice of flat-cake from me.
> Sausage Seller: Here, take this *whole* flat-cake from me.
> Paphlagon: Ah ha! But I bet you won't be able to get hold of any hare meat to give him. Whereas *I* can!
> Sausage Seller: Oh no! Where am I going to get hare meat from? Now, o my soul (*ô thyme*), I need you to come up with a meaty plan!
> *Knights* 1190-4

Here, there is no reason to suspect that any particular tragic passage is being evoked by the Sausage Seller's *ô thyme* (indeed, as Silk points out, it is difficult to imagine how any specific passage could be evoked by such a short and unexceptional phrase as this). Rather, what we have here is probably best understood as a fleeting nod in the direction of tragedy, a high-flown word tossed into an otherwise colloquial line of speech with no further ado. Aristophanes neither seems to be mocking tragedy in this passage nor using high-flown language to endow the Sausage Seller's words with any extra authority (these are characteristics of parody and pastiche respectively: see below). Perhaps the use of a tragic word here is simply to be seen as playful on Aristophanes' part – an example of the way he often employs words from different linguistic habitats in order to enliven his work.[3]

A more sustained instance of paratragedy comes in the prologue of *Lysistrata*. When the women respond far from enthusiastically to the announcement of the planned sex-strike, Lysistrata queries their actions in a series of interestingly phrased lines:

> Well then, we have to give up – cock!
> [*The women react in various ways.*]
> Why are you turning away from me? Where are you going? You there! Why are you pursing your lips and shaking your heads? Why pales your skin? Why are there tears shed? Will you do it or not? Why do you hesitate?
> *Lysistrata* 124-8

6. Tragic Fragments

After the obscenity of line 124 ('cock': *peos* in Greek), Lysistrata uses fairly neutral language. And while there is nothing exceptional about lines 125-6 – nothing positively 'tragic' about them – the absence of colloquialisms (plus the tightening of the poetic metre found in the original Greek) nevertheless means that they would not be out of place in the elevated world of tragedy. In line 127, however – 'Why pales your skin? Why are there tears shed?' – the phrasing is more than simply neutral: this line has a definite tragic ring about it, so much so that critics wonder whether it might in fact be a quotation from a lost play. Whether this is a quotation, an adaptation of a tragic original or simply a line composed by Aristophanes in the tragic style, however, we can nevertheless find a useful label for it: namely, 'paratragedy'.

So *Lysistrata* 127 is a paratragic line – but what effect does Aristophanes produce by the elevation in tone here? Certainly, the language of tragedy provides a strong contrast with 'cock' (*peos*: which happens to be the first obscene word uttered in the play) and therefore serves to heighten this word's effect. But what else? On one view, the use of tragic language could be said to add to the *weightiness* of Lysistrata's proposition – in the context of the play (if not in real life) the sex strike is worthy of being taken just as 'seriously' as any scheme put forward in tragedy and Lysistrata's paratragic words underline just that. But in addition to this, the juxtaposition of the *comic* idea of the sex strike with *tragic* language is surely incongruous: this certainly counts as an instance of playfulness on Aristophanes' part and one that may even have been designed to raise a laugh with his audience – especially if accompanied by some well-judged stage action. To sum up, the tragic language in *Lysistrata* 127 could be said to fulfil a number of different functions simultaneously and this line therefore serves as a good demonstration of just how versatile a tool paratragedy can be in the hands of a skilled comic dramatist like Aristophanes.

In this section we have seen that paratragedy can exist in many different forms. It can exist in miniature (even a single word, *thyme*), or occupy one line of verse (as in the *Lysistrata* example) or more than one line (as in the adapted quotation from *Telephus* we saw in *Acharnians* above). Equally, however, it can pervade a play, as is the case with Aristophanes' use of Euripides' *Telephus* throughout *Acharnians*: this play's borrowed plot lines, quotations and costumes can also be described as 'paratragic'. Indeed, part of the beauty of the term 'paratragedy' is that it is flexible enough to describe all these different phenomena. As we have seen in the case of *Lysistrata* 127, for example, regardless of whether a line *is*, or is *not* – or *might* be, or might *not* be – a quotation from a particular tragedy, if it is tragic in style then we can still label it 'paratragic'.

Tragic parody

'Paratragedy', then, is a useful umbrella-term for all evocation of tragedy. But what are the distinctive qualities of tragic parody? In line with the way that this word is commonly used in English, I shall define 'parody' as some form of *imitation*: be it of a particular passage, plot line, or some other feature of a genre or specific author's work. What is more, this imitation is *negative* in nature: it serves to point out deficiencies. Typically parody *makes fun of* specific features of, say, an author's style, and often *exaggerates* and *misrepresents* to achieve its effects. Silk's definition of parody is worth quoting here: for him, it is 'any kind of distorting representation of an original', and 'works by recalling a more or less specific original and subverting it'. Silk adds that '[n]on-parodic paratragedy is not necessarily subversive or negative at all.'[4]

The Lesson of Lyric: Tragic Parody in Frogs

What does all this mean in practice? Some of the most prominent parodies in the plays are to be found in *Frogs*, where Aristophanes makes huge humorous capital out of having Aeschylus and Euripides deride each others' work. Aeschylus, for instance, comes under attack for composing tragedy that is 'puffed up ... with ponderous and showy vocabulary' (*Frogs* 940) in which ideas are jumbled up rather than presented in a logical order (*Frogs* 945).[5] When Euripides later recites what is supposedly a choral ode of Aeschylus', these qualities are more than evident. Here is the text in full:[6]

> How two Achaean kings united in power, of Hellas' young manhood
> – Phattothrattophlattothrat –
> Sphinx, the bitch that presided o'er days of ill-fortune were sped with
> – Phattothrattophlattothrat –
> Spear and avenging hand by a bird of martial omen
> – Phattothrattophlattothrat –
> Which handed them over to be the brutal air-roaming hound's prey
> – Phattothrattophlattothrat –
> And those who gathered around Ajax
> – Phattothrattophlattothrat.
>
> *Frogs* 1285-95; transl. Sommerstein

What we have here is certainly no Aeschylean ode, but rather a *parody* of an Aeschylean ode. Aristophanes has composed this passage by collecting together lines from a number of Aeschylus' plays,[7] a process which has allowed him to produce verse which has an Aeschylean feel about it, of course (since most of it was written by Aeschylus), but which contains shortcomings that are of Aristophanes' own making. Aeschylean phrases which contain the kind of 'ponderous and showy vocabulary' supposedly typical of the tragedian's work are to be found in abundance here in an ode whose cobbled-together nature means that it also fails to make any real sense: indeed, the passage is more jumbled up and illogical than any real Aeschylean ode could ever be thanks to the way that Aristophanes has put it together. On top of all this, we find a feature in the ode that Aristophanes has simply invented: Aeschylus *does* use refrains in his lyrical passages, yes, but never a *meaningless* refrain like we find here – 'phattothrat-tophlattothrat' – nor indeed does Aeschylus ever repeat *any* refrain which such regularity. So what this passage amounts to is a *negative imitation* of an Aeschylean ode which *exaggerates* and *makes fun of* Aeschylus' style – and which also *misrepresents* it in crucial respects. In short, this passage is a parody.

In *Frogs*' battle of words, it is not just Aeschylus who comes under attack, of course. But whereas Aristophanes parodies Aeschylean lyric by serving up a reconstituted version of the poet's own phrases, the opportunity to parody Euripidean lyric elicits from Aristophanes an altogether more full-blooded response. In the following extract from what is his longest surviving lyrical parody, Aristophanes makes fun of a number of aspects of Euripides' verse. Not least of these is the tragedian's habit of foregrounding lowly characters like women and slaves – a tendency which Aristophanes has Euripides describe as 'democratic' (*Frogs* 952) – and his penchant for 'introducing everyday matters' into his plays (*Frogs* 959). The ode (ostensibly sung by a woman, it transpires) opens with a lengthy question about a god-sent dream of foreboding, but moves on to a very different topic:

> O black-lit dark of Night,
> What is this abominable dream
> Thou dost send me, come forth from obscure Hades
> With a soul that is no soul,
> A child of black Night,
> A terrible vision that makes one shudder,
> Black-funereally-bedecked,
> Gazing murderously, murderously,
> With huge claws?
> Yes, mine attendants, kindle me a lamp,
> Bring fresh dew in pales from the river and make fervent the water,
> That I might wash the holy dream away.
> O august Lord Poseidon!
> Hang on! O, my companions,
> Behold these marvels! Glyce's only gone and
> Robbed my chicken and now it's vanishèd!
> O mountain-born Nymphs,
> And you there, Mania, help me!
> I, wretch that I am,
> Was just attending to my work,
> Wi-i-i-inding a spindle
> Full of thread with my hands ...
> And it flew up, flew up, into the ether on the tips of its wings so nimble,

And sorrows, sorrows did it leave me
And tears, tears, from my eyes
I shed, shed, in my misery. ...

Frogs 1331-49; 1352-5

In this passage Euripides is parodied in a number of different ways, but most strikingly for his 'democratic' style: his portrayal of 'everyday matters'. Aristophanes initially sets up the lyric as elevated in the extreme: in the very first line the compound-adjective 'night-lit' forms part of a lengthy circumlocution ('O black-lit dark of Night'), for example, which is then followed by the heightened 'abominable' (*dystanos*), and so on. However, the tragic tone is eventually punctured by the somewhat prosaic 'Hang on!'. This translates *tout' ekeino* (literally, 'that's it!'), a phrase used by prose writers in the classical era but generally avoided by tragic poets – although not (as Aristophanes has keenly observed) by Euripides. However, whereas the real-life Euripides only ever uses *tout' ekeino* in the spoken parts of his plays (i.e. in dialogue and 'recitative'), here Aristophanes has Euripides employ the phrase in a more elevated context: namely, tragic lyric. By deliberately placing the lowly *tout' ekeino* alongside highly ornate tragic language, Aristophanes exaggerates Euripides' tendency to be prosaic and in so doing strengthens his parodic point.[8]

The 'democratic' parody does not end there, however. Indeed, this slightly incongruous phrase is nothing compared with what is to come: the incident with the chicken. Needless to say, this time there is no precedent:[9] Euripides' surviving plays contain no reference to chickens (stolen or otherwise) and while we do find abundant examples of women and slaves speaking in Euripides' plays (as Aristophanes has Euripides himself admit at *Frogs* 949) we certainly do not find references to contemporary, everyday disputes between women with names like Glyce ('Sweetie') and Mania (generally a slave name).[10] Here, then, we find features typical of parody once more: negative imitation, exaggeration and misrepresentation.

As well as mocking Euripides' 'democratic' instincts in this passage, Aristophanes also makes fun of various Euripidean mannerisms. Euripides certainly grew fond of repetition in the later stages of his career (mimicked here by 'murderously, murderously', 'flew up, flew up', 'sorrows, sorrows', and so on). Flights into the ether, too, were also something of a Euripidean cliché (although not undertaken by chickens, it must be said).[11] The stretching of a syllable over more than one note of a song ('wi-i-i-inding') seems also to have been a peculiarity of Euripidean verse (this feature of lyric is common enough to us, but evidently not to fifth-century audiences) – and fittingly the word sung in this way is a Euripidean favourite, too: 'wind' (*he[i]lissein*) occurs over forty times in Euripides and mostly in plays written after 420 BC.[12] Other features of this ode are perhaps less specifically Euripidean and more characteristic of tragedy in general: the use of compound-words, for example, and oxymoron of the 'soul that is no

110

soul' kind in line 1334. In addition, we find elements which seem to have nothing to do with Euripides at all: triple compound-words like 'black-funereally-bedecked' are not characteristic of tragedy (whereas they *are* characteristic of dithyramb) and the irrelevant address to Poseidon in line 1342 seems designed simply to underline the fact that this passage is badly written (certainly there is no reason to believe that Euripides had done anything similar in his plays).

Close scrutiny of this passage, then, can teach us an interesting lesson. As we have seen, it contains both subtle details (such as the incongruously prosaic 'hang on!') and conspicuous details (such as the chicken incident and the steady stream of repeated words), all of which combined would serve to make it clear enough, even if we did not know in advance, that the target of this parody was Euripides. But there is more to this lyric than well-observed, on-target detail. As well as exaggerating 'real' features of his target's style, Aristophanes (like many parodists since) has also invented details – presumably in order to add to the passage's negative excesses and increase its comic effect. And so for parody to be effective it need not necessarily restrict itself to mimicking and exaggerating genuine features of an author's style. As this passage proves, as long as there is a critical mass of convincing detail, the parodist can also choose to attribute further *invented* negative features to an author. The result is that the constituent parts of the parody are not always easy to unpick – especially for the audience member or reader not intimately familiar with the target's work (in this case, Euripides) – since all the exaggeration, misrepresentation, mockery and invention are bound tightly together in the same parodic package.[13]

Quotations, phrases and words

So far we have been looking at lengthy examples of parody, but can tragic parody also exist in miniature? The answer is apparently 'yes' as is neatly demonstrated by Aristophanes' propensity to send up tragic lines. Some lines are made fun of more than others, a particular favourite of Aristophanes' evidently being a quotation from Euripides' *Hippolytus* (produced in 428 BC). On breaking an oath he made to keep a secret, Hippolytus famously says:

> It was my tongue that swore, not my heart.
>
> Euripides, *Hippolytus* 612

In our surviving plays, Aristophanes has fun with this line on more than one occasion. In *Women at the Thesmophoria*, for example, the Inlaw agrees to attend an all-female festival, dressed as a woman, in order to intervene on the day that Euripides' fate is to be decided. Just as the Inlaw is heading off to this festival (the Thesmophoria of the play's title), he

111

makes Euripides swear by all the gods to 'help save me in every way possible if any trouble befalls me' (270-1). He then adds:

> And what's more, remember this: it was your heart that swore. It's not your tongue that swore, nor did I ask it to.
>
> *Women at the Thesmophoria*, 275-6

The line also is also made a source of humour six years later in *Frogs* where it is turned on its author once again. When Dionysus is on the brink of deciding which poet to take back with him from the Underworld, Euripides reminds him of an oath he made:[14]

> Euripides: Now, remember the gods that you swore by, saying you'd definitely take *me* home: choose your friends!
> Dionysus: It was my tongue that swore; I'm choosing Aeschylus.
>
> *Frogs* 1469-71

These Aristophanic extracts qualify as tragic parody since they constitute an *imitation* of a tragic quotation: indeed in the case of the last extract, several words of the original Euripidean quotation are even reproduced verbatim just as several of Aeschylus' lines were reproduced (also out of context) in the *Frogs* lyric above. What is more, this imitation can be described as *negative* since Aristophanes *makes fun of* and blatantly *misrepresents* the original quotation: in the context of *Hippolytus*, the line has a profound meaning (perhaps something along the lines of 'now I've found out the nature of the secret you wanted me to keep to myself I no longer find myself able to honour my promise'), but for the purposes of humour, Aristophanes disregards this deeper significance and wilfully reads the lines as simply a crafty Euripidean way to justify reneging on a promise.

Examples of recycled tragic quotations abound in Aristophanes, some of which are more obviously humorous than others – and some of which are more obviously parodic than others.[15] However, parodic moments can also occur in units that are even smaller than the *Hippolytus* quotation, namely a short phrase or even a single word. A favourite technique of Aristophanes' is to make fun of tragedy's tendency to refer to everyday objects in heightened ways. Take the way tragedians use the word *ochêma*, 'vessel', for instance: at line 654 of Sophocles' *Trachiniae*, for example, a ship is referred to as a 'vessel of a ship', whereas at Euripides' *Suppliant Women* 662, chariots are referred to as a 'vessels of chariots'. At *Peace* 865, Aristophanes takes this tragic formula and applies it to Trygaeus' dung beetle to create the phrase 'vessel of a beetle'. Aristophanes thus produces a parodic combination of high and low, made all the more playful by the fact that beetles are not normally the stuff of tragedy and that Trygaeus' dung beetle is, in any case, already his comic substitution for Pegasus – the winged horse that featured in the play that *Peace* so extensively

112

parodies: Euripides' (lost) *Bellerophon*. As for individual words with a parodic feel, we need look no further than some of the examples we encountered earlier, such as the 'ragment' (*rhakôma*) of *Acharnians* 432 (here Aristophanes parodies tragedians' habit of coining elevated versions of everyday words by adding the suffix -*ôma*: e.g. *pylôma*, 'gate'; *pyrgôma*, 'tower') or the 'wi-i-i-inding' of *Frogs* 1348 (also *Frogs* 1314: parodic of Euripides' style of musical composition).

Humour, parody and non-parody

A major source of tragic parody in Aristophanes' plays stems from the reworking of tragic quotations, as we have seen. But is it the case that reuse of a tragic quotation to humorous effect *always* qualifies as parody? The answer here is surely 'no' since citing a quotation (even in comedy) does not *necessarily* involve casting it in a negative light. An interesting passage to contemplate in this regard is *Women at the Thesmophoria* 194-6. Here, the cross-dressing tragic poet Agathon is asked to attend the Thesmophoria on Euripides' behalf (prior to the Inlaw volunteering to go) and his refusal comes in the form of a quotation. The line in question is taken from Euripides' *Alcestis* (438 BC), the plot of which revolves around Admetus' search for someone to die in his place. Admetus' father is unwilling to do this for his son and when rebuked, replies:

> You take pleasure in seeing the light, do you think your father does not?
> Euripides, *Alcestis* 693

Aristophanes has Agathon use this same line to reject Euripides' request:

Agathon:	Did you once write, 'You take pleasure in seeing the light, do you think your father does not?'
Euripides:	I did.
Agathon:	Well then, don't expect *us* to bear your misfortune.

> *Women at the Thesmophoria*, 194-6

The key difference between this extract and the examples of tragic parody that we looked at above is that the quotation is not cast in a negative light here; or put another way, there is no subversion of the original line. Although the quotation has been placed in a new context, its essential meaning ('do not expect others to make sacrifices that you are unwilling to make yourself') has not been distorted, nor has its language been mocked in any way. If any mockery is involved it is of Euripides himself – *not* of his poetry. In a multi-layered blurring of fact and fiction, Aristophanes makes Euripides a victim of the so-called 'authorial fallacy': that is, the notion that an author must believe (and in this case should abide by) everything that he or she has written.[16]

To merit the label 'tragic parody', then, a word or line or passage has to meet a specific set of criteria: some form of original text needs to have been evoked (be it a quotation, passage, plot line, play, an author's style more broadly or even the tragic genre as a whole) and then cast in a negative light – or 'subverted' (to use Silk's term). This subversion can take the form of mockery and/or exaggeration and/or misrepresentation of the original. However, the line is not always easy to draw between parody and non-parody, especially since the nature of our evidence means that we are not always as well informed as we might like to be about the particular original text that is – or is not – being parodied by Aristophanes. And even when we *are* well informed about the original, a judgement is still not always easy to make.

A good example of a challenging text comes in the form of the paratragic episodes in the latter half of *Women at the Thesmophoria*, where scenes from Euripides' *Telephus, Palamedes, Helen* and *Andromeda* are reworked. Are these examples of parody? Arguably not, since the humour does not seem to stem from mockery of the plays themselves; rather, it revolves around the mismatch between the tragic roles and the characters playing them (the elderly and bizarrely clad Inlaw, in particular, gets to play a series of youthful tragic heroines).[17] However, without knowledge of how the lines were delivered and how elements like costume and gesture were handled, it is impossible to state with certainty that these scenes were not parodic in any way.[18]

In summary, the line between parodic and non-parodic text is a fine one and some cases are simply more clear-cut than others. Where text cannot necessarily be labelled as tragic parody, however, there is still the useful term 'paratragedy'. Of course all *tragic* parody is, by definition, *also* paratragic; but it should also be borne in mind that parody does not necessarily have anything to do with tragedy at all: a parody of epic poetry, for example, is not para*tragic* (rather it is 'para*epic*').

Let us now leave the subject of parody and look at a quite different form of paratragedy: tragic pastiche.

Tragic pastiche

Pastiche is a term that is often used fairly loosely in common parlance, but for the purpose of this discussion I shall define it as composition in the style of a particular author (e.g. Euripides) or genre (e.g. tragedy). The key difference between parody and pastiche is that pastiche is neither negative nor subversive: it *mimics* but does not *mock*. Indeed, for tragic pastiche to be successful it has to tread a careful line: it cannot afford to make fun of the tragic conventions being imitated or to introduce any non-tragic elements (e.g. humour, colloquial vocabulary or obscenity) for fear of undermining itself. (Note once more that just as not all parody is necessarily *tragic* parody, there are other forms of pastiche besides *tragic* pastiche.)

In case this definition of pastiche appears too abstract, let us look at a

concrete example from the plays. The most prominent examples of pastiche in Aristophanes are no doubt his various attempts at high-style lyric
– most notably those found in *Clouds* and *Birds*. Such passages are
discussed in more detail in Chapter 8, but for now let us look at the
following lyric from near the beginning of *Birds*, the Hoopoe's song. The
ode is sung by Tereus whose son, Itys, was killed and served up to him by
his wife, Procne: this was in revenge for Tereus' rape of her sister. Procne
was subsequently transformed into a nightingale and Tereus a hoopoe, but
despite their turbulent personal history, in *Birds* the two seem to have
patched up their differences – though Procne evidently still mourns for her
son. In the song, Tereus bids her wake.[19]

> Awake, my mate!
> Shake off thy slumbers, and clear and strong
> Let loose the floods of thy glorious song,
> The sacred dirge of thy mouth divine
> For sore-wept Itys, thy child and mine;
> Thy tender trillings his name prolong
> With the liquid of thy tawny throat;
> Through the leafy curls of the woodbine sweet
> The pure sound mounts to Zeus' seat,
> And Phoebus, lord of the golden hair,
> As he lists to thy wild plaint echoing there,
> Draws answering strains from his ivoried lyre,
> And calls from the blessed lips on high
> Of immortal Gods, a divine reply
> To the tones of thy witching melody.
>
> *Birds* 209-37; based on the translation by Rogers

The song (ably translated into rhyming verse by Rogers) is a neat
pastiche of elevated poetry: linguistically it would be at home in many
poetic contexts, including tragedy. Elevated features abound: compound
adjectives such as 'sore-wept', 'golden-haired' (here translated 'of the
golden hair') are far from everyday and the sheer abundance of adjectives
– *'glorious* song', *'sacred* dirge', *'tender* trillings', and so on – also serves to
underline the passage's poetic status. As is fitting for an elevated ode,
there is a mythological reference (to Itys) and numerous mentions of the
gods: in addition to the references to Zeus and Apollo (named here as
Phoebus) there is a plethora of adjectives connected with the divine
('sacred', 'immortal', etc.). Elevation is also achieved by the sombre subject
matter: Procne's 'dirge' to a 'sore-wept' son. On top of all this, Aristophanes
also treats us to a recherché poetic word, *xouthos* (214), here translated
'tawny', but whose meaning – which was probably unclear to Aristophanes'
audience – is less important than its effect: it is a high-flown word taken
from the realm of high-flown lyric poetry and its use here neatly reinforces
the idea that this ode is to be thought of as weighty and elevated.

As a piece of poetry, we may have reservations about this lyric – indeed, the piling up of adjectives, the repetitions and the use of what may essentially be a meaningless word may even to suggest that Aristophanes' primary interest in establishing the lyric's status as elevated rather than producing poetry of genuine quality. However, as a piece of pastiche, the ode is highly effective: elevated features abound and the whole is tonally consistent – there are no collisions between high and low elements, no hint of mockery. What the ode represents is a prolonged elevated moment and as such has much in common with similar odes found in tragedy.[20]

Pastiche can exist in the spoken parts of comedy, too. Towards the beginning of this chapter we looked at a tragic-style line in *Lysistrata*, for example: 'Why pales your skin? Why are there tears shed?' (*Lysistrata* 127). This line may be a quotation from a lost tragedy (a possibility which we regularly have to take into account with tragic-sounding lines) but is more likely to be an example of tragic pastiche: a line that Aristophanes has composed in the style of tragedy but which, I suggest, does not mock tragedy. In our analysis of *Lysistrata* 127, we saw how the two lines preceding it contained neutral language; that is to say, they lacked anything that marked them out as particularly comic, such as colloquialisms, humour, and so on. And this, it turns out, is a key feature of pastiche: a short elevated moment must be built up to (as at *Lysistrata* 127); a longer elevated moment, if it is to last, requires the elevated expression to be sustained (as it is in the *Birds* ode). Any inconsistency in tone (such as the introduction of a low, comic feature) runs the risk of undermining the pastiche: either the moment fails to materialize or, if already established, its spell is broken.

Tragic pastiche is less common than tragic parody in Aristophanes – as perhaps comes as little surprise given the delicate handling it requires. Such instances as there are take a number of forms. Dicaeopolis' exasperated 'o my city, my city!' of *Acharnians* 27, built up to in a similar way to the *Lysistrata* example, is a good example of the phenomenon in miniature – this brief tragic moment serves to highlight the weightiness of the situation which faces Dicaeopolis: apart from him no one in Athens is prepared to lobby for peace. Outside lyric, perhaps the most sustained example of a passage with clearly discernible tragic qualities is the exchange at *Clouds* 1452-64, when the chorus explains to Strepsiades the reasons behind his downfall. The concept of a character (here Strepsiades) learning through suffering is itself tragic in nature and whilst this dialogue is not presented in full-blown tragic idiom, its phrasing nevertheless has clear tragic resonances.[21]

| Strepsiades: | I have suffered all this because of you, Clouds! I put my whole fate in your hands! |
| Chorus: | No, you brought this on yourself by turning (*strepsâs*; cf. Strepsiades) yourself to wickedness. |

Strepsiades:	Why didn't you tell me that at the time rather than tempt-
	ing an old rustic to do wrong?
Chorus:	We always do this whenever we realize that someone is a
	lover of wickedness. We cast him into misery so that he
	learns to fear the gods.
Strepsiades:	Oh, Clouds! These are harsh words, but fair. I should never
	have tried to get out of paying my debts.

Clouds 1452-64

On select occasions, then, Aristophanes uses pastiche to evoke a tragic co-presence in his plays – more often in lyrics, less often in dialogue – presumably with the effect of injecting solemnity and/or highlighting the supposed weightiness of what is being sung or said. More often than not, however, Aristophanes only creates a tragic frame so as to undermine it for the purposes of humour. Such is the case with the following ode from *Peace*, for instance, which begins in elevated, pseudo-tragic style with Trygaeus' injunction for his slave to keep a holy silence while he is flying on the dung beetle. His concerns soon become more earthy, however, as he expresses fears that the beetle (which after all, feeds on dung) might be distracted by certain smells.

> Now you must speak fair and not so much
> As mutter an evil word, but cry for joy.
> Please bid men to keep silent,
> And block up the toilets and alleys
> With new bricks –
> And close up their arses!

Peace 96-101

What begins as something that might reasonably called a pastiche, then, is soon undercut – and as with any passage, as soon as mockery of the tragic idiom is involved, it ceases to be pastiche. This playful undercutting of high-flown language in general, and tragic language in particular, is common in Aristophanes: we shall see this phenomenon crop up in later chapters, such as the discussion of Aristophanes' songs in Chapter Eight.

Uses of paratragedy: the tragic 'frame'

In this chapter we have looked at a whole host of ways in which Aristophanes interacts with tragic drama. As we have seen, tragedy is most commonly used by Aristophanes for purposes of humour: his parodies, his mocking of tragic vocabulary and phrasing, his undercutting of tragic idiom – all of these have great potential to amuse his audience. In many ways, tragedy is an obvious target for Aristophanes' humour: after all, the debunking of traditional sources of authority is commonplace in Old Comedy, and one of these sources of authority – high-minded tragedy – was produced in the very theatre in which Aristophanes' plays were staged. So when it came to parodying a play like Euripides' *Bellerophon*, including as it did the hero's flight to heaven on Pegasus, Aristophanes could simply reuse the relevant theatre equipment – in this case the *mêchanê* (crane) – in order to stage Trygaeus' comic flight on his dung beetle. In the case of *Peace*, then, *Bellerophon* provides a perfect foil for humour: the backdrop of tragedy provides a solemn presence which Aristophanes can continually undercut with humour, with obscenity and with parody – not only of tragic quotations but also the plot and staging of the original play.

For a humorist, then, tragic poetry comprises a useful 'frame': that is to say, tragedy, along with all its elevated pretensions, can be evoked by a poet like Aristophanes and then mocked or undermined to comic effect. But as we have seen, this tragic 'frame' need not necessarily be put to humorous use. Aristophanes also uses tragic pastiche on occasion to evoke – but *not* undermine – the weightiness and solemnity of tragedy: to add a mournful tragic aria to *Birds* (albeit one that is slightly contrived); to underline the importance of Lysistrata's scheme and Dicaeopolis' quest for peace (both of which certainly benefit from being taken 'seriously' for the sake of the plays' plots); or to highlight Strepsiades' learning through suffering in *Clouds* (a tragic rather than a comic motif). In the *parabases* of plays, too, Aristophanic choruses sometimes use tragic idiom with the effect, perhaps, of emphasizing the weightiness of the words they address to the audience.

In these passages of pastiche the tragic 'frame' is appropriated only on a temporary basis: once the tragic-style expression fades or specifically comic features are ushered in (colloquialisms, humour and the like) the tragic moment passes. However, a tragic 'frame' can be put to more substantial use still – such as when whole scenes or whole plays are parasitic on tragic originals, as is the case with *Acharnians*, *Peace* and *Women at the Thesmophoria* (also, it would appear, with the lost *Phoenician Women*, Aristophanes' parody of Euripides' play of the same name). In these cases, Aristophanes is able to interact with tragedy in further sophisticated ways – for example, by linking to, building on, deconstructing and subverting the themes of the original drama as he sees fit and thereby creating a highly complex and resonant text (sufficiently complex and resonant for scholars to have discussed at length the way in which *Acharnians* and *Women at the Thesmophoria* interact with tragic originals, for instance). Of course, what the tragic originals also provide in these cases is a way for a dramatist to structure a play or episode: as a genre, Old Comedy simply eats ideas and so the importance of a template around which a comic plot might be structured (be it borrowed from tragedy or elsewhere) can hardly be overestimated.

The appearance of tragic poets in Aristophanes' dramas may be regarded in a similar light: they, too, constitute an instantly recognizable frame of reference for the audience (as is arguably the case with any real-life individual).[22] What tragic poets also offer, however (unlike many other real-life figures) is a large pool of dramatic works with which many members of Aristophanes' audience would be familiar. With a body of work to draw on (in addition to a poet's 'real-life' persona) the potential for humour is enormous, as is evidenced by the reappearance of Euripides in so many of Aristophanes' plays, where he is portrayed differently each time – and where new ways of mocking him and his work are constantly found.[23]

Conclusions

In this chapter we have made some useful inroads into understanding Aristophanes' relationship with tragedy: we have looked at some key terms, examined a variety of examples of paratragedy and have made some important steps towards appreciating what factors may have attracted Aristophanes to tragic material. All the same, there are many challenging questions we have not addressed, such as what Aristophanes' audience may have made of his sustained paratragic use of certain plays in his comedies (the complex example of *Acharnians'* relationship with Euripides' *Telephus* is a good case in point). Similarly, one might like to see answered the seemingly straightforward, but in reality hugely complex, question of what stance Aristophanes takes towards tragedy in his plays.

This last question concerns the knotty issue of how the Aristophanes we know from the plays relates to the real-life Aristophanes: here, we may feel that the plays are about to yield us some vital clue, but in fact the evidence is far from simple to read. Parody – which appears so extensively in the plays – is essentially negative, as we have seen, and so it might be tempting to see Aristophanes' penchant for parodying not just tragedy in general but Euripidean material in particular as somehow revealing about his personal attitudes towards the tragedian: do these parodic passages betray a dislike of Euripides and his work? Well, maybe. But maybe not. What these parodic passages more obviously reveal, after all, is just how well Aristophanes' knew Euripides' work. And so what it is perhaps safest for us to claim is that Aristophanes was deeply interested in Euripides' tragedies; but whether this fascination was born of affection or dislike or something else – such as the fact that in Euripides he had simply found a target that inspired good parody – is something about which we can only speculate.[24]

7

Talking Dirty: Aristophanic Obscenity

Introduction

There can be few authors who are better known for their use of obscenity than Aristophanes. The outrageous language and scurrilous subject matter of his plays has long been a source of fascination, amusement – *and* embarrassment – for students and scholars of the ancient world. Obscenity, then, can be highly emotive: but how is it capable of rousing such strong feelings? Why does Aristophanes choose to use obscene language in his plays and at what points? And what would the original audience have made of the obscenity in Aristophanes' comedies?

The aim of this chapter will be to suggest some answers to these questions by looking at obscenity from a number of different angles. The first task will be to consider the nature of obscenity and the position it occupied in Greek culture; then, we shall go on to look at the artistic and psychological effects that Aristophanes may have achieved through its use. Much of the power of obscene expression stems from its ability to shock, of course, and Aristophanes was certainly not above using obscenity to provoke, amuse – and even disgust his audience. Indeed, Aristophanes' claims to write comedies that are not only more restrained than those of his 'vulgar' rivals (*Clouds* 524) but also 'chaste by nature' (*Clouds* 537) are difficult to believe given how frequently he uses obscenity to spice up scurrilous humour and vicious insults. But perhaps these claims *are* something more than just idle comic boasts. After all, in addition to its role in enlivening low wit and abuse, obscenity is also used in a variety of complex and sophisticated ways in Aristophanes' plays: to underscore themes; to add to fantasy; and to characterize both individuals and behaviour as unsophisticated and unpleasant, for example.

In this chapter, we shall aim to build up a rounded picture of the nature, use and effects of obscenity in the plays, by looking at a broad range of examples from across Aristophanes' work – from the dirty joke and vicious insult to the more complex ways in which obscenity is employed. In the following discussions, particular attention will be given to four of Aristophanes' more obscenity-rich plays, namely: *Acharnians*, *Knights*, *Peace* and *Lysistrata*.

7. Talking Dirty: Aristophanic Obscenity

Obscenity ancient and modern

What do we mean by obscene language? In modern Western cultures, ideas of what does and does not qualify as obscene are in constant flux, but in general it is certain words which describe sexual organs ('cock', 'cunt'), sexual acts ('fuck', 'wank'/'jerk off') and scatological phenomena ('shit', 'piss') that have traditionally been regarded as obscene. Some speakers of English avoid using such words altogether and – whether we are conscious of it or not – most of us have views on when and where it is appropriate to use obscenity: it is hardly unusual to hear 'fuck' uttered during an argument between two adults, but at children's parties and at the supermarket checkout obscenity tends to be avoided.

What links obscene words is that they refer to areas of activity (and their associated body parts) which are subject to taboo in a society. Sex, masturbation, defecation and urination are activities which tend to take place in private and which most people choose not to discuss openly in public. Indeed, knowledge of what words qualify as obscenities in a language can often help us to pin down which actions and objects its speakers find it awkward to engage with: Classical Greek, for example, has no equivalent to the English 'piss' – that is to say, a truly obscene word with the meaning 'to urinate'. This would suggest a society that has fewer hang-ups about urination than has traditionally been the case in English-speaking cultures.

So far I have talked about obscenity as if it were a universal phenomenon, but as Jeffrey Henderson argues in *The Maculate Muse* (his study of obscene language in Old Comedy) it is important to consider how classical Greeks' relationship with taboo words differed from our own.[1] As Henderson states, whereas we and the Romans think of taboo words as being dirty, staining or polluted (our 'obscene' and the Latin *obscenus*), for the Greeks there were no such associations. Classical Greeks had no special term for 'obscenity' and would, instead, have spoken about taboo words as invoking *aidôs* ('shame', 'modesty') and as therefore being *aischros* ('shameful', 'base'). That is to say, for the Greeks these words were not 'dirty' and so there was no *guilt* associated with their use: rather, a Greek would have avoided using these words purely because they referred to objects and acts which he would sooner keep to himself – and *modesty* meant that he or she would choose to keep these objects and acts private.

An important point to make at this stage is that taboo words in Greek were not used as swear words in the way that they are in English. Old Comedy is certainly full of obscene insults (e.g. 'you tank-arsed bugger', *Clouds* 1330) and no doubt there were occasions when such insults were employed by Athenians outside the theatre, too. However, there is no evidence to suggest that obscene words were used as casually by classical Greeks as they sometimes are by English speakers ('Fuck!', 'No fucking way!', 'What the fuck's that?'). A good illustration of this is the fact that the

121

closest phrase in Classical Greek to the English 'Fuck off!' is *ball' es korakas*: 'Go to the crows!' – the Greek phrase being far more innocuous than the modern-day English equivalent. An important consequence of this is that Greeks of the classical era would not have become numbed to the meaning of their obscene vocabulary in the way that modern English speakers often are, since they would not have been accustomed to hearing such words in ordinary speech. Because a phrase like 'Fuck off!' is used so frequently, we are unlikely to connect the phrase with the sexual act, whereas for a classical Athenian the word *binein* ('fuck') was exclusively used with a sexual meaning.

Obscenity in classical Greece

If obscenities were not routinely used as swear words, in what contexts would a classical Athenian have heard or used obscene language? This is no easy question given the nature of obscenity: private matters tend to be discussed in private, after all, and so our sources for the classical era give us little insight into how and when Athenians used obscenities – in their personal lives at least. Aside from Old Comedy, the two contexts in which we *do* have evidence of obscenity being used, however, are in Ionian iambic poetry (named after the poetic metre in which this poetry was written: see Chapter 8) and in the religious rites connected with particular cults and festivals.

Old Comedy has connections with both these contexts. In the hands of Ionian poets like the seventh-century Archilochus and sixth-century Hipponax, iambic poetry came to be characterized by personal abuse – not to mention sexual and scatological detail. The following fragments of Archilochus, for example, contain some fairly grotesque characterizations – of a woman and a man respectively:

> She was sucking away like a Phrygian or Thracian man sucks barley wine
> Through a straw: bent over and really giving it some.
>
> Archilochus fr. 42

> His dick ...
> Swelled up like the dick of a Prienian
> Grain-fed stud donkey.
>
> Archilochus fr. 43

A famous fragment of Hipponax evokes a situation in which the poet is having a stealthy bout of sex – probably with a woman who was also the mistress of his great rival, Bupalus:

> In case we got caught
> Naked ...
> And she was urging me on ...

7. Talking Dirty: Aristophanic Obscenity

And I was fucking away ... and ...
Pulling out the tip as if I was drying a sausage,
And telling Bupalus to go to hell.

Hipponax fr. 84.13-18

In the course of another fragmentary poem, Hipponax describes his physical reaction to an assault by a foreign woman in gory scatological detail:

Splattering with shit ...
And my arsehole stank. Beetles came buzzing,
Attracted by the smell – more than fifty of them.
Some of them fell upon me
In an attack; others (sharpened their teeth?)
And attacked the gates
Of my *buttr*ess.

Hipponax fr. 92.10-15

Aristophanes' personal attacks on individuals owe much to this poetic tradition and many of the obscene words we find in Aristophanes (as well as in the fragments of other Old Comic poets) have precedents in Archilochus' and Hipponax's work.

As far as religious rites are concerned, obscenity was a feature of a number of festivals – mostly of Demeter (such as the Thesmophoria) and of Dionysus, too (the latter being the god in whose honour drama was performed, of course).[2] In these religious contexts, ritual abuse and mockery seem to have played a role in marking out festival time as something distinct from everyday life, since it signalled the suspension of normal morals and behaviour. Here there is a similarity with the freedom apparently enjoyed by poets like Aristophanes to use obscenities to attack and mock their contemporaries – insults were traded inside the theatre which would plainly have been unacceptable in everyday life. In addition, obscenity may well have fulfilled a so-called 'apotropaic' function in religious festivals; that is to say, ritual abuse was seen as warding off evil from the participants in a religious rite since the gods would not be envious of someone who had been insulted and degraded.[3]

It is interesting to consider for a moment the different ways in which religious rites and iambic poetry influenced the development of Old Comedy. On the one hand, obscene expression was a traditional part of certain religious cults and this may account for both how obscenity came to be incorporated into Old Comedy in the first place and how it was acceptable for it to continue to feature in comic plays throughout the fifth century. On the other hand, iambic poetry evidently had an important influence on Old Comedy, too: the work of Archilochus and Hipponax demonstrated that obscenity could be incorporated into poetry to great effect and no doubt suggested to comic playwrights inventive ways in which it could be used to help them achieve their artistic ends. For the poets of Old Comedy

123

obscenity was no fossilized relic – something they used merely because it was 'traditional'. Rather it was a vibrant and central part of comic drama in the fifth century – an essential ingredient which Aristophanes and his contemporaries used in their plays to a variety of effects.

Types of obscene expression

To enable us to discuss obscenity in greater depth, it will be useful to distinguish between different kinds of obscene expression. In this section, we shall look at the different ways in which taboo acts and objects are referred to in Aristophanes' comedies, some of which are more direct than others.

Primary obscenities

In *The Maculate Muse*, Henderson coins the useful term 'primary obsceni-ties' to describe terms like *kysthos*, 'cunt'; *peos*, 'cock'; *prôktos*, 'arse-hole', and *binein*, 'to fuck'. Primary obscenities are words that refer to taboo objects or acts in a wholly non-euphemistic way. Someone uttering one of these words not only evokes for us the object or act in question but does so in an entirely direct way, with no regard for modesty or shame. Note, too, that for English speakers some of these primary obscenities are them-selves more taboo than others.

Henderson follows a model for understanding obscenity based on a psychological approach first developed by Sigmund Freud.[4] Freud's theo-ries propose that to explain the unique power of obscene words, it is necessary to understand the processes involved in a child's early psycho-logical development. At a pre-verbal stage the child thinks in concrete, pre-abstract images. During this stage the child also experiences his first sexual and scatological pleasures. As the child acquires language he develops a capability for abstract thought – and this process of language acquisition happens at the same time as he learns society's taboos. The child, then, learns to express himself in a socially acceptable manner and not to make direct mention of life's taboo areas. Obscene words, however, refer directly to taboo organs and actions and allow him in later life to experience them again in a concrete, pre-abstract form. So obscenities are, in Henderson's words, 'simply equals-signs cutting through social barriers and pointing directly toward, and invoking in the listener, the basic emotions adhering to the organs and actions themselves'. He adds that: 'their unique power lies in their ability to recall to us a pleasurable time of life' and that obscene words allow us to fulfil 'our occasional need to rebel against the repressions enforced by adulthood.'[5] Whether or not this psychological account of obscenity is found wholly convincing, it does at least provide a possible explanation as to why obscene language can rouse such strong emotions in us.

7. Talking Dirty: Aristophanic Obscenity

Clinical language and euphemisms

A useful point of comparison with primary obscenities is medical terms for sexual and excretory acts and organs: in ancient Greece just like today, these existed alongside obscene terms. Such words are also non-euphemistic, but unlike primary obscenities they are used in 'respectable' contexts such as medical treatises. Articulating the difference between primary obscenities and medical terms provides something of a challenge, however. Henderson is surely right that 'clinical language' is not 'charged with [the same] strong emotional ... feelings' as primary obscenities: in the context of medicine it is sometimes necessary to discuss sex, excretion and the associated body parts and clinical language provides a 'respectable' way of doing just that. Different terms, then, possess different associations and most native speakers of a language will have a similar intuitive feel for when it is appropriate to use a word like *phallos* ('penis') rather than *peos* ('cock'), and *vice versa*. Henderson also talks of a difference in the 'mental picture awakened' by primary obscenities on the one hand and clinical language on the other.[6]

A further useful comparison to make is between primary obscenities and euphemisms. Euphemisms refer to taboo acts and objects only in the most oblique way: genitalia may be referred to as 'privates' (*aidoia*), for example – such as by Better Argument at *Clouds* 978; and the sex act as 'performing the holy rites of Aphrodite' – a phrase used by Myrrhine at *Lysistrata* 898. In Aristophanic comedy, euphemisms are often used by a polite speaker to contrast with a crude one: in *Clouds*, for example, Better Argument's euphemisms stand in stark contrast to Worse Argument's coarseness and in *Lysistrata*, Myrrhine's tone is very different from that of her sexually frustrated husband Cinesias. Alternatively, euphemisms can play a role at the more genteel and/or heightened moments of Aristophanes' plays: in a poignant moment in her argument with the Magistrate, Lysistrata talks of young women being unable to 'enjoy their youth' during war time, for instance (*Lysistrata* 591: see Chapter 5, p. 90) and in a light-hearted lyric passage from *Knights* the chorus says of a supposedly venerable and upstanding trireme that 'she has never been near a man' (*Knights* 1306).

Primary obscenities and obscene slang

There is also a distinction to be made between primary obscenities and obscene slang – although to be sure this is a very difficult line to draw. There are numerous contexts in which most English speakers would avoid using slang words like 'screw' or 'dick' for instance, but neither is as forceful as the equivalent primary obscenities – 'fuck' and 'cock'. Indeed, it is interesting to ponder the difference in our emotional reaction to sets of slang words which all have the same basic (obscene) meaning: what is the difference between the way we use – and the way we react to – words like 'muff', 'twat', 'pussy' and 'snatch'? And how do such terms differ in tone from 'cunt'? Some of these words no doubt seem more forceful than others or perhaps seem more appropriate in particular contexts.

If it is not always easy to make meaningful distinctions between primary obscenities and obscene slang terms in English, the situation in Classical Greek is that much more complicated. Which words qualified as primary obscenities and which as slang for Aristophanes' audience? How can we quantify the difference in tone between various slang expressions – and even between the various primary obscenities we have identified in Greek? After all, as we noted above, not all primary obscenities are found as shocking as each other by English speakers – think of the difference in tone between 'cock' and 'cunt' for instance. With Classical Greek, there is not the option of asking native speakers their reactions to the various words that interest us, and we also lack any explicit comments from the classical era as to the force and nuance of different obscene expressions (perhaps unsurprisingly given the subject matter). Indeed, our major resource for getting to grips with obscene language in the fifth and fourth centuries BC is the work of Aristophanes himself – and so our best chance of answering these questions comes from careful observation of the way in which characters in Old Comedy employ different words: how often is a given word used? In what context? And so on. According to Henderson's analysis of Aristophanes' obscene vocabulary, some of the Greek words that count as primary obscenities (as opposed to obscene slang) might surprise speakers of English. Not only were *skôr*, 'shit', and *dephesthai*, 'wank'/'jerk off', considered primary obscenities, Henderson suggests, but also words whose English translations seem relatively tame, namely: *psôle*, 'hard-on', *styesthai*, 'to get a hard-on' and even *perdesthai*, 'to fart' (though, it must be said, the sheer frequency with which fart references occur in Aristophanes might suggest that *perdesthai* is not as vulgar as some of the other words listed here).[7]

In Classical Greek, slang and metaphorical expressions for sexual organs generally derive from everyday objects. *Balanos*, 'acorn' or 'bolt-pin', for example, is a common term for the penis, as is *erebinthos*, 'chickpea', when the penis is erect, and numerous other expressions for the male member are to be found in Aristophanes' plays, often deriving from phallic-shaped objects and tools. Words for the female genitalia are commonly connected with enclosed and/or dark spaces, doors, fruit and flowers. *Kistê*, 'box', and *myrton*, 'myrtle berry' are typical expressions – as is *choiros*, 'piglet', which denotes hairless female genitalia.[8] It was evidently not uncommon for young women to practise depilation, so hairless genitalia do not necessarily imply that the owner is immature physically, though this certainly is the case with the Megarian scene from *Acharnians* (750-818).[9] Here, the Megarian trader, for want of anything else to sell, tries to sell Dicaeopolis his young daughters, claiming that what he is

126

selling are 'piglets' (*choiroi*: see Chapter 4, p. 71). In an attempt to convince Dicaeopolis, he even has one of the girls make the appropriate noises:

Daughter:	Oink! Oink!
Megarian:	Now ya gotta admit – *that*'s a piglet (*choiros*)!
Dicaeopolis:	Well, it certainly looks like a 'piglet' (*choiros*) now – but when it grows up, it'll be a real cunt (*kysthos*)!

Acharnians 780-2

Double entendres

Double entendres – non-obscene words and phrases which are endowed (usually temporarily) with an obscene meaning – form a particularly interesting category. Aristophanes employs these throughout his plays, but perhaps nowhere in as concentrated a form as in the following passage from *Lysistrata*, where the Magistrate (*Proboulos*) explains to the chorus of old men that husbands only have themselves to blame for their wives' sexual infidelities.

> For when we ourselves help our wives to be wicked and teach them how to play up, such are the plots they are bound to hatch. In craftsmen's shops, for instance, we say things like: 'You know, goldsmith, the necklace you mended? Well, my wife was dancing one evening and the bolt-pin (*balanos*) fell out of the hole. Now, I've got to sail over to Salamis, so if you've got a moment, could you pop over towards evening and – to the best of your ability – fit your pin in her slot?'

Lysistrata 404-13

The humour in this passage relies on a series of double meanings: *balanos*, as we have already seen, can signify either the penis or a bolt-pin; 'hole' (*trêma* in Greek) can stand for the female genitalia; and *enarmottô*, 'to fit something into a slot', can be understood without difficulty as referring to the sexual act. However, none of these words is in itself obscene: *balanos* (with its meaning of 'bolt pin', at least), *trêma*, 'hole', and *enarmottô*, 'slot in', could all be used in polite conversation. However, the passage is structured in such a way that we are invited to understand these not only as everyday words but also as expressions which possess a secondary obscene meaning.

An intriguing feature of *double entendres* is that – in comparison with primary obscenities, say – they require a relatively high level of co-operation from the reader or listener in order to be fully understood. The word 'hole' (*trêma*) does not always – indeed does not even *usually* – signify the female genitalia and so we as readers (just like Aristophanes' original audience) have to work out the secondary obscene meaning of the word for ourselves. So, by using *double entendres* authors can lead their audiences to think about obscene things and can do so *without* using explicitly obscene vocabulary. And in the context of Old Comedy, then, *double entendres* allow Aristophanes to set his audience on the path to thinking about things which are base (*aischros*) and lack modesty (*aidôs*) and to do so using vocabulary which is – on one view – perfectly inoffensive.

With this is mind, it is interesting to note that Aristophanes often seems to prepare the audience for the occurrence of primary obscenities by means of *double entendres*. Perhaps the most striking example comes in the Megarian scene in *Acharnians* that we briefly considered earlier (750-818). Here, the word *choiros* is used a number of times – initially to be understood simply as 'piglet', then as a *double entendre* (since *choiros* can also signify the female genitalia) – before the primary obscenity *kysthos* ('cunt') is finally introduced (782). There is similar build-up to a primary obscenity in the prologue of *Lysistrata*, too. The plan for the sex strike is revealed only at length, after a number of risqué lines and tantalizing allusions, when Lysistrata finally announces:

> Right then: we're going to have to give up – cock (*peos*)!
>
> *Lysistrata* 124

Obscene gesture

Whilst the major concern of this chapter is obscene expression, it is worth bearing in mind other ways in which obscenity was conveyed to the audiences of Aristophanes' plays. Actors' gestures would often have played a prominent role both as an accompaniment to obscene language and in their own right – although, to be sure, gestures are not always easy to reconstruct from the text (as we saw in Chapter 3, the manuscripts handed down to us contain no original stage directions). In *Wasps*, for example, one wonders what stage business might have accompanied Philocleon's request to the flute-girl, Dardanis, with whom he has just run away from the drinking party (symposium).

> Did you see how cleverly I stole you away when you were just about to suck off the dinner guests? Do this cock of mine a favour for that, won't you?
>
> *Wasps* 1345-7

It seems safe to assume that during this *Wasps* scene, the actor playing Philocleon would have had his padded leather phallus on prominent display – and actors' phalluses were evidently used in other plays, too, to accompany obscene language and to make obscene gestures. It is by pointing at his phallus that Trygaeus' slave in *Peace*, for instance, is able to realize a risqué joke about his master's future bride, Opora (Harvest), whom Trygaeus has recently brought back from Olympus.

Slave:	Tell me, should I give her anything to feed on?
Trygaeus:	No point. She won't want to eat bread or barley cakes, since she's too used to licking ambrosia with the gods up there.
Slave:	Well, we'll just have to give her something to lick *down here*, too!

Peace 851-4

The most sustained exploitation of actors' padded leather phalluses comes in *Lysistrata*, where for large sections of the play the sexual frustration of the younger male characters would have been clearly shown by their exaggerated erections. In the following extract, some Spartan envoys arrive in Athens and are soon joined by a delegation of Athenians. The chorus comments on the efforts of both parties to conceal their erect phalluses:

Look! Here come some ambassadors from Sparta with their long beards wearing something like a pig-pen around their thighs.

Lysistrata 1074-5

Look! I can see some native Athenians hunched over like wrestlers, holding their cloaks away from their stomachs.

Lysistrata 1082-4

Note here how actions taking place in the acting space are integrated into the play's dialogue (a dramatic technique we observed in Chapter 3). In this way, Aristophanes keeps all of his spectators informed about the characters' physical actions (and their prominent hard-ons) – even those sitting at the back of the theatre.

Aristophanes' use of obscenity

So far we have been looking at the kinds of obscene expression that appear in the plays, but have yet to engage fully with *why* Aristophanes employs obscenity. One answer to this, of course, is that it was traditional: his rival playwrights used obscene language, as did his predecessors – and so obscenity was simply a conventional and accepted element of Old Comedy. But if we choose to regard Aristophanes as the master rather than the slave of his art (as I think we should), it is also worthwhile asking a further series of questions. How and when does he use obscenity? What might Aristophanes' motives as a poet and playwright be for using obscene expression in the way he does? How might his audience have reacted to its use? In the next few sections we shall look at three major contexts in which obscenity appears in an attempt to shed light on these questions: the role obscenity plays in personal abuse; its relationship with humour; and its use in passages that describe sex acts.

129

Aristophanes: An Introduction

Obscenity and personal abuse

A common use of obscenity in Aristophanes' plays is to abuse figures of authority. Occasionally this is done by simple name-calling (such as Better Argument calling Worse Argument a 'shameless faggot' at *Clouds* 909). At other times, however, an obscenity will be introduced in the course of a heated exchange between two characters – often in a 'climactic' position: that is to say, the obscenity draws a line under the argument and effectively seals victory for the character that has uttered it. The following extract from *Knights*, for example, demonstrates this principle well. Paphlagon (who represents Aristophanes' arch rival Cleon) and the Sausage Seller are trading threats while arguing about who should control Demos (that is to say, the *dêmos* or people of Athens). Eventually the Sausage Seller manages to gain the upper hand by means of a timely obscene joke.

Paphlagon:	I'll tear out your guts with my nails!
Sausage Seller:	I'll scratch your Prytaneum food out of you.
Paphlagon:	I'll drag you in front of the people (*dêmos*) and exact justice from you.
Sausage Seller:	I'll drag you there, too, and outdo you in slander.
Paphlagon:	But [the people] won't believe a word you say, poor thing. Whereas I can make an utter fool out of it if I want.
Sausage Seller:	You really think that the people (*dêmos*) is in your power, don't you?
Paphlagon:	I sure do – I know just what titbits to feed it, you see.
Sausage Seller:	Yes, but it doesn't get fed well by you. You're just like nurses who chew the food first – you place a little bit in his mouth and swallow down three times as much for yourself.
Paphlagon:	Yes, by Zeus, and my abilities are even such that I can make Demos [i.e. the people] expand and contract as I please.
Sausage Seller:	Even my arsehole (*prôktos*) knows *that* trick!

Knights 708-21

Of course, Cleon is not the only real-life figure appearing in Aristophanes' plays to be attacked with obscene insults. Indeed, obscenities clearly play an important role in his drama in undermining the intellectual authority of a whole range of public figures. In *Women at the Thesmophoria*, for example, the tragic playwright Agathon is unflatteringly portrayed as an effeminate transvestite who produces pretentious and essentially vapid poetry. Even before Agathon appears in person his character is maligned, as in the following exchange between Euripides and the Inlaw, where Agathon is characterized not as an intellectual playwright but rather as something approaching a whore. Note that once again obscenity is used in this passage in a climactic joke.

7. Talking Dirty: Aristophanic Obscenity

Euripides:	This is the home of the famous tragic poet Agathon.
Inlaw:	Which Agathon is that?
Euripides:	There liveth a certain Agathon who ...
Inlaw:	You don't mean the tanned, strapping one?
Euripides:	No, it's another one. Haven't you ever seen him?
Inlaw:	Not the one with the bushy beard?
Euripides:	You really *haven't* seen him.
Inlaw:	No, by Zeus, not that I'm aware.
Euripides:	And yet you must have *fucked* him – though perhaps you're not aware.

Women at the Thesmophoria 29-35

The debunking of intellectual authority can also be achieved without resorting to direct personal insults. In *Clouds*, for instance, Strepsiades introduces a comic obscenity into what ought to be a philosophical conversation with his teacher, Socrates: in so doing he not only reveals his own crudeness but also uses language which is far from respectful. Here Strepsiades (who is lying under a cover in bed) is asked by the philosopher whether he has had any intelligent thoughts.

Socrates:	Have you come up with anything?
Strepsiades:	No, by Zeus, I haven't – not really.
Socrates:	Nothing at all?
Strepsiades:	No, nothing [*throwing back the covers*] – except a handful of cock (*peos*)!

Clouds 733-4

There is, then, a tendency for obscenity to be coupled with humour: the character insulted is also the butt of a joke. Sometimes, however, insults are less amusing (if still inventive), such as the Sausage Seller's threat to Paphlagon, 'I'll stuff your arse (*prôktos*) like a sausage case' (*Knights* 364) or Strepsiades calling his son, Pheidippides, 'cistern-arsed' (*Clouds* 1330: implying that he, like Agathon, has an inappropriate and excessive enthusiasm for being buggered).

So, obscenity plays a key role in the abuse of figures of authority and in undermining intellectual discourse. And since this is the case, it is interesting to ponder what sort of a link there might be between this abuse of public figures and the 'apotropaic' function of obscenity we considered earlier: that is, the idea that obscene abuse could ward off the envy of the gods from those who had been insulted and degraded. Was there, for instance, a sense in which the audience would have viewed the humiliation of Athens' intellectuals and politicians as somehow healthy for the city? Some scholars have suggested that the abuse of public figures in Old Comedy fulfilled something of a ritual function in this way – as well as providing an opportunity for hostility towards high-profile and powerful individuals to be played out in a public arena in a non-violent way: a collective letting off of steam.[10]

131

Two further points need to be made at this juncture, however. The first is that it is not only real-life, powerful figures who are on the receiving end of obscene insults in Aristophanes' plays, but also fictional characters (Pheidippides in *Clouds*, to name but one) and people who are relatively powerless (even the audience themselves are insulted as 'wide-arsed' at *Clouds* 1099-1100). This indicates that Aristophanes used obscene language abusively when it was appropriate to his dramatic ends (such as staging a lively argument or making a good joke), not only when he saw fit to insult a well-known figure of authority on stage. And second, it should also be borne in mind that not all insults in Aristophanes' plays employ obscene language. In short, obscene abuse is evidently a weapon which Aristophanes uses to achieve specific effects at specific points in his plays. And so when we meet insults in the plays – whether they are obscene or not – it is always worth asking why Aristophanes has chosen to phrase them in the way he has.

The psychology of obscene abuse

Before leaving the subject of obscene abuse, it will be interesting to look at a psychological account of why Aristophanes' audience might have found such insults appealing. One approach to follow is that of Freud, whose model for understanding obscenity (which we touched on earlier) can be used to explain the role that obscenity plays in degrading figures of authority. The suggestion here is that obscene language can be used to bring about what is called 'exposure': a kind of public humiliation which is to be thought of as a substitute for physical (sometimes sexual) aggression.[11]

So how does 'exposure' work? According to this model, by using obscene language, Person A forces Person B to visualize what is being said. Thus if A says the word 'cock', for example, B is forced to imagine the male sexual organ and, in this way, B's knowledge of a private and taboo matters is 'exposed'. Further to this, B's recognition of the significance of the word 'cock' throws up questions about his character. If he knows what 'cock' means, what other obscene things does he know? Importantly, too, if a third party is present, then B's knowledge of the deeds or objects to which obscene words refer is made public – and B's 'exposure' is all the more degrading. The suggestion is that this 'exposure' is pleasurable for everyone apart from the person 'exposed'. In the context of Old Comedy, then, the suggestion is that by watching one of Aristophanes' plays an audience member would have gained enjoyment from seeing powerful figures such as politicians or gods humiliated in this way. That is to say, by witnessing 'exposure' in the fictional world of a play an audience member could enjoy the fantasy of getting one over on the powers that be.

This Freudian model is not without its weaknesses. Why does Person A's use of obscene language bring shame on Person B but not himself?[12] To what extent do we really 'visualize' obscene words when we hear them used? What pleasure can there really be in seeing fictional characters 'exposed'? But these objections aside, this approach nevertheless goes some of the way to providing an explanation for the prevalence and popularity of obscene abuse in Aristophanes' plays. Certainly appreciating the way in which obscenity can be used to abuse public figures is key to understanding plays like *Acharnians* or *Knights* where almost all of the obscenities are delivered by a single character – Dicaeopolis and the Sausage Seller respectively. These characters spend much of their time exposing the faults and corruption of the world around them – often with the help of obscenity.

Obscenity as humour

One context in which we have already seen obscenity crop up several times is in jokes – the Sausage-Seller's claim that his arsehole could perform the same trick as Paphlagon, for example (*Knights* 721), and Strepsiades' reply to Socrates that he had come up with 'nothing – except a handful of cock' (*Clouds* 734). On both these occasions obscenity heightens the humour of the passage, the surprise of the punch line being added to by a further surprise – a shift in tone from neutral to obscene language.

As I have argued in *Humour, Obscenity and Aristophanes*, humour and obscenity are in many ways natural bedfellows.[13] Both humour and obscenity can be used aggressively to mock or humiliate, for example. Both can elicit laughter (be it through amusement or embarrassment). Both humour and obscenity can play a role in defining an 'in crowd' by differentiating between those in the know and those who are not: sometimes there are people who fail to 'get' the joke, just as there are sometimes people who fail understand the meaning of a *double entendre* or piece of obscene slang. And both humour and obscenity can also be seen as breaking certain unspoken rules of communication – to appreciate humour, listeners must be prepared to release themselves from the bonds of standard logic, whereas to appreciate obscenity they have to be prepared to tolerate breaches of conventional morality. Why obscenity is of particular use to the humorist is because unconventional morality can often be surprising (surprise being an important element of humour, as we saw in Chapter 4). That is to say, in the hands of a skilful comic writer, the shock that obscenities are liable to cause can be pressed into service to create successful jokes.

This ability of obscenity to create an amusing shock is perhaps demonstrated nowhere better than at *Lysistrata* 708-15. At this point in the play the sex strike is in full swing and when Lysistrata emerges from the stage building (*skênê*), she is questioned by the chorus of old women about her apparently anxious behaviour. Both Lysistrata and the chorus speak in the high-flown language typical of tragedy – until the mood is finally punctured by a primary obscenity:[14]

Chorus:	O mistress of this deed and plan,
	Why, pray, dost thou come cross-visaged from thy dwelling?
Lysistrata:	'Tis the deeds of wicked women and the female heart
	That make me walk dejected to and fro.
Chorus:	What dost thou say? What dost thou say?
Lysistrata:	The truth! The truth!
Chorus:	What is thy trouble? Speak to thy friends.
Lysistrata:	It shames me to tell, yet it is weighty to conceal.
Chorus:	Then do not hide from me such woe as we suffer.
Lysistrata:	In brief to tell – we need a good fucking!

Lysistrata 708-15

Aristophanes' use of obscenity here allows the tragic idiom to be suddenly deflated to humorous effect – with the shock (and humour) no doubt heightened by the fact that it is a *woman* who utters the taboo word. It could be argued that the effect of obscenity here is to undermine tragic language and decorum: the lofty phrases may sound impressive, but do not convey meaning nearly as effectively as obscenity, which allows Lysistrata to make her point quickly and clearly. Unlike the undermining of characters such as Agathon and Socrates that we saw earlier, the target being deflated in the *Lysistrata* passage is not an individual, then; rather it is tragic idiom as a whole: the high-flown way in which tragic poets express themselves in their plays.

A similar undermining of traditional sources of authority is also visible in the opening lines of *Frogs* (which we have already seen quoted at the beginning of Chapter 4). Here, Aristophanes creates humour in a number of ways – such as by having the god Dionysus, Olympian deity and patron of the dramatic festival, not only use obscenity himself but also tolerate its use by his slave, Xanthias. Here, then, the humour stems from a clash between high and low. A god – a divine being who inhabits an ethereal world – is seen engaging with the basest realities of man's everyday existence: in this case, shitting and farting. And the use of obscenity makes this juxtaposition of two worlds all the more striking. The obscene words come in a passage where Dionysus and Xanthias (who is carrying a bundle on a pole over his shoulder) discuss which jokes it is permissible to make in front of the audience.

Xanthias:	... Can I tell the *really* funny one?
Dionysus:	Yes, by Zeus, be my guest. Only whatever you do, don't tell
	...
Xanthias:	Which one?
Dionysus:	... the one where you shift your stick from one shoulder to the other and say that you're busting for a crap. ...
Xanthias:	Can't I even say that the burden I'm carrying is so heavy that if someone doesn't relieve me of it then – I'll relieve *myself* in a power-fart?

Frogs 6-10

134

Aristophanes evidently found this clash between the elevated world of the gods and the lowly world of obscenity to be a rich source of humour. In *Peace*, for example, the gods are said to act as pimps (848-50) and Zeus is given the comic epithet *skataibatês*, 'dung-walker' (*Peace* 42) – a corruption of his traditional epithet *kataibatês*, 'he who descends (in lightning)'.[15]

Obscenity and sexuality

Another common use of obscene words in the plays is as an ingredient of Aristophanes' many descriptions of – and allusions to – sex. Here obscenity plays an interesting dual role: it can be used both in a positive way to celebrate sex and sexual freedoms but also in a negative way to highlight certain kinds of sexual behaviour which – in Aristophanes' world at least – seem to be regarded as degenerate. In this section we shall look at how obscene language is used in different sexual contexts and briefly explore the nature of Aristophanes' sexual ethics.

Throughout Aristophanes' plays there is a connection between sex and peace: when war ends and peace is achieved, sex follows. In *Lysistrata* the sex associated with peace is envisaged as taking place between married couples: sex with their wives (and a return to domestic normality) is the reward that the men receive for ending the war. In the other 'peace' plays, however, *Acharnians* and *Peace*, the central figure – after the success of his grand scheme – enjoys a return to youthful vigour and an opportunity to fulfil his sexual desires with attractive and sexually available young women (as discussed in Chapter 5, p. 95). In *Peace*, Trygaeus' reward for re-establishing Peace on earth is to marry Opora (Harvest), one of the beautiful young women that he has brought back from heaven. Trygaeus' slave makes a number of salacious comments about his master's bride (we saw an example of this earlier). Following her bridal bath, the slave uses an obscenity while reporting on the state of the wedding preparations:

> The girl's been bathed, her backside's beautiful, the flat-cake's baked, the sesame cakes are being seen to – as is everything else: the only thing lacking is the cock (*peos*)!
>
> *Peace* 868-70

These comments about Opora are followed by an even more salacious set of remarks – this time about Theoria (Festival), the other girl Trygaeus has brought back to earth. When Trygaeus presents Theoria to the city's council (*boulê*), he makes some highly suggestive proposals as to how she might be treated.

> And next, now you've got her, you can hold a fine athletic contest tomorrow and wrestle her on the ground, set her up on all fours, oil yourselves and fight no-holds-barred, striking and gouging with fist as well as – cock (*peos*)! And in two days' time you can hold a horse race, with *rider outriding rider* and

135

chariots piling on top of each other and *thrusting* together, puffing and panting – and other charioteers will be lying on the ground, their dicks all stiff, after falling down while negotiating the curves.

Peace 894-904

In *Acharnians*, the difference between peace and war is also characterized by sex. Owing to the private peace he has made, Dicaeopolis is able to enjoy the company of two sexually compliant dancing girls in the final scene of the play. He is joined in the acting space by the general Lamachus whose fate is quite different: Lamachus is still bent on waging war with Sparta and instead of sexual success, his reward has been to wound his ankle and hit his head on a stone. He appears in the company of two soldiers who help prop him up.

Lamachus:	Take hold of my leg, take hold! Arrrghhh! Grab it, my comrades!
Dicaeopolis:	Yes, and you two grab my cock right round the middle, my dears!
Lamachus:	I'm dizzy – I've been hit hard by a stone and have got some serious wounds!
Dicaeopolis:	And I want to go to bed – I've been hit hard by a stiffy and have got some serious wood![16]

Acharnians 1214-21

The sex that Trygaeus and Dicaeopolis describe and look forward to enjoying is well and truly the stuff of fantasy. These are poor, old men and while they may both come up with ingenious plans for ending the war, they are evidently not to be thought of as educated – or even remotely sophisticated (as, indeed, the use they both make of obscenity in the early parts of their respective plays makes clear). These characters would have been played by actors wearing grotesque masks with padded bellies and rumps and so they are not even to be thought of as remotely physically attractive. In short, they are figures who in real life would possess none of the charms of youth, wealth, culture or beauty – yet they come to enjoy all manner of sexual benefits. These fantasies may be highly unrealistic, then, but in one sense this is what makes their appeal all the more broad: no man in the audience – however old, poor or ugly – is precluded from imagining himself in Dicaeopolis' or Trygaeus' position. Obscenity plays a crucial role here: it adds colour to these fantasies by making them more earthy and more immediate, whilst also making these passages – and the sexual pleasures they evoke – stand out from the surrounding text.

These are, of course, strictly male fantasies – and while it is interesting to ponder how any women in the audience might have reacted to them, it is clearly male tastes that Aristophanes is catering for here.[17] The formula of 'old man *plus* young girl' was evidently popular with theatre audiences, too, since Aristophanes also presents us with a reinvigorated old man

enjoying the attentions of sexually compliant young women towards the
end of *Knights* (Demos and his 'Peace Treaties' (*Spondai*)) and *Wasps*
(Philocleon and his stolen flute girl). Like Opora, Theoria and Dicaeopolis'
dancing girls these sexually available characters are mute throughout and
were probably played on stage by male actors dressed as voluptuous naked
women (although some scholars have suggested that real-life slave-girls
played these parts). In *Birds* there is a slight variation on the theme:
Peisthetaerus gains a beautiful young wife, Basileia, but no obscene
comments are made about her (perhaps indicating that she is cast purely
in the role of a virginal bride; perhaps that the audience is not invited to
empathize with Peisthetaerus' (sexual) success). In *Lysistrata*, however,
we encounter yet another one of these mute, nude female characters –
Reconciliation – who is ogled by the sexually frustrated Athenians and
Spartans alike.[18]

Athenian:	My hard-on is killing me!

Lysistrata 1136

Spartan:	That's one gorgeous arsehole (*prôktos*)!

Lysistrata 1148

Spartan:	I've never seen a nobler woman.
Athenian:	And I've never seen a prettier cunt (*kysthos*)!

Lysistrata 1157-8

As her name suggests, Reconciliation represents the sexual benefits of
making peace (something she has in common with the girls in *Acharnians*
and *Peace*) and is once more mute: that is to say, she is given no personality
beyond being a sexually available object. As we saw in Chapter 4, the two
sides patch up their differences by using her body as a map to settle their
territorial disputes: the Spartans demand the return of the 'protuberance'
of Pylos, while the Athenians ask for the Malian 'gulf', Megaran 'legs', and
so on (*Lysistrata* 1162-3; 1169-70). The use of obscenity here certainly
reinforces the sexual desperation of the male characters and neatly highlights the basic nature of the instincts they are looking to satisfy.

Sexual fantasies and accounts of past sexual pleasures are to be found
in one form and another throughout the plays – some more developed than
others; some containing obscenity, some not. These can range from
exchanging a glance with a girl whose breast is poking out of a torn
dress (*Frogs* 409-12); to kissing a slave girl while the wife is in the bath
(*Peace* 1138-9); to the full blown sexual assault of a slave girl (*Acharnians* 271-5). Needless to say, even the mildest of these scenarios would
be morally problematic in real life (at least for the woman): in the world
of Old Comedy, however, they are almost exclusively presented in a
celebratory light.

Alongside heterosexual pleasures, we occasionally find homosexual

137

pleasures as the subject of fantasy: a 'good-bollocked boy' is an object of desire in *Knights* (1385), for example, and in *Wasps* the benefits of jury service extend to looking at boys' 'privates' when they are being examined for registration (578). In *Birds*, Euelpides even waxes lyrical about the kind of city he would like to live in:

> A place where a father of an attractive boy, when I bumped into him, would complain that I had done him wrong, saying, 'That was a fine turn you did my boy, sunshine! You met him coming from the gymnasium, freshly bathed, and you didn't kiss him, you didn't talk to him, you didn't draw him close and you didn't finger his balls. And you, an old family friend of mine!'
>
> *Birds* 137-42

The beauty of young men and boys is also praised elsewhere by male characters in Aristophanes (albeit less than the beauty of young women and girls), and this largely reflects broader sexual attitudes amongst classical Athenians who would hardly have thought it unusual for an adult man to find a young person – be they male or female – sexually attractive (it should also be said that a difference in age between partners was evidently accepted in heterosexual relationships and expected in homosexual ones: that is, the pairing of an adult male with a very young woman or youth). This is not to say that attitudes towards homosexuality in classical Athens were straightforward, however. Homosexual relations, especially between free-born males, could evidently prove morally problematic for a whole host of reasons – but perhaps most important was the issue of what role a man played in a homosexual sex act. For a male adult citizen, acting as the passive partner certainly seems to have attracted derision – and in Aristophanes' plays a fondness for being buggered also tends to be coupled with sexual insatiability. Hence 'wide-arsed' is a common insult, indicating a man who has been frequently buggered; and hence the swipe at Agathon we met earlier – 'And yet you must have *fucked* him – though perhaps you're not aware' (*Women at the Thesmophoria* 35) – the implication being that most men have buggered Agathon and that, since no courtship of him was required, not everyone who has done so will necessarily have seen his face. Numerous men are insulted in Aristophanes as frequently enjoying the passive role in anal sex (they are 'cistern-arsed' and have 'gaping arseholes') or as being effeminate (with pale, smooth skin, shaven faces or, in the case of Agathon and Cleisthenes, transvestite tendencies). A running joke, too, is that the most successful politicians are the ones with the widest arseholes – an idea developed particularly fully in *Knights*. The Sausage Seller is said to have stolen a piece of meat as a boy, for example, which he hid up his backside, eliciting the comment from a nearby politician that: 'There's no doubt that this boy will hold the stewardship of the people one day!' (*Knights* 426).[19]

Other sexual behaviour is also ridiculed in the plays, including adultery

(whether the man is the victim *or* perpetrator) and a fondness for cunnilingus, while the practice of masturbation marks a character out as
lacking in sophistication – such as the fictional Strepsiades who handles
his cock in front of Socrates at *Clouds* 734 or the historical Persian leader
Datis whom Trygaeus describes as 'wanking'/'jerking off' at *Peace* 290. In
these contexts, then, obscenity is once more used to add spice to descriptions of 'negative' sexual behaviour: it emphasizes the supposed crudeness
of certain sex acts and is used to insult individuals who engage in them.

Conclusions

The aim of this chapter has been to provide a brief overview of the topic of
obscenity in Aristophanes: both the different kinds of obscene expression
that are found in the plays and the most common uses to which obscenity
is put. As we have seen, obscenity can have very different effects: it can
insult and debunk; it can add to and even create humour; it can be used to
describe sexual fantasy and highlight 'negative' sexual behaviour; and it
can also play an important role in characterizing figures as unsophisticated and vulgar: the obscenities of both Strepsiades in *Clouds* and
Philocleon in *Wasps*, for example, serve neatly to reveal their lack of
refinement. The balance in a play between 'negative' obscenity (e.g. insults, degenerate sexual behaviour) and 'positive' obscenity (e.g. sexual
fantasy) can also be instructive: the scatological obscenities of *Peace*
connected with the dung beetle, for instance, give way to celebratory
obscenities once peace is made, whereas in *Assemblywomen* the grotesque
sexual revolution of the play – where the young and beautiful are forced
to sleep with the old and ugly – is accompanied by a good deal of 'negative'
obscenity.

   As will now be clear, Aristophanes uses obscenity in a far from random
fashion: he employs it noticeably more in some plays than others (*Wasps*
and *Birds* contain relatively little, for instance); more in some *parts* of
plays than others (the last third of *Birds* is almost obscenity-free); and
often restricts its use in a play to one or two characters: in *Acharnians* and
Knights obscenity is almost the exclusive preserve of the central character;
in *Women at the Thesmophoria*, the bulk of the obscene language is found
in the mouth of the Inlaw in the first half of the play, with the Scythian
Archer taking over his role as foul-mouthed buffoon towards the play's
end. Through obscenity the audience of Old Comedy is able to experience
a temporary and collective release from the constraints of normal morality, laugh at the traditional figures of authority that they see insulted and
humiliated in the theatre, and enjoy flights of wild sexual fantasy.

   One of the most fascinating topics we have touched on in the course of
this chapter is the nature of Aristophanic sexual ethics. On the one hand,
outrageous sexual freedoms are often the subject of fantasies and regularly form part of the celebrations connected with the success of the play's

great scheme – especially when the result of that scheme is peace. On the other hand, though, obscenity is used to highlight sexual behaviour that the audience is invited to see in a negative light: above all the insatiable desire for anal penetration which so many characters (often real-life figures) are accused of harbouring. Both positive and negative sex, then, have a key feature in common: an element of outrageousness and excess – and Old Comedy provides us with a unique opportunity to gauge the kind of vocabulary which Athenians might have used to express such sexually 'shameless' thoughts.[20]

So much for Aristophanic obscenity. Let us now turn to a different aspect of the plays – their songs – and look at Aristophanes' abilities and tendencies as a lyricist.

8

Waxing Lyrical: Aristophanes the Songwriter

Introduction

Aristophanes' theatre is musical theatre. The figures speak for themselves: at least 20% of the lines in his fifth-century plays would have been sung, for example, and the number of separate songs found in a play such as *Birds* – perhaps as many as 30 depending on what one counts as a song – makes it more than a match for many modern musicals. In addition to this, numerous passages in the plays were delivered in what is commonly referred to as 'recitative' – a term borrowed from opera and which, in the context of Aristophanes' plays, indicates lines which were spoken, perhaps chanted, with some form of musical accompaniment.

Music and song, then, were a central part of Aristophanic drama – but this was hardly musical theatre in the Broadway tradition. Not only would ancient Greek music strike a modern Western ear as far from melodic but the range of musical instruments used in theatrical performances was also limited by today's standards. The most common musical accompaniment in drama was the *aulos*, an instrument comprising two 'flutes' played simultaneously by means of reeds – and which therefore probably sounded something like an oboe. The *aulos*-player, who wore a special head-strap to help him play his instrument, would have stood alongside the chorus members as they sang and danced in the *orchêstra*. Timpani (drums) and the lyre were also used regularly in comic theatre. The only other instruments we find used in the plays (and then only in a very limited way) are the castanets and the Spartan *physallides* (*Lysistrata* 1244): probably a form of bagpipe.

Another way in which Aristophanes' plays differ from modern musicals is that they rarely, if ever, contain anything comparable to the 'big number'. Lyric passages in Old Comedy are generally short, with few songs comparable in length even to the choral odes found in tragedy. That said, there are exceptions to this rule. For example, the odes which marked the pauses between episodes in *Assemblywomen* and *Wealth* (the vast majority of which have not been preserved for us in our manuscripts) were probably similar in length to tragic choral odes. We occasionally find longer musical sequences at other junctures in his plays as well: sometimes when the chorus enters the acting space (the *parodos*) and, more typically, in the closing stages of the play (the *exodos*). The *parabasis*, too, when the chorus 'comes forward' to address the audience, commonly consists of a mixture of sung lyric passages and recitative – a kind of 'cantata', to borrow another term from the realm of classical music.[1] Such lengthy musical passages are the exception rather than the rule, however, and the majority of Aristophanes' songs are short, written to punctuate the spoken parts of the play rather than to steal the show.

The focus of this chapter is on these shorter lyrical passages rather than larger set-pieces such as the *parabasis*. The terms 'lyric', 'song' and 'lyrical passage' will be used interchangeably to indicate the same phenomenon: namely, any set of lines in the plays that would have been sung rather than spoken, with the term 'ode' used to indicate a song sung by just one party (usually the chorus). In fact, determining exactly which lines were sung, which delivered in recitative and which spoken is not always straightforward but, as we shall see in the next section, locating passages which can be classified as 'songs' is generally unproblematic.

8. Waxing Lyrical: Aristophanes the Songwriter

The purpose of this chapter, then, will be to look at a range of lyrical passages found in Aristophanes' plays – from the ordinary to the exotic, the bawdy to the highfalutin', the good to the bad – in order to gain an impression of what these songs add to his plays and where Aristophanes' strengths and weaknesses as a lyricist lie. Examples will be drawn from across the plays and different ways of viewing, categorizing and understanding Aristophanes' songs will be considered in turn. Lyrical passages are by no means simple to get to grips with – but this chapter will at least suggest ways some starting points.

A note here on translation. Not all translators rise to the challenge of translating Aristophanes' songs into anything approaching lyrical form. This is, I think, a perfectly understandable choice on the part of translators who may – quite reasonably – aim to convey the meaning of the words rather than the 'feel' of a lyrical passage (which is often both hard to pin down and far from easy to put across). Some translators *do* attempt verse – sometimes even rhyme – but regardless of the translator's inclination and abilities one common practice is to set songs out as poetry rather than continuous prose: in that way, the Greekless reader is usually able to spot where a lyric passage occurs in the original text. Such translations of lyrics as I have attempted in this chapter follow the same convention: that is to say they are likewise set out as poetry. In addition, I have generally tried to convey some of the rhythm and poetic 'feel' of the Greek (elements like alliteration, rhyme and the like). In two places I have also made use of pre-existing translations by scholars who have, in my view, conveyed the meaning and feel of a passage particularly well.

Greek verse

As students of the Greek language will know, Greek poetry works on very different principles from most English-language poetry. In this section I offer a brief introduction to the rhythms of Greek verse for the novice. The concepts introduced here will be met again in later discussions of Aristophanes' lyrics, but for those who already have a sound understanding of Greek verse, this section will contain little that is unfamiliar. It should be noted that for the purposes of this discussion, song lyrics are conceived of simply as poetry that is sung.

Before getting to grips with Greek verse itself, it will be useful to look briefly at some key characteristics of English poetry. The most important point to make is that the bulk of English-language poetry displays some kind of identifiable rhythm. Ordinarily, this comes from the positioning of stressed syllables in a sentence. Take the following poem, for example, from William Blake's *Songs of Innocence and Experience*, with the stressed syllables marked:

My móther groáned, my fáther wépt

Ínto the dángerous wórld I leápt
Hélpless, náked píping loúd,
Líke a fiénd hid ín a cloúd.

William Blake, *Infant Joy*

If we wanted to reproduce the rhythm of these lines (with no reference to the words), we could write them out as follows, using 'tum' to represent a stressed syllable, and 'ti' an unstressed syllable:

ti-tum-ti-tum-ti-tum-ti-tum
tum-ti-ti-tum-ti-ti-tum-ti-tum ..., etc.

Like much (but by no means all) English verse, this poem makes use not just of rhythm but also end-line rhyme (here a simple AA BB pattern: wept – leapt; loud – cloud). Of course, rhythms and rhyme-patterns are often far more complex than in Blake's *Infant Joy*, but the point still stands that the rhythm provided by stressed syllables and patterns produced by rhyme are the building blocks of most English poetry – and, by extension, song lyrics, too.

The situation for Greek poetry is somewhat different. First, Greek poetry seldom makes use of rhyme (and when it is used it tends to be found in 'low' verse such as drinking songs rather than in more elevated poetry). Second – and more crucially still – the way that Ancient Greek was pronounced did *not* involve the stressing of syllables: instead, the poetic rhythms of Greek verse are based on what is known as 'quantity'. In a similar way to how native English-speakers intuitively take account of where the stress falls in a given word, Greeks intuitively categorized syllables as 'heavy' or 'light' according to whether a syllable takes a relatively long or a relatively short time to say. When modern scholars write out the rhythm of a line of verse, heavy syllables (often simply called 'long') are marked as '–'; light syllables (often simply called 'short') are marked as '∪'. So to recap, both English and Greek poetry make use of rhythm, the difference being that one relies on the stressing of syllables, the other on the syllables' 'quantity', i.e. heavy or light. For the purposes of conceptualizing Greek metre, it can be useful to think of heavy and light syllables respectively as roughly equivalent to the stressed 'tum' and unstressed 'ti' I used earlier to represent the rhythmical pattern of *Infant Joy*.

In the ancient Greek tradition different poetic metres are created by arranging heavy and light syllables in different patterns. For example, the rhythm of two similar meters called 'glyconic' and 'pherecratean' can be written out as follows. Note that a position in the line where *either* a heavy *or* a short syllable is possible is marked by 'x':

glyconic: – x – ∪ ∪ – ∪ –   (i.e. tum-ta-tum-ti-ti-tum-ti-tum)
pherecratean: – x – ∪ ∪ – –   (i.e. tum-ta-tum-ti-ti-tum-tum)

These two metres are found in together in a lyric from *Knights* (973-84:

discussed more fully below). Here are the first four lines of the ode with the Greek transliterated, syllable divisions marked, and heavy ('long') syllables shown in bold:

hê-dis-ton fa-os hê-mer-as   (glyconic: tum-tum-tum-ti-ti-tum-ti-tum)
es-tai tois te par-ou-si   (pherecratean: tum-tum-tum-ti-ti-tum-tum)
tois-in eis-aph-ik-nou-men-os (glyconic: tum-ti-tum-ti-ti-tum-ti-tum)
ên Kle-ôn a-pol-ê-tai   (pherecratean: tum-ti-tum-ti-ti-tum-tum)

(For a translation of these lines – albeit one which reflects the meaning of the Greek better than its metrical structure – see p. 153 below.)

Other lyric metres are based on far simpler patterns of heavy and light syllables than those found in this ode, however. Common building blocks include the anapaest ($\cup\cup-$, ti-ti-tum), iamb ($x-\cup-$, ta-tum-ti-tum), trochee ($-\cup-x$, tum-ti-tum-ta) and dactyl ($-\cup\cup$, tum-ti-ti). Some rhythms have strong associations with certain kinds of subject matter. Perhaps the best example of this is the dactyl: this is the rhythm found in epic poems such as the *Iliad* and *Odyssey* and so a song written in dactyls might reasonably be expected to deal with elevated subject matter and therefore be lofty in tone.

But why bother to study these metrical patterns in the first place? The primary answer is that, because the tunes that would have accompanied lyrical passages are lost to us, establishing the metre of his songs is the closest we can get to reconstructing the music of Aristophanes' plays. Something of a poor substitute admittedly. What a knowledge of metres and rhythms also allows us to do is to establish when a metrical pattern – and therefore presumably a tune – was repeated in a play (and as we shall see, odes are often found in pairs in Aristophanes). Further, by looking at the metre in which a song is composed we can make informed judgements as to whether Aristophanes was striving for a given effect – it makes a difference, for example, whether Aristophanes has chosen to compose a song in lofty dactyls, for example, rather than, say, glyconics and phere-crateans, which probably had a more popular feel.[2]

Before leaving the subject of Greek verse, one final point ought to be made clear, namely that Aristophanes' plays were written *entirely* in poetic metre. However, the non-sung parts of comedy are generally easy to distinguish from the sung parts (and recitative) since the majority of spoken lines are composed in a metre called iambic trimeter (i.e. three iambs $(x-\cup-)$ per line: ta-tum-ti-tum-ta-tum-ti-tum-ta-tum-ti-tum). This metre, according to Aristotle, approximated the rhythms of everyday speech more closely than any other verse form (*Poetics* 1449a24-5).

Naturally the subject of Greek verse is far more complex than has been outlined here. Nevertheless, this brief introduction should allow us to consider – at least on a basic level – some of the ways in which Aristophanes uses rhythm in his lyrics. In the following discussion, we shall be considering a whole range of songs from a number of different viewpoints.

More often than not, Aristophanes' songs are sung by the choruses of his plays (choral odes), but we shall also look at songs sung by individual characters (monodies) and, first, at duets (which most often consist of a character interacting with the chorus).

Aristophanes' simple lyrics

In her 1997 book, *The Songs of Aristophanes*, Laetitia Parker makes the following comment about Aristophanic lyric:[3]

> A proportion of Aristophanes' song is of virtually no poetic significance. It is in lyric metre because the genre requires it, because that is how choruses express themselves, because lyric metre and song confer of themselves a certain impetus and heightening of excitement.

This far from flattering judgement on Aristophanes' abilities as a lyricist is perhaps a little harsh, but Parker nevertheless makes an important point here – anyone coming to Aristophanes expecting to find an endless supply of engaging lyric poetry will be sorely disappointed. This is not to say that Aristophanic lyric does not have its high points, however, nor that the texture and variety that his odes (with their accompanying music and dance) bring to the plays, plus their ability to create 'impetus and heightening of excitement', are not hugely important to Aristophanic theatre. However, an appreciation of Aristophanes' lyrics, the heights they can scale and the role they play in his dramas, is best reached by starting with an example of one of his more ordinary songs.

In their simplest form, Aristophanes' lyrics can amount to no more than a few lines of spontaneous song, punctuating the spoken lines of a play. A fairly typical example is the following short duet sung during the dispute between the chorus of *Acharnians* and Dicaeopolis about his private peace treaty with Sparta. Dicaeopolis has recently produced a basket of coals that he threatens to slaughter if the chorus members do not surrender their weapons and hear him out – the 'comic logic' being (as explained in Chapter 4) that since the chorus' native deme, Acharnae, is famous for its charcoal, it would be just as sorry to see the slaughter of coals (*anthrakôn:* line 332) as it would the slaughter of people (*anthrôpôn*).

Dicaeopolis:	Yes, kill I will. Scream away – for I'll not listen.
Chorus:	You can't mean that you'd kill my charcoal-friend?
Dicaeopolis:	Did you lot not hear what I said just now?
Chorus:	Well then, tell us whatever
	You like right now,
	Like how come it is
	You like Spartans.
	For I'll never betray
	This charcoal basket.

Acharnians 335-40

146

This short sequence (only half of which is quoted here) could hardly be less remarkable. For example, aside from the coinage 'charcoal-friend' (*phil-athrakês*), the vocabulary consists purely of everyday words and the duet is even relatively unadventurous rhythmically (although, that said, some interest is provided by the contrast between Dicaeopolis' steady trochees ($- \cup - $ x) and the chorus' anapaests ($\cup \cup -$) and cretics ($- \cup -$), perhaps conveying the former's relative calmness). Another feature that helps in a small way to lift the lyric out of the ordinary is some faint alliteration in the chorus' short ode (mimicked in translation here primarily by the repetition of 'like'). For a reader in translation, though, this duet will inevitably lack excitement since the alliteration and rhythms of the original cannot be experienced. However, this makes it all the more important to bear in mind the way in which songs would routinely have been something of a highpoint for the audience – and in the case of this particular lyric, the accompanying music and dance would certainly have helped to mark a point of huge *dramatic* interest in the play: the moment at which the chorus begins to listen to what Dicaeopolis has to say.

Two duets: *Acharnians* and *Peace*

A slightly more adventurous lyric from *Acharnians* comes from towards the end of the play. At this point in the action Dicaeopolis is enjoying the benefits of his private peace treaty, in contrast with other characters who are still suffering the consequences of the war. Perhaps the most notable benefit that Dicaeopolis is now able to enjoy is food – and it is following mentions of cooked hare and the promise of roasted thrushes that the chorus bursts into song:

Chorus:	I envy you your good policy
	Or rather your resplendent tea,
	That I see in front of me.
Dicaepolis:	Why! That's nothing to the delicacy
	To come – hot roasted thrushes!
Chorus:	I daresay you're right about *that*.
Dicaeopolis:	Someone stir up the ashes!
Chorus:	Did you hear how wonderfully cheffishly
	And professionally and connoisseurishly
	He does it all himself?

Acharnians 1008-16

Immediately following this song a farmer, Dercetes, comes along and the mode of delivery in the play reverts to speech. Dercetes begs to be allowed to share the benefits of peace: Dicaeopolis refuses, however, and the farmer departs, eliciting another metrically identical duet between the chorus and Dicaeopolis. When songs are paired in this way, the first song is called the *strophê*, the second song the *antistrophê* (these terms mean 'turning' and 'turning back' and owe their origin to the dancing that would have accompanied the singing).

Chorus:	The man has found sweet pleasure,
	And since he treasures his treaty
	Doesn't care to share it.
Dicaeopolis:	Souse the sausage with honey!
	Cook the cuttlefish!
Chorus:	Did you hear his boasts?
Dicaeopolis:	Go roast the eels!
Chorus:	You'll kill my mates and me with
	The smell – oh, I'm so hungry! – if
	You yell things like that.

Acharnians 1037-45

This second song is followed by a sequence similar to the Dercetes episode. This time, a pair of newlyweds comes along wanting a share of peace, but whereas the groom is refused, the bride gains her wish since, as Dicaepolis says, 'she is a woman and not responsible for the war' (*Acharnians* 1062).

This sequence of short episode + *strophê* + short episode + *antistrophê* is typical of many in Aristophanes' plays.[4] As here, the two short songs are either roughly the same or identical metrically and the short episodes are likewise of a similar or identical length (the Dercetes episode lasts from line 1018 to 1036 of the play, the newlyweds episode from line 1048 to 1066). Also typical is the way in which the scenes framed by these odes both display strong similarities and important differences (here, characters beg to share the benefits of peace in both episodes: in the former the request is refused, whereas in the latter there is limited success). Songs like these evidently play an important role in adding structure, texture and variety to Aristophanes' plays.

But what of the wording and tone of these two lyrical interludes? They are far from elevated with their mentions of 'thrushes' and 'eels', not to mention their use of rhyme and alliteration – which is present in the Greek, too, and not a feature one would expect to find in, say, an ode in tragedy (at least not to any great extent). Their jocular word play, too, adds vigour – 'cheffishly', 'connoisseurishly' – but this jocularity once again separates these lyrics from the world of tragedy and high poetry. But not *in spite of* – rather, I think, *because of* – their worldliness, these odes exercise huge appeal and even recall moments in modern musical theatre when characters also take to song in seemingly spontaneous outbursts of uplifting emotion.

The hills are alive with the sound of music ...
'The Sound of Music' from *The Sound of Music*;
lyrics: Oscar Hammerstein II

8. Waxing Lyrical: Aristophanes the Songwriter

I could have danced all night,
I could have danced all night,
And still have begged for more.

'I Could Have Danced All Night' from
My Fair Lady; lyrics: Alan Jay Lerner

The worldly detail, too, consisting as it does of nice things to eat, may even recall the cosy items listed in a song like *My Favourite Things*.

Raindrops on roses and whiskers on kittens,
Bright copper kettles and warm woollen mittens,
Brown paper packages tied up with string:
These are a few of my favourite things.

'My Favourite Things' from *The Sound of Music*;
lyrics: Oscar Hammerstein II

But whilst there may be similarities between the *Acharnians* duets and these songs from modern musicals, the differences are nevertheless stark. The lyrical exchanges between Dicaeopolis and the chorus are short-lived bursts of song, not big musical numbers, and their lyrics are closely linked with the ongoing stage business of the play – they do not mark a pause in the action, but rather the roasting and sousing is going on as the song is being sung. Odes like this grow organically out of the action and are very much rooted in the here and now.

A further example of a pair of short songs lending structure to an episode is to be found at *Peace* 459-69 and 486-96. The following disarmingly simple lyrics are sung by Trygaeus and the chorus members as they try, unsuccessfully, to pull the goddess Peace from the cave in which she is buried.

Chorus:	Heave-a-ho!
	Heave it is!
	Heave-a-ho!
	Heave it again!
	Heave-a-ho! Heave-a-ho!
Trygaeus:	Hey! The men aren't all pulling equally.
	[*To a section of the chorus*]
	Won't you give it a go? What egos you have!
	You Boeotians had better watch your backs!
Chorus Leader:	Heave it now!
Chorus:	Heave-a-ho!
	[*To Trygaeus and Hermes*]
	Come along, you two, help us haul her up, too.
Trygaeus:	I'm heaving and hauling and dragging the rope,
	And getting stuck in, and giving it gumption.
Chorus:	Then – why's – the – job – not – done – yet?

Peace 459-69

Simple as this song is, it nevertheless displays some interesting features, not least metrically. The underlying rhythmical unit of much of this passage is the anapaest ($\cup\;\cup$ –) but Aristophanes has Trygaeus sing almost wholly in spondees (– –): that is a constant stream of heavy ('long') syllables mirroring, perhaps, his weighty tugs on the rope. The chorus, on the other hand, uses far more light ('short') syllables – until the final line, that is, when they, too, sing wholly in spondees, 'Then – why's – the – job – not – done – yet?': *pôs oun ou chô-rei tour-gon* (– – – – – – –).

This short duet is a precursor to another song occurring eighteen lines later which corresponds metrically (the technical term for this is 'responsion'). This second lyric marks another attempt to haul Peace from the cave, which again ends in failure.

Chorus:	Heave-a-ho!
	Heave it is!
	Heave-a-ho!
	Heave, by Zeus!
	It's hardly budged an inch!
Trygaeus:	Well, some are putting their backs into it,
	But others are slacking – isn't it sad?
	...
Chorus:	There're – some – who're – just – not – with – us.

Peace 486-99

This second song (the *antistrophê*) shares the same characteristic of the earlier song (the *strophê*) in that Trygaeus sings mainly in weighty spondees. This rhythm is again picked up by the chorus in the final line, 'There're – some – who're – just – not – with – us': *all' eis' hoi kô-lu-ou-sin* (– – – – – – –).

This pair of odes may lack the humour and word play of the *Acharnians* passages, but they still neatly exhibit some of the same characteristics: once more they provide structure and texture to the episode in which they occur; once they are more closely linked to the action of the play (the heaving, hauling and slacking are taking place as the words are being sung); and once more the language used is far from elevated. The discussion of the *Peace* songs also helps to demonstrate, on a very basic level, the kind of effects that Aristophanes can achieve through rhythm. In this instance, the fact that the chorus eventually picks up Trygaeus' rhythm, the spondee (– –), suggests that its members are increasingly uniting behind him – and, in performance, their weighty syllables may even have been accompanied by longer, more deliberate pulls on the ropes.

Three choral odes from *Lysistrata*

So far we have looked at duets in the plays, but in this section the focus will be on three lyrics from *Lysistrata* sung entirely by the chorus. Choral odes such as these essentially form a continuum with duets since they share the same metrical variety, ability to structure episodes, and so on. Nevertheless, examination of these odes will allow us to observe an important way in which songs can vary in terms of their relationship to the play's dramatic action.

The following lyric from *Lysistrata* forms part of a group of four songs that come towards the end of that play. Here we meet a set of features we have seen before – mention of everyday food items and the presence of humour, for example – in addition to two further important ingredients that Aristophanes sometimes uses to flavour his unelevated lyrics: namely *obscenity*, in the form of a *double entendre* ('pork'), and *topicality*, in the form of a reference to allied troops from the Euboean town of Carystus who were stationed in Athens at the time of the play's production in 411 BC.

> We're going to entertain
> Some visitors from Carystus –
> Real gents they are.
> There's some pea-soup; and
> If they're the kind of men who like a nice bit of pork
> They can have some lovely stuff spit-roasted on a skewer.
> So come along to mine today; have your wash first –
> Do it nice and early, both you and the kids –
> Then walk right in,
> No need to ask,
> Bold as brass:
> Do just as you would at home,
> 'Coz my door – will be *shut fast!*

Lysistrata 1058-70

The joke here could hardly be more lame – 'you can have what you like, only – *it's not on offer!*' – but nevertheless Aristophanes sees fit to repeat it four times in metrically corresponding odes (*Lysistrata* 1043-57; here at 1058-70; then again at 1188-1202 and 1203-15). As with all sets of songs (be they a pair like the *Acharnians* and *Peace* examples, or like here, a set of two pairs) the subject matter, register and tone of each of the odes is always similar – indeed, these four humorous songs in *Lysistrata* even share the same basic punch line (see Chapter 4, p. 70). Unlike the paired songs from *Acharnians* and *Peace*, however, the two lyrical interludes created by these songs introduce very *different* episodes in the play: the first set comes just before the scene when Lysistrata persuades the Athenians and Spartans to make peace, whereas the second set precedes the drunken celebrations. Here, then, is another use to which songs are put by Aristophanes: to mark a break in the action. A further point of interest is that these *Lysistrata* odes have little or no bearing to the ongoing action of the play and contain no mention of its characters or events. In short, they are essentially *detachable* from the play (and as such once more stand in contrast to the various duets from *Acharnians* and *Peace*).

Lyrics, then, can differ hugely as to extent to which they integrated with, or detachable from, their play. The choral songs of *Lysistrata* run the gamut in this respect. On the one hand there is the fully-integrated entry song of the chorus of old men:

> Why, Strymodorus! Who would ever have expected to hear
> That women ... had seized my Acropolis ...
>
> *Lysistrata* 256-65

This ode's engagement with the here and now is clearly demonstrated by the use of a chorus member's name and mention of the Acropolis' occupation (which is under way as they sing). On the other hand, there is the largely detachable song of the men's chorus about the 'Black Hunter', Melanion, and his loathing of women:

> I want to tell you a story that once I heard
> When still a boy.
> There was a young man called Melanion who,
> Fleeing wedlock, came to the wilds and
> Lived in the mountains.
> And he had a dog
> And hunted hares
> And weaved his nets
> And never ever went back home
> All because of his hatred.
> That's how much he did loathe women:
> And we've got sense, too,
> And hate them no less.
>
> *Lysistrata* 781-96

Arguably, this song could be sung by *any* misogynistic chorus at *any* appropriate juncture in a play (and a similar thing could be said of the corresponding anti-male song sung by the man-hating female chorus at lines 805-20). However, it should also be noted that in a play where men are pitted against women the ode's thematic relevance is more than apparent – unlike the 'visitors from Carystus' ode quoted above (*Lysistrata* 1058-70). So, detachability and integration are, then, two important respects in which lyrics of all kinds – choral odes, monodies *and* duets – vary between themselves; but in addition, detachable lyrics can also vary as to their relevance to the ongoing action and, indeed, to the themes of the play as a whole.

Abusive songs: *Knights, Frogs* and *Acharnians*

As the Melanion ode (quoted above) may serve to remind us, some of the more prominent lyric passages in Aristophanes' plays are those which contain abuse. Whilst insulting odes are scattered throughout the plays, the *parabasis* is no doubt the most common place where songs of invective are found, their most frequent targets being prominent citizens and rival playwrights (in Chapter 1 we met some mild abuse of comic playwrights, for example, from the *parabases* of *Wasps* and *Clouds*). Certainly, lyrics of this type vary not just in their targets but, more importantly, in their tone, register and degree of savageness. At the restrained end of the spectrum, for example, comes a lyrical attack on Cleon, the rhythms of which have already been discussed earlier at the beginning of this chapter:

> Most pleasant will be the light of day
> For those who dwell here
> And those who come here
> Should Cleon be destroyed.
> That said, I heard some older men
> Of the most vexatious kind
> Suggesting in the place
> Where justice is bought and sold
> That if he weren't the city's biggest
> Fish, we all would lose
> Our two most useful tools:
> A pestle and a spoon.
>
> *Knights* 973-84

This jaunty ode is sung by the chorus of *Knights* and marks the only mention of Cleon's name in the whole play (in the rest of the play he is attacked in the guise of 'Paphlagon'). The chorus sings of its wish for Cleon to be destroyed and sarcastically suggests the way he 'benefits' Athens: as a pestle to mash up the city's affairs and as a spoon to stir Athens into confusion.

What makes this ode particularly interesting is the way it combines high and low elements. The rhythms (glyconics, $-$ x $-$ ∪ ∪ $-$ ∪ $-$, and pherecrateans, $-$ x $-$ ∪ ∪ $-$ $-$) are not uncharacteristic of drinking songs, for example, and it has been suggested more than once that Aristophanes might have hoped that this song would catch on and come to haunt his adversary outside the theatre:[5] certainly it displays the characteristic of detachability, making it a perfect candidate for recitation at a symposium (drinking party), for instance. The mention of a living person's name (Cleon), lawsuits (here 'justice') and everyday items (the pestle and spoon) are also elements alien to elevated poetry – as is the sarcasm of the closing lines. However, taken as a whole the expression is somewhat restrained: there is no obscenity here, no mentions of food and even the humour is wry rather than ribald. What is more, this ode also contains hints of elevated expression: most notably the opening line, 'Most pleasant will be the light of day', which has an unmistakable tragic ring to it (indeed, the scholiast even claims that it is a Euripidean quotation). We will look more closely at this blend of high and low elements later.

153

Few of Aristophanes' lyrical invectives display the kind of restraint noted in the *Knights* ode, however. A far more scurrilous example comes from the *parabasis* section of *Frogs* shortly after the arrival of Xanthias and Dionysus in the Underworld (where the play is mostly set). Here the chorus' targets are a politician, Archedemus; the much-maligned Cleisthenes (who, as we saw in Chapter 4, was ridiculed for being effeminate); and an extravagant spend-thrift, Callias. The chorus addresses the audience, singing:

> Would you like us all to make fun of Archedemus
> Who still hadn't grown Athenian teeth at the age of seven?
> Now he's rabble-rousing up amongst the dead
> And has reached pole position as far as villainy is concerned.
> And I hear that Cleisthenes' arsehole was in the graveyard, too,
> Mourning his master in a womanly way, tearing at his cheeks.
> And he was bent over and beating his head and weeping and wailing
> Looking out for Mr. Roger M. E. Senseless – whoever that is.[6]
> And they say that good old Callias, son of Horsecock,[7]
> Was battling away at sea, dressed in a lion-skin made of – *cunt!*[8]
>
> *Frogs* 416-30

The exact meaning of these attacks is not fully understood: Archedemus' credentials as a true-born Athenian are evidently being questioned (the suggestion is that he was not registered as a member of his father's tribe until suspiciously late in life); Cleisthenes is being maligned for his passive homosexuality (as elsewhere in Aristophanes' plays), but the significance of the comments about Callias are simply lost in the mists of time.[9] However, where we can be more confident is about the tone of this lyric: here topicality, the naming of individuals, colloquialism, obscenity and even the run of the mill iambic metre serve to establish the tone as low in the extreme – there are no hints of tragic phrasing here!

These two songs neatly represent the extremes of Aristophanes' lyrical invective: on the one hand there can be elevation, restraint and a subtlety in the way in which the target is undermined ('A pestle and a spoon'); on the other, Aristophanes can adopt a no-holds-barred approach where his overriding concern seems to be scurrilous abuse. A further point to note is that lyrics of invective tend to display the characteristic of detachability – either of these songs could be sung in a different context (and in the case of the *Knights* ode, this may even have been the intention). That said, the *Knights* ode does have strong thematic links to the rest of the play: its target is Cleon (who is pilloried throughout *Knights* in the character of Paphlagon) and the capacity of politicians to mash and stir is no more evident than in the occupation of Paphlagon's main rival for political power, the Sausage Seller, whose job – involving as it does mashing and stirring low grade meat and offal – supposedly makes him so suitable as a leader of men. Passing references to the dead aside, the *Frogs* lyric shows no such thematic resonance with the rest of the play.

154

8. Waxing Lyrical: Aristophanes the Songwriter

Elevated lyrics: religious songs and high lyrical pastiche

So far we have mainly been looking at songs from the tonally low end of the spectrum with lyrics full of topical allusions, everyday detail, obscenity, and so on. But as well as maintaining tonal neutrality in his lyrics (as is arguably the case in the Melanion ode from *Lysistrata*) or giving them splashes of tragic colour (as in the *Knights* song), Aristophanes is also capable of producing songs whose subject matter and language is far from informal. Perhaps the most straightforward examples of elevated lyrics are to be found amongst the religious songs in which his plays abound. The following, for instance, is part of the song that the chorus of *Women at the Thesmophoria* sings as it dances in honour of various goddesses:

> Step forward as you sing and praise
> Artemis, mistress of the lyre,
> Archeress and virgin queen ...
> And let us hymn, as hymn we should,
> Hera, goddess of the marriage bed,
> Who sports with us in all our dances
> And holds the keys of wedlock.
>
> *Women at the Thesmophoria* 969-76

The chorus of *Knights* also sings hymns to Poseidon and Athena:

> Lord Poseidon, god of horses, whom
> The clatter of bronze-shod horses
> Doth please ...
>
> *Knights* 551-3

> Pallas, guardian of the city, o
> Sovereign of the holiest of
> All lands ...
>
> *Knights* 581-5

In a similar vein we find the Spartan's song from the end of *Lysistrata*, full of local detail: there is mention of Sparta's Mount Taÿgetum; its township of Amyclae; its bronze temple of Athena; its mythical founder, Tyndareus, and its river, Eurotas:

> Leave your home on Taÿgetum once again,
> My Spartan Muse, and in befitting way,
> Help celebrate Amyclae's god
> And brazen-housed Athena
> And those who tread Eurotas' banks –
> Tyndareus' noble sons.
>
> *Lysistrata* 1296-1301

155

Aristophanes' religious songs have received remarkably little attention from scholars, the principal reason being, no doubt, that they contain little out of the ordinary worthy of comment: they are conventional in the extreme. Gods receive their traditional epithets – as is conventional; and are given appropriate praise – as is conventional. In the *Women at the Thesmophoria* passage, for example, Artemis is 'mistress of the lyre', 'archeress' and 'virgin', whereas Hera is 'goddess of the marriage bed' and appropriate epithets are similarly evoked in the *Knights* lyric. Likewise, in the *Lysistrata* lyric mention of Sparta elicits references to the city's most famous features: its highest mountain range, its river and its mythical founder. These songs may well hold a certain charm, but few surprises.

Certainly, religious songs serve important functions. They can underline the solemn nature of cult proceedings, for instance, as is the case with the lyric from *Women at the Thesmophoria*; or they can help to characterize the chorus members of *Knights* as good citizens through their connections with the two gods of Athens' ancient Acropolis, Athena and Poseidon; or they can help to mark highpoints as is the case with this upbeat hymn at the end of *Lysistrata*, where during the peace celebrations Athens' and Sparta's shared worship of Athena is also brought to the fore. Similarly a wedding hymn can add excitement and a sense of occasion to a play's finale (as in *Peace* or *Birds*). However, for all the thematic and dramatic relevance of these lyrics – and for all the opportunity they provide for music and dance – they are nonetheless fairly unexceptional as lyrics go: the fact that they are *tonally* high does not make them high *quality*.

What these religious lyrics amount to are well executed pastiches:[10] Aristophanes takes the traditional building blocks of devotional lyric – its heightened vocabulary and phrasing, conventional epithets, and so on – and reproduces perfectly competent (if essentially unoriginal) versions of his own at appropriate junctures in his plays. And importantly, this tendency of Aristophanes to produce well judged pastiche (rather than poetry of substance and resonance) carries over into his other attempts at tonally high lyric, too.

The deficiencies of Aristophanes' more elevated odes were originally pointed out by Michael Silk in 'Aristophanes as a Lyric Poet'.[11] In this influential article, Silk undertakes a detailed evaluation of a number of songs from the plays with the intention of highlighting what he regards as Aristophanes' strengths and weaknesses as a lyricist. One of the odes he subjects to close analysis is the *parodos* of *Clouds*.[12] Both *strophê* (quoted here below) and *antistrophê* are sung by the chorus of Clouds offstage, as Socrates and Strepsiades listen:[13]

We Clouds ever floating in the blue,
Lift we up our dewy essence, airy-bright, for all to view,
Let us rise from father Ocean with his hoarsely-booming roar,
Till we reach the lofty hill-tops, forest-clad for evermore.

Thence gaze we on the peaks far seen across the plain,
And on holy Earth refreshing her crops of golden grain,
And the bright majestic Rivers, ever singing in their glee,
And the hoarsely-sounding murmur of the everlasting sea.
For the never-resting Eye of Ether in the sky
Is shining mid the dazzle of its rays;
Let us shake the misty showers from these deathless forms of ours,
And sail upward on the wide world to gaze.

Clouds 275-90; transl. Rogers

As Silk points out, this song has woven something of a spell on scholars in the past and has even been called 'one of the most beautiful lyric passages of Attic literature'.[14] Perhaps this is understandable. After all, there is no doubting the fact that the lyric is impressive: its expression is elevated, the subject matter timeless rather than everyday and its metre (mainly dactyls, $- \cup \cup$) dignified (as mentioned earlier, dactyls are associated with epic poetry, such as Homer). What Silk's discussion highlights, however, is the ode's tendency to triteness and repetition. On the one hand, Aristophanes makes use of a string of conventional epithets: Ocean is 'father Ocean', hill-tops are 'lofty' and 'forest-clad', Earth is 'holy', and so on. On the other, we find 'hoarsely-booming' *and* 'hoarsely-sounding'; 'hill-tops' *and* 'peaks'; 'everlasting' *and* 'never-resting' *and* 'deathless'. This repetition and excess of predictable epithets suggest that Aristophanes is making doubly sure that his audience knows that this is 'serious', high-flown lyric; but as Silk says, this is not the same as it being great poetry.[15]

This is not to write off this *Clouds* lyric, however. The song serves a key dramatic purpose in that the Clouds need to come across as deities noble enough to impress not only the country bumpkin Strepsiades but also the sophisticated Socrates – and what better way to do this than by means of a tonally elevated, metrically dignified song? And as Silk points out, the very fact of an ode sung by a chorus of clouds is in itself highly original. Characteristically, then, Aristophanes shows an excellent instinct as a dramatist and real imagination in the way that this ode is conceived; but, also characteristically, when Aristophanes attempts high-style lyrics what he typically produces is little more than a competent pastiche packed full of conventional language and repetitions.[16]

Hybrid lyrics: *Acharnians*' phallic song

If Aristophanes' strengths as a lyricist do not lie in high-style lyric, then where do they lie? To a large extent, no doubt, in the domain of upbeat low lyrics, where he has an opportunity to display his relish for word-play and his infectious enthusiasm for life's pleasures and enjoying the moment. The paired duets from *Acharnians* (see above) are good examples of this type of uplifting song, where coinages, alliteration and rhyme lend Aristo-

157

phanes' lyrics real energy.[17] Many of Aristophanes' abusive songs are also attractive for their sheer vitality.

For Silk, however, Aristophanes' most notable achievement as a lyricist is in the creation of what he calls 'hybrid lyrics' or 'low lyrics *plus*', that is, songs which combine high and low elements. We have already met an example of an ode which blends high-flown and everyday language in the form of the Cleon ode from *Knights*.

> Most pleasant will be the light of day
> For those who dwell here
> And those who come here
> Should Cleon be destroyed.
> ...
> A pestle and a spoon.

Knights 973-84

Here, everyday detail (Athenian lawsuits) and topicality (Cleon) are wedded to tragic-sounding phrases ('Most pleasant will be the light of day') to create a type of lyric not found elsewhere in Greek literature. Silk himself waxes lyrical on this point, commenting that 'the vigour and the other positive attributes of the low, together with the formal elegance of the high ... offers an enlarged tonal and expressive range all round'.[18] According to Silk, then, these hybrid lyrics combine energy *and* elegance. What is more, the collision of two linguistic worlds – the high and the low – allows ideas to be expressed creatively and in novel ways. Importantly, too, high-flown language and phrasing can serve to raise the status of the everyday: in a hybrid lyric, Cleon and Athens' lawsuits acquire something of a timeless quality.

As Silk demonstrates, hybrid lyrics are characteristically sparing in their use of high-flown language (hence his term 'low lyrics *plus*') and, what is more, such high-sounding language as there is tends to occur at the beginning of the ode. The *Knights* ode follows this pattern closely, as does the following choral song from the *parabasis* of *Peace*, with its swipe at the tragic poet Carcinus and his dancer sons.[19]

> O Muse, thrust wars aside and dance
> With me, thy friend,
> Celebrating the weddings of gods, the banquets of men,
> And the festivities of the blest; for these have been thy chosen themes from the first.
> But if Carcinus comes
> And begs you to dance with his children,
> Do not listen to them nor go
> To aid them in their work,
> But regard them all as
> Home-bred quails, dwarfish dancers
> With hedgehogs' necks, snippets of dung-balls, hunters after gimmicks. ...

Peace 775-90; transl. Sommerstein

As with the *Knights* ode, an audience member hearing the opening phrase, complete with its address to a Muse, might justifiably expect a high-style lyric.[20] However, a surprise is in store as the song progresses: the elevated tone evaporates – and in this instance its place is taken by a series of insults directed at a fellow poet.

So far the examples of hybrid lyrics we have looked at have been songs of invective. Let us now look at a very different passage, however, one of Aristophanes' most discussed lyrics: the so-called Phallic Song from *Acharnians*. This extraordinary ode is sung by Dicaeopolis as he celebrates his own, personal Country Dionysia as his family look on, his return to his rural deme having been made possible by the private peace treaty he has made with Sparta.

> O Phales, comrade of Bacchus,
> Fellow-reveller, night-wanderer,
> Adulterer and pederast,
> After five full years I finally face you,
> Returning happily to my deme,
> Having made myself my private peace,
> Free from fights and from fusses
> And from Lamachusses.
> For it's far sweeter, O Phales, Phales,
> To find a blooming girl sneaking off with stolen wood –
> Strymodorus' Thratta from the Fell-land –
> And to catch her by the waist, raise her up,
> Cast her down, and de-pip her grape!
> O Phales, Phales,
> If you drink with us, for your hangover
> Come the morning you'll drain a draft of peace;
> And I'll hang my shield up in the ashes.

Acharnians 263-79

This ode is a full-blooded celebration of peace and the benefits it brings: a rural homecoming, wine and sex. The addressee is Phales, the personified Hard-On, who is immediately linked to comedy's patron deity, Dionysus. Unlike the epithets in the religious and high-style lyrics we met earlier, there is nothing clichéd about the tags Phales is given, each of which is more scurrilous and remarkable than the last: first 'fellow-reveller' (hardly a surprising epithet for a follower of Bacchus), then 'night-wanderer', (which perhaps *hints* at irrespectability), then the racy climax, 'adulterer' and 'pederast'. The image conjured up of 'a wild revelling-band wandering the streets at night in search of sexual opportunity'[21] stands in striking contrast to Dicaeopolis' current rural isolation (just as the sexual imagery of this passage is striking given the presence of his wife and daughter).

No sooner are Phales' scurrilous associations mentioned than the tone changes, and Dicaeopolis talks of his happy return to his deme with the highly alliterative phrase 'After five full years I finally face you' (*hectô s'etei proseipon eis ...*: lit. 'in this *sixth* year I address you ...').[22] With this line there also begins a dazzling combination of concrete specifics and elements of fantasy: the general Lamachus and the sixth year of the war are realities for the audience, whereas the private peace treaty, the return to the countryside and the release from troubles are fantasies that Aristophanes has created for his play.

Next, Phales is appealed to again (and by implication his associations with Dionysus and sexual wrongdoing evoked once more), and it is suggested that there is something even *more* sweet than the images of peace and freedom we have encountered: illicit sex. The discovery of a slave girl stealing wood provides a perfect opportunity for a man to indulge his sexual desires (and while a modern reader might be shocked at the sexual assault envisaged by Dicaeopolis here, issues of consent are hardly likely to have troubled an ancient male audience). The description of the assault, which Silk suggests is 'intensely physical in its effect',[23] culminates in the extraordinary coinage *katagigartisai*, translated here as 'de-pip her grape'. This word connects elements from throughout the ode – it is suggestive of wine, which is in turn suggestive of peace, Phales and, of course, the god who unites all these elements: Dionysus. The rich, allusive imagery, with its concreteness and physicality, continues in the last lines of the ode and themes and images important to the play are evoked once more– the sparks of the fire remind us of the charcoal-burning Acharnians, dawn reminds us of Dicaeopolis' lonely wait on the Pnyx at the beginning of the play and the overarching theme is again that of peace.

This song is certainly notable for its pace, conciseness, exuberance – and for the fact that it contains both tonally high and tonally low elements. At the high end come the ode's opening compound-epithets, 'fellow-reveller' and 'night-wanderer', which have an elevated feel, as does the phrase 'comrade of Bacchus'. At the low end we find the subject matter (sex and drinking), topical allusions, the presence of rhyme (reflected here in translation: 'fusses ... Lamachusses') and words such as 'adulterer', 'pederast' and 'hangover' (although it is interesting that – as in other hybrid odes – truly low elements such as obscenity are avoided). The combination of high and low is even reflected in the opening phrase, 'O Phales', which is repeated throughout the ode: an address to a god is characteristic of elevated lyric, but the associations of this particular 'god' are sexual, that is to say, very much *unelevated*.

Certainly not all of Aristophanes' hybrid lyrics are of the quality of the *Acharnians'* Phallic Song. Here, the best tendencies of this original mode are on show: energy *and* elegance; ideas expressed creatively in a novel way. And there are perhaps few better examples in Aristophanes of the raising of lowly themes to a higher plain. In this ode, carefree sex and drinking are effortlessly lifted to the level of the universal.

Confines of space do not allow for further discussion of 'low lyrics *plus*', but a brief examination of the other examples discussed by Silk is no doubt the best way to get to grips with these hybrid lyrics. These include: *Acharnians* 692-702 (the song of the Marathon fighters: quoted in Chapter 9, p. 175) and 971-99 (the chorus' song on the benefits of peace), *Peace* 582-600 (the chorus' hymn to Peace), *Birds* 227-59 (Tereus summoning the birds) and *Frogs* 209-23 (the 'brekekekex' frog chorus) and 814-29 (the introduction to the tragic contest).

Conclusions

This brief introduction to Aristophanic lyric can do no more than scratch the surface of this engaging and challenging topic. As with so many other aspects of Aristophanes' work, there are no neat ways of classifying his songs and so in this chapter I have simply aimed to cover some of the important ways in which lyrics differ from each other: detachability and integration, for example, high, low and hybrid – good and bad, even. Lyrical passages can often be offputting as they routinely employ conventions which are unfamiliar to the modern reader. What is more, the act of translating into English what is often complex Greek – rich in rhythms, alliteration and allusions – can often serve to make the text seem that much more unfathomable: what aspects of the original song has the translator included in their translation and which have they left out? With lyrics, perhaps more than with any other aspect of Aristophanes' work, we have to be careful to look at scholars' notes on the passages which interest us and – if we are studying the plays in English – to get used to looking at more than one translation.

Tracing the way in which Aristophanes' lyrics change over the course of his career is also a fascinating business. As we observed in Chapter 5, the most noticeable difference between his earlier and later plays is the fact that his last two surviving plays – the fourth-century comedies *Assemblywomen* and *Wealth* – have gaps in the manuscript where the choral odes would have been delivered, marked simply by *chorou* ('of the chorus'). The text of these odes has not been recorded – possibly because they were not even written by Aristophanes. Between *Frogs* (405 BC) and *Assemblywomen* (392/1? BC), then, a major sea change occurred in comedy: in imitation of tragedy, these plays developed formal choral odes marking pauses in the action. What is just as interesting, though, is that whilst the number of sung lines fluctuates from play to play, there is nothing to suggest that song became any less important to comedy as time went on (if anything the number of sung lines in each increases ever so slightly towards the end of the fifth century).[24] To be sure, the kind of songs Aristophanes wrote does change in character (in the later fifth-century plays there is more and more parody of tragedy and of new musical movements, for instance),[25] but song remained as central as ever to the Aristophanic experience. They may well be challenging, but the songs of Old Comedy cannot be ignored.

9

Getting the Message: Aristophanic Politics

Introduction

According to an ancient anecdote, when Dionysius I of Syracuse expressed a desire to find out about Athenian politics, Plato sent him a copy of Aristophanes' plays.[1] Whether true or not, this story reveals a view of Aristophanic comedy that we would no doubt be inclined to share: namely, that it is hugely revealing about public life in the ancient city of Athens. The personalities of Athens loom large in Aristophanes' plays, as do so many of the political debates and social issues that were evidently under discussion at the time. Indeed, the contemporary world is no mere back-drop in the plays – Aristophanes' main characters often express discontentment with the city in which they live and hatch plans to change it: they seek peace, or new leaders, or a redistribution of wealth, and so on. What is more, we also find Aristophanes making numerous claims in the plays to be offering the city good advice. In short, Aristophanic comedy is political to its core.

The exact manner in which both Aristophanes and his plays interact with the real world of Athens, however, has been the source of an enormous amount of scholarly debate. What picture of Aristophanes' own political and personal views emerges from the plays? What impact did Aristophanes seek to have or actually wield in the city of Athens? To what extent can Aristophanes' claims to educate and advise the city be taken 'seriously'? This chapter will look at some of the more significant factors to be taken into account when attempting to answer these questions and examine a number of Aristophanic passages key to the debate. The topics that will be considered in this chapter include: Aristophanes' portrayal of real-life figures; the general value system that emerges in his plays; passages in which specific political advice is offered; and the biases that Aristophanic comedy displays in its choice of targets. In addition, we shall look at the fit between the likely prejudices and expectations of the audience and the stances that we find adopted in the plays. Lastly in this chapter, we shall consider how Aristophanes' contemporaries viewed Old Comedy and, in particular, the extent to which they thought that the abuse, satire and political advice we find in comic drama had an impact outside the theatre.

To be clear from the outset, what this chapter does not provide is a simple series of clear-cut 'answers' to questions that are still the subject of

162

intense debate amongst scholars. The aim here is to provide an overview of the issues that the plays throw up and to allow readers to come to their own, informed opinions as to where the best answers and solutions lie. The principal plays discussed in this chapter will be *Acharnians*, *Knights*, *Lysistrata* and *Frogs*, with *Clouds*, *Wasps* and *Peace* also coming under scrutiny.

Introductory points: Athenian 'politics' and Aristophanes' personal views

There are some introductory points that need to be made before we go on to discuss Aristophanic politics in earnest. First, we need to take stock of what 'politics' and 'politician' mean in an ancient Athenian context. The nature of the radical democracy in fifth-century Athens meant that it was open to any citizen to attend and even address the assembly (*ekklêsia*). However, the number of men who took the opportunity to speak in public on a regular basis was relatively small – and it is these men who will be referred to as 'politicians' in this chapter. Unlike modern political figures, most of these men would have been private individuals with little or no *official* public role. Someone like Aristophanes' arch-rival Cleon (who features prominently in the discussion in this chapter) was therefore in the minority: for several years in the 420s he held office as a general (*stratêgos*), an influential annually elected post. The point should also be made that the *participatory* nature of Athens' democracy made it quite unlike modern *representative* democracies where professional politicians are voted for and then act on the electorate's behalf; indeed, the ability of every citizen to vote on proposals put forward in the assembly meant that it was often characterized by its critics as little short of mob rule. As we shall see, major political tensions existed in late fifth-century Athens between democrats, who were supporters of the city's radical democracy, and the more traditional elements in society who favoured rule by the social élite (an aristocracy) and/or the monied classes (an oligarchy).

A further important point to make at this stage is that the plays can only tell us a limited amount about what Aristophanes 'really' thought. Indeed, in this chapter, I shall shy away from making firm pronouncements about Aristophanes' own views on the world or intentions as an author since – in the absence of any independent evidence – these are impossible to ascertain with any real certainty. However, to make a subtle but important distinction, what we *can* talk about are the views on politics and people that we find expressed in the plays (which may or not have represented what the real-life Aristophanes 'really' thought himself). There is also a distinction to be made, of course, between the opinions expressed in the plays and how Aristophanes' audience would have reacted to them. How Aristophanes' contemporaries perceived the relationship between comedy and politics is a hugely interesting topic and will be considered towards the end of the chapter, but we should certainly be careful not to assume unquestioningly that Aristophanes actually achieved any political effect that he may have hoped to have had on his public. In any case, different members of the audience will no doubt have understood and reacted to the plays in different ways.

Personal abuse and caricature

The nature of Athenian democracy means that there is no hard and fast line to be drawn between what we in the modern world might think of as 'politics' and the affairs of the city-state (*polis*) more broadly defined. With this in mind, let us first look at perhaps the most prominent way in which Aristophanic comedy engages with the city of Athens, its abuse of real-life individuals, by looking at two examples of comic jibes: one aimed at a 'politician' proper, the other at someone who was *not* (as far as we know) active in the sphere of 'politics'.

The first insult is directed at Cleonymus (a political associate of Cleon's) who is regularly accused in Aristophanes' plays of having thrown away his shield in battle. The chorus of *Birds* sings:

> There is an extraordinary tree
> ... the Cleonymus
> Useful for nothing ... .
> In the spring it always
> Blossoms with false accusations,
> But in winter, quite the opposite occurs:
> It sheds a foliage – of shields!

Birds 1473-80

The second insult is made against Ariphrades (who may have been a comic poet).

> He maltreats his own tongue with shameful pleasures, licking the 'detestable dew' in brothels, staining his beard and stirring up the women's hearths ... Whoever does not detest such a man shall never drink out of the same cup as me.

Knights 1284-9

For many ancient scholars reading Aristophanes *after* the classical era, attacks like these on named individuals (*onomasti komoidein*, 'mocking by name') were the most striking feature of Aristophanes' plays.[2] In an attempt to explain why ancient Athenians tolerated such extensive personal abuse in comedy, later readers commonly supposed that it had a moral dimension: that is to say, the individuals attacked were generally presumed to be deserving targets.[3] Underpinning this belief is a further

164

assumption: namely, that attacks in comedy must reflect 'facts' about their targets – or at the very least views that were commonly held about them at the time. Working on this basis, one of the tasks that ancient scholars of Old Comedy set themselves was to compile biographical details of mocked individuals (*komodoumenoi*) in an attempt to discover what real-life behaviour had inspired the abuse in the plays.

It is interesting to consider the assumptions that this approach to Old Comedy entails: most notably that the individuals mocked were mostly guilty as charged – that Cleonymus really *did* throw away his shield, for example, and Ariphrades really *did* engage in cunnilingus with prostitutes – and that the exposure and discouragement of morally questionable behaviour was part of Aristophanes' job as a comic poet. When phrased in these terms, however, things start to look problematic. To be sure, Cleonymus *may* have thrown his shield away (indeed, a number of modern scholars have concluded that he probably did) – and, furthermore, many in Athens (including perhaps Aristophanes) *may* well have considered such behaviour reprehensible – but in point of fact an accusation in a comic play neither proves that Cleonymus was a shield-thrower (*rhipsapsis*) nor that everyone – or perhaps even *anyone* – thought that he deserved condemnation.[4] Indeed, in the case of Ariphrades, why should we assume that the allegations are true at all, let alone that this behaviour merited exposure on moral grounds?

Fact and fiction

This difficulty of establishing the 'truth' behind comic reputations is just one of the problems that confront us when we consider the political content of Aristophanes' comedies. On the one hand, we are often inclined to believe that allegations made about individuals had at least *some* basis in fact – the 'no smoke without fire' principle. Indeed, we often have independent confirmation that a 'fact' we learn about an individual in comedy is indeed true (Cleon's populist oratorical style is a good case in point: other sources, such as Thucydides, choose to portray him as a rabble-rouser, too). But on the other hand, some comic reputations clearly owe very little to reality indeed.

The case of Euripides demonstrates well the extent to which a comic reputation can be almost entirely fictional. Aristophanes' portrayal of him in *Acharnians*, for instance, is a wonderful comic caricature, but we are hardly tempted to take at face value the idea that Euripides composed plays surrounded by the costumes of his own characters or that he littered his everyday speech with tragic words and phrases (*Acharnians* 395-479). Similarly, we know that the portrayal of Socrates in *Clouds* is far from accurate. The real-life Socrates neither ran a school nor charged money nor taught science; but he *does* in this play, where the character 'Socrates' is probably best understood as representing 'philosophers' as a type. Here, it transpires that Aristophanes has bundled together a number of different intellectuals' beliefs and practices, added a liberal sprinkling of ridiculous, invented attributes (like an interest in gnat's intestines), and given the resulting package the name 'Socrates'. In short, Aristophanes' portrayal of Socrates in *Clouds* may well be highly effective as a caricature, but it is hardly a reliable portrait.[5]

Aristophanes' satirical targets

To take the discussion further, it will be helpful at this point to consider personal abuse from the perspective of a comic writer. How did Aristophanes choose his victims? Certainly it is plausible that personal animosity played a role here – but there are clearly more factors than this to bear in mind. For example, Aristophanes would no doubt have taken his audience's reaction into account, too. From this point of view, it may even have made sense to target someone who was unpopular in the city and/or who could easily be portrayed as morally bankrupt – indeed, in a proportion of cases ancient scholars may have been right to assume that Aristophanes' satirical targets did in fact deserve their abuse. Tradition and habit would also have been key factors: for instance, comic poets prior to Aristophanes had routinely targeted politicians and this was a tradition that Aristophanes upheld. What is more, if Aristophanes (or indeed another comic poet) made a successful joke about an individual, that joke might well bear repeating: Cleonymus, for example, is mocked no fewer than nine times in Aristophanes' eleven surviving plays for his alleged shield-throwing.

All this said, the largest single factor for a satirist like Aristophanes is most likely to be the need to find a target around which he can build an effective attack – an attack that is both biting and humorous. Aristophanes was no doubt inspired to choose his victims for a whole host of reasons: something they said, or did, their reputation, their physical appearance or even their name might have provided the spark of an idea. As a dramatist, he would then have developed his attack, adding fiction to fact when the situation suited. And so it is no doubt the case that some individuals, like Socrates for example, simply provided excellent raw material for satire. Whatever Aristophanes' views were about the man in real life, Socrates' unique brand of philosophizing, his striking physical appearance (many sources talk of his ugliness), and the fact that he – unlike so many of the other philosophers of the day – was a relatively well-known figure in Athens must surely have sealed his fate: that is to say, all these striking characteristics of the real-life Socrates taken together would have formed an excellent basis around which to build the mainly fictional character we find in *Clouds*.

9. Getting the Message: Aristophanic Politics

Mockery of politicians

Having considered the way in which real-life figures in general are attacked and satirized by Aristophanes, let us now turn to the portrayal of politicians in particular, many of whom are abused in the plays and some of whom even appear as characters. Ultimately, jibes against politicians provide the same difficulties as all of Aristophanes' personal abuse: that is, it is not always clear how much they owe to fact and how much to fiction.

When it comes to political mockery, however, one important point to bear in mind is that certain allegations are essentially standard. Amongst the charges routinely made against political figures in Old Comedy, for example, are that they are corrupt, that they are of foreign descent and also that they prostituted themselves in their youth. These are all allegations which, if proven to be true, would have had dire consequences for the men concerned – but the fact that they are repeated so often in respect of a whole range of politicians suggests that it would be unwise to take them at face value.[6] Indeed, one could even argue that it is only when specific, non-standard allegations are made that there is any reason to pursue the notion that they might have some basis in truth.

Cleon and Knights

Discussion of political targets brings us to the subject of Cleon, the individual who is attacked more extensively and more viciously than any other in Aristophanes. Cleon features as a satirical target in all five of the Aristophanic plays that date from the 420s, the last of which, *Peace*, was produced in 421 BC, shortly after Cleon's death. The dispute between Cleon and Aristophanes (or perhaps Callistratus, the producer of Aristophanes' early plays) has already been outlined in Chapter 1: this seems to have simmered for a number of years, presumably fuelled in no small part by Aristophanes' depiction of the politician in his plays. Here, for once, we appear to have a clear-cut case of personal animosity: someone targeted by Aristophanes because of a personal feud whose reputation our poet would have been keen to damage.[7] That might be so, but given that we have no independent means of knowing what Aristophanes' views about Cleon actually were, can we at least safely claim that Aristophanes' plays constitute a meaningful attack on this influential political figure?

The most sustained attack on Cleon comes in *Knights* (424 BC) where he appears in the thinly veiled guise of a Paphlagonian slave – a new arrival at the household of Demos ('The People') who manipulates his master in such a way as to profit at the expense of the other slaves. The play is essentially a fantastic allegory with the contemporary world of Athens lying just beneath its surface – not least the recent events at Pylos where Cleon had claimed a surprise military victory leading to the capture of around 120 Spartan citizens.[8] As we learn in *Knights*, Cleon was afforded certain public honours as a result of this action (such as maintenance at the state's expense and privileged seating at public spectacles: *Knights* 280-1, 702-4, 709, 766, 1404-5), whereas the efforts of Demosthenes, his fellow commander at Pylos, won no such recognition. In *Knights*, Demosthenes is portrayed as one of the slaves of Demos whose lives have been adversely affected by Paphlagon's arrival. In the prologue, for example, he complains:

> Paphlagon snatches whatever one of us has prepared and makes a gift of it to our master. Just the other day when I'd kneaded a Spartan barley cake in Pylos, he ran past me as brazenly as you like, snatched it up and served it up himself – the cake that *I* had kneaded!
>
> *Knights* 52-7

The plot of *Knights* initially concerns the search by Demosthenes and another slave (probably to be identified with the aristocratic politician, Nicias) for someone to take Paphlagon's place in Demos' affections, the comic logic of the play being that the only suitable candidate would be someone even *more* base, *more* low-born and *more* shameless than Paphlagon. The arrival of a Sausage-Seller provides them with the ideal candidate – although in the first instance this low born man is in need of some persuading that he has what it takes for the job.

> Sausage-Seller: I don't consider myself worthy to hold power.
> Demosthenes: What do you mean? Why on earth do you say that you're not worthy? You don't have something *good* on your conscience, do you? Please tell me you're not a gentleman!
> Sausage-Seller: No, by the gods, I'm as rough as could be.
> Demosthenes: Good news. That's a stroke of luck! What an advantage you've got for political life!
> Sausage-Seller: But I must tell you, my friend, that I haven't had any education – except for some reading and writing, and I'm right bad at that.
> Demosthenes: That's the only thing that counts against you, that you can read and write at all – even 'right bad'. You see, the leadership of the people is no longer a job for a man of accomplishment, but for someone who's uneducated and disgusting.
>
> *Knights* 182-93

The bulk of the play then consists of a contest (*agôn*) between Paphlagon and the Sausage-Seller to decide who should be foremost with Demos: this involves establishing who is the more unscrupulous as well as competing for Demos' affections.

It is interesting to trace how Paphlagon is portrayed in this play.[9] An important point to make in this regard is that the portrayal of Paphlagon consists of a complex mixture of plausible and implausible elements and that his characterization therefore works on a number of levels. At times, for instance, we find him having recourse to the kind of low tactics that we can easily imagine were employed by real-life public figures in Athens – perhaps even by Cleon himself. At one point he threatens the Sausage-Seller, saying:

> Well, I'm off to the council right away. I'm going to tell them about the conspiracies you've all been hatching, and about your nocturnal anti-state meetings, and all the things you've been plotting with the Medes and their King ...
>
> *Knights* 475-8

At other times, however, we find him making 'admissions' that no politician would plausibly make – even if they were true.

> Sausage-Seller: I know full well that you got ten talents [60,000 drachmae] out of Potidaea.
> Paphlagon: What of it? How about I give you one of those talents to keep your mouth shut?
>
> *Knights* 438-9

Paphlagon also recites oracles and quotes them at length, however ludicrous they may seem:

> 'There is a woman shall bear a lion in sacred Athens,
> Which shall fight with many gnats on behalf of the people (*dêmos*) ...'
>
> *Knights* 1037-8

And at other times still, he acts in a way in which Cleon – or indeed anyone who hoped to hold sway with the people of Athens – can hardly ever have acted in real life, such as engaging in violent slanging matches with the Sausage Seller in public.

> Sausage-Seller: I'll yell three times as loud as you.
> Paphlagon: I'll shout you down with my shouts.
> Sausage-Seller: I'll yell you down with my yells.
> Paphlagon: I'll slander you, if you're made a general.
> Sausage-Seller: I'll beat your back like a dog's.
>   ...
> Paphlagon: If you so much as grunt, I'll tear you in pieces.
>
> *Knights* 285-90; 294

The point being made here is not that *Knights* fails to present us with an 'accurate' portrait of Cleon: that much is self-evident. It is rather that, within the inaccurate portrait that we *do* have, the level of reality is constantly shifting (in a 'recreative' way, we might say: see Chapter 5). In addition to plausible elements (such as Paphlagon's willingness to stir up

169

the council) we find numerous invented details, some of which may possibly map on to something in real life (maybe Cleon *did* misuse public funds or squabble in public) and some of which probably do not (he is unlikely to have admitted to embezzlement or threatened his political opponents physically, for example). Impressionistically, then, we might say that the attack on Cleon in *Knights* is vitriolic – but when it comes down to the level of detail it is less easy to make definite claims about what Cleon is alleged to have done wrong, beyond the fairly bland charge of taking too much credit for the Pylos episode. Crucially, too, many of the other faults he is assigned (flattery and deception of the people; playing on fears of conspiracy; dishonesty and financial misdealing; brashness and shamelessness) feature regularly in attacks on politicians in general in Old Comedy – and probably reflect in an exaggerated form the kind of allegations politicians themselves made about their rivals in public.[10] Indeed, in the fictional world of *Knights*, many stock, political insults have simply become realities: the Sausage Seller really *has* been a prostitute (e.g. *Knights* 1243), for example, and Cleon really *is* of foreign descent (the name Paphlagon indicates a slave from Asia Minor as well as evoking the Greek word *paphlazô*, 'boil' or splutter', as we saw in Chapter 4). In short, the relationship of the portrayal of Cleon here to the 'real' world of Athens is highly problematic, since it involves a heady mixture of reality, convention and invention.

So how are we to make sense of this complex caricature? This fundamental question has been approached in different ways. To simplify somewhat, the assumption of some scholars is that these different elements can largely be unpicked and that the original audience would therefore have had a good idea of what the 'real' accusations against Cleon were (his tax-and-spend policies and use of oracles in public life are plausible candidates for specific targets; his abrasive style and self-serving manipulation of the *dêmos* plausible as more general complaints). However, the approach of others has been to emphasize the complex interplay of fictional elements in the play. On this view, put crudely, it is essentially impossible to unpick the various components of the caricature successfully in order to discover what the 'points' being made against Cleon are.[11] Clearly this is a complex issue and one that will not be resolved here – as stated in the introduction, the purpose of this chapter is not to provide a ready 'answer', but rather to highlight some of the problems with which students of Aristophanic politics are forced to grapple.

There is one final point worth emphasizing before we move on, and that is the way in which Aristophanes as a dramatist uses the figure of Cleon in his comedies. As mentioned above, Aristophanes' dispute with the politician surfaces time and time again in his plays during the 420s – almost as if Aristophanes were serving up a new instalment with each new comedy in the manner of a soap opera. Whilst we can never know the extent to which the real-life Aristophanes 'really' hated the real-life Cleon, what we *can* confidently claim is that the dispute made for compelling drama (so compelling, we might say, that we are still talking about it 2,500 years later). The interweaving of fact and fiction in the portrayal of Cleon may even have added to the appeal for the original audience, for whom it must have been thrilling to see a public fight between a leading playwright and a leading politician played out at regular intervals in the high-profile context of the theatre.[12] Whatever the challenges of reading *Knights* as a political play, then, one thing is clear: Aristophanes evidently has excellent instincts as a playwright. If nothing else this is fantastic drama.

So much for Old Comedy's attacks on politicians. Let us now take a look at another way in which politics surfaces in comedy: namely the viewpoints and policies – both general and specific – that are given a sympathetic airing in Aristophanes' plays.

General policies: Aristophanes and the Good Old Days

Towards the end of *Peace*, Trygaeus emerges from the *skênê* door dressed for his wedding. After asking for his bride to be fetched he sings:[13]

> And now we should all take our things back to the countryside
> Once we've danced and poured libations and got rid of Hyperbolus
> And prayed that the gods
> Give wealth to the Greeks
> And that we all grow plenty of barley
> And make plenty of wine
> And chew figs
> And that our wives bear us children
> And that once again, as in the past,
> We can gather all the good things we lost
> And say farewell to glittering steel.
>
> *Peace* 1318-29

This passage is typical of many in Aristophanes which bundle together a similar collection of positive values. Here, as elsewhere, the good things the world has to offer include the countryside and an abundance of food, wine and sex (here, as befits a bridegroom, it is fertility *within* marriage that is praised – elsewhere extra-marital sex is favoured). It is the absence of war (represented here by the 'glittering steel') that makes all this possible, but this is not the only kind of 'peace' that is prized: 'getting rid' of politicians like Hyperbolus will also mean that Trygaeus and his companions will be able to live *peacefully*, free from disturbance and interference. Once they have all returned to the countryside, life will be like it was in 'in the past': in other words, peace will allow a return to the Good Old Days.

The charm of this passage is undeniable – and the appeal of this cluster of values must have been enormous to Aristophanes' audience in 421 BC

171

who for the last ten years had been living with war, privation and uncertainty. The Attic countryside, in particular, must have held a special significance for a city-state whose urban residents and country-dwellers alike had been forced to live within Athens' city walls for many of the early war years to protect themselves from Spartan invasions. Athens' glorious past, too, especially its victory over the Persians at Marathon (in 490 BC), was a potent symbol throughout the classical era, Aristophanes being just one of a number of classical authors who looks back to this era with nostalgia. As we noted in Chapter 5, however, whilst a glorious battle like Marathon may have been good *then*, peace and tranquillity are what is sought *now*.

What we find in this and other passages, then, is a positive picture, painted in broad brush strokes, of an ideal world characterized by tradition and peace. And to link this with attacks on individuals, figures like Cleon and Socrates might usefully be seen as standing in contrast to this positive picture, since they represent new and negative forces in society (a new style of politics; new ways of thinking) that might be said to threaten these traditions. So in short, the traditions of the Good Old Days are to be prized, the innovations of the modern world despised. Does what we have here amount to a coherent system of values – or even a political agenda?

Unfortunately, things are not that straightforward. To focus on one minor point, for example, the fact that Aristophanes is evidently a highly inventive poet must make us wary of accepting the view that there is a simple contrast between 'good' tradition and 'bad' innovation to be found in his plays. Aristophanes even boasts about his 'new ideas' as we saw in Chapter 1 – so perhaps it is more accurate to say that both tradition *and* innovation can be presented as positive virtues when the situation suits. More fundamental, though, is that part of the power that these positive images of peace, food, wine, sex and the Good Old Days hold stems from the fact that they are essentially uncontroversial and vague. 'Life was great in the Good Old Days', 'It's good to have access to lots of food, wine and sex', 'Peace is better than war' are presumably propositions that few members of Aristophanes' audience would have taken exception to, but taken together they hardly amount to a political manifesto. In order to make the claim that Aristophanes plays' engaged with Athenian politics in any meaningful way it will be necessary to look not at the broad picture, but at the precise policies that are advocated. In other words, the devil is in the detail.

Specific policies: political advice in the *Parabasis* and beyond

There are in fact plenty of places in Aristophanic comedy where precise advice *does* seem to be offered. In the *parabases* of his plays in particular, the chorus 'comes forward' (*parabainô*) and claims to speak frankly to the audience – sometimes in character (as birds or clouds, etc.), sometimes as chorus members in a play and sometimes in the first person (either 'I' or 'we'), apparently speaking on behalf of the poet. The topics discussed in *parabases* are hugely diverse: we learn about Aristophanes' rivalries with Cleon in the *parabases* of all five plays from the 420s, for example, and we are also offered views on other comic poets (e.g. in *Clouds* and *Peace*) as well as a myriad of other topics, including contemporary politics. Sometimes the political views are relatively general and bland but, as we shall see below, in the *parabases* of plays like *Acharnians* and *Frogs* we find some very specific pieces of political advice offered. It should be mentioned, however, that any discussion of the *parabasis* is hugely complex: it is a part of Aristophanes' plays that has come under intense scrutiny and, just as scholars differ in their approach to Cleon's characterization in *Knights*, widely different opinions are held about how we should understand the *parabases*' interweaving of fact and fiction, their apparent mix of sense and nonsense and the changing perspectives of the chorus (who, as I mentioned, can switch between speaking as characters, actors and playwright).

Aside from the *parabasis*, statements about contemporary politics are sometimes found in the main body of the plays, too, some of the most significant of which occur in speeches delivered by the central character. Two such speeches which contain particularly striking examples of detailed political advice are also discussed in the following sections: *Acharnians* 497-556 and *Lysistrata* 568-70 and 574-86.

Comedy and justice: the case of *Acharnians*

Acharnians contains two passages of enormous interest to the present discussion: the *parabasis* (626-718) and the speech delivered by Dicaeopolis at lines 497-556 of the play. Let us focus on this speech first, the premise of which is that Dicaeopolis has staked his life on his ability to justify to the chorus the private peace treaty he has made with Sparta. As he starts speaking, Dicaeopolis (whose very name combines the elements 'just', *dikaios*, and 'city', *polis*) appears to claim that what he is about to say will be important not just in the fictional world of the play but in the 'real' world of contemporary Athens, too.

> Even comedy is concerned with justice (*to dikaion*). And what I shall say will
> be shocking, but will also be just (*dikaia*).
>
> *Acharnians* 500-1

Dicaeopolis then goes on to speak as if he were the poet of the play, referring to the dispute with Cleon:

> This time Cleon will not slander me … .
>
> *Acharnians* 502

173

After this, he broaches another 'real-life' topic, the war with Sparta, giving an account of how the hostilities began – but not in a way that is easy to understand. The thrust of Dicaeopolis' narrative certainly seems to be that Athens is at least as much to blame for starting the war as Sparta ('why do we hold the Spartans responsible for all this?' *Acharnians* 514), but the garbled account he then gives of the war's origins is difficult to unravel. The theft of prostitutes, for example, seems to loom large in his version of events (524-9) which certainly differs somewhat from the account of these events in Thucydides![14] Perhaps the overarching theme of the speech is that the war sprang from a combination of trivial events and posturing on the part of the Athenians – but understanding the 'point' of this speech is complicated by the fact that Dicaeopolis seems to speak not only as himself, but *also* as the poet, and *also* as the title character of Euripides' *Telephus* (Dicaeopolis is wearing Telephus' rags over his own comic costume while he delivers his speech and also uses both actual and adapted lines from the original Euripidean play). To make things more complex still, disguise, dishonesty and the ability of clever speakers to deceive the Athenian people are also recurrent themes in the play. Indeed, it has even been suggested that Dicaeopolis is an anti-hero who is wearing a transparent disguise (the rags of Telephus) to deliver a 'transparently' confusing speech in order to bamboozle the chorus and justify an essentially selfish act (the making of a private peace treaty).[15] According to this view, the 'point' of the speech would be to expose the tricks that clever speakers employ in order to convince their audiences of untruths. While this interpretation of the passage has its own appeal it is ultimately problematic, however: Dicaeopolis is, after all, a hugely sympathetic figure with whom it is difficult not to side. But the very fact that the speech *can* be read in this way demonstrates just how complex this passage is: certainly scholars have come to a whole host of diverse yet subtly argued conclusions.

Scholarly opinion may be divided about the significance of the speech, but in the context of the play it lays the groundwork for Dicaeopolis' eventual triumph. At first only half the chorus is won over to Dicaeopolis' side, but following his speech Dicaeopolis persuades the other half to support him, too: this happens during a brief exchange in which he makes several swipes against the excessive public pay drawn by Athens' ambassadors (597-619: a theme already aired in the play's prologue). Following this, the chorus delivers the *parabasis* which, like Dicaeopolis' speech, is also said to contain much of importance for the people of Athens. Addressing the audience directly, the chorus says:

> For in his comedies [the poet] will make just points (*dikaia*).
> He says he'll teach you many things, so that you'll be happy:
> Not flattering you or offering you pay or conning you
> Or doing you down or brown-nosing you – but teaching you what is *best*.
>
> *Acharnians* 655-8

But what exactly *are* these 'just points' and 'best' things? The essence of what the chorus says is that Aristophanes has advised the Athenians well, teaching them not to be taken in by rhetoric and 'foreign words' (634-5) – which may simply be a jibe at politicians who, as we noted, are often portrayed in comedy as being of foreign descent. However, specific 'points' are thin on the ground and, what is more, one of the more substantial claims that *is* made by the chorus is surely fictitious: namely that both the King of Persia and the Spartans believe that Aristophanes' good advice will play a decisive role in the war (646-54). Indeed, it is only when the chorus returns to speaking in its fictional personality – as old men from the deme of Acharnae – that it begins to make any weighty points at all. With great pathos, they complain that the old of Athens have recently become the victims of clever young speakers in the city's law courts (676-718: a theme explored in Chapter 5). Alluding to the water-clocks by which speeches were timed in court they sing:

How is that right?
To ruin a grey-haired old man
Next to a water-clock,
One who has put in more than his fair share of toil
And has wiped off warm, manly
Sweat and plenty of it –
A brave man who fought
For the city at Marathon?
Is this what things are like now? When we were
At Marathon, we were the *pursuers*,
But we now are the ones who are *pursued* –
By truly wicked men who make sure
We are convicted as well.

Acharnians 692-702

Much as the chorus' grumbling might reflect a genuine anxiety in contemporary Athens, we should note, however, that we are now back in the realm of nostalgia: their complaint is consistent with the idea that life has changed for the worse since the Good Old Days – and as men who fought at the Battle of Marathon they deserve better.

Acharnians demonstrates well the difficulties thrown up by Aristophanes' plays when we try to assess their political content. Bold claims are made about the good advice offered by the poet, but when we look closely at passages which deal with recent or contemporary politics they often resist straightforward interpretation. Furthermore, where we *do* seem able to detect value judgements (such as the complaint that old men are being financially ruined in the law courts), these tend to be part of a simplistic pattern which pitches the Good Old Days against the restless Modern Age. On one level, then, *Acharnians* is evidently a deeply political play in which the contemporary world of Athens, its democratic institutions (e.g. the assembly, law courts) and above all the war with Sparta take

175

centre stage. But for all the play holds up peace as an ideal, and for all the claims that are made about the poet's good advice, it provides little practical guidance or analysis as to how that peace might be achieved (such as what demands or concessions Athens might look to make in a peace treaty with Sparta).[16] For specific advice on policy we need to look elsewhere.

Political advice in *Lysistrata* and *Frogs*

In contrast to *Acharnians*, in *Lysistrata* we find a character outlining what seems to be a practical programme for political reform. This appears in a much-discussed speech in which Lysistrata suggests that the city's problems should be worked on in the same way as women work on a skein of wool (see also Chapter 5, pp. 87-8). In the course of this extraordinary extended metaphor she suggests ways in which the war with Sparta could be brought to a peaceful conclusion and details how specific groups both inside and outside the city might be treated:

> First of all, just like a raw fleece, you have to wash the sheep-dung out of the city in a bath, then putting it on a bed, card out the villains and pick off the burrs – and as for those who combine and mat themselves together for political gain, you should card them out and pluck off their heads. Then card general goodwill into a basket, mixing everyone together: the immigrants (*metoikoi*), any foreigner who is friendly to you, and anyone who is in debt to the public treasury – mix them in, too. And, by Zeus, don't forget the cities that are colonies of this land: you should recognize that these are lying around all by themselves like tufts of wool. So, from each of these you should take the citizen-flock, bring them together here and join them all together to make one big ball of wool from which you can then weave a nice warm cloak for the people to wear.
>
> *Lysistrata* 574-86

It is interesting to try to establish the precise nature of Lysistrata's advice here. Just before this passage, she has suggested sending embassies 'now this way and now that' (570), presumably to sue for peace. And now here she suggests that 'villains' and 'those who combine and mat themselves together for political gain' should be removed from the citizen body: here the target seems to be public figures who belong to political factions and who conspire to gain money and power. Next she mentions groups who, she says, should be included in the citizenry but are currently excluded. Four groups are listed: (i) resident immigrants ('metics'); (ii) foreigners who are well-disposed to Athens; (iii) debtors (who were disenfranchised at Athens, hence the need for the reinstatement of their citizen rights), and (iv) Athens' colonies. These suggestions are certainly striking and, perhaps, in the recent years of crisis following the failure of the Sicilian Expedition in 413 BC, Athenians had grown used to suggestions for wide-reaching reform (and a radical oligarchic coup actually did take place in 411 BC just a few months after *Lysistrata* was staged). But the sending of embassies aside, could any of them have been taken 'seriously' in contemporary Athens?

This question becomes even more complex when we try to clarify exactly what Lysistrata is proposing. What 'foreigners' does she mean? What does she mean by 'colonies' (scholars are unsure)? More importantly, what status do Lysistrata's words have here? As we have seen, Athenian theatre-goers would have been used to hearing sincere-sounding pieces of 'advice' in Aristophanes' plays, but these were normally delivered either by the male protagonist (such as Dicaeopolis) or, more commonly, by the chorus in the *parabasis* (an element missing from *Lysistrata*). So how would the various members of Aristophanes' audience have reacted to these suggestions of Lysistrata's – made ostensibly in earnest, but presented in the form of an involved metaphor by a female character in the midst of a bawdy comedy? Once again, there are no easy answers here.

If the advice offered in *Lysistrata* proves difficult to interpret, perhaps we stand a better chance with *Frogs* 674-737 – a passage that has been called 'the most political *parabasis* in the surviving works of Aristophanes' and one which certainly contains 'specific, practical proposals'.[17] Not that the *parabasis* begins in an exceptional way: the chorus first attacks one of the leading politicians of the day, Cleophon, making a number of standard accusations (i.e. they claim that he is dishonest, foreign and a brash speaker: *Frogs* 678-85). However, they then go on to make a set of very precise points. They say that the Athenian people were right to grant citizen status to those slaves that had fought at the recent sea battle of Arginusae (406 BC) – 'I congratulate you on it; it's the only sensible thing you've done' (*Frogs* 696) – but also highlight the fact that there are men in the city who are true born Athenians, and whose fathers fought in many naval battles on Athens' behalf, but who no longer have citizen status. Here the reference is to a number of men who were deprived of some or all of their citizen rights for supporting the oligarch coup in 411 BC (which was overthrown the following year). The chorus appeals for these men to have their citizen rights restored ('it's only right for you ... to pardon them this one wrong', *Frogs* 697-9). What is more, they also imply that these men were misguided in their actions rather than wicked – victims rather than criminals.

Here we have a passage that seems, for once, to represent a clear and unambiguous piece of advice – so much so that a scholar like Malcolm Heath (whose general approach is that Aristophanes' comedies have only a 'tenuous attachment to reality' and not intended by their author to influence the audience's political outlook) takes the view that the *Frogs parabasis* is the one place in Aristophanes where he can detect 'serious intent'.[18] But if Aristophanes is capable of expressing 'serious intent' here (and the passage certainly looks heartfelt and to be taken at face value), then why not elsewhere? Potentially, then, this passage raises a whole series of difficult questions about how we should approach those other sections of Aristophanes' plays where the city appears to be offered advice.

The *Frogs parabasis* is not only remarkable for the clear and detailed nature of the policies it advocates. What makes it even more noteworthy still is that the advice it contains was apparently acted on later that year: in the autumn of 405 BC full citizen rights were indeed restored to most of the men who had been disenfranchised for supporting the coup of 411 BC. And what is more, we also learn that the playwright and his play were granted special honours: we are told by later sources that, *because of the advice* that the *parabasis* contained, Aristophanes was 'formally commended and crowned with a wreath of sacred olive'[19] and *Frogs* was even given an official restaging the following year – a quite exceptional occurrence. Is this evidence that the people of Athens, at least on this one occasion, not only understood Aristophanes to be making a sincere proposal in a play but also took this piece of advice to heart? And does this anecdote therefore establish that comic plays could and did play a role in shaping public policy?

Maybe. But a postscript should urge us to be cautious about how we interpret this story. In early 404 BC, around the time that *Frogs* was restaged and Athens was under siege, the politician most strongly attacked in the play's *parabasis*, Cleophon, was arrested on a trumped-up charge, tried and executed by men who would soon, after the fall of Athens, be implicated in a harsh oligarchic regime. There may, then, be reason to suppose that Aristophanes' comic advice was deliberately linked to a policy that was being enacted anyway – namely the restoration of the men's citizen rights – so as to justify the restaging of what was evidently a popular play; and that the restaging of *Frogs* was, at least in part, a politically motivated move in a propaganda war against one of the city's democratic leaders. If this is indeed the case, this whole story may tell us far more about how Aristophanes' drama could be manipulated by self-serving political agitators in times of crisis than it does about how this piece of Aristophanic advice was initially perceived by the public at large. Of course, if there *was* an element of propaganda behind the restaging of the play, the question we would dearly love to be able to answer is whether Aristophanes approved of his play being used in this way or, on the contrary, was deeply embarrassed about the way his drama was exploited. But on this point we can only speculate.

Aristophanic biases

So far in this chapter we have seen just how complex discussions of Aristophanic politics can be: the manner in which individuals are presented and the context in which specific policies are put forward make drawing firm conclusions about the political stances adopted in the plays highly problematic. In this section, however, let us consider the topic of

178

politics from a potentially more productive angle, namely the general biases that Aristophanes displays in his plays. These biases concern the institutions, practices and kinds of people that Aristophanes chooses to satirize.

In his 1996 article, 'How to avoid being a *komodoumenos*', Alan Sommerstein makes important inroads into categorizing the so-called *komodoumenoi* ('mocked individuals') of Old Comedy.[20] As we might expect, he concludes that the largest single category of *komodoumenoi* comprises people who are active in the institutions of the *polis*. Amongst these are included not only men like Cleon who can be classed as 'politicians', but also office holders, military men and priests. The next largest category is that of men active in the theatre: we have seen in previous chapters how Aristophanes mocks both his rival comic poets (Chapter 1) and tragedians and their poetry (Chapter 6) – and along with these we also find actors, dancers and *chorêgoi* targeted. Other significant categories include men active in given trades or professions, Athens' conspicuous consumers, and those held in high regard either for their wit or beauty. As Sommerstein comments, 'virtually anyone in the public eye could expect to become a target of comic satire'.[21]

Where Sommerstein's study becomes particularly interesting for the present discussion is when he looks at the category of politicians in more detail. As he points out, those politicians satirized for a whole or a substantial part of a play are all radical democrats like Cleon rather than supporters of the more socially and politically conservative aristocracy. More telling still are the few occasions that politicians are praised in Aristophanes. For the most part, it is only dead politicians that attract admiration (Pericles, for example, gets a good press in Aristophanes, whereas he was regularly the source of biting satire in comedy while still alive). Of the three living politicians who receive positive mentions in Aristophanes, however – Archeptolemus, Ulius son of Cimon and Thucydides son of Melesias – all are opponents of the radical democracy. Nor would it appear that these trends are exclusive to Aristophanes: his rival poets' plays also attack radical democrats (most notably Hyperbolus) and the one instance we find outside Aristophanes of a living politician praised in comedy is the aristocratic general and politician Nicias (Eupolis fr. 193).[22] Notable, too, in our surviving fragments is the almost complete dearth of attacks by comic poets on one of the most controversial figures of the day: the flamboyant aristocrat Alcibiades.[23]

This striking collection of data at last seems to point us in a definite direction: an anti-democrat stance – or, if we wish to phrase things more cautiously, an 'anti-establishment' bias, which for most of the late fifth century amounted to much the same thing.[24] What is more, opposition to democrat politicians also fits neatly with other biases we find in Aristophanes, most notably recurrent attacks on a specific branch of the democratic system: Athens' law courts. *Wasps* contains a sustained critique of the legal system, for example, and we find attacks on the courts in a number of other plays, too – such as *Acharnians* (e.g. the chorus' 'waterclock' song, quoted above, p. 175) or *Birds*, where Peisthetaerus constantly distances himself from Athenians' predilection for law suits (e.g *Birds* 41, 110). 'Sycophants', too, come in for repeated attacks in Aristophanes. As we saw in Chapter 4, these were men who brought prosecutions against the rich for personal profit and regularly feature in Aristophanes' plays as characters trying to spoil the hero's plans: sycophants are fought off by Dicaeopolis in *Acharnians*, Peisetaerus in *Birds*, and Carion in *Wealth*, for instance. Another aspect of the legal system which is regularly criticized is the pay received by jurors[25] – and this seems to form part of a broader set of attacks on economic matters in Aristophanes' plays. In addition to stock charges of financial mismanagement by politicians there are also more specific comments made about the nature of public pay: for example, as we saw in our discussion of *Acharnians*, the pay given to public servants such as ambassadors is often portrayed as excessive. Interestingly, though, the pay of common soldiers and sailors *never* comes under fire.

Taken as a whole, these biases would suggest that the plays are fundamentally hostile towards democrat politicians and elements of Athens' democratic system – especially the excesses of public pay and the lawcourts. These biases even chime with the plays' attacks on Cleon, who was responsible for increasing jurors' pay and who had also supported moves to increase taxes on Athens' subject states in order to fund increased public expenditure. Have we finally located a meaningful political stance here?

To a large extent the answer must be 'yes' – although there are some important points to bear in mind. First, we must be clear about what we are saying 'yes' to. What we cannot claim to have located is Aristophanes' views – instead, what we have identified here is better defined as the existence of certain viewpoints that are routinely adopted in his plays. Second, the fact that one of the central biases in Aristophanes' plays – namely, hostility towards living, democrat politicians – seems to be repeated in the work of other comic poets is also important. This might simply suggest that comic poets routinely took an anti-establishment stance – which makes sense from the point of view of satire, too, since there is a tendency for satirists to attack the *status quo* and use as material for their comedy things that can be portrayed as going wrong in the here-and-now. A further interesting perspective on these biases is the way they map on to the Good Old Days philosophy we noted earlier. Once more we find antipathy towards the modern world (such as the new style of leaders that the radical democracy has thrown up) and hostility towards forces in society that stir up conflict (such as the possibility to make money by exploiting the legal system) coupled with praise of the traditional (such as conservative aristocratic politicians).

This Good Old Days view of the world may even be the source of one of the more puzzling biases we find in Aristophanes, namely the extraordinarily (if not exclusively) positive press that Sparta and Spartans receive throughout his plays (which is particularly remarkable given that Athens was at war with Sparta when most of the plays were produced).[26] As we have seen, Aristophanes' plays seem to adopt a pro-aristocratic stance – and since the aristocracy at Athens had traditionally been relatively well-disposed towards Sparta, the positive portrayal of Sparta could be seen as yet another example of aristocratic leanings.[27] However, another way to understand the pro-Spartan sentiments of the plays might be to see them as part of the pervasive tendency in Aristophanes to look back to the Good Old Days – specifically, that is, the glory days when Athens and Sparta co-operated to ward off the Persian invaders in the early years of the fifth century. To make another suggestion, the readiness of characters to make peace with Sparta – such as in *Acharnians*, *Peace* and *Lysistrata* – could also be said to be another example of comedy taking an anti-establishment stance. After all, these 'peace plays' were written while the war was being fought – and the decision whether to continue fighting or to sue for peace ultimately rested with the 'establishment', i.e. the democracy.

To sum up, Aristophanes' plays display a bias towards aristocratic politicians and a surprisingly positive view of Sparta. Attacks, on the other hand, tend to be reserved for democrat politicians and certain aspects of the democratic system (such as the law courts and the payment of jurors and ambassadors). Whilst an anti-establishment stance may have been a traditional aspect of comedy (and might make particular sense from the point of view of satire) one question looms large: what did Aristophanes' audience make of these standpoints? If Aristophanes' aims included winning over his audience – and even winning first prize – how could he afford to criticize the democracy and its institutions in this way?

Criticizing the democracy: the audience perspective

Making sense of the anti-democratic stance of Aristophanes' plays lies at the heart of many discussions of Aristophanic politics. One view that can be adopted is to see Aristophanes as a moral crusader – someone prepared to speak out and tell the truth about people and policies, however unpalatable and unpopular this truth may be. This certainly fits with claims made about Aristophanes by the choruses of his plays, of course.

Our poet ... dares to say what is just (*ta dikaia*).

Knights 509-10

Now then, o people, pay attention to us, if you're ready to hear some honest talk.

Wasps 1015

181

As we have seen, however, many scholars are uncomfortable with this view and choose to emphasize the posturing and playfulness of Aristophanes' comedies, the conventions that govern Aristophanes' choice of targets and the lack of substance underpinning many of the seemingly political positions taken in the plays. In a different vein, much has also been made of the special licence Old Comedy evidently had to abuse and attack, the *parrhesia* (freedom of speech) it enjoyed, and its carnivalesque nature.[28] In this light, Old Comedy can be seen as playing a subversive role: comic poets were *expected* to abuse the establishment and they did just that. However, does this really account for comedy's anti-democratic and pro-aristocratic leanings? Did the aristocracy not form part of the 'establishment', too?

A helpful way to look at these questions will be to consider the Athenian political scene from the point of view of Aristophanes' audience.[29] As outlined in the introduction to this chapter, whilst most Athenian citizens will have participated in one way or another in Athens' democratic institutions at some point in their lives (e.g. as part of the assembly or even members of the council, *boulê*), the number of men who had the ability and courage to stand up and speak in the assembly must have been very small indeed. 'Politicians', then, formed a relatively small and self-selecting group about whom there would no doubt have been a certain amount of suspicion and resentment amongst ordinary Athenians.

In the Greek-speaking world the general rule was (and always had been) that it was men of noble birth who guided public policy and made executive decisions. In the 420s, therefore, there must have been a great deal of nervousness in Athens about the new kind of politician that was emerging: men like Cleon who, whilst hardly being of humble origins (contrary to his depiction in *Knights*), was nevertheless no aristocrat.[30] Cleon was evidently a persuasive speaker who used his gift for stirring up the crowd to great effect – but he was also a character who clearly did not meet with everyone's approval (Thucydides' damning portrait of him as populist and brash is good evidence of that).[31] Aristophanes' attacks on Cleon, then (just like other comic poets' attacks on Hyperbolus), need not necessarily be thought of purely in terms of an anti-democratic stance: comedy might better be said to be tapping into a broadly held anxiety about Athens' new breed of leaders.

We can take this principle one step further, I think. The criticisms that are made of public pay, the power of the law courts, and even the preparedness of the Athenians to continue the war with Sparta, might usefully be seen in a similar light. That is to say, by putting certain policies, institutions and decisions under the spotlight, Aristophanes is tapping into contemporary anxieties in Athens. It is perfectly plausible that many of the citizen members of the audience watching *Knights* had supported measures put forward by Cleon in the assembly and even went on to help elect him general (*stratêgos*) in 424 BC shortly after *Knights* was staged, but at the same time did not feel wholly at ease with his political methods and policies. And in the same vein, there is every reason to suppose that many Athenians were anxious about the increasing financial demands that the city was making on its allies to meet the growing demands of public pay, the changing nature of the legal system and the continuation of the war in the 420s – even if they had been in favour of the relevant policies themselves (and let us also remember that not all of Aristophanes' audience had the opportunity to vote: amongst the spectators were also immigrants, youths and maybe women).[32] In short, Aristophanes' plays need not be thought of as positioning themselves in opposition to popular feeling in the city by adopting an anti-democratic stance. Quite the opposite. There may be good reason to suppose that the political stances taken in the plays are, at least in part, informed by current anxieties and tensions in the city – and that, far from challenging the views of the most ordinary Athenians, Aristophanes often sought to align his plays with important undercurrents of popular sentiment.

Some would go further still. For Jeffrey Henderson, for instance, comic criticism should be seen as playing a key role in the democratic processes of Athens – its personal attacks helping to hold Athens' leaders to account, and its choice of themes alerting them to widely held public concerns.[33] In this light, Old Comedy might also usefully be thought of as acting as a safety valve, allowing alternative political views to be aired – albeit in a far from straightforward way.

External evidence: contemporary views of Comedy

Lastly in this chapter, let us look beyond Aristophanes' plays and gather together what threads of evidence we have about how Aristophanes' contemporaries reacted to the personal attacks and political stance of Old Comedy. The following is a brief survey of some of our more important sources.

Outside the plays themselves, the only substantial pronouncement about Old Comedy we have from the fifth century comes in the *Constitution of Athens*: this is a political pamphlet written sometime in the late fifth century (probably the 420s) by an anonymous author who, owing to his political leanings, has become known as the Old Oligarch. One of the anxieties expressed in this work centres on the personal abuse contained in Old Comedy: as far as the Old Oligarch is concerned, the same sections of society are targeted all too often.

> [The Athenians] do not allow the people (*dêmos*) to be made fun of in comedy (*komoidein*) so as to avoid being spoken ill of themselves. But they allow anyone wishing to mock a private individual to do so in the full knowledge that the person mocked (*komodoumenos*) is not usually one of the common people (*dêmos*) or the masses but rather is rich, noble or powerful. A few of

the poor and common people are mocked but only if they engage in public affairs or look to rise above their station in life, so it does not bother them if men like this are made fun of.

Old Oligarch, *Constitution of Athens* 2.18

So the Old Oligarch evidently thinks that Old Comedy displays strong biases: for him comic writers are all too ready to attack important men in the city but were slow to criticize the masses. Interestingly, he does not seem to have spotted Old Comedy's pro-aristocratic leanings, however. Quite the reverse: for this spectator at least, Aristophanes and his fellow poets are too harsh on 'rich' and 'noble' (as well as 'powerful') Athenians. Clearly, then, what we have here is essentially a personal reaction to the plays from a very particular (aristocratic) perspective. What is more, we also note that the Old Oligarch fails to address the questions to which we would most like to know the answers: that is to say, he neither talks about the intentions of the comic poets themselves (i.e. whether they sought to have an impact on contemporary politics) nor about any effects that comic attacks might have had on public opinion.

The other evidence we have about contemporary reactions to Old Comedy is difficult to interpret but nevertheless important. As detailed above, there is, for example, the story about Aristophanes being rewarded by the city for the advice he gave in *Frogs* – and whilst we have seen that this episode can be viewed in different lights, the fact that lines spoken in one of Aristophanes' plays were capable of being linked to a change in public policy (whatever the circumstances were) is nevertheless instructive. Here it is clearly the case that advice offered in a comedy was, at least on this one occasion, capable of being viewed as meaningful and sincere.

A more problematic example of comedy allegedly interacting with the real world comes in *Apology* (Plato's version of the defence speech that Socrates delivered at his trial in 399 BC). Here we find Socrates saying that some of the most notable accusations against him in the past came from 'a comic playwright' (*Apology* 18d). Some scholars have taken this statement at face value; that is to say, as evidence that Aristophanes' portrayal of Socrates in *Clouds* adversely influenced the way that the philosopher was thought of in Athens. However, others have argued that this passage should be interpreted ironically: that Socrates is effectively saying that the worst accusations ever made against him in the past were those in *Clouds* – and that since no-one would be inclined to take much notice of these, other things said about him should also be given little credence.[34] It is also the case that, in another work, *Symposium*, Plato portrays Aristophanes and Socrates as engaging in banter at a dinner party in 416 BC (seven years after *Clouds* was staged). Does this indicate that Plato thought that there would have been no personal animosity between the two? Or is he instead keen to portray Socrates as rising above the comic slander?

Finally, we come to Old Comedy's relationship with the law. Perhaps the best evidence we have that Aristophanes' contemporaries thought that comedy could add to political tensions in the city is the passing of a decree in 440 BC placing certain restrictions on comedy. The detail of the decree is unclear: all we have is a fleeting reference by a scholiast which says that it forbade *komoidein*, probably best understood as 'mockery' – but mockery of what, we are unsure.[35] Our best guess is that the decree, which was repealed three years later, was a reaction to a specific set of sensitivities surrounding the events of Samian War of 440-439 BC: perhaps it forbade comic references to the war altogether, or to the actions of Athenian generals, or to Athens' crushing of the Samians. Some scholars maintain that a similar decree was passed in 415 BC,[36] perhaps forbidding mention of individuals involved in the infamous scandals in which Alcibiades and other young aristocrats were implicated – the Profanation of the Mysteries and the Mutilation of the Herms – but this is much disputed.[37] The key point here is that if the Athenians legislated even once about what comic poets could and could not say, then comedy was clearly perceived by at least some of Aristophanes' contemporaries as having the potential to cause trouble. On the evidence available, the most we can claim, however, is that limited censorship was imposed on Old Comedy in times of perceived crisis.

Lastly, we come to Cleon's legal dispute with Aristophanes (or perhaps Callistratus) over *Babylonians*.[38] Once more, the details are hazy, but the charges made by Cleon seem to have revolved around the attitude taken in the play towards the city (*Babylonians* evidently attacked public officials and the behaviour of Athens towards its empire, made allegations of corruption and portrayed the Athenian citizenry as foolish).[39] What exactly lay behind this dispute we shall never know, but for the purposes of the present discussion the most significant element of this incident is the fact that it was possible for Cleon to mount a legal prosecution at all (even one that ultimately failed). Evidently he was able to make a plausible case that Aristophanes' play had overstepped the mark and contained inappropriate allegations – in other words, Cleon's legal action was underpinned by the notion that words spoken in a comedy could do harm in the real world.

Taken as a whole, these different strands of evidence suggest one important conclusion: namely that there was a recognition amongst at least some of Aristophanes' contemporaries that Old Comic abuse could be excessive and could have an effect outside the theatre. Whether these concerns were well founded, however, is less easy to establish. Certainly two notable butts of comic abuse, Hyperbolus and Socrates, both met with sticky ends (the one murdered in 411 BC, the other executed in 399 BC) but to make a direct connection between their comic reputations and the fates that befell them in the real world would surely be taking things too far. This said, we simply cannot know the extent to which different comic reputations took on a life of their own outside the theatre and/or had any influence over the way in which given individuals behaved: presumably this varied hugely from case to case. Nor, perhaps, should we assume that individuals always reacted negatively to the abuse that was meted out to them by the poets. Indeed, for some, being satirized in comedy may have constituted a welcome sign that they had 'made it', with comic mockery both confirming and reinforcing their status as public personalities.

Conclusions

This chapter has no doubt raised more questions than it has answered, its central purpose having been to illuminate some of the key issues that arise when discussing Aristophanic politics. Historically, one of the central debates that the plays have generated, of course, concerns the extent to which Aristophanes sought to influence his audience – a question whose complexity resides not least in the fact that we can neither establish Aristophanes' intentions with any certainty nor hope to reconstruct the diverse ways in which different members of the audience would have reacted to and understood his plays. And this is not to mention the difficulties of interpreting the plays themselves, with their intricate interplay of fact, fiction, convention and innovation.

With all these layers of complication, perhaps it is inevitable that scholars have come to such diverse views about Aristophanic politics. As we noted earlier, for example, for Malcolm Heath Aristophanic comedy has a 'tenuous attachment to reality' and the seemingly political stances taken in the plays stem from 'certain traditional concepts of the poet's role' whilst also playing to 'the prejudices and expectations of the majority of Aristophanes' audience'.[40] In short, for Heath: 'politics was the material of comedy, but comedy did not in turn aspire to be a political force'.[41] For Jeffrey Henderson, however, Aristophanes is a different creature altogether. For him, the poets of Old Comedy 'regard themselves as genuinely political voices' and 'argue vehemently ... about the most important and divisive issues of the day'; comedy being an institution that offered the people of Athens a 'yearly unofficial review' of the establishment.[42] The discussion in this chapter shows, I hope, how both these positions can be argued for – and how they also share a number of common assumptions.

What I also hope that this discussion has provided is a means of understanding approaches to Aristophanic politics that lie outside the much-quoted positions of Heath and Henderson. In particular, one idea that surfaces in various forms in the work of different scholars is that ambiguity is central to the way in which Aristophanes writes his plays. On this view, the fact that there are different ways of reading and understanding the plays is not to be seen as a problem to be solved, but rather as one of their essential qualities. Does such an approach allow us to stop looking for a neat 'answer' about the relationship between the plays and the 'real world'? Should we simply accept that different views can be taken on this issue and devote our efforts instead to understanding how Aristophanes deliberately creates these different ways of reading and understanding his plays?

Maybe. But as much as it is important to examine the plays as works of literature with their own internal dynamics, it is nevertheless the case that the plays both claim to interact with the real world of Athens and were evidently perceived by at least some of Aristophanes' contemporaries as having an impact on contemporary society. What is more, I think it is natural for us to be curious about biographical details – especially when the conflict with Cleon, for example, looms so large in the early plays. Exploring the complex relationship between Old Comedy and Athenian society therefore remains an important topic for students of Aristophanes to tackle. In short, the problem of Aristophanes' personal views and politics is not about to go away.

Aristophanes in the Modern World:
Translation and Performance

Introduction

As feminists it's our duty to use
Every weapon we have ...
Stockings, suspenders, wonderbras, thongs,
Boned basques with underwired cups, frilly babydolls,
Baroque bustiers, chemises with frou-frou ruffles –
Playing the vamp might be a cliché,
But once the men see us, it won't be war they want, no way!

Blake Morrison, Lisa's Sex Strike

In 2007, the theatre company Northern Broadsides toured the UK with a production of *Lisa's Sex Strike* by Blake Morrison, a play based on Aristophanes' *Lysistrata*. The piece takes as its setting a Northern English town where racial tensions are bubbling over – a theme which is linked into broader global-political issues, above all the War on Terrror and the consequences of the 2003 American-led invasion of Iraq. For many in the audience this would have been their first exposure to Aristophanes, and the heady mix of musical numbers, risqué humour and social comment (with its strong anti-establishment bias) will have left a lasting impression. For the most part, *Lisa's Sex Strike* follows the structure of *Lysistrata* fairly closely and part of the interest for classicists in the audience lay in seeing how Morrison had updated original elements, changed the play's emphases and blended the old with the new. The words of the women's chorus quoted above provide a neat illustration of how a passage of the original play (*Lysistrata* 149-54) is expanded and adapted by Morrison in such a way as to speak directly to a twenty-first-century audience.[1]

Performances, adaptations and translations of Aristophanes' plays: the reason why these are all of such vital importance to students of Old Comedy is that this is how most of us encounter Aristophanes for the first time and go on encountering him whenever we read a new translation or see one of his plays performed. Since these encounters play such a key role in forming our own and others' perceptions of Aristophanes it makes sense to reflect on the processes involved in translation and theatrical production: this way we can understand better the forces that shape the finished products that we find on the page and the stage. An awareness of issues that confront translators also equips us to ask more informed questions of

Fig. 6. Becky Hindley as Lisa (standing) and Sally Carman as Carol
(seated) in Northern Broadsides' production of *Lisa's Sex Strike*,
2007. Photograph reproduced courtesy of Nobby Clark.

the translations and adaptations that we read and so brings us yet another step closer to understanding the original texts.

   This chapter covers a series of topics relating to translation and performance. After a brief overview of the history of Aristophanes in print and in the theatre, I shall look at some of challenges involved in translating Aristophanes' plays and how different translators have tackled them (including discontinuity and sexual ethics). Two of the biggest difficulties presented by the plays – humour and lyrics – will be considered in particular detail. Towards the end of the chapter, I shall also go on to look at four adaptations of Aristophanic plays written specifically for theatrical

189

performance and reflect on the way in which they were staged. A number of Aristophanes' comedies feature in this chapter in one form or another, but in order to provide a focus for discussion, one play takes centre stage – *Lysistrata* – with *Birds* and *Acharnians* playing supporting roles.

Aristophanes in translation and performance: an overview

The systematic translation of Aristophanes' plays into English began in earnest in the nineteenth century – before then only three of his plays existed in English versions: *Wealth, Clouds* and *Frogs*.[2] Whilst the Victorian era was a boom time for Aristophanic translation, it was not until the early twentieth century that Aristophanic studies was to acquire its first set of truly 'classic' translations: the editions of the eleven plays by the English barrister Benjamin Bickley Rogers. These were published between 1902 and 1916 and later reprinted as part of the bilingual Loeb series of classical texts in 1924.[3] Roger's translations are notable for their poetic qualities, their extensive use of blank verse – and also for the fact that obscenities are either avoided, 'cleaned up' or replaced by euphemisms (Rogers even chose to leave out some of Aristophanes' more scurrilous passages altogether and, for the Loeb reprint, parts of *Lysistrata* and *Women at the Thesmophoria* had to be anonymously translated and reinserted into the text).

Performances of Aristophanes had also gained a degree of popularity in Britain towards the end of the nineteenth century – a fact due in no small part to revival performances at Oxford and Cambridge universities.[4] A particular success came in 1883 with the Cambridge production of *Birds*, performed in a translation by Henry Fleeming Jenkin and noted for its spectacular music and costumes. Although Old Comedy has never enjoyed the same popularity as Greek tragedy on the British stage (or elsewhere, for that matter), in the early years of the twentieth century certain Aristophanic plays nevertheless caught the attention of translators and directors, attracted by their apparently feminist and pacifist themes (topical issues at the time). Indeed, the lure of the anti-war stance of certain plays continued to be strong throughout the twentieth century, with *Peace* enjoying a number of landmark productions in France in particular.[5]

The growing interest in the issue of female equality was not the only aspect of a play like *Lysistrata* to attract producers and audiences in the early twentieth century. The risqué nature of the play also served to make the play commercially viable. In Athens, a version was staged at the Municipal Theatre as early as 1905 (with an all-male cast and female spectators forbidden) but for many decades subsequently the play became the preserve of the city's more disreputable theatres where it was produced in a titillating cabaret style.[6] In the English-speaking world, too, the

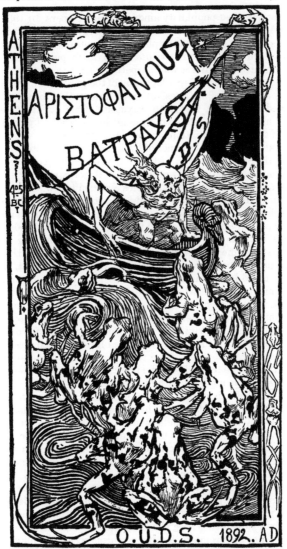

Fig. 7. Poster for the Oxford Union Dramatic Society (OUDS) production of *Frogs* (1892). Reproduced courtesy of The Bodleian Library, University of Oxford (G.A. Oxon b. 9/1884-1926).

play gained modest popularity amongst theatre-goers. In 1934, for example, the American writer and critic Gilbert Seldes, in his introduction to a visually stunning edition of the play which contains a series of etchings by Picasso, could claim that *Lysistrata* had a 'fairly permanent place in the modern theatre' and that it was 'perpetually produced ... as a living play'.[7] Seldes' version is more of an adaptation of the play than a translation, and certainly a product of its times: although he says that his version had been performed as 'a rowdy farce',[8] the sexuality of his *Lysistrata* is relatively subdued and elements not so prominent in the original play, such as the pathos of the wives' situation, are brought to the fore.

Inevitably, the sexual themes of *Lysistrata* also attracted the attentions of the authorities. This was certainly true of Seldes' version, whose play fell victim to the censors in a number of American cities – indeed, one performance of the play in Los Angeles even led to a warrant being drawn up for the arrest of Aristophanes himself! It is these risqué elements not just of this play but Aristophanes' comedies in general which no doubt held a special appeal for readers of the late 1950s and early 1960s when social attitudes towards obscenity and sexuality were changing rapidly: tellingly, this is a time from which a number of translations of the plays date. Perhaps part of the appeal of a play like *Lysistrata* was that, as a classical drama, it could lay claim to a degree of respectability. This in turn meant that in times and places where the full effects of sexual liberation were still to be felt, it could be performed more readily than a non-classical play of comparable content. In her article 'Greek Drama in Rhodesia/Zimbabwe', for example, Jessie Maritz talks of a performance of *Lysistrata* which took place in Sailsbury (modern-day Harare) in 1964 in which girls wore bikinis – a daring move, she notes, since these had been banned at public swimming baths four years earlier.[9] The play, although not universally praised by reviewers, was a big hit with the public.

This ability of Aristophanes' comedies to play a subversive role is hugely important to their performance history in many countries, but perhaps especially in Greece. As Gonda Van Steen has documented in her book *Venom in Verse*, in the turbulent three decades following the Second World War in particular, Aristophanic comedy came to be seen as something quintessentially Greek – a repository of ancient folk traditions – and provided a vehicle through which the establishment was often severely criticized by directors like Koun and Solomos.[10] A particular *cause célèbre* was Koun's 1959 production of *Birds* in the ancient Herodes Atticus Theatre in Athens: his radical production featured a priest dressed in Greek Orthodox garb whose chanting parodied the music of the church liturgy.[11] After the premiere, further performances of the play were banned by the government and the incident led to front-page discussions in the press for some time afterwards about the rights and wrongs of both the production itself and the subsequent act of censorship. Over forty years later in 2002, a production of *Frogs* in Sicily also came under scrutiny from the authorities: in this case it would appear that the director, Ronconi, was pressured into removing panels from his set containing caricatures of four prominent right-wing Italian politicians.[12]

The performance history of Aristophanes' plays in the English-speaking world has certainly been less headline-grabbing than in Greece and Italy but none the less healthy – especially from the late 1980s onwards, since when there has been a marked increase in the staging of classical drama of all types. We shall look in detail at some English-language productions of Aristophanes' plays towards the end of the chapter. Scholarly interest in modern stagings of Greek drama has also been intense since the 1990s and now forms a major part of the academic discipline of 'Reception Studies'. For the amateur and professional researcher alike there exists an abundance of online resources and databases: the University of Oxford's *Archive of Performances of Greek and Roman Drama* and the Open University's *Classical Receptions* websites are particularly useful starting points for investigating British productions.[13]

This revived interest in staging plays was also prefigured by a growth in the number of published translations of Aristophanes. From the 1960s onwards there has been a steady stream of English language versions of the plays, partly inspired no doubt by the increased scholarly interest in Aristophanes, which in turn has led to large numbers of students in British and American universities studying his comedies in translation. In short, the market has been buoyant.

This increased translation activity means that there are a whole range of editions of Aristophanes for a reader to choose from. The two most prominent bilingual editions of the plays (with facing page Greek and English) are the Loeb series translated by Jeffrey Henderson (five volumes, including fragments) and the Aris and Phillips series translated by Sommerstein (eleven volumes, including commentaries on the text, plus a further volume of indices).[14] Both these scholars-cum-translators have translated the plays in different formats, too, Sommerstein and Barrett's Penguin series being the most widely read (Sommerstein's *Lysistrata and Other Plays*, originally published in 1973, has sold over 300,000 copies).[15] Other translations of note include volumes by McLeish (published by Methuen),[16] Meineck (Hackett),[17] Halliwell (Oxford World Classics)[18] and those included in the Penn University Series (edited by Slavitt and Bovie).[19] It is these and other published translations that will form the basis of the discussion in the following sections.

Issues of translation: theoretical perspectives

With their humour, colloquialisms, obscenities, topicality and literary allusions, Aristophanes' plays present the translator with a unique set of challenges. And this is not to mention the added complications involved in translating for the stage: how is a translator to make a drama which is a product of a very different culture and theatrical tradition 'work' in modern performance?

Arguably, these difficulties simply serve to underline the importance of translation – and not just for the Greekless reader, either. The act of translating, reading a translation, or seeing an Aristophanic play transposed onto the stage as a piece of living theatre, keeps the challenges and questions posed by a text fresh in the mind, providing what Lorna Hardwick describes as 'a contemporary means of understanding and responding to the ancient work.'[20] Translations, then, need not be regarded as inferior imitations of the original text: rather they play a pivotal role in negotiating the status and meaning of a text in the receiving culture – and, more than this, they are usefully regarded as works of literature in their own right. Rather than simply ask of translations what has been lost in comparison with the original, it is now a commonplace to ask with equal vigour what has been gained and, if we then look back to the original work, to ask how the translation can reinform our understanding of it.

This growing interest in translation has also touched some of the translators of classical texts themselves, who voice informed, and sometimes challenging, opinions in the introductions to their works. David West, for example, in the preface to his version of the *Aeneid*, reconfigures traditional views of 'faithful' translation to include responsibility to the sound, pace and poetic feel of the original.[21] West thus gives new life to the age-old issues of the 'letter' and 'spirit' of the text so central to discussions of translation, reminding us that to convey a literal meaning of a literary work from source to target language is only one model of translation – and often an unsatisfactory one at that.

But what of these age-old debates? Terms such as the 'letter' and 'spirit' are still widely used in discussions of translation for the good reason that they neatly encapsulate different views as to what it means to be 'faithful' to the original text. At one extreme, it has been argued that a translation should take the form of a heavily footnoted word-for-word rendering of the text in question, accompanied by towers of explanatory footnotes (this is the position taken by the novelist Vladimir Nabokov); at the other extreme, that a translation should be conceived as a 'rewrite' designed to convey the underlying energies of the original (the position of the poet Ezra Pound, who famously advised a translator, 'Don't bother about the WORDS, translate the MEANING').[22]

Debates about 'letter', 'spirit', 'literalness' and 'faithfulness' continue to be reshaped by scholars working in the thriving academic discipline of Translation Studies and for those wishing to describe the ways in which translators approach their work, there are any number of ways in which translations can be categorized. Is the translation 'Source-Text orientated', for instance (that is, does it aim to reflect the assumptions and values of the society that produced it, e.g. classical Athens) or is it 'Target-Text orientated' (that is to say, adapted to the norms and expectations of the receiving culture, e.g. the modern English-speaking world)?[23] A slightly different distinction is made by Lawrence Venuti who coins the terms 'foreignization' and 'domestication'. 'Foreignization' involves translating the text in such a way as to make readers aware that they are reading a text in translation (e.g. by including anachronisms or by reflecting the word order of the original text), whereas 'domestication' involves 'reduc[ing] ... the foreign text to target language values' so as to make it 'immediately recognizable and intelligible' to a reader. In short, 'domestication' means that the translated work is given the illusion of not being a translation at all, but rather a work originally written in the target language: that is to say, something 'domestic' rather than 'foreign'.[24]

These complex theoretical issues are not just academic problems: they represent live practical concerns for the translator of Aristophanes' plays. How is a translator to cope with all the culturally-specific everyday objects mentioned in Aristophanes' plays, for example, or with colloquial expressions? In his bilingual Loeb edition of *Frogs*, Henderson uses words like 'minestrone', 'munchies' and 'lummox' (lines 62, 510, 1037): these are far from bland words, I would suggest, and represent an attempt to make the dialogue lively and contemporary for a reader (in the same way that Aristophanes' Greek would have struck *his* audience as lively and contemporary). Ironically, such 'faithfulness' to the original 'spirit' of the original (if we choose to view it in those terms) could also be seen as an example of 'foreignization': for many people, modern colloquialisms like 'munchies' or a word such as 'minestrone' will no doubt seem out of place in a translation of an ancient text – with the result that Henderson's readers will be more rather than less conscious that what they are reading is a translation. And here it is worth gauging our own personal reactions to Henderson's strategy and reflecting on any preconceptions that we may have: do we consider translations like 'psychopath' and 'salsa' (*Assemblywomen* 250 and 292) to be an acceptable and engaging attempt to render Aristophanes' Greek or do we find them *un*acceptable and unappealing?

Whatever we might make of Henderson's efforts, what he produces in his Loeb editions is very much a *translation* of Aristophanes' plays: each line of English clearly corresponds to a line in the Greek. This is not the strategy adopted by everyone, however. Sometimes translators – while leaving the plays largely intact – choose to omit and/or rework elements of the original text (topical references, for example), so much so that the word 'version' probably describes more accurately what they have written. Sometimes writers go further still, producing a self-consciously new work of art, like Tony Harrison's *The Common Chorus* (written 1988; published 1992) or Blake Morrison's *Lisa's Sex Strike* (2007: discussed above) both of which are based on Aristophanes' *Lysistrata*. These are probably best described as 'adaptations' of *Lysistrata* – works which, while inspired by Aristophanes, are recognizably distinct from the Aristophanic original. It should be said, however, that these are loose categories: there is no hard-and-fast line to be drawn between a 'translation', 'version' and 'adaptation' and scholars tend to use the terms if not indiscriminately, then fairly interchangeably.[25]

Faithfulness can work at deeper levels, too. Translators and adaptors may have strong opinions about the extent to which *their* versions of the plays (like Aristophanes' originals) should strike *their* audiences as humorous or political, for example, and addressing these issues – especially in the context of a performance translation – might lead to the inclusion of substitute jokes or references to contemporary politics (we shall see both of these strategies in operation below). Most translators for the stage would also see producing a play that works well in performance as an important aspect of being 'faithful' to the Aristophanic original – even if this entailed making significant changes to the 'letter' of what Aristophanes wrote. In short, translating Aristophanes consists of a whole series of difficult decisions, both large and small, and a translator needs to have a clear idea of what they think to be the 'spirit' of an Aristophanic play if they are to produce a coherent version of it. Only in this way can the translator make intelligent decisions about what aspects of the play they will choose to enhance and which to underplay.

Lysistrata: stage directions, discontinuity and dialect

To help us think about these issues further, let us begin by looking at the opening lines of *Lysistrata* and consider some of the issues that these raise. Here is how Sommerstein translates the first 17 lines of the play in his 1990 Aris and Phillips volume (a scholarly edition with facing page Greek and English text).

> [*Lysistrata comes out of one of the flanking doors of the stage-house. She looks off to right and left, but sees no one approaching.*]
> LYSISTRATA [*annoyed*]: Now if someone had invited them to a Bacchic revel, or to Pan's shrine, or to Genetyllis' shrine at Collias – you'd never have been able to get through the crowd, what with the drums! But as it is, there's not a woman turned up here.
> [*Seeing the far door open*] Except that here's my neighbour coming out.
> [*Calonice comes out.*] Good morning, Calonice.
> CALONICE: Same to you, Lysistrata. [*Coming closer*] What's disturbed you so terribly? Don't look cross, child. Knitted brows don't look good on you.
> LYSISTRATA: My heart's burning, Calonice, and I'm feeling *very* sore about us women: because in men's opinion we're thought to be such utter rascals –
> CALONICE: And so we are, by Zeus!
> LYSISTRATA: But when they've been told to meet here to have a discussion about a far from trivial matter, they lie asleep and don't come.

There are a number of items of interest in these lines. To take them in order, the first point to consider is the inclusion of stage directions in the

English text. Of course, all ancient drama presents us with the problem of reconstructing stage business, but with Old Comedy our lack of knowledge about the actor's movements (the 'blocking' of the original play) and comic business such as slapstick is a particularly significant loss. Importantly, the manner in which we think of a line as being delivered can also effect whether we perceive it as, say, serious or humorous, weighty or light – an issue with particular resonance for Aristophanic drama, where the boundaries between playful and non-playful, seriousness and humour are often difficult to discern (or even deliberately blurred). A translator's stage directions therefore gain special importance by acting as a commentary on the text, steering the reader's perception of, and reaction to, the words spoken.

In this passage we note that whilst Sommerstein includes a number of stage directions – indeed, more than many translators – his tendency is to play safe: he simply conjectures that Lysistrata 'looks off to right and left' and that in her initial delivery she is 'annoyed'. He then adds a series of notes concerning Calonice's movements, all of which are envisaged in terms of the ancient rather than the modern stage – just as we might expect, perhaps, from a scholarly edition of the text such as this.

To put Sommerstein's intial stage direction into context, let us look at the opening of the play as translated by X.J. Kennedy is his 1998 translation for the Penn Greek Drama series, edited by Slavitt and Bovie:

ACT I

(Athens, a public square. In the background the Propylaea, main gate to
the Acropolis. Lysistrata, a young matron, is alone
walking up and down impatiently.)
LYSISTRATA
 No doubt if I'd asked them over for an orgy
 in honour of Dionysus, Pan-pipes and drinks,
 a little Aphrodisiacal wild party,
 they'd be here with bells on – you couldn't
 move for the mob of them. But now
 not a woman in creation shows her face.

Kennedy's translation of the play has a different set of aspirations from Sommerstein's. In his introduction, he says that he hopes his translation 'will be a fairly readable, possibly playable version' of the play,[26] to which end he uses as an idiom modern American colloquial English. Put simply, Kennedy has chosen accessibility and performativity over any archaeological faithfulness: certainly he seems to envisage the action in a modern theatre, since his stage direction would suggest a set and perhaps even a curtain, after the raising of which Lysistrata can be seen 'walking up and down'.

Providing stage directions appropriate to the modern stage is not the only way in which Kennedy adapts his translation for a modern audience.

Like many others, he also omits the place names mentioned in the original text ('Pan's shrine' and 'Genetyllis' shrine at Collias' in Sommerstein's translation), divides the play into two acts and gives the action of the play a location: a square in front of the Propylaea. And again, like many others who employ the convention, he also has the second act take place five days after the first (for the simple reason that Cinesias comments to his wife at line 881 that their baby has not eaten for six days). By adopting this policy, of course, Kennedy either fails to take into account – or, to give him the benefit of the doubt, deliberately chooses to underplay – a key aspect of Aristophanes' plays: the way in which time and place are sometimes only weakly defined. As we saw in Chapter 3, in Old Comedy the location of the action is not always fixed (especially at the beginning of the play) and can alter (often rapidly) during the course of the play – and similarly, such lapses of time as take place during the course of the play are generally unsignalled and unaccounted for (only the most literal-minded spectator would think to ask how Dicaeopolis manages to get from place to place so fast in *Acharnians*, for example, or why the gods get perturbed so quickly by Peisthetaerus' actions in *Birds*). And whilst *Lysistrata* may not display the shifts of time and place of a play like the *Acharnians*, there is nonetheless something un-Aristophanic about having the location and timing of the episodes rigidly specified. In Aristophanes' play (as compared to Kennedy's translation of it) it is not until around line 240 – about one-fifth of the way through – that the stage building is identified as the Acropolis; before then the location of the play is simply not fixed with any certainty. Likewise, in the original play the action is simply presented as a continuous stream of sequential events rather than being structured into two separate acts – let alone ones that are formally identified as taking place on different days.

One response to Kennedy's translation strategy is to see him as having failed to grasp an essential element of the play that he is translating, but perhaps this is doing him a disservice. On another view, he could be seen as translating the play in such a way as to be more comprehensible to directors and audiences unused to the traditions and conventions of ancient theatre. His division of the play into acts might even be seen in a pragmatic light: after all, for a theatre an interval (and the increased drinks sales it represents) can often be essential to the commercial viability of a production.

Related to the shifts in time and place is a further feature of Aristophanic comedy: the 'recreative' nature of many of Aristophanes' characters – that is, the fact that his characters do not always act in a consistent and psychologically plausible way (as outlined in Chapter 5). As an example of this, let us take another look at a short exchange from towards the beginning of *Lysistrata*, this time in Kennedy's 'modern American colloquial' idiom (a passage we looked at in Chapter 5):

LYSISTRATA
>Oh, Kally, darling, this just burns me up.
>What a disgrace! That women won't turn out
>to save their reputations! Menfolk say
>we're just a pack of conniving schemers.

KALONIKE
>Ain't it the truth!

LYSISTRATA
>And now, when I invite
>all the girls here for an important conference,
>the dumb clucks stay home dozing.

Lysistrata 9-15

Calonice's interjection, translated as 'And so we are, by Zeus!' by Sommerstein – 'Ain't that the truth!' in Kennedy's version – is a subtle example of 'recreativity'. In a real-life exchange – or one which is aimed at realism – we might expect Lysistrata to challenge Calonice as to what she means or to reproach her for her lack of solidarity. But in the 'recreative', discontinuous world of Aristophanic drama, Lysistrata resumes speaking and Calonice's comment is simply not reacted to. Much as these instances of discontinuity are a characteristic feature of Aristophanic drama, they are obviously capable of making some translators uncomfortable. Fitts, for example, in his 1959 translation feels the need to make both characters' comments less pointed, with the result that Calonice seems merely to be sympathizing with Lysistrata's sentiments.

LYSISTRATA: ...
>Kalonikê,
>the way we women behave! Really, I don't blame the men
>for what they say about us.
KALONIKE: No, I imagine they're right.

Seldes, in his 1934 adaptation for the stage, also reconfigures the exchange to make it more naturalistic:

LYSISTRATA: ... Oh, Kalonika, my heart is broken. I'm ashamed of our sex.
>Men have always said that we are untrustworthy and sly and trivial –
KALONIKA: Just between ourselves, don't you think that they're right?

So far we have been dwelling on loss: the fact that a potentially challenging quality of Aristophanes' plays – their 'recreative' nature – is not always reflected in translations as well as it might be. (Indeed, this tendency to iron out difficulties presented by the Source Text is a quality common to many translations, not just those of Aristophanes: this is also characteristic of 'domestication', as discussed above). Natural as it might seem to dwell on what we might feel is missing from a translation, however, we should not forget that there are other points we might usefully make about these passages, too. As Lorna Hardwick comments, '[i]t is a commonplace to say that something is lost in all translations. However, asking precisely what is lost in a particular work and comparing this with what is gained, makes for a far more interesting inquiry.'[27] So here it is also worth noting an important quality which versions like those of Seldes, Fitts and Kennedy may have gained from the alteration of details: performativity. Adopting modern dramatic idiom and stage conventions no doubt makes the action more comprehensible and more immediate to an audience unacquainted with the ancient stage.

To look for gain, however, is not abandon our critical faculties: we may, for example, have strong views about the decisions a translator makes and the rationale (or, indeed, lack of rationale) underpinning the choices made. Our personal reactions (however well thought through they may be) are also worth balancing, no doubt, with a different kind of judgement: namely an assessment of the extent to which the translator's own objectives are achieved. As Seldes explains in his introduction, the radical changes that *he* makes to *Lysistrata* are done self-consciously as part of a programme with clear objectives. One of these was to produce a play that would work successfully on the contemporary stage – an objective he apparently achieved (his *Lysistrata* was even staged on Broadway). It strikes me that the work of Kennedy, on the other hand, has certain responsibilities which are not fulfilled. His translation is published as part of the Penn Greek Drama series which, we are told by the editors, aims 'to make ... cultural treasure accessible, restoring as faithfully as possible the original luster of the plays ...'.[28] In part this goal is achieved (the play is no doubt 'accessible'), but there must be a concern that some of the 'lustre' of Aristophanes' play has been translated away. Certainly the changes Kennedy makes are not highlighted as being at odds with contemporary scholarly approaches to the play and often seem arbitrary rather than informed. For example, he opts to render the speech of the Spartans in the dialect 'of the streets of Brooklyn or Jersey city' on the basis that this is 'a dialect likely to strike most Americans as barbarous'.[29] Why Spartans should need to come across as 'barbarous', he does not explain, and whilst his Brooklyn-cum-Jersey City dialect may have the potential of being found amusing by modern audiences – especially audiences unused to hearing this particular working-class accent used in the context of classical drama – his readership ought to be warned that Aristophanes himself apparently makes no comic capital from Spartan dialect whatsoever.

This last topic, that of the rendering of Spartan dialect, raises fascinating issues of perceived cultural equivalence. Historically, British translators have tended to employ Scots dialect and American translators that of the Deep South. Kennedy's departure from this at least has the merit of novelty, but Halliwell's solution in his 1997 translation for the Oxford World Classics series is more radical still. He simply translates the Spartan's speech into standard English since, he argues, 'no appropriate equivalent, making sense in both linguistic and cultural terms, is readily available'.[30] As someone who teaches in a Scottish university, his decision is also pragmatic, as he points out. Halliwell's is essentially a page rather than a stage translation, but presumably it would make even *more* sense for authors of performance-orientated translations to allow the matter of the attribution of Spartans' accent to be decided by a director.

Obscenity, sexual ethics and *double entendres*

Perhaps the most striking way in which translations of *Lysistrata* have changed over the years is in the rendering of obscenities. The most climactic obscenity of the play, the *peos* uttered by Lysistrata as she reveals what she is asking the women to forgo (*Lysistrata* 124), has changed from Benjamin Bickley Rogers' 'the joys of Love' (1902) to Sommerstein's 'cock and balls' (1990) and Halliwell's 'prick' (1997). Proudest of the directness of his expression is Henderson who states in the introduction to his 1996 'Staging Women' edition of the play:[31]

> In my translation I have ... made no attempt to spare the modern reader by censoring or translating around potentially disturbing material; instead I have tried to render each of Aristophanes' linguistic registers by using the nearest English equivalent.

Perhaps it is no surprise that Henderson singles out his full-blooded approach to translating obscenities: after all Halliwell was still able to comment in 2000 that there are 'few [translators] who shirk nothing in this area'.[32] It may be telling that British translators often seem less inhibited than their American counterparts – with the obvious exception of Henderson. That said, one of the complicating factors surrounding obscene language is how effectively to render Greek obscenities like *peos* and *prôktos*. As far as *peos* is concerned neither 'cock', 'dick' nor 'prick' is particularly obscene in modern English (unlike its Greek counterpart) and as for *prôktos*, 'ass-hole' has lost much of its force in American English.

Here we are encroaching on one of the central decisions which translators have had to make over the years when translating Aristophanes: that is, how to deal with the sexual content of his plays. The increasing tendency from the 1960s onwards to square up to Aristophanes' obscenity has not always been matched with a willingness on the part of translators to represent the less politically correct aspects of what Halliwell has called Aristophanes' 'erotics of shamelessness'.[33] A key passage here is the Phallic

Ode of *Acharnians*, where Dicaeopolis fantasizes about sexually assault-
ing a slave-girl (a passage examined in detail in Chapter 8); the relevant
extract – complete with its address to Phales, personified god of the
Hard-On, is robustly translated by Henderson in his 1998 Loeb edition as
follows:[34]

> Yes, it's far more pleasant, Phales, Phales,
> to catch a budding maid with pilfered wood—
> Strymodorus' Thratta from the Rocky Bottom—
> and grab her waist, lift her up, throw her down
> and take her cherry.

> *Acharnians* 271-5

However, in the translation of the ode by Jack Flavin for the Slavitt and
Bovie Penn University series (also published in 1998) the nature of the
assault is considerably softened:[35]

> O Phales, how much sweeter it is
> to catch a pretty thieving maid
> and lie in a soft inviting glade
> and make her pay a fine of kisses.

There are any number of reasons why Flavin may have chosen to translate
the lines in the way he has, but a good candidate must surely be a desire
to avoid confronting the morally problematic rape in these lines head on.
In a similar vein, it is not unknown for North American translations to
underplay the ethnic and sexual stereotyping so prevalent in Aristophanes' plays – presumably to accommodate cultural sensitivities (in a
2002 article, for example, Elizabeth Scharffenberger looks at the controversy surrounding William Arrowsmith's portrayal of the Scythian archer
as African-American in his version of *Women at the Thesmophoria* and
highlights some particularly interesting aspects of the debate surrounding
race).[36] Even in the modern era, Aristophanes' comedy still has the power
to shock, it would appear.

Double entendres appear to cause translators fewer qualms than obscene language and matters of sexual ethics. The following passage from
Lysistrata (a more literal translation of which appears in Chapter 7, p.
127), is delivered by the Magistrate (*Proboulos*) as he explains how men
only have themselves to blame for their wives' infidelity. The lines appear
here in the version of Horace Liverlight whose work was privately published (at the time anonymously) by the Athenian society in 1912.[37] Of interest
is that this translator avoids outright obscenity in his version the play (his
Lysistrata simply says, 'We must refrain from the male altogether') but he
nevertheless preserves at least some of the force of the *double entendres* in
his translation of this passage.

MAGISTRATE

We men must share the blame of their [wives'] ill conduct; it is we who teach them to love riot and dissoluteness and sow the seeds of wickedness in their hearts. You see a husband go into a shop: 'Look you, jeweller,' says he, 'you remember the necklace you made for my wife. Well, t'other evening, when she was dancing, the catch came open. Now, I'm bound for Salamis; will you make it convenient to go up to-night to make her fastening secure?'

Lysistrata 404-13

The relative lack of inhibitions which translators display in relation to *double entendres* has a straightforward explanation, of course: unlike obscenity, *double entendres* refer to taboo objects and acts only obliquely.

The challenge of humour

An added interest that this passage of *double entendres* represents is that it is an example of humour. The humour of this last passage from *Lysistrata* seems to me to have been preserved remarkably well in the version quoted – but this contrasts markedly with an exchange such as the following from the play's prologue, the humour of which proves challenging for translators to convey. Here, Lysistrata is bewailing the fact that none of the women that she has asked to come to her meeting has yet shown up, singling out those from two particular places in Attica for their non-arrival: the coastal region (Paralia) and the island of Salamis.[38] A rough, literal version might read:

Lysistrata: Well! There's not a single woman from Paralia here yet –
                nor from Salamis.
Calonice: I'm sure that they'll have been going over on their *kelêtes*
                since the early hours.

Lysistrata 58-60

The humour here lies in some clever word play in the Greek: *kelês* (pl. *kelêtes*). This can denote a kind of swift-moving boat, hence one way to understand the last line is that the women have been 'crossing over on their yachts'; but *kelês* also means 'race-horse' and as such refers to a sexual position in which the woman straddles the man (a position for which prostitutes could apparently charge a large amount of money) – so the women have also been 'spread over their rides'. In addition, Salamis is a place that evidently had erotic connotations of its own.[39] Here, then, we have a pun which relies on a nexus of cultural references to allow it to be realized – and the lack of a single straightforward English phrase that can convey the complexity of the pun in the Greek ('crossing over on their yachts'/ 'spread over their rides') means that translators are forced to be inventive. Halliwell's version, for example, reads:[40]

203

LYSISTRATA.   Not a single woman has come from the coastal region,
               And no one's here from Salamis yet.
KALONIKE.   I bet
               That they were up at dawn for an early ride!

Halliwell's solution is both simple and effective – but we should not let the slickness of his rendering of these lines disguise the difficulty which puns can cause a translator. The pun of Sommerstein's Aris and Phillips version, for instance, is less direct (if none the less ingenious) and the reference to horses lost. Exploiting the fact that the word 'pinnace' (which is a kind of light boat) shares a formal similarity with the word 'penis', he has Calonice reply:[41]

Oh as for them, they'll have been working over on their pinnaces well before daylight.

Henderson, on the other hand, in his 1996 'Staging Women' translation, jettisons the reference to boats, but effectively maintains the pun nevertheless:[42]

Oh them: I just know they've been up since dawn, straddling their mounts.

Lastly, Fitts seems to miss the joke altogether:[43]

LYSISTRATA: ...
    There's no one here from the South Shore, or from Sálamis.
KALONIKE:
    Things are hard over in Sálamis, I swear.
    They have to get going at dawn.

These two instances of humour – the Magistrate's *double entendres* on the one hand, and the pun concerning the women of Salamis on the other – would appear to represent quite separate challenges for the translator. To help us account for the differences in their translatability, it will prove useful to refer to a distinction often made by humour theorists, namely one between 'verbal' and 'situational' humour. This division of humour into these two categories (which we encountered briefly in Chapter 4) makes its first appearance in Cicero's *On Oratory* – though is probably Greek in origin, possibly originating with Aristotle. In the treatise, Cicero talks of jokes either relying for their effect *de verbis*, 'on the words' or *de re*, 'on the thing'.

For the joke that, said in whatever words, is nevertheless funny, is contained in the thing (*res*); the joke that loses its wit if the words are changed, has all the funniness in the words (*verba*). ...

                                    Cicero, *De Oratore*, 2.62 (252)

Cicero's test, then, for deciding whether a joke is verbal – *de verbis* – or situational – *de re* (also called 'referential' humour) – is whether it can be cast in different words and still retain its wit. And whilst Cicero is not talking about translation as such, we nevertheless have here a potentially useful distinction when considering the translation of humour into a foreign language. According to Cicero's principle, a 'situational' piece of humour ought to be straightforward to translate, since 'if the words are changed' – its funniness is still apparent. This is the kind of humour we witnessed in the passage of *double entendres* just now – a passage whose humour is so hardy that even the most bashful of translators seems unable to kill it off. However, since the second instance of humour we looked at – the lines about the women of Salamis – is a *pun* and therefore belongs to the category of 'verbal' humour. And since 'all the funniness' of the original joke was 'in the words' (i.e. the double meaning of *kelês*) it seems reasonable that it caused problems for its translators, as this is the very kind of humour which, in Cicero's terms, is capable of losing its funniness when rephrased.

So far so good: but things are not always as straightforward as this divide between 'situational' and 'verbal' humour might initially suggest. Sometimes, for instance, a translator is fortunate enough to find that there is a English equivalent for the word or phrase which is the subject of the pun in the Greek – equivalent, that is, inasmuch as it has a similar range of meanings as the Greek word. In such cases (rare as they might be in the case of two languages that differ as much as English and Classical Greek) translation of verbal humour is relatively unproblematic. A prime example of a piece of 'translatable' verbal humour comes towards the end of *Acharnians* when Dicaeopolis, who is now enjoying the benefits of his private peace treaty, is mocking the war-mongering general Lamachus. Aristophanes puns on the word *xymbolê*, which can mean both 'encounter, engagement' (i.e. in battle) and also 'contribution, subscription'. The stroke of luck enjoyed by the translator of these lines is that there is a corresponding English word that possesses these same multiple meanings: namely, 'charge'. In the Penguin version of the play, Sommerstein translates:[44]

Lamachus: O dreadful, fatal charge –
Dicaeopolis: What, you've been *charged* for your entertainment on
              Pitcher Day?
                                                    Acharnians 1210-11

So, a translator can sometimes be fortunate in finding that a verbal joke can be transferred from the source language to the target language relatively easily. When the translator is *un*fortunate, however, and no natural correspondence exists for the humorous phrase or word they are faced with translating, a decision must be taken as to how to convey the humour effectively. We have already seen how a series of translators have grappled with the same essentially untranslatable pun on *kelês*, for example.

Verbal humour, and puns in particular, would appear to cause great anxiety for translators of Aristophanes – and for good reason, given both the difficulty they present in and of themselves and the added fact that, as Stephen Halliwell notes, it is 'the verbal details of the text ... which cumulatively create the flavour of Aristophanic humour'.[45] In their introductions, translators sometimes proudly single out instances of puns they feel they have successfully transferred from Greek to English while preserving most of the letter and the flavour of the original. They are seldom as candid about their less admirable efforts, however, as Robin Bond, a New Zealand academic who has translated a number of plays by Plautus and Aristophanes for performance. Reflecting on his translation work, he says:[46]

> ... in comedy one has to adapt and change to a certain extent. As a matter of technique the hardest thing, of course, is puns. Occasionally translations of puns fly into your head but sometimes they don't. Sometimes therefore you ignore the pun in the Greek or the Latin and sometimes you import one which is not there, because whatever you've lost you can compensate for by invention.

Sommerstein makes similar comments in his 1973 article, 'On translating Aristophanes: Ends and Means', in which he explains the approach he takes to translation in the original Penguin volumes of the plays.[47]

> To give an idea of the verbal humour ... I have found it necessary to adapt his jokes, or, where even this is impossible, to compensate for their loss by adding something elsewhere. I have generally at such points given an idea in the notes of what the author wrote.

Douglass Parker, recalling his work with William Arrowsmith on their various translations of the comedies from the 1950s onwards, expresses this strategy of 'compensation' more starkly still, calling the technique 'the surrogate joke':[48]

> The *fact* of the joke is more important than the particulars of that joke. ... But verbal jokes are normally lost. So, we were to *compensate*. Put in other jokes.

Here we come back once more to the issues of the compromises which must be made to maintain something of the 'spirit' if not the 'letter', with adapted and substitute jokes being emblematic of a whole series of additions – large and small – which translators either choose to make or are forced to make in order to communicate key aspects of the original text. Faced with the problem of conveying Aristophanes' humour, Bond, Sommerstein and Parker all make the similar pragmatic decision – they *compensate* – though in very different ways, as can be judged from the diverse nature of the resulting translations (the Parker/Arrowsmith versions of plays in particular are highly experimental). A further key difference is that Bond is translating for the stage and so does not have the option afforded to Sommerstein and Parker of appending notes to their texts.

Humour and cultural transfer

Before we leave the topic of jokes we should note that there is sub-category of humour which, while being situational, fails to transfer into the Target Language. This is when there are allusions in the Greek to objects, concepts or people which have a different or no resonance in the modern world. The extent to which such cultural transfer breaks down is naturally dependent on the audience – a scholarly translation can afford to assume some knowledge of Aristophanes' world in a way in which a translation for the stage rarely can. The following quip from *Lysistrata* serves as a good illustration of this phenomenon. When Cinesias is being tormented by his wife, Myrrhine, with promises of sex which she keeps failing to fulfil, he says:

> Well, is this Heracles' cock you're entertaining?
>
> *Lysistrata* 928

The joke makes sense only when we know that Heracles often features in Old Comedy as a character who was promised a meal, but either received it too late or not at all. Henderson's device of including necessary information in the text of his translation – the so-called 'intruded gloss' – is a common one. In his Loeb edition, he translates:[49]

> KINESIAS: Is this cock of mine supposed to be Herakles waiting for his dinner?

The problems of rendering the humour of this line in English neatly illustrate the point that translation is a process of cultural as well as linguistic transfer: that is, the successful translation of humour often depends on the existence of certain shared cultural assumptions or knowledge between the original and new audiences. If a modern audience is likely to lack a piece of vital knowledge, then the text needs to be adapted (e.g. by the addition of an 'intruded gloss') for the joke to be put across successfully.

Translating Aristophanes' lyrics

Songs throw up an interesting set of challenges for the translator of Aristophanes. Not least of these is how to convey in a written translation (as opposed to performance) any sense that Aristophanes was writing a form of musical drama. Of course, since the tunes of Aristophanes' lyrics are lost to us there is no imperative for the translator to come up with a version which reflects the rhythms of the original – although this is still an option, as many of the translations by Benjamin Bickley Rogers in particular bear out (one of Rogers' lyrical translations appears on pp. 156-7 of this book). More recent translators tend to play down the musical aspect of the lyrics, however – but not all. The following comments made by Stephen Halliwell in the introduction to his Oxford World Classics volume are worth quoting at length on this point. He maintains that, as far as translating lyric is concerned:[50]

> ... it would be pointless to follow Rogers and several of his Victorian predecessors in aiming for anything like a consistent correlation with Greek rhythms, since too many ... make no recognizable pattern to a modern ear. In some passages, however, it is feasible to capture part of the rhythmical ethos in at least an approximate manner, either by the general 'shape' and length of metrical phrases or by some of their dominant rhythms. My strategy here has been to employ marked English stress patterns in a few contexts where they can provide an intelligible match for the original ... but often to allow myself a more fluid, free-verse technique.

So Halliwell's strategy is, as a rule, to employ rhythm in his translations of lyric and for this to reflect the rhythm of the original when appropriate but by no means always. One of the issues that Halliwell is wrestling with here is one with which we are already familiar (albeit in a different guise): cultural transfer. Some cultural items – like the *double entendres* of the *Lysistrata* passage and certain simple poetic rhythms – transfer from Classical Greek to Modern English with comparatively little difficulty; other items, however, such as the Phallic Ode's sexual assault and more complex poetic rhythms, may need more careful handling before being presented to a modern English-speaking audience.

So what effect does Halliwell achieve? Here is his version of *Birds* 209-22, the Hoopoe's song (discussed in Chapter 6, p. 115, where it is quoted in Roger's 1906 translation). In the lyric, Tereus (the Hoopoe) calls on his wife, Procne (a nightingale) to wake up and sing her accustomed dirge to their dead son.

HOOPOE. Come, nest-mate of mine, wake up from your sleep!
Issue forth all the strains of the sacred chants
In which you lament, with a mouth that's inspired,
For the child of us both, oh piteous Itys!
Let your voice thrill the air with its liquid notes,
Through your vibrant throat! For your song is so pure
As it echoes around, through the rich-leaved trees,
Till it reaches the throne of lord Zeus up above,

Where Phoibus as well, gold-tressed god of song,
Hears your grief and responds on his ivory lyre,
As he summons the gods to take part in the dance.
Then is heard from above an immortal choir,
   All in unison clear,
As the gods cry in grief for your plight.

Birds 209-22

Here, Halliwell employs the ode's original rhythms (anapaests, ∪ ∪ –, and spondees, – – : see Chapter 7) to create an accomplished pastiche (even for the least poetically-minded reader, the rhythm, with its four stresses to the line, comes alive on reading this passage aloud). Halliwell pays homage to the Aristophanic original in other ways, too: his version is elevated in tone, for example, and translates most, if not all, of the compound adjectives in the Greek with compound adjectives in English ('rich-leaved', 'gold-tressed').

As far as other lyric passages are concerned, Halliwell sets many out in verse form but does not always choose to translate them with any consistent rhythm (especially when the original rhythm is iambic and therefore metrically similar to the play's spoken parts). An example of this can be seen in his version of an ode from *Lysistrata* in which the defiant chorus of old men claims that it will see off the women from the Acropolis just as they did King Cleomenes of Sparta nearly a century before. This is a passage which is far less elevated both metrically and lexically than the *Birds* lyric.

Old men.   I swear that while I live their plot will fail.
                  Why, even when Kleomenes seized this hill,
                     He did not leave unscathed.
                     For all his Spartan puff and prowess,
                     I made him drop his weapons.
                     He wore a little, patchy cloak;
                     He starved, he stank, he hadn't shaved
                     For six full years.

Lysistrata 271-80

The passage is not wholly prosaic, however: in case a reader should forget that this is poetry (albeit unelevated and relatively unexceptional poetry), Halliwell has gently coloured it with bursts of rhythm and alliteration.

Amongst modern translators, Halliwell is rare in his ambitions to produce literate poetry – indeed, it is no coincidence that, in the comments cited above, he mentions 'Rogers and ... his predecessors': who else would he compare his work in this area to? Hardly that of a performance translator like Peter Meineck whose version of the *Birds* lyric may well be jaunty and irresistible, but certainly no counterpart to the Aristophanic original in terms of linguistic elevation:

HOOPOE
> *Come my darling, rise from slumber,*
> *Fill the air with your holy number.*
> *Cry the keen from lips divine,*
> *Sing for Itys, both yours and mine.*
> *Pour forth the melody, honey-sweet,*
> *Raise the warble, chirp the tweet. ...*

This is not to say that Meineck's translations are inferior to Halliwell's – we are not comparing like with like. Meineck's translation is written for the theatre and part of the responsibility he evidently feels towards the original material is to make the play performable and accessible for a wide audience. What Meineck's translation of this passage loses in complexity it no doubt gains in immediacy.

To pick cruelly on the early Penguin translations, there is also clear blue water between Halliwell's approach and that of the young Alan Sommerstein, who translated so many of Aristophanes' lyrics to the tune of popular songs. His 1973 version of the Cleomenes ode from *Lysistrata*, for example, can be sung to the tune of *The Grand Old Duke of York*.

CHORUS:
> The grand old Spartan king,
>> He had six hundred men,
> He marched them into the Acropolis
>> And he marched them out again.
> And he entered breathing fire,
>> But when he left the place
> He hadn't washed for six whole years
>> And had hair all over his face ...

Lysistrata 273-80

Presumably the answer to the perfectly reasonable question 'What *was* he thinking?' is that Sommerstein was, on the one hand, keen to convey to his readers that the lyric parts of Aristophanes' plays were something distinct from the spoken parts and, on the other, was (like Meineck) conscious to make his translations performable – and saw sung lyric passages as a key part of any performance. It is striking how many translators when commenting on their work highlight performativity as central to their mission – but the effects of this emphasis are uneven when it comes to the treatment of lyric. To be sure, translators tend to mark the difference between the spoken and lyric parts of Aristophanes' plays in *some* way. The rhythm, rhyme and italics of Meineck's translations of lyric lie at one end of the spectrum; the typographical setting out of the lines as if they were free verse at the other. The most uniform use of this latter convention comes, perhaps unsurprisingly, in parallel texts, such as Sommerstein's Aris & Phillips edition and Henderson's Loeb translations (an extract from whose version of the

Phallic Song was quoted earlier), but this technique is also used freely elsewhere, including by Halliwell, as we have seen.

One key issue that lyric passages raise is how to convey specifically poetic and 'highfalutin' language – an area where modern translators understandably struggle to find suitable expression given the relative foreignness of high-flown language (as opposed to merely technical language) to most speakers today. Indeed, the language of high poetry was no doubt far more familiar to, and easily assimilated by, Rogers' readers in the early twentieth century than it is by modern readers. The result is that Rogers was able to reflect the registers and poetic expression of Aristophanes' lyrics in a way which would be difficult for a modern translator (for whom, of course, the obscene and sexual strata of Aristophanes' plays are, on the other hand, far easier to convey).[51] Here we return yet again to issues of cultural transfer – and perhaps the lesson to be learnt here is that we must resign ourselves to the fact that certain aspects of Aristophanes' work are simply more 'translatable' – linguistically and/or culturally – in certain societies, languages and eras than others.

Adapting Aristophanes for the stage

In this final section I want to consider briefly how adaptations of Aristophanes' plays have been staged. Naturally, amateur and student productions play a huge role in keeping Aristophanes alive in the modern theatre, but here I shall concentrate on larger scale productions for which versions of the plays have been specifically commissioned. Of interest here is the recurring importance of rhyme, music and spectacle to the productions and also the ways in which directors have changed and shaped the text with which they are working. Not all productions of Old Comedy have met with equal success with critics and audiences and this snapshot of four productions may serve to illustrate some of the reasons for this: making Old Comedy 'work' on stage is no easy task.

One adaptation that has a particularly rich performance history is Ranjit Bolt's *Lysistrata*, which premiered in Liverpool in 1993 before transferring to the Old Vic Theatre in London.[52] Bolt, a classicist by training, had previously enjoyed successes with adaptations of plays from a number of languages and was commissioned to write his *Lysistrata* by the renowned theatre director Peter Hall. Bolt's lively script is written in a contemporary idiom and makes extensive use of rhyme. The opening exchange, for example, reads as follows.[53]

LYSISTRATA

Where the fuck are these women? If they'd been
Invited to some orgy – some obscene
Bacchanalian ritual, the air would have been thick
With frenzied female cries – it makes me sick!
I don't believe it ... Here's Kalonike –
There's still some hope for Greece. Well possibly.
Morning.

KALONIKE

Morning, Lysistrata. What's wrong?
Don't scowl! A look like that does not belong
On a lovely face like yours!

Bolt's adaptation of the play follows the outline of the play fairly closely. While taking great pains to preserve the classical 'feel' of the play, he neither completely shies away from anachronistic detail ('barbecue', 'stocking') nor from inserting elements into the play that have no direct parallel in the original. Perhaps most striking in this regard is the way in which he reworks *Lysistrata*'s musical elements: songs play a particularly prominent part in Bolt's adaptation but their lyrics often differ hugely from what we find in Aristophanes. The following lyric, for instance, is taken from the Magistrate's song and is inspired by a *spoken* section of the original play: the *double entendres* passage discussed earlier (pp. 202-3; cf. p.127). Here, men's indulgent behaviour towards their wives' infidelity is said to have inspired the women's plan to seize the Acropolis.

SONG

Say you're married to a nymphomaniac –
She's given you a second heart attack –
You're out of action and she's in heat –
And just to make your misery complete –
Her latest lover's coming round tonight –
You haven't got the guts to stand and fight.

You go on bended knee to him
And grovel shamefully to him;
You're sweet as sweet can be to him;
You hand an extra key to him
And take a cup of tea to him
Or even two or three to him.
Say: 'rather you than me!' to him
Why don't you simply veto him?

Behaviour such as this beyond a doubt,
Has brought this latest escapade about.

Of course, when we are talking about a staged play, the script is only one element we need to consider. In addition, there is also an important respect in which the director, actors – even the set and costume designers – also take part in the process of 'translation' by shaping the audience's understanding of, and reaction to, the play. In Hall's production of Bolt's *Lysistrata*, for example, the anti-war theme was given particular emphasis. At the beginning of the play Lysistrata, played by Geraldine James, was to be seen daubing pacifist slogans on the wall of the set and this theme was picked up once more in the production's extraordinary finale, in which Hall subverted the play's celebratory ending. As one reviewer recounts: [54]

> As the actors lined up on the stage of the Old Vic to toast their treaty, clutching cheerfully phallic balloons and embracing one another, the audience, which had been spontaneously applauding and laughing heartily throughout the production, was ready to explode. And then suddenly the balloons popped and recorded machine-gun fire blasted out over the loudspeakers as the lights went down. The spectators were baffled, halted mid-clap as a wave of embarrassment and confusion swept the theater. Finally, hesitantly, the applause began, picking up energy as the actors appeared, masks in hand, for their curtain call.

Another interesting feature of Hall's production is the way in which it both evoked and played with ancient theatrical practices: as in many of his productions of classical plays, Hall had the actors wear masks, for instance; but in an exciting twist, the chorus removed these masks when addressing the audience in order to convey something of the effect of an Old Comic *parabasis*. This regard for the play's fifth-century BC context is also apparent in the script itself: at times Bolt even includes *more* detail about the contemporary political situation than is in Aristophanes' play, dwelling on the failure of the Sicilian Expedition in 413 BC, for example (a significant turning point in Athens' conflict with Sparta which took place two years before the original production of *Lysistrata* in 411 BC). Both adapter and director, then, were deeply concerned to convey something of the play's 'ancientness' as well as to make it 'work' as a piece of living theatre.

'Ancientness' is not always apparent in adaptations of Aristophanes' plays, however. Blake Morrison's decision to relocate *Lysistrata* in a Northern English town, for example, in *Lisa's Sex Strike* (Northern Broadsides) has already been described in outline in the introduction. The updating of the play allowed Morrison to explore issues of sexual and racial tensions in modern Britain and to bring new emphases to the play, but the relocation of the action also created its own difficulties. Above all, there was a mismatch between the ancient and modern contexts: as one reviewer remarked, '[i]t doesn't ring quite true because the women don't seem to work',[55] and the pitching of whites against non-whites (the central

213

conflict of the play) required blacks and Asians of all creeds to be lumped together in a rather contrived way. That said, the production was remarkable for its sheer energy, its inventiveness and the quality of the music, all of which were praised by reviewers. Also remarkable was the play's strongly politicized, anti-establishment stance: there was mockery of the supposed incompetence and brutality of the British police, for example, and biting condemnation of the war in Iraq – both of which themes were highly topical at the time that the play was staged.

The politicization of Aristophanic comedy was also a feature of another important Aristophanic production: *The Birds* produced by London's National Theatre in conjunction with Mamaloucos Theatre in 2002. This was based on a commissioned adaptation of the play by the poet and playwright Sean O'Brien who, like Bolt and Morrison, also wrote his dialogue in rhyming verse. The lively idiom employed by O'Brien owes much to the English spoken in Newcastle (a city in the North East of England) – as does the description of the utopian 'mega party town' that Pez (Peisthetaerus) and Eck (Euelpides) are searching for.[56]

Pez
Well, that's what we've been travelling to find –
We're looking for a mega party town,
Entirely occupied with getting down –
Where the party policemen throw away the keys
Unless you end up guttered on your knees
My life's ambition is to puke my ring –

Eck
I'd rather die a pisshead than a king.
Let's not forget we'll need some canny birds,
Susceptible to charm and honeyed words,
In party gear with neither fronts nor backs,
Some nice lap-dancing nymphomaniacs.

The play was staged as an extraordinary piece of physical theatre, using actors with circus and acrobatic skills swinging in the air on cords, riding trapezes and trampolining. The production was not a hit with reviewers, however, who consistently complained that the play was miscast, the words often unintelligible, and that the physical elements and the script simply did not gel (as one reviewer put it: 'this production simply uses the text as a trampoline').[57] Perhaps in compensation for the inaudibility of many of the words, the director, Kathryn Hunter, used bold symbolism to flesh out a script that already had a political edge: when the tyrannical Pez (Peisthetaerus) married Sovereignty (Basileia) at the end of the play, his bride was dressed as the Statue of Liberty and money rained down from the ceiling. The finale thus became a far from subtle attack on American economic colonialism.[58]

The 2007 production of *Clouds* by Kaloi k'Agathoi, a small company based in Hereford (a city in the West of England), was quite a different proposition from these well-financed productions. Here, the hard-edged anti-establishment undercurrents of Northern Broadsides' *Lisa's Sex Strike* and Mamoloucus' *Birds* were certainly not in evidence. Instead, this production was characterized by spirited humour, with a vibrant script complemented freely by well-judged ad libs delivered by an energetic cast. Sam Pay in particular in the role of Strepsiades injected real pace into the show with his lively performance of both dialogue and song – such as the regretful and revengeful lyric that Strepsiades sings when he realizes that his plan has backfired.

> I thought I'd come up with a foolproof plan
> To help me get out of arrears
> But now my whole scheme has gone arse-over-tit
> And it's all going to end in tears
>
> But there must be a way to make it turn out
> That they're Socrates' tears and not mine
> As I cannot accept and I will not admit
> It was my stupid fault all the time
>
> I'll pay the bastards back! ...
>
> I'll slag them all off to my local MP
> Or I'll write to the Mail and the Times
> I'll make up a story that Socrates touched me
> I'll make them all pay for my crimes.

While its backdrop was fifth-century Athens, the play included much topical humour and contemporary references to politics, music, television shows and even the floods suffered in the West of England which had been a recent media obsession in the UK (an authoritative newscaster's voice at one stage announced that 'this is the worst flood since records of this flood began'). The production, billed as 'a dazzling new musical', included songs in a mixture of musical styles, both old and new, in addition to a spontaneous *parabasis* delivered by a Hereford-based rap duo called the *Anomalies*, who took as their subject matter suggestions called out by the audience. Both song and dance was provided by the cloud chorus, too, who effortlessly shape-shifted from Georgian ladies to a sassy girl-group – but it was as curiously posh cheerleaders that they introduced themselves to the audience, spelling out various obscene acronyms as they sang:

> Tedious Intelligentsia Taking Shit
> We're totally out of touch but we think we're it!
> T. I. Tits, are us!
> You won't catch us with the people, on a public bus!

215

Kaloi k'Agathoi presents

a dazzling new musical based on Aristophanes' classic comedy

featuring *The Anomalies*

19 September, 8pm - Borough Theatre, Abergavenny (box office/swyddfa docynnau 01873 850805)
21 & 22 September, 8pm - Greenwood Theatre, London (call Kaloi k'Agathoi on 01432 363564)
28 & 29 September, 8pm - Courtyard Theatre, Hereford (box office 0870 11 22 330)

www.kaloikagathoi.co.uk

Supported by
The National Lottery®
through Arts Council England

Fig. 8. Poster for the Kaloi k'Agathoi production of *Clouds* (2007).
Reproduced courtesy of Kaloi k'Agathoi.

...
Capitalism Unchecked? No Thanks!
We've had it up to here with your merchant banks.
C. U. Ooh, yes please,
We're upper middle-class revoluntion'ries!

The Kaloi k'Agathoi *Clouds* was hugely appealing and demonstrates well two points. First, that Aristophanes' plays can be staged successfully for a modern audience even on a relatively low budget. But second, that a production that does Aristophanes justice simply eats ideas – and so this twenty-first-century *Clouds* makes us appreciate all the more the enormous amount of energy that Aristophanes (along with his various casts and crews) must have ploughed into his plays years after year in fifth-century Athens.

Conclusions

In this chapter we have looked at some of the key issues raised by the translation, adaptation and performance of Aristophanes' plays. What is striking, I think, is the number of decisions that translators and adaptors make in the course of producing their text, some of which can have a huge effect on the end product – with performance involving yet another set of decisions in terms of the set design, direction, acting styles, and so on. Certainly there is no single 'correct' formula for translation and there are clearly all sorts of reasons why some versions of the plays 'work' better than others: some translations are more suited to some particular contexts, for example (such as the classroom or the theatre), but it must also be admitted that some translators are simply more skilled at what they do. Part of the aim of this chapter has been to reflect on why different translators and adaptors tackle their work in the ways that they do and to suggest questions that might be asked of translations and productions in order to assess their strengths and weaknesses. However, it is also true that much of our reaction to a particular version of a play will depend on our own personal preferences, and so before we pass judgement on the efforts of translators and theatre directors, it is also important to reflect on any preconceptions or prejudices we might have about the process of translation and/or the way in which ancient drama is staged in the modern world.

The humour, colloquial language, topical references, literary allusions and political bite of Aristophanes' plays: all these aspects of translations need constant updating if they are to remain meaningful to a reader or audience member. It is often said that new translations of works are needed every generation, but in the case of Aristophanes the immediacy of some versions and adaptations (above all those written for the stage) can evaporate within a far shorter time than that. But this only makes the task of producing new versions of the plays all the more important. And whilst the work of scholars will continue to inform our view of Aristophanes' comedies, it will remain the job of translators to bring his plays to life for modern readers and to provide audiences with a truly direct way of responding to his drama.

Notes

1. Aristophanes and Old Comedy

1. 'Deme' is the name given to the 139 administrative regions into which the city-state of Attica was divided.

2. Ararus also produced at least two of Aristophanes' later plays.

3. No other Greek dramatist – not even Euripides – has such a large proportion of his work extant.

4. Also referred to in a fragment of Aristophanes' rival comic poet, Eupolis (fr. 78).

5. Possibly it was the play's producer, Callistratus, against whom Cleon took legal action. Our knowledge of these events comes from the text of *Acharnians* and various scholia, not all of which are equally reliable. In the play, Dicaeopolis (who may have been played by either Aristophanes or Callistratus or neither) uses the first person to refer to these events, whereas the chorus, confusingly, refer to the injured party as both 'producer'/'teacher' (*didaskalos*: 628) *and* 'poet'/'maker' (*poiêtês*: 633). If Cleon's adversary was indeed the playwright rather than the producer, then it is possible that the antipathy between the two arose from a dispute between Cleon and Aristophanes within the deme of Cydathenaeum.

6. The accused is one Labes, 'snatcher', cf. the real-life Laches whom Cleon had recently accused of profiting from recent military operations in Sicily (the alleged stolen object in *Wasps* is a Sicilian cheese).

7. Or perhaps Callistratus: see n. 5 above

8. The claims to originality may stem from the fact that *Clouds* was an unusual play: Silk, for instance, maintains that 'only in *Clouds* is satire truly dominant' and calls the play 'an extreme and extraordinary ... experiment' (M.S. Silk, *Aristophanes and the Definition of Comedy* (Oxford, 2000) 369).

9. The matter is of course complicated by the fact that this passage is taken from the revised version of *Clouds* (the only version we possess). One scholar has argued that in this *parabasis* Aristophanes is outlining all the types of low humour that he has included in the revised version of the play in order to broaden its comic appeal (T.K. Hubbard, 'Parabatic Self-Critisim and the Two Versions of Aristophanes' Clouds', *Classical Antiquity* 5 (1986) 182-97): a thesis that is certainly not universally accepted.

10. The controversial topic of Aristophanes' political views is considered separately in Chapter 9.

11. In place of a *parabasis*, *Lysistrata* has two epirrhematic syzygies (614-705).

12. W. Arrowsmith, 'Aristophanes' *Birds*: The Fantasy Politics of *Eros*', *Arion* 1 (1973) 119-67: 137.

13. K. McLeish, *The Theatre of Aristophanes* (Bath, 1980) 50.

2. Putting on a Show

1. The strongest piece of evidence we have that there were five plays performed at the Lenaea is an inscription detailing the placing of plays in the dramatic

competition of 284 BC (*IG* II2 2319 col. i): it is possible that fifth-century practice varied. As outlined below, many scholars believe that only three plays were performed at the Lenaea during the Peloponnesian War: certainly the *hypotheses* to *Acharnians*, *Knights*, *Wasps* and *Frogs* give only the names of the plays that placed first, second and third in the comic competition, but this need not *necessarily* imply that only three plays were entered.

2. A small but perhaps important detail is that *ikria*, temporary wooden benches, are mentioned at *Women at the Thesmophoria* 395. Some scholars have taken this to imply that this and other Lenaea plays were in fact performed to spectators sitting on collapsible stands in the agora rather than on permanent seats in the Theatre of Dionysus.

3. Aristophanes evidently entered two plays in the Lenaea of 422 BC: the first hypothesis to *Wasps* tells us that the play was beaten into second place in the competition by *Proagôn* – which we know to be the name of another play by Aristophanes. Presumably our playwright was able to exploit a loophole of the competition rules by entering these plays under the names of different producers (*didaskaloi*): on which see below.

4. This said, a papyrus fragment from Oxyrhynchus is taken by some to suggest that the Great Dionysia held more prestige for comic poets, too. POxy fr.1 2737 col. ii lines 10-17 tells us that *Rabdouchoi* (*Rod Bearers*), a play by the comic poet Plato, placed fourth in the City Dionysia with the consequence that he was 'pushed back' to the Lenaea. Interpretations of this fragment vary hugely, however, and the fact that comedies both predated and outnumbered tragedies at the Lenaea would suggest that this festival in fact held a certain importance for comic playwrights.

5. An important source for this is the orator Isocrates. Writing in the fourth century (after the collapse of Athens' empire and therefore at a time when the tribute display no longer took place), he states (*On the Peace*, 82): '... [The Athenians] passed a decree to divide the funds obtained from the tributes of the allies into talents [i.e. units of 6,000 drachmas] and to bring it into the *orchêstra*, when the theatre was full, at the festival of Dionysus; and ... at the same time they brought in and paraded the sons of those who had died in war ... .'

6. Thus it seems that the tribute money referred to by Dicaeopolis in *Acharnians* (504-7, quoted above; also referred to at *Acharnians* 643) was brought to the city in early spring for the express purpose of being shown off in the theatre during the Great Dionysia – and that the 'foreigners' that Dicaeopolis refers to as being absent from the Lenaea but present at the Dionysia would therefore probably have included ambassadors sent by subject states.

7. The orator Aeschines, writing around 330 BC when the ceremony was clearly no longer practised, recalls the words addressed to the audience by the herald (*Against Ctesipon*, 154): '... as the tragedies were about to be performed ... the herald used to come forward ... and make a proclamation that was extremely honourable and a genuine incentive to virtue (*aretê*), saying, "the state has supported these young men, whose fathers were courageous men and died in war, until their coming of age; and now it has clad them in full armour and sends them out with its best wishes, each to make his own way in life, and invites them to occupy seats of honour (*prohedria*) in the theatre." '

8. In J.J. Winkler and F.I. Zeitlin (eds) *Nothing to Do With Dionysos?* (Princeton, 1990) 97-129.

9. Metics were permitted to be both *chorêgoi* and chorus members at the Lenaea, however (scholiast on *Wealth* 945): this perhaps lends weight to the idea expressed by Dicaeopolis that (at the Lenaea, if not at the Great Dionysia) metics

could justifiably be considered as the 'citizen bran', i.e. as forming a continuum with Athenian citizens.

10. D.M. MacDowell, *Aristophanes and Athens: An Introduction to the Plays* (Oxford, 1995) 9-11.

11. The fact that the author of this law varies the order in which the tragedies and comedies are listed is itself significant: why else does he do this if it is not a reflection of the order in which the plays were produced?

12. This view is based largely on the fact that *hypotheses* to plays of this period name only first, second and third placed plays; in support of a five-play Dionysia, however, can be cited the fact that a play of Plato's *Rabdouchoi*, which dates from 427-12 BC, is said to have placed fourth (see n. 4). Needless to say, the evidence for both points of view is thin.

13. D. Wiles, *Greek Theatre Performance: An Introduction* (Cambridge, 2000) 33.

14. The speaker of Cratinus fr. 17 complains that Sophocles had been denied a chorus in favour of the supposedly inferior Gnesippus.

15. Two *chorêgoi* evidently shared the costs for *Frogs* (405 BC), at a time of what must have been severe economic hardship in Athens.

16. Lysias 21.4, in which the speaker makes numerous other boasts about expenditure on choruses. He claims to have spent 3,000 drachmae on a tragic chorus, for example, at the Great Dionysia of 409 BC (presumably this would have entailed funding three tragedies plus a satyr play).

17. The fact that the actors wore masks also gives rise to the possibility that these 'extra' lines were simply spoken by one of the three speaking actors in a modified voice.

18. In certain tragedies, the three actor rule must have required the same character to have been played by different actors at different stages in the play (a phenomenon made possible by masked acting): in *Oedipus at Colonus*, for example, if only three speaking actors were used in the production, all three would have had to take turns to play Theseus. The only possible instance of role-sharing in Aristophanes' extant plays comes in *Wealth*, where Wealth/Ploutos may well have been played by a different actor during lines 771-801.

19. G. Mastromarco, 'L'esordio "segreto" di Aristofane', *Quaderni di Storia* 10 (1979) 153-96; S. Halliwell, 'Aristophanes' Apprenticeship', *CQ* n.s. 30 (1980) 33-45.

20. This ingenious interpretation of the evidence for the voting process – along with the mathematical case for its viability – is made by C.W. Marshall and S. Van Willigenburg, 'Judging Athenian Dramatic Competitions', *JHS* 124 (2004) 90-107.

21. In fact, both these characteristics – the choosing of post-holders by lot (a process called 'sortition') and their selection from across the ten tribes – can be seen time and time again in the Athenian democracy: Athens' Archons, jurors and members of its council (*boulê*) were all chosen along similar lines.

22. The fact that Plato deems it necessary to advise judges not to be swayed by the audience at *Laws* 659a is no doubt testimony to the influence that the spectators' reactions to a play could exert on them.

23. Plutarch, *Life of Pericles* 9.3. The payment in the fourth century was two obols (a third of a drachma): see also the scholiast on Demosthenes 1.1.

24. It may have been the case that would-be theatre goers who could not afford the entrance fee could find space to sit on the Acropolis slopes behind the theatre (the proverbial 'view from the poplar': Cratinus fr. 372).

25. Other relevant passages include *Peace* 966 and *Women at the Thesmophoria*

395-7. For a balanced and concise survey of the evidence, see S. Goldhill, 'The Audience of Greek Tragedy' in P.E. Easterling (ed.) *Cambridge Companion to Greek Tragedy* (Cambridge, 1997) 54-68, who is ultimately sceptical about the presence of free women in the audience, with which contrast J. Henderson, 'Women and the Athenian Dramatic Festivals', *TAPA* 121 (1991) 133-47.

26. Aelian, *Varia Historia* 2.13.

27. According to the play's hypotheses – as well as the ancient *Life of Aristophanes* – *Frogs* was given a second staging, but this would appear to be an exceptional event.

3. Setting the Scene: Theatre Space and Costumes

1. *Eisodos* (pl. *eisodoi*) is the name which Aristophanes' uses to refer to these gangways, but in modern accounts of the Greek theatre the later term, *parados* (pl. *parodoi*) is often used (not to be confused with the part of the play when the chorus appear, also known as the *parodos*: see Chapter 1).

2. Since no *skênê* was required for the dithyrambic performances which preceded the dramatic contests, this building may have been collapsible.

3. Philocleon's attempt to escape from the house at *Wasps* 156-73 and the scene where the girl argues with the hags at *Assemblywomen* 877-1111 both seem to require a window.

4. It has been suggested, however, that the Greek word used here, *anabainô*, could simply mean 'come up*stage*'.

5. Wiles, *Greek Theatre Performance*, 104-9.

6. Wiles, *Greek Theatre Performance*, 106.

7. In tragedy, the chorus enter through the *skênê* doors in Aeschylus' *Eumenides* and Euripides' *Trojan Women*, though this is never the case in extant comedy. Some choruses in comedy exit by means of the *eisodoi*, others through the *skênê* doors.

8. The assumption has been made here that plays presented in the Lenaea festival were also staged in the Theatre of Dionysus in the late fifth century: if, as some scholars argue, these plays were in fact staged in the Athenian *agora*, or indeed elsewhere, then naturally the theatre space would be different from that described here (see Chapter 2, n. 2)

9. N.J. Lowe, 'Aristophanic Spacecraft' in L. Kozak and J. Rich (eds) *Playing Around Aristophanes: Essays in Celebration of the Completion of the Comedies of Aristophanes by Alan Sommerstein* (Oxford, 2006) 48-64.

10. This point is made well in a fragment of the comic poet Antiphanes, fr. 189: once a tragedian introduces a character such as Oedipus, the audience automatically knows his personal history, the names of his family members, and so on. A comic poet has no such luxury and has to invent things anew for every play.

11. Lowe, 'Aristophanic Spacecraft', 54.

12. For further possible instances if its use, see C.W. Dearden, *The Stage of Aristophanes* (London, 1976) 75-85.

13. See especially Dearden, *Stage of Aristophanes*, 50-74.

14. T.B.L. Webster, 'Staging and Scenery in the Ancient Greek Theatre', *Bulletin of the John Rylands Library Manchester* 42.2 (1959-60) 493-504: 502-4, suggests 2.55 x 1.30 m as a maximum on the basis of the holes in the nose of masonry ('T') projecting from the fifth/fourth century remains of the Theatre of Dionysus' long wall ('H').

15. A suggestion supported by the scholiast, who uses the verb *ekkykleô*.

16. Aelian, *Historical Miscellany* 2.13, relates an anecdote that Socrates stood up during the performance of *Clouds* when he heard foreigners murmuring that they did not know who he was. Aelian assumes that mask-makers were capable of producing an 'excellent likeness', though K.J. Dover, *Aristophanes Clouds* (Oxford, 1968) xxxiii, points out that Socrates' actions are consistent with his wishing to demonstrate how *little* he resembled the stage Socrates – in physical appearance and otherwise. At *Knights* 230-3, Demosthenes explicitly tells the audience that Paphlagon will *not* be wearing a portrait mask: ostensibly because mask-makers were too frightened to make a likeness of Cleon, but perhaps in reality because Cleon's features were not striking enough to caricature (unlike those of Socrates).

17. There were no doubt ways to keep expenditure down, such as by reusing costumes and properties from previous productions.

18. Wiles, *Greek Theatre Performance*, 159.

19. Wiles, *Greek Theatre Performance*, 149.

20. Whether or not the women would actually have had tanned 'male' masks, however, is unclear – a joke is made later in the play that the disguised women looked like cobblers (i.e. men who worked indoors) with white faces: *Assemblywomen* 385-7.

4. Aristophanes the Humorist

1. Silk, *Aristophanes*, 312-16.

2. This assumption is particularly noticeable when comedy is compared with tragedy: Aristotle, for example, talks of the precursors of tragedians being 'more serious-minded', whilst the precursors of comic dramatists were apparently 'more trivial' and wrote about 'meaner types of people' (*Poetics* 4: 1448b24-8).

3. For a particularly engaging study of humour which covers a number of sociological angles, see M. Mulkay, *On Humour: Its Nature and Place in Modern Society* (Cambridge, 1988).

4. Key works are: V. Raskin, *Semantic Mechanisms of Humor* (Dordrecht, 1985); S. Attardo, *Linguistic Theories of Humor* (Berlin, 1994) and *Humorous Texts: A Semantic and Pragmatic Analysis* (Berlin/New York, 2001); S. Attardo and V. Raskin, 'Script Theory Revis(it)ed: Joke Similarity and Joke Representation Model', *Humor* 4 (1991) 293-347.

5. Section 54.

6. The classic 'social' theorist is Henri Bergson, who in *Le rire* (Paris, 1899) argues that laughter is a form of 'social corrective'.

7. This approach is adopted by L. O'Higgins, *Women and Humor in Classical Greece* (Cambridge, 2003), for example (see below).

8. L. Feinberg, *The Secret of Humor* (Amsterdam, 1978), for example, is a book-length study which proposes that all humour has an aggressive undertone.

9. S. Halliwell, 'The Uses of Laughter in Greek Laughter', *CQ* 41 (1991) 279-96 and *Greek Laughter: A Study of Cultural Psychology from Homer to Early Christianity* (Cambridge, 2008). The distinction made by Halliwell is classical in origin: Plato distinguishes between laughter which is *aneu thymou* (Halliwell's 'playful') and *meta thymou* (Halliwell's 'consequential') in the *Laws* (935d-6a) when discussing what can be tolerated by the laws of the city.

10. Cambridge, 2003. The major role of humour, O' Higgins suggests, was to define the female cultic group both by vilifying outsiders and breaking down internal hierarchies.

11. Comic caricature in general and the portrayal of Cleonymus in particular are discussed further in Chapter 9, pp. 164-5.

12. Such scenes are still 'painless' for the audience: the violence is neither real nor do the spectators suffer in any way.

13. Interestingly, however, the slave does not remain the straight guy for long and he soon switches to making quips of his own.

14. The English pun, 'oxpedition', is that of A.H. Sommerstein, *The Comedies of Aristophanes*, vol. 3: *Clouds* (Warminster, 1985).

15. A.H. Sommerstein, *The Comedies of Aristophanes*, vol. 10: *Ecclesiazusae* (Warminster, 1998)

16. Indeed, surprise items are regularly used by Aristophanes to create humour – and not just in lists. As Trygaeus is flying to Heaven on his dung beetle, for instance, he promises his daughter that, if his trip is successful, on his return he will give her 'a nice big bread roll and … a smack in the gob' (*Peace* 123).

5. The People of Aristophanes

1. London and Berkeley/Los Angeles, 1972: 59-65.

2. G.W. Dobrov, 'The Poet's Voice in the Evolution of Dramatic Dialogism', in G.W. Dobrov (ed.) *Beyond Aristophanes: Transition and Diversity in Greek Comedy* (Atlanta, Georgia, 1995) 47-97: 56.

3. M.S. Silk, 'The People of Aristophanes', in C.B.R. Pelling, *Characterization and Individuality in Greek Literature* (Oxford, 1990) 150-73; reworked in Silk, *Aristophanes*, ch. 5 (207-55).

4. Silk, *Aristophanes*, 213-14.

5. Silk, *Aristophanes*, 212.

6. Silk, *Aristophanes*, 243.

7. Perhaps it is not so problematic to talk about the thoughts of some of Aristophanes' more 'realist' creations – Strepsiades, or even Lyistrata – but it is not a practice easy to defend for his more 'recreative' characters.

8. As I have argued in J.E. Robson, *Humour, Obscenity and Aristophanes* (Tübingen, 2006) 45-7, whilst 'recreative' highpoints are certainly not always humorous, instances of humour *are* usefully be described as 'recreative', displaying as they do qualities such as discontinuity, binary reversal and apparent absence of logical consequentiality.

9. J. Henderson, 'Pherekrates and the Women of Old Comedy' in F.D. Harvey and J. Wilkins, *The Rivals of Aristophanes: Studies in Athenian Old Comedy* (London, 2000) 135-50, provides a thoughtful summary (and convincing chronology) of the development of female characters in the comic theatre in the late fifth century. The kind of female figures we find in Aristophanes' extant plays are probably (very broadly) representative of those found in comedy as a whole during this period, though some character-types, such as mythological women and hetairai (prostitutes), are notable by their absence.

10. As Henderson says, these Aristophanic plays of 411 BC may represent the first time that respectable citizen wives were portrayed in comedy ('Pherekrates and Women', 141).

11. In the case of *Lysistrata* it is worth mentioning that women make a good vehicle through which to explore the theme of war and its effects: a technique adopted by Homer in Books 3, 6, 22 and 24 of the *Iliad*, for example.

12. The fact that citizen wives are discussed as a single group in this section should not be taken to imply there are no differences between the way in which older and younger women are portrayed in Old Comedy: on this topic see J. Henderson, 'Older Women in Attic Old Comedy', *TAPA* 117 (1987) 105-29.

13. Henderson, 'Older Women', 128, suggests that the 'protests heard in the plays of 411 ... echo real female discontent, even rebelliousness' in the aftermath of the unprecedented loss of life suffered in the Sicilian Expedition in 413 BC.

14. Though interestingly, as T.K. Hubbard points out in 'Old Men in the Youthful Plays of Aristophanes' in T.M. Falkner and J. de Luce, *Old Age in Greek and Latin Literature* (New York, 1989) 90-113, 90, at the beginning of their plays, old men often ally themselves with 'new political and intellectual leaders' (such as Cleon in the case of the chorus of *Wasps* or Socrates in the case of Strepsiades in *Clouds*): the plays then tend to plot the old men's rejection of these figures.

15. The subject of Aristophanic pathos is explored in M.S. Silk, 'Pathos in Aristophanes', *BICS* 34 (1988) 78-111.

16. Or as Hubbard puts it ('Old Men', 104), they are 'victims manipulated by the system'.

17. A.W. Schlegel, *On Dramatic Art and Literature* (1808); F.W. Nietzsche, *The Birth of Tragedy* (1872).

18. Quoted in a different translation in Chapter 8, pp. 156-7.

19. A.H. Sommerstein, *The Comedies of Aristophanes*, vol. 7: *Lysistrata* (Warminster, 1990) 5.

20. The role of the chorus in the fourth-century is discussed by K.S. Rothwell 'The Continuity of the Chorus in Fourth Century Attic Comedy', in Dobrov, *Beyond Aristophanes*, 99-118, esp. 110-16, where he challenges the view that the chorus' importance in comedy underwent a sharp decline following the end of the fifth century.

6. Tragic Fragments

1. M.S. Silk, 'Aristophanic Paratragedy', in A.H. Sommerstein et al. (eds) *Tragedy, Comedy and the Polis* (Bari, 1993) 477-504: 477-8. As Silk notes, various lost plays of Aristophanes' also seem to have centred on tragedy: a second *Women at the Thesmophoria*; a *Phoenician Women* parodying Euripides' play of the same name, and two further plays in which Euripides purportedly appeared as a character: *Proagôn* (422 BC) and *Dramas* (although which of Aristophanes' two lost plays called *Dramas* is unclear). Interestingly, it is only in the lost *Gerytades* that Aristophanes seems to have made *non*-tragic poetry the subject of a play – here, the audience met a group of assorted poets in Hades.

2. In the Euripidean play, Telephus, King of Mysia, evidently disguises himself as a beggar to infiltrate the Greek camp at Troy. After his disguise is penetrated, he snatches the baby Orestes in order to force the Greek leaders to listen to a speech; he then takes the chance to appeal for Achilles' help to cure a wound (the purpose of his visit). The motif is used again in *Women at the Thesmophoria* where the hostage snatched by the Inlaw turns out to be a wine-skin that one of the women has dressed as a baby.

3. The way in which Aristophanes has his characters use unusual items of vocabulary is both a symptom and cause of their 'recreativity': see Chapter 5.

4. Silk, 'Paratragedy', 477 and 478.

5. At *Frogs* 837-9, Aeschylus is also described as 'a man who is uncultured and stubborn-lipped, with an unbuttoned, unbridled and unshuttable mouth, a champion babbler and boundless bundler of bombastic phrases'; cf. *Clouds* 1366-7.

6. A.H. Sommerstein, *The Comedies of Aristophanes*, vol. 9: *Frogs* (Warminster, 1996)

7. 1285, 1289 are from *Agamemnon*; 1287 from the lost *Sphinx*, an Aeschylean

satyr play; whereas 1291 is wrongly ascribed in the scholia to *Agamemnon* (perhaps a scribal error for *Memnon*).

8. *Helen* 622 (and 788); *Ion* 554; *Medea* 98; *Orestes* 804 and *Trojan Women* 624: on this phrase see Silk, 'Paratragedy', 488-9.

9. Interestingly, it is Euripides who earlier accuses Aeschylus of talking about chickens in his plays: *Frogs* 935.

10. The name is the female version of Manes and denotes Phrygian origin. Perhaps Aristophanes has a freedwoman or foreign wife in mind here: see A.H. Sommerstein, *The Comedies of Aristophanes*, vol. 9: *Frogs* (Warminster, 1996) 278 (note on line 1345).

11. See Sommerstein , *Frogs* 279 (note on line 1352-5).

12. Aristophanes makes the same joke at line 1314 in an earlier parody of Euripidean lyric: *heieieieieieilissete*, 'you wi-i-i-i-ind'.

13. On the basis of his discussion of various parodies of English poetry, Silk, 'Paratragedy', suggests the categories 'imitative' and 'deconstructive' parody. To paraphrase his argument somewhat, there is a spectrum between closely observed parody (which nevertheless exaggerates a poet's mannerisms, juxtaposes elements that are not juxtaposed in the original, and so on) and parody which invents characteristics for effect: one end of this spectrum is 'imitative parody', the other end 'deconstructive'. As Silk himself maintains (492), these categories are far more useful for discussing his English-language examples of parody than those in Aristophanes.

14. At *Frogs* 68-9 Dionysus does state his strong desire to retrieve Euripides from the Underworld, although he neither swears to do so by the gods nor makes this statement in front of Euripides.

15. Parody is a river fed by many streams. Euripides is often mocked for his supposed 'sigmatism', for example; that is, his overuse of the /s/ sound (sigma). A particularly sigmatic pair of lines from *Medea* (476-7: 'I saved you as all those who sailed in the same vessel, Argos, appreciate': *esôsa s', hôs isasin Hellênôn hosoi/ tauton syneisebêsan Argeion skaphos*) is gently parodied at *Peace* 865-7 (a particularly sigmatic little ode in the Greek), although the best parody of these lines surely belongs not to Aristophanes but the comic poet Plato, who wrote 'I saved you from the sigmas of Euripides' (*esôsa s' ek tôn sigma tou Euripidou*, fr. 29 KA).

16. The Euripidean line *is* put to parodic use at *Clouds* 1415, however.

17. In turn, humour also stems from the fact that Crytilla and the Archer seem incapable of comprehending what is going on. This links in to some of the main themes of the play: the power of disguise and *mimêsis* (imitation).

18. Indeed, the fact that Euripides' *Helen* is extant (unlike the other plays that are reworked here, of which we only possess fragments) does not make passing judgement on the parodic or non-parodic status of Aristophanes' take on the *Helen* scene any the easier (*Women at the Thesmophoria* 850-928).

19. B.B. Rogers, *The Birds of Aristophanes* (London, 1930) 27 and 29. These lines may have been delivered as recitative rather than song: Dunbar, *Aristophanes Birds* (Oxford, 1995) 203.

20. Specifically an ode in Euripides' *Helen* (lines 1107-21) that was produced two years later in 412 BC, where the phrase 'liquid (notes)' also occurs (1111). The two odes may share a common source, or alternatively Euripides has copied Aristophanes' unusual phrasing (either deliberately or unconsciously).

21. On which passages, see Silk, 'Paratragedy', 497-503.

22. For more on caricature, see Chapter 9.

23. Euripides also appears as a character in at least two plays besides those extant: see n. 1.

24. For a useful survey of Aristophanes' interaction with tragedy, see R.M. Rosen, 'Aristophanes, Old Comedy and Greek Tragedy' in R. Bushnell (ed.) *A Companion to Tragedy* (Oxford, 2005) 251-68. Here, Rosen also makes the point that paratragic language is often used by Aristophanes (esp. in longer speeches and the play's *parabases*) to help him achieve his satirical ends, providing as it does a 'serious'-sounding backdrop which thus gives the impression that weighty points are being made (261).

7. Taking Dirty: Aristophanic Obscenity

1. *The Maculate Muse: Obscene Language in Attic Old Comedy* (New Haven: Yale University Press, 1975: 2nd edn, 1991).

2. On these cults, see Henderson, *Maculate Muse*, 13-17, and O'Higgins, *Women and Humor*, ch. 1: 'Cultic Obscenity in Greece, especially Attica' (15-36).

3. This apotropaic use of obscenity was a feature of Roman institutions too, such as the Fescennine Iocatio, a typical feature of the Roman wedding (found, for example, at Catullus 61.120).

4. Henderson, *Maculate Muse*, 36-9: S. Freud, *Jokes and Their Relation to the Unconcious* in J. Strachey et al. (eds) *The Standard Edition of The Complete Psychological Works*, vol. 3 (trans. by J. Strachey et al. from *Der Witz und seine Beziehung zum Unbewussten*, 1905) (London, 1960).

5. Henderson, *Maculate Muse*, 38.

6. Henderson, *Maculate Muse*, 35.

7. Henderson, *Maculate Muse*, 35.

8. Part of the appeal of *kistê* may lie in its similarity to *kysthos*.

9. The chorus of Old Women in *Lysistrata* lays claim to neatly singed genitalia, too, despite their age (825-8).

10. See Chapter 9, pp. 182-3.

11. This is the approach adopted by Henderson, for example (*Maculate Muse*, 10 and 36-8): post-Freud these ideas were developed by Sándor Ferenczi.

12. Henderson does talk of 'self-exposure', though this is not a concept he develops theoretically.

13. Tübingen, 2006: ch. 3.

14. In his commentary on these lines J. Henderson, *Aristophanes Lysistrata* (Oxford, 1987), comments that, 'the whole passage is typically tragic and we need not suppose that the spectators were expected to recall any particular source(s).'

15. McLeish translates 'Lord of the Thunder-Crap' (*Theatre of Aristophanes*, 95). Part of the humour may be an allusion to Zeus' pederastic attachment to the boy Ganymede: there has already been a joke at lines 11-12 about the excrement of a boy prostitute being 'well pounded'.

16. In the Greek the pun hinges on the similarity between the verbs *skotodineô*, 'to feel giddy', and the coinage, *skotobineô*, 'to fuck in the dark'.

17. On the question of whether women attended the plays, see Chapter 2, p. 27.

18. In this passage the Spartan consistently displays a keen interest in anal sex, whereas the Athenian's preferences are clearly vaginal.

19. Such insults no doubt owe much to a common form of slander aimed at prominent politicians, namely that they had prostituted themselves in their youth. This slur was particularly biting since, if proved true, a man could lose many of his citizen rights. This fate befell the politician Timarchus in the fourth century, the prosecution speech against whom is preserved as Aeschines' *Against Timarchus*.

20. 'Shamelessness' is the term that Halliwell uses to characterize Aristophanic

sexuality: S. Halliwell, 'Aristophanic Sex: The Erotics of Shamelessness', in M.C. Nussbaum and J. Sihvola (eds) *The Sleep of Reason: Erotic Experience and Social Ethics in Ancient Greece and Rome* (Chicago and London, 2002) 120-42.

8. Waxing Lyrical: Aristophanes the Songwriter

1. Lengthy passages of songs, sometimes interspersed with speech or recitative, also occur outside the *parabasis*, such as at *Wasps* 273-345, *Lysistrata* 1247-1321 and *Frogs* 316-459.

2. Also of interest is when a rhythm predominates in a play: perhaps the most outstanding example is *Acharnians* in which there is extensive use of cretics ($- \cup -$) – a verse form found only rarely in tragedy.

3. Oxford, 1997: 10.

4. Alternatively the sequence is reversed: *strophê* + short episode + *antistrophê* + short episode, or an episode is simply framed by two matched songs (see below on *Lysistrata* 1043-70 and 1188-1215).

5. A.H. Sommerstein, *The Comedies of Aristophanes*, vol. 2: *Knights* (Warminster, 1981), note on *Knights* 976, relaying an observation of B.B. Rogers; Parker, *Songs of Aristophanes*, 176.

6. In Greek the name used is Sebinos of Anaphlystos (also found at *Assembly-women* 979-80), which seems to have been a way of referring to an anonymous lover.

7. 'Horsecock' translates the Greek *Hippokinos* – which combines elements of 'horse' (*hippos*) and 'screw' (*kinein*) – a distortion of the name of Callias' father, Hipponicus.

8. The meaning of this line is unclear.

9. For a more detailed discussion of personal abuse (esp. of politicians), see Chapter 9.

10. On pastiche, see Chapter 6, pp. 114-17.

11. *YCS* 26 (1980) 99-151. In the following discussions I draw on various aspects of Silk's argument from this article and his reworked discussion of the same topic in *Aristophanes*, 160-206.

12. Arguably this is not a true *parodos* (entry song), since the chorus do not physically enter the acting space until later in the play.

13. The translation quoted here is that given in a footnote of B.B. Rogers' 1916 translation. Rogers introduces this version with the comment that (41): '... the Strophe may be more literally, if more prosaically, rendered as follows' (*The Comedies of Aristophanes*, vol. II, London, 1916).

14. C. Segal, 'Aristophanes' Cloud-Chorus', *Arethusa* 2.2 (1969) 143-61: 148.

15. Silk talks of the ode's 'pervasive absence of point' (*Aristophanes*, 170).

16. A more positive analysis of this and other elevated lyrics is made by G. Matthews in 'Aristophanes' "High" Lyrics Reconsidered', *Maia* 49 (1997) 1-42.

17. Interestingly, though, Parker chooses the *Acharnians* duets as examples of Aristophanes' least remarkable efforts as a lyricist (*Songs of Aristophanes*, 11); Silk's assessment is more positive, however (*Aristophanes*, 165-6).

18. Silk, *Aristophanes*, 180-1.

19. The translation here is from A.H. Sommerstein, *The Comedies of Aristophanes*, vol. 5: *Peace* (Warminster, 1985). It is unclear to me whether Silk would classify this as an example of 'low lyrics *plus*': it certainly has structural similarities with odes that he discusses under this heading, but at the same time lacks much of the sophistication of the examples he chooses to highlight.

20. According to the scholia on *Peace* 797, the opening lines of this ode are adapted from Stesichorus – possibly his *Oresteia*. Intriguingly, Parker includes this passage in her discussion of 'parody' calling it (*Songs of Aristophanes*, 7): 'a sort of domesticated version of high lyric.'

21. S.D. Olson, *Aristophanes Acharnians* (Oxford, 2002) on *Acharnians* 263.

22. Olson, *Acharnians* (commenting on line 266 of the play) reasons that the last such Rural Dionysia would have been celebrated in late 432 BC and thus 'sixth' here is possibly 'evidence ... of a somewhat casual attitude towards chronology'.

23. Silk, *Aristophanes*, 123.

24. *Knights* and *Clouds* appear to have the fewest sung lines, *Birds* and *Frogs* the most.

25. Tragic parody is particularly prominent in *Women at the Thesmophoria* and *Frogs*. Extensive parodies of the New Music are found at *Birds* 1372-1409 and *Frogs* 1348-55. Presumably Agathon's song at *Women at the Thesmophoria* 101-29 is also (among other things) a musical parody.

9. Getting the Message: Aristophanic Politics

1. *Life of Aristophanes* fr. 42-5 KA.

2. The following discussion incorporates many of the points made by S. Halliwell in 'Ancient Interpretations of *onomasti kōmōidein* in Aristophanes', *CQ* 34 (1984) 83-8. See also 'Comedy and Publicity in the Society of the Polis', in Sommerstein et al., *Tragedy, Comedy and the Polis*, 321-40.

3. Although, to be sure, we do find some Roman writers complaining that the abuse went too far and that the wrong men were sometimes criticized: e.g. Horace, *Art of Poetry* 281-4, claims that 'freedom degenerated into licence' and Cicero, *On the Republic* 4.11, considers Old Comedy's attacks on Pericles to be shameful.

4. There are grounds for believing that Cleonymus was an associate of Cleon: S. Halliwell, 'Comedy and Publicity', 332 n. 28. Outside Aristophanes, Cleonymus' name appears in comedy only at Eupolis fr. 352 KA and Com. Adesp. 64 (Kock): in other words, jokes about him may well have been a largely Aristophanic preserve.

5. On caricature, see S. Halliwell, 'Aristophanic Satire', *Yearbook of English Studies* 14 (1984) 6-20: 9-14.

6. Evidently there is an extent to which scandalous comments were tolerated in comic plays in a way in which they would not be outside the theatre (*parrhesia* is the Greek word for the 'freedom of speech' from which comic playwrights benefited at these festivals). The precise nature of this *parrhesia* (e.g. whether comedians enjoyed some form of legal immunity from prosecution if they made slanderous accusations) has been the subject of substantial debate: see below.

7. Not all scholars are convinced that Aristophanes' tussle with Cleon was an historical truth: R. Rosen, *Old Comedy and the Iambic Tradition* (Atlanta, 1988) 78, suggests that 'the details of the quarrel between Aristophanes and Cleon can easily be seen as an elaborate fiction'.

8. Thucydides comments (4.40) that 'this event caused more surprise amongst the Greeks than almost anything else that happened in the war' (transl. R. Warner, *History of the Peloponnesian War* (London, 1954)): the Spartan military had a formidable reputation and the 300 Spartans at Thermopylae had famously chosen to die rather than surrender.

9. The following discussion takes as its point of departure Silk, *Aristophanes*, 334-46.

10. Malcolm Heath, 'Aristophanes and the Discourse of Politics' in G.W. Dobrov

(ed.) *The City as Comedy: Society and Representation in Athenian Drama* (Chapel Hill and London, 1997) 230-49: esp. 232-6. Halliwell, 'Aristophanic Satire', 17, suggests that Aristophanes' claims to benefit and advise the city also find their origin in political oratory.

11. Something approaching this position is taken by M. Heath (e.g. *Political Comedy in Aristophanes* (Göttingen 1987); 'Some Deceptions in Aristophanes', *Papers of the Leeds Latin Seminar* 6 (1990) 229-40); S. Goldhill, *The Poet's Voice* (Cambridge, 1991), and Silk, *Aristophanes*, in different forms – notwithstanding the fact that the conclusions reached by these scholars differ hugely.

12. There is no reason to suppose, I suggest, that reaching firm conclusions about the relationship between the world of the play and the 'real' world of contemporary Athens would have been significantly easier for ancient Athenians than it is for us.

13. Compare this passage with *Knights* 1333-4 as discussed by Silk, *Aristophanes*, 301-2.

14. For an excellent overview of Thucydides' and Aristophanes' account of the origins of the Peloponnesian War, see Olson, *Acharnians*, xxxi-xxxix.

15. Here I baldly summarize the argument of H.P. Foley, 'Tragedy and Politics in Aristophanes' *Acharnians*', *JHS* 108 (1988) 33-47.

16. With the possible exception of *Acharnians* 652-5 which appears to be advocating the rejection of a peace treaty that involved Athens giving up sovereignty over Aegina.

17. Sommerstein, *Frogs*, 13-14.

18. Heath, *Political Comedy*, 23; Heath discusses the *Frogs parabasis* at 19-21.

19. *Life of Aristophanes*: Ar. testimonia 1.35-9 KA.

20. *CQ* 46 (1996) 327-56. On Aristophanes' biases, see also Sommerstein, 'An Alternative Democracy and an Alternative to Democracy in Aristophanic Comedy' in U. Bultrighini (ed.) *Democrazia e antidemocrazia nel mundo greco* (Alessandria, 2005) 195-207: 197-202.

21. A.H. Sommerstein, 'How to Avoid Being a *Komoudomenos*' *CQ* (1996) 46 (ii): 327-56.

22. Sommerstein, '*Komoudomenos*', 334.

23. This said, Alcibiades may have featured as a figure of ridicule in Eupolis' *Bathers* of 415 BC.

24. As mentioned above, the radical democracy was briefly overthrown by oligarchic coups in 411 and 404 BC, but none of the plays we possess were composed or produced under oligarchic rule. Personal abuse is least prevalent in the 411 BC plays, *Lysistrata* and *Women at the Thesmophoria* (Aristophanes' choruses even point out their restraint at *Lysistrata* 1043-9 and *Women at the Thesmophoria* 962-4). This is perhaps explained by the tense political atmosphere of that year.

25. *Knights* 51, 255, 798-807; *Wasps* 300, 606-9, 661-4, 700-12; *Lysistrata* 624; *Frogs* 1466.

26. See F.D. Harvey, 'Lacomica: Aristophanes and the Spartans', in A. Powell and S.J. Hodkinson (eds) *The Shadow of Sparta* (London, 1994) 35-58.

27. As the Old Oligarch comments in the *Constitution of Athens* 2.14 '... in the present situation the farmers and the wealthy Athenians are more inclined to make up to the enemy, but the common people live without fear and do no such thing because they know that none of their property will be burnt or destroyed'. (transl. J.M. Moore, *Aristotle and Xenophon on Democracy and Oligarchy* (London, 1975)).

28. See Halliwell, 'Aristophanic Satire' and C. Platter, *Aristophanes and the Carnival of Genres* (Baltimore, 2007).

29. The following discussion takes as its point of departure C. Carey, 'Comic Ridicule and Democracy' in R. Osborne and S. Hornblower (eds) *Ritual, Finance, Politics: Athenian Democratic Accounts Presented to David Lewis* (Oxford, 1994) 69-83: 75-7 and 80.

30. The fact that Cleon's family owned a tannery suggests that they were fairly wealthy.

31. E.g. and esp. Thucydides 3.36-40: other unsympathetic portraits include Old Oligarch, *Constitution of Athens* 28.3 and Plutarch, *Life of Nicias* 8.6. Carey, 'Comic Ridicule', 70-1 and 77-9 points out that Cleon's *style* is attacked more than his policies.

32. Jeffrey Henderson calls the dramatic festivals 'supracivic' owing to their inclusion of all sections of society, not just citizens ('Attic Old Comedy, Frank Speech, and Democracy', in D. Boedeker and K.A. Raaflaub (eds) *Democracy, Empire and the Arts in Fifth-Century Athens* (Harvard, 1998) 255-73: 268).

33. J. Henderson, 'Comic Hero versus Political Élite' in Sommerstein, *Tragedy, Comedy and the Polis*, 307-19: 317.

34. Fourth-century oratory provides us with two examples of speakers claiming that the comic reputations of their adversaries should be taken as established truths (Lysias fr. 53 about the poet-cum-politician Cinesias and Aeschines 1.157 about Timarchus). The rhetorical context would once more urge against taking these statements at face value.

35. Scholia on *Acharnians* 67. For discussion of this decree, see S. Halliwell, 'Comic Satire and Freedom of Speech in Classical Athens', *JHS* 111 (1991) 48-70: 58-9 and 63.

36. J.E. Atkinson, 'Curbing and Comedians: Cleon versus Aristophanes and Syracosios' Decree', *CQ* 42 (1992) 56-64. The debate centres on a scholiast's comment on Phrynicus fr. 26 KA.

37. On Old Comedy and the law, see S. Halliwell, 'Comic Satire', Henderson, 'Frank Speech', 262-3, and A.H. Sommerstein, 'Comedy and the Unspeakable' in D.L. Cairns and R.A. Knox (eds) *Law, Rhetoric and Comedy in Classical Antiquity* (Swansea, 2004) 205-22.

38. On which see A.H. Sommerstein, 'Harassing the Satirist: The Alleged Attempts to Prosecute Aristophanes', in I. Sluiter and R.M. Rosen (eds) *Free Speech in Antiquity* (Leiden/Boston, 2002) 145-74: 145-54.

39. On which see Sommerstein, 'Comedy and the Unspeakable', 206-7 and 209-10

40. Heath, *Political Comedy* 23, 42 and 40.

41. Heath, *Political Comedy*, 42.

42. Henderson, 'Frank Speech', 260 and 'The *Dêmos* and Comic Competition' in Winkler and Zeitlin, *Dionysos*, 271-314: 273 and 307.

10. Aristophanes in the Modern World: Translation and Performance

1. It is interesting to note in this extract that the items of female underwear seem to be taken from a range of historical periods, with boned basques and baroque bustiers lying alongside thongs and wonderbras, for instance, thus giving this list something of a timeless quality.

2. For an overview of the translation of Aristophanes into English, see the entry on 'Aristophanes' by S. Halliwell in O. Chase (ed.) *Encyclopedia of Literary Translation into English* (London and Chicago, 2000). E. Hall, 'Introduction:

Aristophanic Laughter across the Centuries' in E. Hall and A. Wrigley (eds) *Aristophanes in Performance 421 BC – AD 2007* (London, 2007) 1-29 also provides a useful summary of the translation and performance history of Aristophanes. For lists of translated plays, see also V. Giannopoulou, 'Aristophanes in Translation before 1920', in Hall and Wrigley, *Aristophanes in Performance*, 309-42. J.M. Walton also provides a list of published English-language translation of Aristophanes in his appendix to *Found in Translation: Greek Drama in English* (Cambridge, 2006) 253-67.

3. London, 1902-16 and London, 1924 (Loeb). On the early history of the Loeb Aristophanes, see Sommerstein, 'How Aristophanes got his A&P' in Kozak and Rich, *Playing Around Aristophanes*, 126-39: 130-1.

4. On which see A. Wrigley, 'Aristophanes Revitalized! Music and Spectacle on the Aristophanic Stage' in Hall and Wrigley, *Aristophanes in Performance*, 136-54.

5. M. Bastin-Hammou, 'Aristophanes' *Peace* on the Twentieth-Century French Stage: From Political Statement to Artistic Failure', in Hall and Wrigley, *Aristophanes in Performance*, 247-54.

6. G. Van Steen, 'Aristophanes on the Modern Greek stage', *Dialogos* 2 (1995) 71-90: 74-5. In Chapter 3 of *Venom in Verse: Aristophanes in Modern Greece* (Princeton, 2000), Van Steen looks at the fascinating production history of the play in Greece in more detail, especially the playing of the lead role by transvestite actors (76-123).

7. *Lysistrata by Aristophanes: A New Version by Gilbert Seldes with a Special Introduction by Mr. Seldes and Illustrations by Pablo Picasso* (New York, 1934) 5.

8. Seldes, *Lysistrata*, 5.

9. J. Maritz, 'Greek Drama in Rhodesia/Zimbabwe' in J. Barsby (ed.) *Greek and Roman Drama: Translation and Performance* (Tübingen, 2002) 197-215: 205.

10. A point continually underlined in Van Steen, *Venom in Verse*.

11. For a detailed account of the incident, see G. Van Steen, 'From Scandal to Success Story: Aristophanes' *Birds* as Staged by Karolos Koun', in Hall and Wrigley, *Aristophanes in Performance*, 155-78.

12. An incident recounted by F. Schironi, 'A Poet without "Gravity": Aristophanes on the Italian Stage', in Hall and Wrigley, *Aristophanes in Performance*, 267-75.

13. To be found at: www.apgrd.ox.ac.uk and www2.open.ac.uk/ClassicalStudies/GreekPlays/ respectively.

14. Loeb: London, 1998-2002; Aris & Phillips: Warminster, 1980-2002.

15. D. Barrett, *The Wasps, The Poet and the Women, The Frogs* (Penguin: London, 1964); A.H. Sommerstein, *Lysistrata, The Acharnians, The Clouds* (Penguin: London, 1973; revised by Sommerstein 2002); A.H. Sommerstein and D. Barrett, *The Birds and Other Plays* (Penguin: London, 1978; revised by Sommerstein 2003).

16. *Plays, 1: Acharnians; Knights; Peace; Lysistrata*, introduced by J.M. Walton; translated and introduced by K. McLeish; *Plays, 2: Wasps; Clouds; Birds; Festival time (Thesmophoriazousai); Frogs*, introduced by J.M. Walton; translated and introduced by K. McLeish (London, 1993). A separate volume of translations by McLeish also exists: K. McLeish, *Aristophanes Clouds, Women in Power, Knights* (Cambridge, 1979).

17. *Clouds, Wasps, Birds*, translated, with notes, by P. Meineck ; introduced by I.C. Storey (Indianapolis and Cambridge, 1998)

18. *Birds and Other Plays* (Oxford, 1998)

19. *Aristophanes, 1: The Acharnians, Peace, Celebrating Ladies, Wealth*, D.R. Slavitt and P. Bovie (eds) (Philidelphia, 1998); *Aristophanes, 2: Wasps, Lysistrata,*

Frogs, Sexual Congress, D.R. Slavitt and P. Bovie (eds) (Philadelphia, 1999); *Aristophanes, 3: The Suits, Clouds, Birds*, D.R. Slavitt and P. Bovie (eds) (Philadelphia, 1999).

20. L.P. Hardwick, *Translating Words, Translating Cultures* (London, 2000) 12.

21. D. West, *Virgil: The Aeneid, A New Prose Translation* (Harmondsworth, 1990) xii.

22. These two positions are discussed in greater detail by S. Underwood, *English Translators of Homer* (Plymouth, 1998) 3-4 and can usefully be seen as developments of the concepts appealed to the seventeenth century poet and critic John Dryden: 'metaphrase' (word-for-word translation); 'paraphrase' (translation of the sense rather than the words) and 'imitation' (a version that aims to convey an overall equivalence of the original). Quotations come from V. Nabokov, 'Problems of Translation: Onegin in English', *Partisan Review* 22 (1955) 504-12 and H. Kerner, *The Pound Era* (London, 1972) 147-53.

23. T. Hermans, *Translation in Systems* (Manchester, 1999), reformulating the 'adequate' v 'acceptable' distinction made by G. Toury, *Descriptive Translation Studies – And Beyond* (Amsterdam and Philadelphia, 1995).

24. L. Venuti, *The Translator's Invisibility* (London and New York, 1995) 20, who very much argues for 'foreignization' as a translation strategy, i.e. that translators should lose what he calls their 'invisibility' and make readers aware that they are reading a text in translation.

25. A further complicating factor for anyone trying to make a distinction between a 'translation', a 'version' and an 'adaptation' is that many translators/adapters tackle different parts of a play in different ways.

26. Slavitt and Bovie, *Aristophanes, 2*, 90.

27. Hardwick, *Translating Words*, 17.

28. These words are taken from Slavitt and Bovie's summary of the aims of the series which appear on the first printed page of each volume.

29. Slavitt and Bovie, *Aristophanes, 2*, 90.

30. Halliwell, *Birds*, liii. Translators of bilingual editions of plays tend to render the speech of Spartans into standard English, too.

31. J. Henderson, *Three Plays by Aristophanes: Staging Women* (New York and London, 1996) 30.

32. 'Aristophanes' in Chase, *Encyclopedia of Translation*.

33. Halliwell, 'Aristophanic Sex'.

24. J. Henderson, *Aristophanes: Acharnians, Knights* (Cambridge, Mass., 1998)

35. Slavit and Bovie, *Aristophanes, 2*: Flavin's version evidently owes much to Rogers' version of nearly a hundred years earlier (published in various formats from 1902-24).

36. E. Scharfenberger, 'Aristophanes' *Thesmophoriazousai* and the Challenges of Comic Translation: The Case of William Arrowsmith's *Euripides Agonistes*', *AJP* 123 (2002) 429-63: esp. 435 and 456-60. Arrowsmith's work on the play began some time before 1960 and was resumed again in the late 60s/early 70s: however, the translation was never finished.

37. *Aristophanes, The Eleven Comedies, Now for the first time translated literally and completely translated from the Greek into English by Horace Liverlight* (London: Athenian Society, 1912).

38. Paralia and Salamis are probably chosen, as Sommerstein notes (*Lysistrata*, 157) because they evoke the names of two of Athens' swift triremes, *Salaminia* and *Paralus*: since the triremes move fast, then the women from these

demes might also be expected to be among the earlier arrivals (an example of 'comic logic': see Chapter 4).

39. *Lysistrata* 411; *Assemblywomen* 33-8.

40. Halliwell, *Birds* 97.

41. Sommerstein, *Lysistrata* 21.

42. J. Henderson, *Staging Women,* 45.

43. To be sure, an actor could deliver the phrase 'Things are hard' in a nuanced way, but owing to the lack of any word play in these lines such a strategy might run the risk of striking an audience member as baffling or crude rather than amusing.

44. Sommerstein, *Lysistrata, The Acharnians, The Clouds,* 103.

45. Halliwell, *Birds,* lii.

46. R. Beacham, R. Bond, M. Ewans, 'Translation Forum', in Barsby, *Greek and Roman Drama,* 168-82: 178.

47. Sommerstein, *Lysistrata, The Acharnians, The Clouds,* 36.

48. D. Parker, 'WAA – an intruded gloss', *Arion* 3 2.2&3 (1992/3) 251-6: 253.

49. J. Henderson, *Aristophanes III: Birds, Lysistrata, Women at the Thesmophoria* (Cambridge, Mass./London, 2000) 395.

50. Halliwell, *Birds,* li.

51. That said, Halliwell, 'Aristophanes' in Chase, *Encyclopedia of Translation,* criticizes Roger's tendency to use archaic words such as 'ye' and 'thou' in his translations.

52. Bolt's play has been performed in a number of contexts, including at the Guthrie Theatre in Minneapolis, Minnesota in 1999; the Arcola Theatre, London in 2005 (set in an Athens car park) and on the BBC World Service in 2005, performed in what the press release described as 'fiery version with an all-Asian cast'.

53. *Lysistrata by Aristophanes,* adapted by Ranjit Bolt (London, 2006).

54. S. Goetsch in *Electronic Antiquity* (August 1993): scholar.lib.vt.edu/ejournals/ElAnt/V1N3/goetsch.html (accessed 5/2/08).

55. H. Loxton writing for The British Theatre Guide (2007): www.britishtheatreguide.info/reviews/lisagreenwich-rev.htm (accessed 5/2/08).

56. S. O'Brien, *The Birds by Aristophanes* (London, 2002) 13-14.

57. S. Clapp in the *Observer,* 4/8/02.

58. O'Brien himself gives his account of the production in 'A Version of *The Birds* in Two Productions' in Hall and Wrigley, *Aristophanes in Performance,* 276-86.

Bibliography and Abbreviations

The following bibliography gives titles of works cited more than once and which therefore appear in abbreviated form in the notes. In addition, it provides a key to other abbreviations, such as those of journal titles, found in the book.

AJP = *American Journal of Philology.*
Barsby, *Greek and Roman Drama* = J. Barsby (ed.) *Greek and Roman Drama: Translation and Performance* (Tübingen, 2002).
BICS = *Bulletin of the Institute of Classical Studies.*
CQ = *Classical Quarterly.*
Carey, 'Comic Ridicule' = C. Carey, 'Comic Ridicule and Democracy' in R. Osborne and S. Hornblower (eds) *Ritual, Finance, Politics: Athenian Democratic Accounts Presented to David Lewis* (Oxford, 1994) 69-83.
Chase, *Encyclopedia of Translation* = O. Chase (ed.) *Encyclopedia of Literary Translation into English* (London and Chicago, 2000).
Com. Adesp. = Comica Adespota (fragments of comedy not assigned to any particular author).
Dearden, *Stage of Aristophanes* = C.W. Dearden, *The Stage of Aristophanes* (London, 1976).
Dobrov, *Beyond Aristophanes* = G.W. Dobrov (ed.) *Beyond Aristophanes: Transition and Diversity in Greek Comedy* (Atlanta, Georgia, 1995).
fr. (frs) = fragment(s).
Hall and Wrigley, *Aristophanes in Performance* = E. Hall and A. Wrigley (eds) *Aristophanes in Performance 421 BC–AD 2007* (London, 2007).
Halliwell, 'Aristophanic Satire' = S. Halliwell, 'Aristophanic Satire', *Yearbook of English Studies* 14 (1984) 6-20.
Halliwell, 'Aristophanic Sex' = S. Halliwell, 'Aristophanic Sex: The Erotics of Shamelessness', in M.C. Nussbaum and J. Sihvola (eds) *The Sleep of Reason: Erotic Experience and Social Ethics in Ancient Greece and Rome* (Chicago and London, 2002) 120-42.
Halliwell, *Birds* = S. Halliwell, *Aristophanes Birds and Other Plays* (Oxford, 1998).
Halliwell, 'Comedy and Publicity' = S. Halliwell, 'Comedy and Publicity in the Society of the Polis', in Sommerstein et al. (eds), *Tragedy, Comedy and the Polis* (Bari, 1993) 321-40.
Halliwell, 'Comic Satire' = S. Halliwell, 'Comic Satire and Freedom of Speech in Classical Athens', *JHS* 111 (1991) 48-70.
Hardwick, *Translating Words* = L.P. Hardwick, *Translating Words, Translating Cultures* (London, 2000).
Heath, *Political Comedy* = M. Heath, *Political Comedy in Aristophanes* (Göttingen 1987; updated text available at http://eprints.whiterose.ac.uk/3588/, 2007).
Henderson, 'Frank Speech' = J. Henderson (1998) 'Attic Old Comedy, Frank Speech, and Democracy', in D. Boedeker and K.A. Raaflaub (eds) *Democracy, Empire and the Arts in Fifth-Century Athens* (Harvard, 1998) 255-73.
Henderson, *Maculate Muse* = *The Maculate Muse: Obscene Language in Attic Old Comedy* (New Haven: Yale University Press, 1975: 2nd edn, 1991).

Bibliography and Abbreviations

Henderson, 'Older Women' = J. Henderson, 'Older Women in Attic Old Comedy', *TAPA* 117 (1987) 105-29.

Henderson, 'Pherekrates and Women' = J. Henderson, 'Pherekrates and the Women of Old Comedy' in F.D. Harvey and J. Wilkins (eds) *The Rivals of Aristophanes: Studies in Athenian Old Comedy* (London, 2000) 135-50.

Henderson, Staging Women = J. Henderson, *Three Plays by Aristophanes: Staging Women* (New York and London, 1996).

Hubbard, 'Old Men' = T.K. Hubbard, 'Old Men in the Youthful Plays of Aristophanes' in T.M. Falkner and J. de Luce (eds), *Old Age in Greek and Latin Literature* (New York, 1989) 90-113.

IG = *Inscriptiones Graecae*.

JHS = *Journal of Hellenic Studies*.

KA = R. Kassel and C. Austin, *Poetae Comici Graeci*, Berlin and New York 1983-.

Kozak and Rich, *Playing Around Aristophanes* = L. Kozak and J. Rich (eds) *Playing Around Aristophanes* (Oxford, 2006).

Lowe, 'Aristophanic Spacecraft' = N.J. Lowe, 'Aristophanic Spacecraft' in Kozak and Rich (eds), *Playing Around Aristophanes*, 48-64.

McLeish, *Theatre of Aristophanes* = K. McLeish, *The Theatre of Aristophanes* (Bath, 1980).

O'Higgins, *Women and Humor* = L. O'Higgins, *Women and Humor in Classical Greece* (Cambridge, 2003).

Olson, *Acharnians* = S.D. Olson, *Aristophanes Acharnians* (Oxford, 2002).

Parker, *Songs of Aristophanes* = L.P.E. Parker, *Songs of Aristophanes* (Oxford, 1997).

POxy = Oxyrhynchus Papyrus.

Seldes, *Lysistrata* = G. Seldes, *Lysistrata by Aristophanes: A New Version by Gilbert Seldes with a Special Introduction by Mr. Seldes and Illustrations by Pablo Picasso* (New York, 1934).

Silk, *Aristophanes* = M.S. Silk, *Aristophanes and the Definition of Comedy* (Oxford, 2000).

Silk, 'Paratragedy' = M.S. Silk, 'Aristophanic Paratragedy', in Sommerstein et al. (eds) *Tragedy, Comedy and the Polis* (Bari 1993) 477-504.

Slavitt and Bovie, *Aristophanes, 2* = D.R. Slavitt and P. Bovie (eds) *Aristophanes, 2: Wasps, Lysistrata, Frogs, Sexual Congress* (Philidelphia, 1999).

Sommerstein, 'Comedy and the Unspeakable' = A.H. Sommerstein, 'Comedy and the Unspeakable' in D.L. Cairns and R.A. Knox (eds) *Law, Rhetoric and Comedy in Classical Antiquity* (Swansea, 2004) 205-22.

Sommerstein, *Frogs* = A.H. Sommerstein, *The Comedies of Aristophanes*, vol. 9: *Frogs* (Warminster, 1996).

Sommerstein, '*Komoudomenos*' = A.H. Sommerstein, 'How to Avoid Being a Komoudomenos', *CQ* (1996) 46 (ii) 327-56.

Sommerstein, *Lysistrata* = A.H. Sommerstein, *The Comedies of Aristophanes*, vol. 7: *Lysistrata* (Warminster, 1990)

Sommerstein, *Lysistrata, The Acharnians, The Clouds* = A.H. Sommerstein, *Lysistrata, The Acharnians, The Clouds* (Penguin: London, 1973; revised by Sommerstein 2002).

Sommerstein, *Tragedy, Comedy and the Polis* = A.H. Sommerstein et al. (eds) *Tragedy, Comedy and the Polis* (Bari, 1993).

TAPA = *Transactions of the American Philological Association*.

Van Steen, *Venom in Verse* = G. Van Steen, *Venom in Verse: Aristophanes in Modern Greece* (Princeton, 2000).

Wiles, *Greek Theatre Performance* = D. Wiles, *Greek Theatre Performance: An Introduction* (Cambridge, 2000).

Winkler and Zeitlin, *Dionysos* = J.J. Winkler and F.I. Zeitlin (eds) *Nothing to Do With Dionysos?* (Princeton, 1990).

YCS = *Yale Classical Studies*.

Index of Principal Passages Cited

References to the pages and notes of this book are in bold type.

Index of Principal Passages Cited

General Index

240

241